Alifa dared to m...

She was stunned by the passion blazing there. His hand cupped protectively around hers and he leaned closer, his obvious intent making her heartbeat staccato.

"Alifa," he whispered, and his breath fanned across her lips.

Alifa could not deny him. Everything within her surged in anticipation of his kiss. Just one taste, she told herself as her eyes fluttered closed.

Just one, for what might have been, in another time and place.

Yusef's arms closed possessively around her at her submission. His kiss was dark and sultry, like the night claiming the mountains around them. He tasted of forbidden spices, of hidden secrets, of nameless treasures to be found in the dark....

Dear Reader,

The enigmatic hero and less-than-perfect heroine of
The Magician's Quest were first introduced to readers as
minor characters in Claire Delacroix's *Honeyed Lies*.
Now the two of them share their own story in this tale of
a man who must come to terms with the legacy left him
by his father, and his love for a woman of questionable
virtue. *The Talisman* called the romance that grows
between these two people "as warm and overpowering
as a desert storm." We hope you will enjoy it.

With *Playing To Win*, author Laurel Ames returns to the
Regency period to tell the story of a new wife who will
do anything to win the love of her husband, a rakish duke
with an uncanny conscience. Don't miss this delightful
story of trust and love.

Our featured Women of the West title this month is
Cassandra Austin's *Trusting Sarah*, the story of a young
woman who heads west on a wagon train, trying to escape
her past, only to run headlong into it again, in the form
of the man who wrongly sent her to jail years before.

And for Catherine Archer fans who have been eagerly
awaiting her next story comes *Velvet Bond*, a medieval
tale of passion and honor.

Whatever your taste in historical reading, we hope
you'll enjoy all four titles, available wherever Harlequin
Historicals are sold.

Sincerely,

Tracy Farrell
Senior Editor

Please address questions and book requests to:
Harlequin Reader Service
U.S.: 3010 Walden Ave., P.O. Box 1325, Buffalo, NY 14269
Canadian: P.O. Box 609, Fort Erie, Ont. L2A 5X3

CLAIRE DELACROIX

THE MAGICIAN'S QUEST

Harlequin Books

TORONTO • NEW YORK • LONDON
AMSTERDAM • PARIS • SYDNEY • HAMBURG
STOCKHOLM • ATHENS • TOKYO • MILAN
MADRID • WARSAW • BUDAPEST • AUCKLAND

ISBN 0-373-28881-6

THE MAGICIAN'S QUEST

Copyright © 1995 by Deborah A. Cooke.

Books by Claire Delacroix

Harlequin Historicals

Romance of the Rose #166
Honeyed Lies #209
+Unicorn Bride #223
The Sorceress #235
Roarke's Folly #250
+Pearl Beyond Price #264
The Magician's Quest #281

*The Rose Trilogy
+Unicorn Series

CLAIRE DELACROIX

An avid traveler and student of history, Claire Delacroix can be found at home when she has a deadline, amid the usual jumble of books, knitting needles and potted herbs.

Chapter One

Ceuta, North Africa
June 1085

Yusuf considered the mint tea before him with disinterest and reflected sourly on the mess his life had become.

It was almost impossible to believe that so many things could turn out so badly at the same time. Not only had the woman he loved married someone else, but Rebecca was actually happy with the match she had made. More than happy, in fact. Yusuf took a grim satisfaction in twisting the knife within his own wound. Rebecca and Jacob were madly, deliriously, in love.

What an inspired idea that had been, to go with them to Tunis, he congratulated himself ironically. With Jacob's family greeting Rebecca with open arms and Jacob being so intent on pleasing his new bride, any feeble hope Yusuf had had that she might reconsider her match had died a quick death.

He should have just continued with his own life and spared himself that tender scene. Yusuf drained the glass of tea in one swallow and set the empty vessel deliberately back on the table.

And to make matters worse, the one mission he had promised to fulfill for his father, the single deed that would finally free him from any lingering bonds to his past, was now completely and utterly impossible to achieve.

Curse the man for extracting that promise from Yusuf before their last fight. Yusuf would have given anything to avoid going back there ever, but a promise made must be kept.

Even if after twelve years of seeking that ridiculously obscure book his father had demanded he find, after two years of knowing where it was and carefully awaiting his moment, it had been completely destroyed. Burned. Gone. Yusuf shook his head, hating the inevitable conclusion that drew.

He would have to go home to tell his father. There was no other choice.

The very thought of returning to the backward little village of his birth, for any reason at all, irked Yusuf beyond reason—let alone needing to go there to confess that he was a failure. Although the simplicity of life there was not the issue. Yusuf resolutely avoided the real reason he had walked away from that life, and frowned.

One small favor, his father had called it, with that coy smile playing over his features, yet Yusuf had absolutely failed to fulfill it. He should have known better than to make the promise. But he had been young and the temptation too much. One small favor that would have shaken the dust of his roots from his feet forever.

How the old man would laugh. Yusuf squirmed inwardly, feeling all of six summers old. Truly, Yusuf had failed in more ways than one.

So overwhelming was his annoyance with himself that when the barkeeper asked if he wanted another drink, Yusuf's response shocked them both.

"Make it *eau-de-vie* this time," he growled. He was as surprised at his words as the barkeeper appeared to be.

But why? Yusuf scowled. Certainly, the faith denounced consumption of alcohol, but he had been pushed too far this time. And Allah surely knew that Yusuf had drunk enough spirits up in the mountains before his conversion.

Of course, there was a risk in imbibing again—there was always a risk when he relaxed his self-control in any way—but on this night of nights, Yusuf was beyond caring. The barkeeper's gaze rose dubiously to Yusuf's green turban, an unmistakable sign of his faith, and the Berber gritted his teeth angrily as he stared the man down.

That's right, Yusuf thought viciously as his lips tightened. *That's right. Regardless of my faith, tonight I need a drink.*

Satisfaction rolled through him when his glare sent the barkeeper positively scurrying to get the liquor. The fierce response was so reminiscent of what he had struggled to leave behind that Yusuf worried for a heartbeat.

Had his control already slipped?

Ridiculous. The man was in the business of selling libations and one more sale was one more coin in his pocket. It was no more than that. Regardless of his failure to acquire this book, Yusuf knew the dark side of his past was solidly behind him.

Right where it belonged. He was a scholar, a translator, a teacher, an educated man. His father's nonsense had no place in Yusuf's life. Certainly he was not the same kind of creature as his sire.

Those stories were precisely that. Hadn't he lived fourteen years without any sign of that dreaded affliction his father reveled in?

Yusuf silently toasted his victory in leaving superstition behind him before quaffing the liquor. The *eau-de-vie* was satisfyingly good, the heat it sent surging over his skin an almost forgotten sensation. Yusuf savored every welcome tingle. It was so good, in fact, that he indulged in two more shots, fired back in rapid succession, before his annoyance began to diminish in the slightest.

He pictured his father's smug grin and threw back the fourth shot in frustration. Wouldn't the old man just love this! How he would delight in commenting on the failure his son with the lofty ambitions had become. Yusuf could already hear the mockery that would greet his turban, not to mention every other article of his dress, every element of his speech, and who knew what else.

The old man would accuse Yusuf of running away from himself. He growled in annoyance and turned the glass within its wet ring on the tiled table.

The old man was wrong. Yusuf had become what he ought to have been all along.

Home was the last place he wanted to go, now or ever. The squalor of that life would never leave Yusuf's memory, despite his efforts to start fresh and wipe the taint of his origins from his skin. And there was the other...kept in check so easily in town. Yusuf scowled at the tiled counter, telling himself that certainly returning to the mountains could make no difference. None at all.

And there was no other way to let his father know the truth. Surely he owed the old man that much, at least. It was a question of respect, and regardless of whatever else had passed between Yusuf and his sire, he still respected the old man.

Or maybe he was afraid of him. Yusuf winced and vainly tried to coax another sip of *eau-de-vie* out of his empty glass.

"Well, well, well," came a vaguely familiar and thoroughly sarcastic voice. "Praise be to Allah—look what the cat dragged in."

Yusuf gritted his teeth and turned slowly to meet the knowing gaze of a dancing girl. His heart skipped a beat at the familiarity of her features. She propped one hand on her hip, the defiant light in her dark eyes reminding him of how she had confronted him for the first time several months ago.

Still as fiery as ever, he concluded, taking in the gloss of her loose hair, the ripe curves of her breasts. Her scantily cut red top left her flat midriff temptingly revealed, despite the array of coins dangling from it.

Yusuf felt the old quickening within him that signified the awakening of the beast, but stubbornly ignored it. He certainly had no intention of losing the upper hand he had taken so long to gain.

Despite that conviction, he could not look away. Her *chalwar* trousers were cut full, but were so sheer that Yusuf could discern the silhouette of her shapely legs. He cast a disparaging glance over her and spied the delicate arch of her bare feet. Desire flickered deep within him, but he stamped out the flames, more than certain of precisely what kind of woman confronted him.

He had never had any use for whores.

"I thought you would be unemployed," he said tersely, not in the least pleased that she had chosen to address him. People would think he was in the habit of hiring such women, and his shoulders stiffened at her effrontery.

But she merely laughed easily at his reference to the burning of the tavern where she had previously been employed—the same fire, incidentally, that had seen to the loss of his book, he thought sourly. It was troubling to think that he and this woman actually had something in common.

Her laughter was even more disconcerting. It made her look unexpectedly young and mischievous, a twinkle quite at odds with her usual demeanor lighting her eyes. She was younger than he had originally thought, he realized with astonishment. Yusuf's surprise held him in captivity when she leaned toward him confidentially, those dark eyes dancing.

"I'm not yet old enough or fat enough to be out of work," she whispered devilishly. She swung her hips provocatively to make her point and the coins swinging from her knotted sash jingled. She winked audaciously at Yusuf and against his will he felt compelled to glance over her. His mouth went dry as what he saw fanned the flames of desire anew.

"I suppose your kind can find employ as long as you have the strength to spread your thighs," he commented harshly, taking refuge in argument without considering the move. The twinkle went out abruptly and her eyes flashed with anger. Yusuf was momentarily embarrassed for his hurtful comment.

But she was a whore, he reminded himself forcefully, knowing he had no reason to feel guilty. Facts were facts.

But still the sight of her tightened lips and narrowed eyes reminded him only too well that it had been his remark that prompted the return of her hardened expression.

"Really?" she inquired archly. "And you, of course, are so *perfectly* ethical that you can presume to judge me?"

"I endeavor to live a clean life," Yusuf retorted stiffly. And he did. A perfectly proper and respectable Muslim life—no whores, no swearing, no gambling, no drinking. It was the mark of a convert to follow the creed so fastidiously.

He was faithful. And he was ethical. It was only right.

Especially since the taint of markedly less ethical practices haunted his line.

Yusuf's glance strayed guiltily to the empty *eau-de-vie* glass. The vast majority of the time, he lived a highly ethical life, he reminded himself. Surely a single transgression was not a crime?

It seemed he was not alone in noticing the evidence of his having strayed from the true road. Yusuf was unable to restrain himself from inhaling sharply when the dancer's gaze dropped pointedly to the empty glass before him. She *would* show up when he made one small concession to the pressures of his life. In fact, he remembered quite well that she had a tendency to be annoying.

"Yusuf *Khudabanda,* wasn't it?" she demanded softly. Yusuf could only nod, telling himself that she would not dare to make an issue of his momentarily lapse. She wouldn't. She couldn't.

And he knew just as well that she could.

Malice flashed in those dark eyes and the dancer plucked the glass from the counter. She deliberately sniffed the remnant of its contents and her eyes widened with mock surprise. Yusuf hated her in that instant with all his heart and soul.

"Khudabanda—*the hand of God,*" she mused thoughtfully and rolled the glass between her finger and thumb as she met his gaze knowingly. She wouldn't. "Isn't that what your name means?" she inquired mildly.

Yusuf nodded dumbly. She wouldn't dare, he told himself one last time. She straightened and he knew he had hoped in vain.

"One would think that a man with such a lofty name would not frequent this sort of establishment, let alone be so indulgent of spirits," she hissed. Her eyes narrowed dangerously and Yusuf gritted his teeth.

She had done it. He couldn't believe that she would insult his integrity. A dancing girl, a whore, had presumed to judge him. He glared at her, his embarrassment at his earlier churlishness turning on its heel and feeding his anger.

"Khudabanda," interjected the man beside him before Yusuf could respond. The man glanced over Yusuf and sneered indignantly. "Leave it to a Berber to be so ashamed of his father that he would change his name," he muttered disparagingly and turned back to his drink.

The barb struck particularly close to home, given Yusuf's current troubles. A Berber? Yes, he was a Berber, and all the better for it! Never had he denied his sire, although he had wished more than once that he could shake the old man's influence over his life. And to be Berber was to be blessed with the most noble lineage, regardless of his family's taint.

A fierce and almost forgotten pride in his race brought Yusuf upright without another thought. The liquor running hot through his veins compelled him on when otherwise he might have stopped.

At least it was easier to tell himself that than to acknowledge the roar of the beast within.

"How dare you presume to judge me?" Yusuf demanded. The man made the mistake of glancing up again.

"They should never have let your lot out of the hills," the man snorted. He muttered an expletive that roused a sympathetic chuckle around the bar. "Barbarians."

Yusuf's fist plowed into the man's soft face before Yusuf knew what he was about. It felt better than he had anticipated and Yusuf was stunned to find the urge to land another punch raging within him. It certainly was less than an ethical thought. And respectable scholars did not brawl in taverns.

But the beast demanded blood.

The dancer gasped in surprise at Yusuf's movement. Before Yusuf could make sense of the maelstrom within him, another man swore and lunged for him.

Sides were quickly chosen and the tavern erupted into chaos, the occupants evidently welcoming the distraction. The injured man shouted an accusation, someone grabbed Yusuf by the shoulder and spun him around. Yusuf was ready, landing a solid punch to this new assailant's belly before he could strike a blow.

"Now, wait just a moment," the barkeeper protested, too late to influence the outcome.

A heavy green glass sailed past his head and shattered on the wall behind. His objections fell silent as he ducked to a crouch and scurried away for protection.

Yusuf deflected another blow, his pulse pounding jubilantly in his ears. He punched another assailant, and kicked the feet out from beneath still another.

A wary space appeared around Yusuf and he permitted himself a slow smile of satisfaction. His palms prickled with the beast's awareness and Yusuf felt more alive than he had in years.

His gaze landed on the dancer still standing to one side of him, and she grinned unrepentantly. "Feel better?" she demanded pertly. When she smiled like this, it was easy to forget what she did for a living and he cast a newly appreciative glance over her curves.

"Yes," he admitted with a measure of surprise. He ducked out of the path of a stool crashing toward the floor and took a step closer to her without intending to do so.

"I knew you'd have to let loose one of these days," she informed him, her voice warm and confidential. Yusuf looked to her with surprise. "It's just not healthy to keep all that male aggression bottled up inside," she said teasingly.

Yusuf made the fatal mistake of glancing down into her eyes. That infectious twinkle was there again, and the sight of it triggered his lust twofold. He was seized by a wave of desire so strong that it stunned him. Even as he tried to tell himself that its source must be the liquor burning through him, he knew better.

Just as he knew that he couldn't possibly walk away without tasting her.

Just once. After all, it had been so long. Such was the price of an ethical life. But if he was breaking rules tonight, surely one taste would not be too much.

Yusuf gripped the dancer's upper arms before he could change his mind. He savored the little murmur of surprise she made, the way her eyes widened just before his lips closed relentlessly over hers. She was softer than he had expected and Yusuf hesitated for an instant, wondering if he had misunderstood her occupation.

The press of her hips against his and their suggestive roll laid any such doubts to rest and he pulled her purposefully closer. The mingled scent of feminine skin, jasmine and incense flooded his nostrils and threatened to drown him as his tongue plunged into the sweet depths of her mouth.

She was intoxicating, her effect upon him more intense that he could have imagined, and his one kiss showed no signs of being readily put to an end. Yusuf was lost in sensation and he knew it, the press of her full breasts against his chest, the soft sounds of capitulation she made deep in her throat, only urging him on and on.

His palms positively itched.

The dancer tore her lips from his and he panicked briefly, until she ran her teeth provocatively along his jawline. The feel of her breath in his ear when she paused to nibble his lobe inflamed Yusuf beyond his wildest dreams. He tightened his grip on her, cupping her buttocks, her breast, pressing her back against the table and letting her feel the fullness of his arousal.

This was what he wanted tonight, regardless of the consequences. He bent her back and kissed her hard. Her response was more than he had bargained for, the way her tongue tangled with his telling him that she was his to take.

The old power surged through him, making him feel invincible in a way he had almost forgotten. The beast was breaking free of his careful domination, but Yusuf didn't care.

He wanted her now.

The sounds of fighting finally forced themselves into his consciousness when a stool was smashed over the table directly beside them. Yusuf caught himself reluctantly, marveling that he had almost taken her here. Mercifully, the interruption had pulled him back from the brink just in time.

He had almost coupled with a whore, no less. Yusuf willed himself to feel shocked at his own behavior as he stepped deliberately away from the dancer. The beast was displeased but he stubbornly ignored its protests. He fully intended to walk out of the chaotic tavern.

Yusuf's hands, however, showed no inclination to abandon her skin. They slid over her shoulders in an unwilling caress, the soft warmth of her flesh inviting his touch even after he had willed himself to stop. His fingers slipped up the length of her golden throat as he watched them helplessly. They cupped her jaw and tipped her face upward. Yusuf met her eyes then, the smoldering desire in those dark depths stunning him.

She wanted him.

That alone was enough to tip the scales the other way. Something proud and primitive surged through him that he recognized but would not name. Yusuf could not tear his gaze away when she slowly slid the tip of her tongue over the fullness of her lips. The blatant invitation was his undoing and he hauled her close once more, kissing her with a bruising, possessive intensity.

He would show her male aggression, he thought grimly when he finally lifted his head and noted the drowsy passion in her eyes. He would show her lovemaking as she had never known it before. Before she could protest, Yusuf scooped her purposefully into his arms and stalked out of the rowdy tavern.

Virility was certainly something Berbers in general, and he in particular, had in abundance, Yusuf thought with no small measure of pride. This one would learn that before this night was through. The dancer smiled coyly up at him as he strode through the moonlight and kicked her feet like a young girl. Yusuf returned her grin confidently, certain that his lovemaking would wipe the smug smile from her face.

This night would be worth the price of awakening the beast.

* * *

Much later, Alifa burrowed contentedly in the cushions, a satisfied smile playing over her lips. The house was silent, the hour late, the room flooded with velvety darkness. The man behind her rolled over. His breathing changed and Alifa knew he was awake. Her pulse quickened in anticipation.

She stretched beneath the weight of the hand that swept firmly over her hips and emitted a sound of pleasure that was completely out of her usual repertoire.

Alifa never moaned. At least not unintentionally. But tonight she had moaned. She had cried, she had caressed and been caressed with a thoroughness she had never experienced. And all the while she had been aware of the glow of desire in Yusuf's green eyes.

Had a man ever desired her for herself? Alifa suspected not. Had a man ever pleasured her the way he had? Had anyone ever taken the time to leisurely explore and tantalize, as Yusuf had all of this night? Alifa knew none had.

His breath on her nape sent goose pimples rising all over her flesh. Alifa chuckled and spread her legs wide as she felt his hardness nudge against her buttocks. She smiled against the pillows, knowing she had never before enjoyed lovemaking.

She would not feel ashamed of this night and that was a welcome change.

Yusuf was on top of her, his hands exploring her, his strength within her, his lips on her earlobe. Alifa felt her passion rise once again. She writhed beneath his weight and felt rather than heard his answering moan. His heartbeat thudded against her back, his chest hair tickled her flesh. They rose to their knees as one, Alifa's hips bucked of their own accord. Her pulse quickened, she stretched for the ceiling, and the blessed heat flooded through her.

Yusuf gripped her hips and thrust against her an instant later, his entire body tightening against hers. He gave a hoarse cry that pleased her immensely, coming as it did from one who seemed so formal and reserved. That silly smile played over Alifa's lips once more and she allowed her eyes to drift closed as she collapsed back onto the pillows.

She was exhausted, yet curiously replete. She felt clean. The sensation was novel and entirely welcome.

Maybe there was more to Yusuf than she had guessed. Maybe on an instinctive level she had known it could be special between them. Maybe he was feeling a similar wonder.

Alifa rolled to one hip to see Yusuf, and met the steady green gaze of a black panther instead.

Her heart stopped cold in disbelief.

The great cat sat atop the cushions, precisely where she had expected to see Yusuf, and watched her avidly. Alifa's mind boggled. What was this? Where was Yusuf? How had this creature slipped in? For a long moment, her mind could not make sense of what her eyes perceived. Then all her senses rose together in a flash.

Panthers could kill.

Her mouth went dry, her heart pounded. She had to get out of Yusuf's room! Alifa stumbled to her feet and raced for the door. It was farther than she had thought.

No! She felt the panther leap in pursuit and her breath stopped. Not here, not now. She couldn't be caught! The others needed her! Alifa lunged for the door but the weight of one heavy paw landed on her shoulder too soon.

No! Alifa twisted in a desperate attempt to escape. She cried out as the claws dug reflexively into her skin. Alifa tried to twist away but the claws etched a burning path down the length of her back.

Alifa gasped with the pain. It seemed time had stopped as she stared into those fathomless green eyes and she felt awareness slipping away. The lines on her back raged as though they had been seared into her flesh.

But she couldn't faint! Alifa fought to remain conscious. She had to run! She had to get home somehow!

Despite Alifa's resolve, the darkened room tipped and swirled around her. She stumbled on the threshold of the room and fell to the floor.

The last thing Alifa saw before the darkness closed in was the black panther pacing across the floor before her. Its tail lashed at the night air agitatedly and its green eyes glowed with an unnerving luminescence as it fixedly watched her.

There was no escape.

Yusuf awoke feeling as though he had slept with the camels.

He rolled over and groaned at the pounding that erupted between his ears, feeling the cushions wind conspiratorially between his ankles, as though they would make his morning more difficult than it already threatened to be. He dared to open one eye, only to be lambasted by a ray of sunlight and fall bonelessly back against the pillows, groaning anew.

Everything he had hurt.

Even his conscience. Although in his current state, Yusuf couldn't exactly pinpoint why.

"Not much of a morning person, are you?" a woman inquired cheerfully. Startled, Yusuf sat up with a jolt that did his headache no favors.

The dancer stood at the foot of the bed, fully dressed and disgustingly fresh-faced. Memories flooded his mind, the very thought of her stretched beneath him assaulting his mind and bringing at least one part of his anatomy wide-awake. The jolt that ripped through him did no favors for either his muddled thinking or his headache. Even more confusing was a very masculine ripple of pride that their mating had been spectacular.

At least what Yusuf could recall of it had been spectacular. His recollection was admittedly incomplete. He flatly refused to recall when he had last had a similarly impaired memory of a night.

It was the effect of the liquor, no more than that. The dancer spared him a calculating glance, her wary expression reminding Yusuf of one detail.

One relatively important detail.

Not only had he imbibed of spirits, but he had coupled with a whore. Guilt writhed within Yusuf at his own failure and his lips twisted angrily. *She* had tempted him. She had led him astray from his convictions. He felt his color rise in indignation, but the dancer had already turned her attention to his purse and was dumping silver dinars into her hand.

That captured his attention rather thoroughly. She intended to take his coin, as well?

"Wait just a moment," Yusuf protested hotly. His mind might be jumbled this morning, but he *knew* their coupling had been something special.

She must have thought so, as well. In fact, the more he reflected upon it, the more convinced Yusuf became that this could not have been simply another business transaction for her.

There had been a special magic between them, he knew it. Of course. The attraction had been inescapable. Although Yusuf certainly had no intention of continuing on the same path, it was suddenly critical to him that the dancer acknowledge that magic. After all, if he paid her, then he would have simply used a whore and Yusuf Khudabanda didn't hire whores.

He was quite certain she would understand. After all, she must have enjoyed the ride. There had been days, or rather nights, before he converted to his austere life, when he had refined his technique to an art.

It must have been the best she had ever had. Yusuf tried to stand to make his point, feeling less than his usual composed self as he stumbled his way free of the clutch of his discarded clothing.

"What do you think you're doing?" he demanded, when she did not glance up from emptying his purse. The dancer smiled condescendingly and added another dinar to the three already in her palm, much to Yusuf's scandalized disbelief.

Four dinars? No woman was worth that much. This had to be an ill-conceived joke. He considered the possibility that she should pay *him* for his prowess.

"Surely you didn't think you'd get it for free?" she demanded archly.

Something uneasy in her manner triggered Yusuf's suspicions, but then she was boldly confident again. What precisely had happened the night before? Unless... He stared into her eyes, but found no clue to her thoughts. He couldn't have. He wouldn't have. The beast could not have regained control so easily.

But he couldn't remember. Yusuf went cold at the realization. He eyed the dancer, not in the least reassured by her frosty demeanor. Had she seen anything?

Was she covering a nervousness or was he reading something into her manner that wasn't really there?

A casual observer would readily have concluded that a whore stood before him, brashly negotiating her fee. Her dark eyes flickered as they audaciously held his gaze though, and Yusuf wondered if she was really as certain of herself as she would have him believe.

His gaze dropped to the four dinars she rolled in her palm and his annoyance rose again. How dare she help herself to such a shocking sum of silver?

"I thought..." He halted for a moment to collect his thoughts, not having any idea how to present his point given the muddled state of his mind. "I didn't think it was a business arrangement," he managed to argue, feeling the statement was hopelessly weak.

She actually laughed aloud, although the sound was harsh. This morning there was no sign of the playfulness that had so attracted him in her demeanor. This whore was all business.

Yusuf's guilt grew by another increment. The foul beast was markedly silent in all of this and he cursed his own weakness in indulging its desires.

"Not a business transaction? What other kind is there?" the dancer asked, shaking her head in amusement as she dropped the coins into her own purse.

"I thought—" Yusuf struggled to find the words for a conversation he had never in his life expected to have "—that it was *good*. That you liked it, I mean." Seeming to sober, the dancer paused on the threshold and turned, propping one hand on her hip and regarding him skeptically.

"Good enough to not charge you, you mean?" she inquired bluntly.

Yusuf nodded in response to her question, and felt his mouth go dry when her lips twisted in wry amusement. There was more of a concession that he wanted from her than that, but he didn't know how to ask for it.

"Believe me," she confided in a low voice that had an undercurrent of steel, "it's *never* that good."

The cold words shocked Yusuf, as she had surely intended them to. With that, she turned and made for the door. But had she seen anything? The very thought of her just leaving sent an irrational panic through Yusuf.

This was not going at all as he had intended. What had happened to his usual suave charm?

"Wait a moment!" He darted across the room in pursuit and grabbed her arm just as she opened the door.

She stopped and looked up at him. Yusuf was reassured by the very touch of her skin and when her eyes met his, he knew without a doubt that there had been something magical between them. How he wished he could remember more! An unexpected glimmer of warmth lit her eyes when she noted his intensity. Yusuf took encouragement from her expression and ran his hand slowly up her arm. She shivered and he pulled her closer with a thrill of victory, telling himself that he had been right all along.

Maybe he could coax her back to bed *and* reclaim his four dinars.

"You really thought it was special, didn't you?" she asked softly, a measure of awe in her tone. Yusuf could only nod.

"Yes. Yes, I really did...." He hesitated, fully intending to add her name to the claim, but was brought up short by the realization that he couldn't remember it.

Or didn't even know it.

This was not good. Yusuf glanced to her in panic, his heart sinking when he saw that she had evidently guessed his difficulty. The meager warmth in her eyes died and her lips twisted cynically. The moment was gone.

"That's Alifa." She enunciated with a vicious clarity that resonated in his pounding head. "*A-li-fa*. Simple enough name, really." She twisted her arm from his grip and sailed out onto the landing, pausing at the top of the stairs to regard him scornfully.

"And to tell the truth, Yusuf Khudabanda," she said with a sneer. "I've had better." The remark stung, but Yusuf lunged after her nonetheless.

"You can't just leave," he protested, not even daring to question why the idea troubled him so. She tossed an arch look over her shoulder.

"Watch me," she challenged. Yusuf was appalled to find his gaze being dragged to the graceful sway of her hips beneath her enveloping white *djellaba*.

Or was that one of his white *djellabas?* Yusuf didn't remember her wearing one the night before, but then, he didn't remember much of the night before.

Maybe he hadn't shown her enough consideration, he concluded wildly, wondering whether the *eau-de-vie* had made him act more selfishly than he had intended. In truth, he could recall only the curiously replete sense their love-making had left.

He realized in that moment that he wanted Alifa again, that he wanted her without delay. He wanted to remember precisely what is was like to have her beneath him. Yusuf started purposefully down the stairs after those swinging hips, certain that just one more bout in bed would convince her that he had pleasured her more than any other.

"Good morning," Alifa said completely unexpectedly.

Startled by her greeting, Yusuf managed to tear his gaze reluctantly away from his target and directed it to the woman Alifa addressed.

Any thought of pursuing the dancer was summarily dismissed when he met the disgruntled eyes of his landlady. Her disgusted expression made him abruptly recall his state. Yusuf's color rose as he glanced down, as though disbelieving what he knew he would see.

He stood stark-naked on the stairs.

Surely this morning could get no worse.

"Well." The landlady huffed. "Well. I honestly never believed that I'd see the day that someone who appeared to be a decent scholarly man would bring this sort of nonsense into my home...."

Yusuf straightened proudly, desperately trying to think of some way to talk himself out of this mess. The flicker of a red skirt caught his eye and he caught the barest glimpse of Alifa's cheeky wave before she ducked out the door to the street.

Rage flooded through Yusuf at her audacity in leaving him here in such a situation. He spun abruptly on his heel, deaf to his landlady's recriminations and stalked up the stairs. It was Alifa's fault that he had been so embarrassed. Yusuf intended to make sure she paid the price, not him.

He would get those four dinars back, one way or the other.

Chapter Two

The tavern was deserted when Alifa slipped in the back door and she breathed a sigh of relief. Reassured by the darkness of the abandoned common room, she strode back to the dancers' room, running one hand tiredly through her hair.

How much longer could she continue?

"I hope you're not forgetting my percentage of your night," a dry voice commented. Alifa stopped dead in shock at finding herself not alone. Her gaze flicked over the tavern until she spied Hakim shrouded in the darkness. His eyes gleamed and the glass he lifted to his lips reflected an errant beam of light.

Trust him to be waiting for her.

"I didn't have much of a night," Alifa declared with false bravado. Curse Hakim, anyway. She needed this silver and there was precious little of it. Only four dinars. Good money for a night, but not nearly enough for what she needed. She gritted her teeth and cursed her own foolishness in not taking every piece of silver that barbarian possessed.

It would only have been fair, after all.

"Alifa, Alifa..." Hakim mused under his breath. He set his glass deliberately on the bar and shook his head, but Alifa held her ground stubbornly. She would not surrender the coins. Not today. Not after the night she had had.

And if she could come through that, she could put up with anything Hakim might choose to do.

"You know the rules of the house," Hakim declared softly in the darkness. Alifa heard the threat underlying his tone, but she lifted her chin stubbornly.

"You don't want a part of what I got last night," she insisted. Hakim's brows rose and he spared her a considering glance.

"Bitter, Alifa? How unlike you." He rose to his feet languidly and strolled across the floor toward her with affected nonchalance. He paused before her, consideration and something else in his gaze. Alifa did not look away. "Surely you're not trying to cheat me?" he asked with feigned surprise.

Alifa shook her head. "I wouldn't dream of it," she said flatly and turned to walk away. Hakim snatched at her elbow and hauled her to a stop before she took two steps. Alifa stiffened and spared him a suspicious glance.

"I'm hoping you'll do well enough tonight to make up the difference," he said silkily. His eyes were cold and Alifa schooled herself not to shiver. "A night off once in a while is fine, but we both know how much you need this job," Hakim added.

Alifa's chin snapped up and she twisted her arm out of his grip. "Then neither of us should have any doubts about tonight," she snapped. Hakim smiled a very predatory smile, but Alifa chose to ignore him as she stalked proudly to the back room.

How she wished Husayn hadn't decided to leave the tavern business. Things had been much simpler when she worked in his tavern.

Alifa's lips twisted at the awareness that she hadn't known how lucky she was.

"Remember, Alifa," Hakim called quietly in the shadows behind her, but Alifa didn't look back.

She would remember. How could she forget, after all? She had more than four dinars as a souvenir of her night.

Alifa shoved aside the curtain covering the doorway to the back room and let it fall behind her, breathing a sigh of relief that she had gained even this meager sanctuary. It was all so familiar—the faded velvet cushions, the abandoned sweets on the table, the honey that had leaked from them to melt and congeal on the tray. Tambourinelike *tars* were scattered on the floor amid a jumble of discarded veils, there was a nub of kohl abandoned beside the crookedly hung mirror with the whorl in its center.

Alifa caught a glimpse of herself in the large glass and forced herself to take a deep breath. She looked as though she had been to hell and back.

Had she? She wasn't even sure. For a moment there, when Yusuf struggled with his argument that there had been something special between them, Alifa had almost been tempted to believe. Despite what had happened, the memory of that sense of repleteness would not abandon her. And there had been the way he touched her, the way he ran his hands over her with a kind of admiration that left her feeling clean, not despoiled.

Tenderness. That was something Alifa had never felt before and for one short moment this morning, when he struggled for words, she had thought of that and almost hoped...

But Yusuf had simply been haggling. Alifa snorted at her own stupidity. She should know better than to expect anything else from men after all these years in the business. Always looking out for themselves or their purses. There was no more to it than that.

And then there was what had happened—whatever it had been. When she awakened this morning, the panther had been gone. To her surprise, just Yusuf's snores had filled the room, and his gloriously sculptured body, sprawled across the cushions, as nude as the day he was born.

Surely he hadn't? Surely he couldn't have? All the old tales she had learned as a child had flooded into Alifa's mind and she had stood mutely in his rooms as she fought against the evidence.

Had she coupled with one of the ancient ones?

Then the *muezzin* had cried out his summons to morning prayers and brought her back to the present. She had wanted only to escape, but Yusuf, curse him, had awakened.

It could not have happened. Yusuf could not be one of the gifted ones. He was just a man. He could not have shape-shifted. The old stories had no place in town. They belonged in the hills when everyone clustered closely around the fire. They were only stories told to frighten children and keep them tight in their beds.

Weren't they? Alifa admitted that she wasn't as sure of that as she had been just a day past.

She had four dinars, Alifa reminded herself fiercely. That was what mattered. It was half of the coin she needed and more than enough of a reminder of what had passed between herself and Yusuf.

But Alifa knew she had one other reminder of the night they had shared.

She swallowed and eyed the mirror, knowing that she had to look. Slowly, as though she feared to startle herself, Alifa unfastened Yusuf's *djellaba*. The scent of his skin rose from the garment to tease her, but she resolutely ignored the quickening of her pulse. She half wished that she had dreamed the entire incident, that she would bare her back to find nothing at all, but some corner of her mind knew better. Alifa lifted the white wool deliberately from her shoulders, her gaze flicking assessingly over every increment of skin as it was revealed.

She didn't have to look to know where the marks were, for she could feel them burning into her flesh. Alifa bit her lip and cast the garment aside, turning gradually until her bare back was exposed to the mirror. She met her own dark gaze over her shoulder and saw the surprise in her own expression at the length of the ugly red gashes.

Tenderness. Here was a vivid denial of that nonsense. Alifa watched her own lips twist cynically in acknowledgment of her souvenir.

Four scratches from shoulder to buttock, evenly spaced and each outlined by a red trickle of blood. Alifa inhaled sharply and touched the end of the longest scratch with a tentative fingertip, as though to confirm that it was really there. It stung and she winced, refusing to permit herself a tear.

No, Alifa concluded with a wry twist of her lips. She couldn't imagine that Hakim wanted any part of what she had earned the night before.

"What do you mean, she isn't here?" Yusuf demanded impatiently. The thin proprietor of the tavern spared him a glance of disinterest.

The tavern where Alifa danced was deserted in the late morning, its cool shadows remarkably at odds with the bright sunlight flooding the busy *souk* outside. Yusuf's eyes still hadn't completely adapted, the glimmer of sunbeams forcing their way between the latticed wooden blinds not helping in the adjustment.

There was no sign remaining of the fight of the previous night, although he imagined there were fewer stools and tables than before. Yusuf could smell the countless spilled goblets of sweet wine that had left their remnants between the flagstones of the floor, and a lingering vestige of incense mingled with the dampness of the cool room.

He couldn't detect even the faintest hint of jasmine, but refused to speculate on why that troubled him.

The sounds of the *souk* drifted through the shutters, as well, sounding curiously distant and otherworldly despite their proximity. Voices rose as they bargained, children laughed, women gossiped, but the tavern seemed to hold its breath.

As though the building itself were waiting for the man before Yusuf to make a move.

The proprietor looked as though he had been born to the darkness and seldom deserted it. Time seemed to be stopped or at least slowed here, its passage measured only by the periodic sips this man took from his glass. In fact, this haven appeared so attuned to him that Yusuf fancied in that moment that the tavern had been wrought around him, to suit his own needs. Or maybe he had been wrought within the tavern, and had never stepped outside.

The proprietor was slender, his movements were lethargic, and his skin darker than most, and smooth. His aloof manner reminded Yusuf of a lizard one might find out basking on the rocks, with the notable exception that lizards sought heat and sun. This one seemed predisposed to linger in cool darkness. Only his eyes glittered as he stroked the length of a glass of *eau-de-vie* with one long finger and watched Yusuf assessingly.

"I mean, she isn't here," he said softly. Despite his low tone, there was a thread of resolve underlying his words and Yusuf understood that this was not a man to be crossed.

The man's brow quirked and he returned his attention to his glass, as though the matter were adequately settled. Yusuf quelled an uncharacteristic surge of impatience, but mustered his calm. Anger would get him nothing here.

And he wanted his four dinars back.

"I thought she worked here," he satisfied himself with saying, hoping the other man couldn't tell he had gritted his teeth.

"She does," the proprietor conceded.

Yusuf waited, but the man clearly had no plans to say anything further. He sipped from his glass, a trace of amusement flickering in his dark eyes as he regarded Yusuf.

It seemed this would not be as easy as Yusuf had expected. The two men stared at each other for a long moment. Then the proprietor's lids drooped carelessly and he tipped his glass once more. The amber liquid swirled as he took a languid sip.

"Well?" Yusuf prompted when he could wait no longer. The man's lips twitched.

"Well?" he returned mildly, as though he had no idea what Yusuf wanted to know.

"Where is she?"

The man shrugged nonchalantly and glanced pointedly around the deserted tavern. "Not here," he said mildly. He frowned at a mark on the table and brushed his fingertips absently across it. Yusuf had a sense that the man had lost interest in the discussion.

"I thought she worked here," Yusuf repeated tightly. That bright gaze swiveled back to his and the man's eyes flashed briefly.

"The women," the proprietor said incisively, "work at night."

With that, he set his glass solidly on the table and scowled openly at the mark on the tile. Despite the apparent dismissal, Yusuf was not quite ready to leave.

"Where does she live?" he asked. The proprietor looked genuinely surprised for the briefest instant, before he managed to conceal the expression with boredom once again.

"I don't know." He glared at Yusuf. "And why would I care?"

"She works for you."

The thin man snorted and spared Yusuf a knowing smile. "No," he said slowly. "Alifa works for whoever has coin in his pockets and something between his legs."

The remark angered Yusuf more than he thought it should have, but he rationalized his response quickly. Undoubtedly it was because the man thought him a customer of the sort of woman Alifa evidently was. It was no small insult to be regarded in such a light.

That must be what had prompted this dull glow of rage. There was no other possible explanation.

"You have no idea where she lives?" he forced himself to ask calmly, finding the task harder than he had expected. The proprietor arched a brow high.

"Too anxious to wait until this evening, are you?" he commented slyly. An insidious smile wound its leisurely way across his features and made Yusuf's gut writhe with its implication. "Our Alifa must have outdone herself." Yusuf felt his color rise in the shadowy darkness, but he refused to be deterred. It was none of this man's business what had transpired between them.

"I just wanted to talk to her," Yusuf insisted. About a shocking sum of silver. The man's smile widened another annoying increment.

"They all want to talk," he confided easily, then shook his head before he turned away with disinterest again. "Check the slums," he said and his voice was harsher than it had been before. "That's usually where you can count on finding their kind."

"You really should be more careful around loose nails," Tabeta scolded. Alifa allowed herself a deprecating smile, knowing that her younger sister couldn't see the gesture. How much longer would the children believe whatever Alifa told them?

Alifa was laying on her stomach on the pallet they shared when she was home. Tabeta was dabbing vinegar along the length of each scratch to ensure that the wounds were clean and clucking like a mother hen all the while. Kasilo watched avidly from the other side of the small room and Alifa spared her baby brother a wink.

"Why didn't you come home last night? I was worried." All of eight summers old, and Tabeta had more maternal instinct than any six women Alifa knew put together. Herself included.

"We had to work late," Alifa fabricated. "Doing an inventory. I didn't want to walk home alone so late so I slept at the shop."

The children knew nothing of where she went at night or what she did when she got there and Alifa aimed to keep it that way. As far as they knew, Alifa worked for a cloth merchant in the Jewish quarter. She had deliberately chosen the location for the shop because she knew they would have no way of checking her story.

"You shouldn't work so hard," Tabeta scolded. "It's not good for you. You probably didn't even have a proper dinner there in the shop."

"I ate," Alifa protested mildly.

"And these scratches," Tabeta continued. "You really need to take better care of yourself, Alifa." The reminder was less than a welcome one and Alifa's reply was more curt than she intended.

"Just clean the cut, Tabeta," she ordered flatly.

"I *am* cleaning it," the younger girl said. "Lucky for you it's a really clean cut. Sometimes nails can be jagged and rusty, but this looks more like it was cut with a knife."

Alifa was well aware that Tabeta paused deliberately and she knew her sister was hoping for an explanation.

Maybe she hadn't fooled the girl as readily as she thought. Maybe those days of innocent acceptance were already slipping away. Kasilo's eyes were bright and Alifa fancied now that they were lit with curiosity, but she ignored both of her siblings.

She had nothing further to say.

She would not give voice to the speculation that filled her mind. She would not tell anyone that she feared she had spent the night with a shapeshifter. It was too implausible. Such things didn't happen in real life. Alifa had clearly misinterpreted. Somehow the panther had gotten into Yusuf's room. At exactly the same time he had inexplicably left.

Even though that made absolutely no sense.

But the idea that Yusuf had changed form made even less sense. The ancient ones, the truly gifted ones, were gone, or at least hidden away in the mountains. The shaman in town, the one who wanted eight dinars to heal Kasilo, didn't shift to work his magic. Of course, Alifa had very real doubts about his effectiveness. It seemed her mother's rural convictions clung tenaciously in her own mind, despite the changes in her life.

"A really sharp knife," Tabeta prompted. Alifa stubbornly maintained her silence.

"Maybe one of those long knives with the silver handles, like the ones in the *souk,*" Tabeta added. Alifa's lips thinned in irritation. Would they never leave the matter be?

"Like the one Sinhaj had the other day," Kasilo contributed enthusiastically.

Alifa frowned, her attention caught by the unexpected reference. Sinhaj had a knife? She didn't much like the sound of that, especially since that troublemaker and her other brother had been spending a lot of time together.

Too much time, to Alifa's mind, but Jaraw was deaf to her recriminations.

"Sinhaj didn't have a knife," Tabeta said, with a self-righteousness that told Alifa the girl was lying. Mercifully, she told tales so seldom that they were readily discerned.

But why was Tabeta protective of that troublemaker Sinhaj?

Suddenly Alifa was concerned for Jaraw and a cold trickle of dread slid down her spine. What had those boys been up to in her absence?

"Yes, he did," Kasilo insisted. Alifa felt rather than saw the look that was fired across the room and cringed inwardly. "Oh, maybe it wasn't him," Kasilo amended hastily. Alifa heard the exasperation in Tabeta's sigh and didn't like it one bit.

"But this still looks like it was cut with a knife," Tabeta insisted. Alifa stiffened.

"I *told* you it was a nail on the wall of the shop. I backed into it by accident."

There was one of those little silences that told Alifa she had not been believed. "Four nails," Tabeta pointed out softly. Her sister was getting far too cheeky for Alifa's taste.

"Four nails," Alifa agreed in a tone that brooked no argument. She imagined that her sister shook her head in disapproval but refused to unbend. That was her story and she would stay with it. The truth was far too upsetting and incredible even to speak about.

Alifa did not imagine that her sister attacked the last scratch with more force than was necessary and she winced as the vinegar stung the wound. She made no sound, knowing Tabeta sought a response in retaliation for Alifa's refusal to confide in her.

The way Alifa had flinched would have to satisfy her.

"Has the shaman come this morning?" Alifa asked, forcing herself to use a conversational tone, despite her stinging back.

"Not today. Was he supposed to?"

"Yes," Alifa replied tightly.

"Is he going to do anything?" Tabeta asked. The fear lurking in her voice made her sound younger than she was and twisted Alifa's heart.

"I hope so," Alifa said. Certain the scratches were adequately cleaned, she rolled over and sat up abruptly. She ignored her sister's inquisitive gaze as she matter-of-factly pulled a loose shirt over her shoulders.

No sleep for her today. The sun was already high. Alifa had yet to find the shaman and make at least a partial payment for Kasilo's blessing. Whether it would be effective or not was anyone's guess, but it was her last alternative.

Maybe she could convince him to start to heal her brother before she earned the rest of the coin.

Maybe.

Then the children needed to be fed, the hearth swept out, their lessons attended to. Alifa set her lips, recognizing the truth when she saw it. She'd be lucky to get through it all before darkness fell and she was due back at the tavern.

And tonight, she had best not get any sleep at all, if she was going to pay the remainder of the debt to the shaman. Let alone satisfy Hakim.

"Is Kasilo going to be all right?" Tabeta whispered, her eyes wide. Well aware that Kasilo himself was attending their conversation, Alifa summoned a brisk smile.

"Of course," she said firmly. She turned to the bright-eyed little boy who had been abed the past two months, and winked again. Kasilo smiled with his usual cheerfulness. "Aren't you going to get better just to prove to your sister that you can?" she demanded brightly.

He nodded with characteristic enthusiasm. "Is the shaman going to help me?"

"Of course," Alifa insisted, certain of no such thing. The shaman had demanded no less than eight dinars for his cure. Alifa couldn't even imagine when she would have another four that she didn't need immediately for something else.

Some frippery, like food for her siblings.

She should have taken every single dinar that barbarian had, she concluded viciously. He owed her as much for the scars on her back. Especially if the sight of them kept her from earning much tonight.

The thought was a chilling one and Alifa shoved to her feet purposefully. Somehow she would have to convince the shaman to begin his treatment with a partial payment.

Would it never end?

The couple next door began to quarrel yet again and she struggled to block her ears against the sound of the beating that would inevitably follow. It wasn't that their home was humble that troubled her, for they hadn't had much more in the mountains. The difference had been outside the door. Where there had been mountains to climb and streams to splash in and green spaces for the children to run in, now there was filth, bad influences and danger.

The man shouted next door, the woman yelping as his first blow fell. Alifa's eyes met Tabeta's and she saw a reflection there of her own failure to do better for her siblings.

If she had had a man, she thought ferociously, she would have taken them back up into the mountains. But Alifa didn't have a man, and the road was and had always been too dangerous for a woman to travel alone. And even if she could have managed to make the journey safely after the death of their parents, the realities of living in the mountains required male assistance. It was a hard life, but Alifa missed it all the same.

If only her parents hadn't decided to seek their fortune in town. She turned and matter-of-factly picked up a water vessel. There was no use fretting over things she couldn't change. Her parents had brought them all here, and then they had died, leaving Alifa to do the best she could in their absence.

Never mind that things hadn't turned out quite the way her mother had planned.

"Find the shaman and tell him that I need to speak with him," she ordered Tabeta. The younger girl nodded quickly. Alifa frowned. "And where *is* Jaraw? He should be at his lessons. If he's done, he can help with dinner."

"I think he went to the *souk* with the other boys," Tabeta confided, her hesitant manner capturing her older sister's attention thoroughly.

"*What* boys?" Alifa demanded.

Tabeta's eyes dropped and Alifa muttered an expletive under her breath. Curse him! Not again.

"Not Sinhaj," she said tersely. "Tell me it wasn't Sinhaj and his gang."

"I don't know," Tabeta confessed miserably. Alifa's heart wrenched at the evidence that her sister was lying yet again. Twice in one afternoon.

Kasilo piped up cheerfully from the other side of the room. "It *was* Sinhaj. I saw them go together. They were talking about the silversmith's."

"The silversmith's!" Alifa repeated in shock.

What business had a pair of penniless young boys at the silversmith's? Unfortunately, Alifa didn't need much imagination to guess, since she knew far too much about Sinhaj. She had told Jaraw countless times that his friends were no good, but it seemed that he was ignoring her, as usual. With a repressed sigh, Alifa hefted the empty water jug onto her shoulder and pulled her hood over her hair.

"It's all right," Kasilo informed her breezily as she turned to leave the house. "They've been there before."

Alifa went still. "What do you mean?" she asked, forcing herself to remain outwardly calm.

"That's where he got the bracelet," the young boy supplied blithely.

"Kasilo!" Tabeta hissed. Alifa dropped a hand on her sister's shoulder to silence her. Later she would find out how much this pair had known and for how long. But she would deal with the root of the problem first.

Bless Kasilo and his loose tongue.

"What bracelet?" she asked coldly. Kasilo seemed to realize for the first time that he had said something amiss and he flicked a glance of trepidation at his oldest sister.

"It was nothing, really. Something someone gave him, I think," he prevaricated hastily and poorly. "Maybe I got confused and remembered wrong." Tabeta rolled her eyes and Alifa tightened her fingers slightly on the girl's shoulder in warning.

"What bracelet?" she demanded again. Kasilo's glance flicked away nervously and he licked his lips. "You know that I'll find out sooner or later," Alifa added silkily, the look her brother shot her revealing that he knew she spoke the truth.

"Tell me, Kasilo," she prompted more kindly, but still with steel in her tone. "You started the tale, and now you will finish it."

"It's just a bracelet," he mumbled miserably.

"Where is it?"

"Over there." He pointed and Alifa tightened her grip on Tabeta's shoulder in a silent demand before releasing her. The younger girl obediently slipped out from under the weight of Alifa's hand to rummage mutinously in Jaraw's clothes. "He moved it under there this morning," Kasilo directed when she did not immediately retrieve it.

Alifa saw the flash of silver when Tabeta followed her brother's direction, and she struggled to maintain her temper. He could *not* have stooped to thievery. But the evidence to the contrary glinted in Tabeta's hand. What would Alifa do? What would she say to Jaraw? How would she make this come right? The younger girl stood and turned slowly, a gleaming bracelet in her hand. Alifa's heart sank at the thickness of the silver band, seeing even at this distance that it was worth a goodly amount of coin.

Jaraw had done it. He had stolen. If he hadn't stolen the bracelet itself, he had stolen the money to purchase it, for she knew that there was not a spare coin to be had here. Alifa gritted her teeth, half convinced she would kill him herself for his stupidity. How could Jaraw not understand that he was throwing his life away?

She put out her hand imperiously. Tabeta's gaze met Alifa's before it skittered away.

"Did you know about this?" Alifa asked with Herculean calm. Tabeta nodded once and Alifa saw the glimmer of tears on her lashes. She bit down on her own disappointment that they had all participated in this in some small way and extended her hand once more.

"Give it here," she ordered. Tabeta stepped forward with evident reluctance and dropped the circle of silver into Alifa's outstretched palm without ever meeting her eyes.

"I expected better of you," Alifa whispered harshly. A tear splashed over Tabeta's cheek before she turned hastily away.

"I'll get the shaman," she mumbled and ran out of the house.

Alifa turned the bracelet over in her hand, absently admiring the workmanship, even as she wondered what she could do to turn Jaraw away from this path he seemed determined to follow. He was so headstrong and sensitive about any criticism she rendered. The times they had talked about Sinhaj had evidently just served to increase that vagabond's appeal.

If only she could get him away from Sinhaj and his band of troublemakers, the battle would be half won.

"Is Jaraw in trouble?" Kasilo asked meekly, his voice interrupting Alifa's thoughts. She fired a glance across the shadowed room.

"What do you think?" she asked. Kasilo frowned and looked away.

"I shouldn't have told you something that would get Jaraw in trouble," he said quietly.

"Jaraw is in trouble for what he did, not for what you said," Alifa corrected. The little boy's gaze met hers tentatively and Alifa smiled slowly in an attempt to reassure him. "You know I would have found out one way or the other," she reminded him in a confidential tone and he smiled tremulously.

"You *always* know," he said with a measure of awe.

"And thanks to you, I might know this in time to make a difference," she added. Kasilo was a loyal little soul and

Alifa was determined to show him that he had not betrayed his brother.

"I don't want Jaraw to be in trouble," he said unevenly. Alifa dropped to her knees beside the bed and brushed the thick hair back from the boy's brow affectionately. She refused to note the pallor of his skin or the weight he had lost over the past months.

"But Jaraw seems determined to find it," she mused. Kasilo looked up at her uncertainly. "Maybe being in a little trouble now will keep him from being in bigger trouble later," she said solemnly. The little boy held her gaze for a long moment while he considered her words.

"Is he going to lose his hand?" he whispered. To her horror, Alifa realized that she had no ready answer.

"I don't know," she admitted, knowing that she had an uphill battle to avoid that outcome. "I hope not," Alifa whispered. If the authorities were notified, there would be no doubt of the result. Something died within her at the realization that she might not be able to save Jaraw from the consequences of his actions.

Had she failed her parents? Had she failed Jaraw? Had she made the wrong choice by staying in town? To Alifa's surprise, Kasilo threw himself into her arms and buried his face in her shirt.

"I don't want him to lose his hand," he mumbled. Alifa gathered him close, his next words sending a pang through her heart. "You will fix it, won't you, Alifa?"

"I'll certainly try," she vowed, even as she recognized the limits of what she could do. She closed her eyes and held her youngest brother close, hoping Jaraw hadn't done anything even more foolish today to cement his fate.

Unfortunately, if he was with Sinhaj again, the chances seemed rather good that he had.

Chapter Three

If she made four dinars a night, she had no business living in a slum.

Four dinars. Four *silver* dinars. Yusuf stomped irritably through the *souk,* his foul mood increasing with every step he took. How dare she take such a sum from him?

Yusuf flicked his red cloak as he turned a corner, savoring the feel of the wool dramatically billowing behind him. He would show her. He was Berber, after all.

No, he was *Imazighen,* Yusuf corrected himself. He enjoyed rolling the Berbers' name for themselves around in his mind again. Imazighen. Men of the land. The noble ones. Yes, much better than merely *Berber.*

It had been a long time since he had even permitted himself to think in the tongue of his childhood, but Yusuf did not let himself dwell on that. What was important was that he had been duped. Duped by a woman who was undoubtedly Arabic, probably because she thought herself better than he.

Yusuf knew better. The Imazighen were, after all, the noblest race of all. The most virile. The most disciplined. The most worthy of respect. He barely realized that the assertions echoing in his mind were his father's, as his annoyance rose another notch.

The insult could not be allowed to pass. Not only was Yusuf Imazighen, but he had *baraka,* the aura of kings, as well. Was he not the son of a magician? Had it not been foreseen that he, too, had the mystical presence of kingship? Was it not openly acknowledged that the force ran stronger within him? Had they not said from his earliest days that he would follow in his father's footsteps and lead the tribe to prosperity?

Of course, that had been before he left, before he had converted. Before he had cut all ties with his past and his father's whimsical foolishness. Before he had turned his back on his legacy and denied that part of himself.

But still. Regardless of his own choices, Yusuf was not a man to be toyed with and cast aside. The whore should have known better.

Yusuf scowled as he passed through the wooden gates and entered the dingy shadows of the poor quarter. It didn't matter that he had turned his back on his heritage, he told himself determinedly. The woman had no right to his money, whether he was a proper scholar or a noble Berber.

A pair of shabbily dressed urchins dared to beg, but Yusuf silenced them with a cold glance. As if he would leave more money here. He snorted under his breath at the very thought. Yusuf had come to retrieve his silver, not cast more to the winds. His eyes narrowed and the children scuttled backward into the shelter of a filthy doorway.

Vermin. How could they live like this? Why did they live like this? Why didn't they simply find work, learn to read, better themselves and fight their way out of such destitution?

Yusuf reached the square, where water sparkled in a tiled fountain for all to use, and surveyed the cluster of people there critically. His lip curled with disdain at their disordered and dirty state, and he squared his shoulders proudly under the weight of their perusal.

Even the tiles in the fountain were chipped, and their design less elaborate than in the other quarters of the city. Undoubtedly they were more cheaply made. The fountain was a simple one, the trickle of water emanating from it brown and feeble. The adjacent baths looked similarly run-down and Yusuf was glad that he was not forced to use such shabby facilities.

No, he didn't belong here and he didn't care whether these people realized it. He met the gaze of each who dared to look to his face in turn and watched their expressions harden before they turned away. Did they sense his judgment of them? Yusuf rather thought they did and permitted himself a moment of self-congratulation.

It might make a difference, after all.

Ignoring the silence that had fallen on the group at his arrival, he stalked to the side of the fountain where the greatest cluster of women were gathered. Several scurried backward, out of his way, one stared him down, but Yusuf was busily checking the faces of them all.

She wasn't here. He didn't allow himself to be disappointed. There wasn't time. He had an errand to accomplish and the sooner his money was retrieved, the sooner he could get out of this miserable quarter. He certainly didn't want to be caught here at dusk when they closed the gates.

"Do you know a woman named Alifa?" he demanded of the woman who boldly held his gaze. She blinked at his abrupt manner.

"And if I do?"

"Then you can tell me where to find her."

"Why?" The woman's eyes narrowed with suspicion and Yusuf nearly laughed aloud. What threat could he possibly make to Alifa? Had she not already done as badly for herself as an individual might manage? She was a whore who lived in a slum. Surely life couldn't get any worse for her with his arrival.

Except for the retrieval of a bit of silver that this woman knew nothing about.

"I would like to talk to her," Yusuf said carefully.

The woman snorted. "No gentleman comes calling on a single lady just to talk." Yusuf was momentarily puzzled. Lady? Alifa was no lady, that much he knew for certain. Could there be two Alifas living here?

"I am seeking the Alifa who works at the tavern on the other side of the *souk*," he explained. The woman's expression relaxed slightly.

"That explains that then," she said amiably. "We don't have any whores living in this neighborhood."

"I beg your pardon?" Now it was Yusuf's turn to be skeptical. The woman took on a hostile air at his manner and jabbed one finger in the direction of his chest while the others watched silently.

"You *heard* what I said," she spat. "We have no whores or otherwise dirty people living around here. We're respectable folk, whatever you might think, and we have children to raise."

Yusuf flicked a glance over the assortment of women gathered around him, and acknowledged that none of them were attractive enough to make much of a living in Alifa's business. They looked tired and worn-out before their time. He stubbornly quelled an uncharacteristic twinge of sympathy for their lives here and propped his hands on his hips.

He had to get his silver back. That was the point of this little adventure.

"So, you have no idea where I might find this woman?"

The woman squared her shoulders. "If it's more of *that* you want, why don't you go back where you found her the first time? Whores tend to work the same locale for exactly that reason." Her eyes narrowed to hostile slits. "Repeat business, I understand, is the foundation of a successful career."

Yusuf saw the judgment in the woman's glittering eyes and drew himself up proudly. How dare she presume to make assumptions about him? "I said that I wanted to talk to the woman."

The woman laughed harshly. "Of course," she said with a sneer. "Everyone hires whores for the conversation." The surrounding crowd tittered until Yusuf glared at them. The silence that followed was filled with nervous little rustlings as people fidgeted, uncertain whether they wanted to stay, but afraid to leave, lest they miss something.

Yusuf gritted his teeth in annoyance and fought against the beast's demand to be unleashed. "She robbed me," he confessed tersely, knowing the words to have been a mistake as soon as they left his mouth.

The woman before him hooted with laughter.

The crowd took up the chuckle and Yusuf felt his color rise with embarrassment. He was not in the least comfortable with this development, especially knowing that he had only himself to blame. He should have kept his mouth closed and left this nameless peasant with her own unflattering assumptions.

"Robbed by a whore!" she chortled. "You don't look like you were born yesterday, but I suppose one never can tell."

Yusuf had an urge to explain that he merely felt he had been overcharged, but determinedly shoved it aside. That could not make matters any better. Nor would telling of his conviction that their lovemaking had been extraordinary enough that he had been stunned she took any money at all.

This definitely was not going as he had planned.

Yusuf stiffly turned and stalked away from the gleeful crowd of women around the well, his ears burning at the taunting cries that followed in his wake.

This was twice that Alifa had been responsible for Yusuf looking like a fool. It wasn't a role he enjoyed playing and his ire redoubled as he made his way through the twisting alleys of the quarter. He stepped into the sunlight in the *souk,* feeling as relieved as though he had returned safely from the land of the damned, and his gaze landed on the glinting silver displayed for sale at a nearby booth.

Four dinars wasn't enough for what he had suffered at Alifa's hand, he resolved. He would have his four back and two for the embarrassment she had caused him. And he would retrieve all of it this very night, at the tavern.

Somehow he suspected Alifa would not be surprised to see him.

Alifa was late. She was exhausted, but there was nothing for it. She still had to work. The cursed shaman had declared *after* he had pocketed her four precious dinars that he needed the entire sum before he could begin. After all, Alifa wouldn't want him to be troubled about anything mundane and be distracted from casting his spell, would she?

Alifa gritted her teeth, wishing she had some other option. But Kasilo was getting weaker by the day and there was an outside chance that, despite his blatant opportunism, the shaman might have some healing powers.

Although Alifa was heartily beginning to doubt that. Of course, having effectively paid half for the spell already, she might as well pay the rest so that the money wasn't completely wasted. Her frustration rose and threatened to choke her as she pushed her way into the crowded tavern.

Another night, another round of customers, another paltry sum of silver to add to the pile. Think of Kasilo, she reminded herself determinedly. Instead, she wondered whether he would even be sick now if she hadn't chosen to stay in town. Alifa didn't know whether that was true or not, but in her current state, the very idea fed her guilt.

She shoved aside a hand that pinched her buttocks, forcing a smile as she assessed the size of the crowd. It might be a good night, she concluded before her flesh began to creep.

He was here. Somewhere. She could feel his presence.

And he had already seen her.

Alifa's panic rose with this unexpected certainty. Her pulse raced erratically and she hastily scanned the group of men, not caring who saw her agitation.

She found those startlingly green eyes with frightening speed. Alifa swallowed nervously as Yusuf smiled a coldly mercenary smile. It seemed to her that everyone else in the room faded away and that even the boisterous sounds of the busy tavern dropped in volume. There was nothing in her universe but those piercing green eyes.

The scratches on her back began to itch in that very moment.

She had to escape! Alifa took a step backward, hoping he couldn't see her shiver of trepidation. Yusuf unfolded himself from his stool as though he had all the time in the world, exhibiting a catlike grace that was a less than welcome reminder of what she thought she had seen the night before.

Suddenly it all seemed real. Any doubts Alifa had had in the bright daylight about what she had witnessed faded to nothing under the weight of Yusuf's piercing stare.

He had been waiting for her. She was sure of it. Her heart began to beat a staccato. Why was he waiting for her? What did he want? To finish what he had begun? Fear stopped Alifa's breathing and she felt her hand clench reflexively.

But still she couldn't look away. There was something about him that drew her like a moth to a flame. Alifa hesitated, her warring impulses leaving her uncertain what to do.

Yusuf took a step across the tiled floor, his red cloak fluttering, his gaze not wavering from her. Alifa's flesh went cold.

It was enough to break her indecision.

He was coming for her! And there was nothing she could do to stop him. A primal desperation to survive flooded through her and, for the first time in her recollection, she took the coward's way out.

Alifa ran.

She shoved her way through the crowd of jovial men, knowing all the while that Yusuf followed her relentlessly. The sound of footfalls echoed in her ears and she told herself that they were his. There was ultimately no escape—Alifa had known that last night—but she had to try.

Alifa gained the street abruptly and gulped in the chill night air. Her cloak conspired against her, but she hauled it up above her knees in two fistfuls and ran. She had everything to lose, after all, and modesty was the least of her problems.

She heard someone else in the street behind her. A man's boots rang on the cobblestones. Alifa's eyes widened and she tried to run even faster. She wished she had managed to get out of sight, wished the sound of her own footfalls didn't give her away, but knew better when those boots echoed in pursuit.

"Alifa!" Yusuf roared as if to dispel any lingering doubt in her mind about who followed her. Alifa gulped and ran as though she hadn't heard him.

Her mind began to race as she ducked past homes draped in darkness. Where was she going? She couldn't go home—he would follow her there. What would happen to the children? The thought almost paralyzed her with fear.

She couldn't lead him there. Whatever the cost to herself.

What would he do now that he knew she knew his secret? She had half forgotten all of the old tales from up in the hills, mostly because she had put no stock in their truth, but Alifa knew well enough that anyone who witnessed a shapeshifter's change was marked. What was the price the spy had to pay? She wished she could remember, but that part of the tale had faded from her mind.

No, Alifa shook her head, hearing her breath come in little pants of terror as she rounded yet another crooked corner. Not home. Anywhere but there. She had never taken evil home to her siblings and she wouldn't start now.

Stones scrabbled behind her and she knew by the volume of the sound that he was getting closer. The mosque? The docks? Back to the tavern? None of them offered any real sanctuary. Alifa couldn't decide.

Why had she run? She should have confronted him in front of everyone at the tavern. Alifa cursed her impulsiveness too late to make a change. Yusuf swore as he stumbled behind her and her panic redoubled.

He was too close! Alifa imagined she could feel his warm breath on her neck, just as it had been the previous night when she lay beneath him. She flicked a glance over her shoulder to find him directly behind her.

Those green eyes flashed fire, too reminiscent of the cat for her taste. Yusuf lunged forward and Alifa screamed.

She tripped over unexpected stairs and tumbled to her knees. He landed on top of her with a vehement curse and she closed her eyes tightly so that she wouldn't have to see him change. His anger bore down on her, much as his passion had, and Alifa had no doubt what would happen next. She twisted and bit, in a futile attempt to break free, but Yusuf quickly rolled her onto her back and pinned her shoulders to the ground with his hands.

Not paws.

Alifa glanced tentatively through her eyelashes to find very masculine hands gripping her shoulders. No claws. She looked skeptically up to her attacker's face, only to find a very annoyed Berber holding her down, his teeth gritted in evident frustration. It was the same man she had spent the previous night with, to be certain, but tonight he appeared perfectly average.

Well, maybe not quite average, Alifa conceded reluctantly as relief restored her usual attitude. She spared her attacker an assessing eye and was pleased despite herself with her conclusions. Yusuf Khudabanda was admittedly better-looking than most and certainly better attired. She remembered only too well his superb physique and eyed his broad shoulders appreciatively. His hands flexed and a flame flickered to life within her at the memory of those long fingers trailing across her skin.

If nothing else, Alifa certainly had picked a fine man to be sprawled beneath.

Except for that one eerie occurrence. Alifa met Yusuf's eyes hesitantly, their vivid green color still shocking her. Was it possible that she had imagined his change? Was it possible that she had just had a strange dream?

Alifa could not be certain and didn't like the feeling one bit.

Yusuf's eyes still glittered angrily and his shoulders heaved from the effort of chasing her. His knees were braced on either side of her hips in a pose that did no favors to Alifa's attempts to rid her mind of thoughts of the night before. Her gaze wandered over his broad chest and lean hips. Alifa licked her lips, knowing that if she dared to touch his black *chalwar* she would find strong thighs beneath the full cut cloth.

She smelled the heat rising from his skin and the warmth of desire spread within her. Yusuf's red cloak fluttered and settled over them both as he glared down at her, making Alifa fully aware of the intimacy of their positions. Her pulse tripped, not from fear this time, but from anticipation.

What was she thinking? How could she even imagine such a thing after the night before?

But Alifa was forced to acknowledge an errant niggling of satisfaction. Before he frightened her, Alifa had been feeling remarkably replete herself in Yusuf's bed. She bit her lip and studied him through her lashes, not in the least comfortable with the memory of his tenderness.

She wanted to be with him again.

It was inexplicable. It was wrong. It was incredibly stupid, but it was the truth.

Alifa fidgeted, as much against her troubling thoughts as anything else. She felt the edge of a stone stair digging into her back and welcomed the excuse to push Yusuf away impatiently. "Let me up," she demanded crossly. "I'll be bruised from head to toe from these stairs."

Surprise flickered over Yusuf's expression before he scowled and complied. "You're the one who ran," he observed irritably. He brushed dirt fastidiously from his black *chalwar* as he stood before her and spared Alifa a sharp glance. "Any particular reason we just raced halfway across town?"

Alifa's mouth worked for a moment as she sought a plausible reply, the sardonic light in his eyes doing little to encourage confidences. "I thought you were somebody else," she retorted with a toss of her hair. Fully aware that he was watching her carefully, Alifa stood up and straightened her own attire as she turned away.

"Someone with more than four dinars in his pocket, maybe?" he drawled. The barb found its mark, for all his casualness.

Alifa spun indignantly on her heel to face him. "You think I was worth more, then?" she demanded archly. Her companion snorted.

"Hardly. I want that silver back." Yusuf braced his hands on his hips as he confronted her. "Those four dinars and two more." Despite the fact that he was taller than she and clearly annoyed, Alifa was insulted enough to not even consider backing down.

"You want it back?" she repeated in amazement. "I told you that I *always* charge."

"And I'm telling you that you charged too much," he snapped.

Alifa snorted. "I should have charged you *double* that," she retorted. His eyes blazed, but she jabbed her chin in the air, undeterred. "I should have charged you for an entire week," she asserted boldly. Yusuf's eyes narrowed.

"You weren't that memorable." He bit the words out cruelly.

"Well, neither were you," Alifa answered scornfully, an idea occurring to her while she argued. "But the marks you left will probably keep me from working for a week. I think you should pay for *that*." It was a nice, neat solution, all the more so for being true. Alifa folded her arms across her chest and waited for the inevitable reaction.

To her surprise, Yusuf's manner turned wary instead of angry.

"What marks?" he asked carefully. She could see that he was not as ignorant of them as he might like her to think.

Maybe she had seen what she thought she had seen. But that was insane.

"The scratches you made on my back," she retorted defiantly.

"I don't remember making any scratches," Yusuf muttered, but Alifa saw the increased awareness reflected in his eyes. He might not specifically recall the night before, but he knew what he was capable of and wasn't surprised by her accusation. This disturbing conclusion fueled her fear anew, but Alifa refused to take a step backward.

"I remember well enough for both of us," she said confidently.

Yusuf's lips thinned. "Show me the marks," he demanded tersely.

"I will not." Alifa took that step backward, and regarded him with shock when his expression didn't change. What did he expect her to do? "I will not bare my flesh in the streets, just because you ask me to," she added indignantly.

Yusuf smiled coldly. "Really? I had understood your type did anything you were asked to do."

Alifa slapped the smug smile from his face with a resounding crack. His eyes blazed and she stumbled backward up the stairs as she realized the foolhardiness of what she had done. Would anger prompt his transformation this time? And how would she manage to outrun that lean and agile panther?

But when Alifa glanced fearfully over her shoulder to Yusuf, she found only a man glaring back at her. An angry man, certainly, but a man nonetheless. Alifa had expected something quite different and she carefully reconsidered her conclusion.

Was it possible she hadn't seen what she thought she had seen the night before?

The glint in Yusuf's eyes was too knowing to let Alifa completely believe that she had been mistaken. Was he just toying with her, the way a cat toyed with a mouse? The image was too apt, to Alifa's thinking, and she took a wary step backward. How far could she run before he caught her? And where could she run to escape?

Yusuf took the first stair and purposefully closed the distance between them. Alifa's pulse began to flutter and she heartily regretted her impulsive action.

"No woman has ever struck me before," he growled. Alifa took another backward step, hoping that she managed it with nonchalance.

"Then maybe someone should have," she retorted breathlessly, determined not to let him see her fear. Yusuf's lips thinned and she already knew enough of him to react. By the time he darted up the remaining stairs, Alifa had already turned and fled.

The hardened leather soles of her shoes clattered on the cobblestones and she almost slipped in her haste to take a corner. Yusuf's footsteps were too close and she knew she wouldn't get far before he claimed her. Alifa spotted the darkened entrance to the tannery and ducked inside with relief, hoping her memory didn't fail her now.

The tannery! What luck to find herself here! Her fingers were immediately unknotting the belt around her waist, with its jingling coins, as she crossed the threshold. Alifa cast it aside and kicked off her shoes in the cool shadows beneath the gate. Shed of telltale noisemakers, she ran silently down one of the side corridors. Yusuf came into the entryway behind her and halted uncertainly.

He would never find her here. Alifa stopped and waited in the shadows, bracing herself against the smell of rotting meat. She closed her eyes so that she would be able to hear him better and melted back against the wall, not even daring to breathe.

She prayed he wouldn't be able to hear her pounding heart.

Mercifully, he seemed indecisive and Alifa dared to hope. She heard the rasp of his breathing and could feel his annoyance almost as a tangible force. Alifa clenched her hands and willed herself to remain motionless.

She was on familiar turf and, given a chance, might even manage to elude him. She allowed a crest of satisfaction to well within her as she curled her toes around the corners of one of the cold flagstones in the old floor.

He would never catch her here.

The smell of the hides filled her lungs, the pungency of the tanning solution stinging her nostrils. It was all too familiar. Alifa let her recollection of the tannery flow through her mind, every nook, every cranny in its convoluted halls as clear as if she had been here yesterday. It had been years since she had played here while her father worked, but she knew the old place hadn't changed. It would never change. She pressed her back against the wall and waited for Yusuf to make his move.

Finally he stepped in the opposite direction. Alifa smiled victoriously.

She waited until he had taken a dozen cautious steps, then scurried silently away from him. Alifa wanted nothing better than to put as much distance between them as possible.

And she knew there was another exit on the other side of the courtyard, where the skins were dyed in the sun.

All she had to do was cross the courtyard without being seen.

Alifa came to a halt at the end of the corridor that hugged the perimeter of the courtyard and hung back in the shadows while she caught her breath. The moon came out from behind a cloud with cursedly poor timing, casting the open courtyard in its pale silver glow.

The large, round dried-earth pits were dug out like a honeycomb, the various liquids within them gleaming ominously in the moonlight. Alifa knew the solutions to be of various colors, but they all looked dark orange at night. The smell might have been overwhelming to one who had not spent as much time here as she.

Alifa visually traced a weaving path between the pits that made short work of the distance, then spared a glance to the moon. She gritted her teeth as she realized there wasn't another cloud in the sky and listened carefully as she eyed the opposite doorway.

Silence. And it couldn't be more than twenty running steps across. She could just barely discern the darkness of the hall in the shadows of the far corridor.

Just twenty steps to the doorway. Then down the hall and out the door to freedom. The alley beyond was filthy with discarded carcasses, but she knew her way back to the main thoroughfare.

And freedom. It was worth it. Alifa licked her lips and waited another half-dozen heartbeats.

Nothing. Maybe Yusuf had left.

She shook her head decisively. Not likely. But he wasn't close. She didn't question her certainty that she would sense his presence as she had in the tavern.

Maybe he wouldn't even see her dart across the courtyard.

Maybe.

She didn't have many other options. Alifa squared her shoulders and slipped into the shadow cast by one of the supporting columns that lined the courtyard.

Nothing moved. She tapped her fingers for an endless moment on the cold stone, then took a deep breath. It was now or never. Alifa clenched her teeth, took a breath and ran.

She was no more than halfway across the courtyard when she heard it.

Something—or someone—sniffed. The hairs on the back of Alifa's neck stood on end and she nearly stopped in her flight, before the sound came again.

It was louder. And closer.

She was being hunted!

Terror lent speed to Alifa's steps and she was across the courtyard in a flash. She lunged down the short stretch of corridor and threw open the door.

Something hit the ground behind her with a soft thud and she burst out into the alleyway, oblivious of the smell of carrion. Alifa hauled the door closed behind her and felt something land heavily against it. Her heart stopped, her eyes widened in horror, but she had no time to stop and reflect. Before the door could be opened, she ran down the filthy alley.

Something scratched at the closed door and the sound carried clearly to Alifa's ears. Her feet flew as she fought to put distance between herself and the sound, her heart filling with a dreadful certainty that she would never escape.

There was no doubting that it had happened again.

Yusuf had wondered when Alifa made her accusation about the scratches he had given her, but he hadn't wanted to believe that the old curse was revisiting him. It had been so long and he had hoped so fervently that it had abandoned him. Although the transformation had been far from complete tonight, that pricking in his palms was enough to convince him of the truth of her tale.

The beast he had hoped had departed had only been slumbering all these years.

And now it was awake again.

He watched dispassionately as the dreaded talons changed slowly back to his familiar nails. The blue-black pads on his palms lightened gradually to the normal hue of his skin.

What about the rest? How much his father's son was he? The possibilities of embracing the power were tempting, but Yusuf refused to indulge the thought. The price was too high. He would not become what his father had become.

It was wrong.

And bearing this curse alone was enough of a price for one man to pay. The moonlight danced over his flesh with its surreal light, defying him to believe what he had just witnessed. Yusuf flexed his hand, amazed yet again at how perfectly normal it looked.

Normal.

Yusuf stifled a laugh. It seemed that, despite his efforts, that was never destined to be. He straightened and stretched, some vestige of feline grace lingering in his movements, although he was unaware of it. He felt compelled to touch the warmth of his skin, as if his own eyes could not be trusted. By habit, he brushed his fingertips across his face and felt that old surge of relief that there were no whiskers.

And Alifa was gone. There was no sound of her flight carrying to his ears anymore. With one long fingertip, Yusuf touched the latch that had effectively halted his pursuit. Where had she run?

Perhaps more importantly, what had she seen?

She was terrified of him, that much was clear and Yusuf supposed she had a good reason to be. He had scratched her.

His eyes narrowed speculatively, but still any specific recollection of that incident evaded him.

What had she done to affect him so strongly? Almost fourteen years since he had last had the change—fourteen years since he had left the village of his birth behind in disgust—and now it had happened twice in as many nights. Both times before Alifa. What was it about her? Last night there had been the *eau-de-vie* to eliminate his control, but tonight he had no such excuse.

The smell of rotting meat was almost overwhelming here. Noticing it for the first time, he winced at its pungency and turned back to the tannery.

Alifa remained the single common factor between the two unwilling transformations.

Yusuf frowned and strolled back along the colonnade to the tannery door they had entered. He picked up Alifa's abandoned belt, smiling to himself at the way it jingled. It was only too easy to remember the noise it made when she danced and the provocative sway of her hips that was responsible. A waft of jasmine mingled with Alifa's own scent rose from the belt to tease his nostrils and Yusuf felt the beast rear back and roar.

That was what she did to him. She awakened his dark side and reminded him of the past.

He shoved the belt into his pocket and scooped up her shoes in poor humor before stalking out into the night. They were small and worn, the colored leather bent to the shape of her foot from use, but Yusuf refused to speculate upon them. He shoved them into his other pocket and made his hands abandon them there. He forced himself to walk through the quiet, twisting streets while he regained his control.

She had struck him.

It was shocking that even knowing what she did, she was not afraid to push him. Yusuf could still feel the echo of the rage that had swept through him at her audacity. When she fled, he had thought of nothing but catching her. And when she disappeared into the tannery, his hunter's instinct had come to the fore.

Of its own accord. Which was frightening, to say the least. Yusuf shook his head and scowled at his own foolishness in thinking this demon banished from his life. Books. Learning. Social prestige. He snorted with disdain. Could such things really change anything as fundamental as who, or what, he was?

He had even changed his faith. How the old man would laugh when he heard. It seemed Yusuf was going to look like a fool on his return home for more than one reason. The prospect of that inevitable trip dulled even further.

He was an urban man, he reminded himself forcefully. He had put the past behind him, and there it would stay. He would not follow his father. Yusuf had made his choice and one whore was not going to throw all of his life into disarray.

Yusuf found himself fingering the instep of Alifa's shoe before he knew what he was doing. He imagined her tiny arched foot within it and readily pictured how she would laugh if he caressed her this way. Certainly she would be ticklish there. Certainly that would summon that girlish twinkle to her eyes once more. He smiled to himself as he pictured her eyes bright with saucy laughter, but then he caught himself up short.

What was he thinking? Yusuf hauled his hands out of his pockets in disgust at the direction his thoughts were taking. Alifa tempted men for money. It was as simple as that. She certainly had no regard for her clients. Hadn't she told him as much this morning?

And didn't she still have his four dinars? Yusuf frowned. Why hadn't he managed to retrieve them?

It didn't matter. He shook his head hastily and recalled the items in his pockets with a slow smile. Yusuf didn't know what the belt and shoes were worth, but he couldn't help wondering whether they were worth four dinars to Alifa.

If nothing else, he certainly aimed to find out.

Chapter Four

"Well, well, well ... Look who decided to make an appearance."

Alifa froze on the threshold of the tavern at the sound of that familiar drawl and glanced across the room. She was momentarily surprised that the tavern was virtually empty, the vestiges of smoke still making the air hazy in the light cast by the lanterns.

Alifa supposed it must be later than she had thought.

"Good evening," she said carefully when she picked out Hakim's shadowed silhouette. He unfolded himself leisurely from his chair and Alifa knew to expect the worst.

"Good morning, more like," he said pointedly. Alifa had no response to that. Hakim paused before her and eyed her disheveled state dispassionately before meeting her eyes. His disdain was clear from his expression.

"I had thought I had made myself clear, Alifa," he said slowly. She knew he was enjoying this moment, but she refused to back down.

"About what?" she demanded defiantly.

"About your working tonight. Or maybe I should say *last* night." There was a new, harsher edge in his voice that sent Alifa's chin proudly into the air.

"I was unavoidably detained," she maintained haughtily. He stepped closer and she saw that he was smiling sardonically.

"It doesn't matter," he whispered. His eyes widened slightly as he leaned closer and Alifa saw more of the yellowed whites than she really wanted to. "It just doesn't matter anymore."

He couldn't mean... Alifa was one of his best earners and she knew it. Just two nights wasn't too much to ask after all this time.

Or was it?

"I don't understand," she said stonily. Hakim chuckled to himself as he strolled away. He eyed her with amusement as he refilled his glass.

"Oh, but I think you do," he said softly.

"I want to understand exactly what you mean," Alifa insisted. Hakim shot her a sharp look that did not bode well.

"Your customer came back yesterday morning," he informed her icily. Alifa straightened. Yusuf had come looking for her here.

And Hakim knew that she had worked the night before.

"You lied to me, Alifa," he charged. Alifa found she had no response to that, so she waited silently. Their gazes met through the smoke and held for a long moment before Hakim arched a brow high.

"I can't afford to have unreliable women working here," he said finally. The words seemed to entangle themselves in the thick smoke and hang there, daring Alifa to comprehend them.

"I'm not unreliable," she insisted, struggling to choke back her feelings.

The proprietor shook his head. "Not until very recently, you weren't," he admitted. He fired a glance across the tavern. "But now you are." He paused and sipped his drink, his eyes unwavering from her face. "And deceitful," he concluded pointedly.

"It was just two nights." Alifa hated the plea in her voice, but was powerless to stop it. "It won't happen again, I promise you."

"You promised that already and have broken your word," Hakim pointed out coldly. "Pay me my percentage of the business you had from that Berber."

"I can't."

"You won't," Hakim corrected with a curl of his lip.

"The money is gone," Alifa protested. She watched Hakim's face set and knew before he spoke that she could make no argument that would win her case.

"Then so are you," he said flatly. "It's over, Alifa. Three customers walked out tonight when they found out that you weren't here. I can't afford to lose business like that just because you arbitrarily decide not to show up."

"I didn't arbitrarily decide—" Alifa began, but Hakim interrupted her.

"No? Then you planned it?"

"Don't be ridiculous," she responded crossly.

"Then what? Something came up? Something unexpected? Something that might come up again at any moment?" Hakim opened his eyes wide and Alifa saw that he really wasn't interested in anything she might say. He had already decided.

And she didn't work here anymore.

"I'll get my belongings and leave," she said tightly.

She would find another tavern. As distasteful as her occupation was, it put food in her siblings' mouths and kept a roof over their heads. Alifa would go to one of the other taverns and continue to do the same thing.

Alifa wished she had a choice, but life had dealt her enough that she knew the truth when it confronted her. She had no other options. Somehow she would make it work. Unable to begin to face her disappointment, Alifa turned to go to the dancers' room and do precisely that, but Hakim's words brought her up short.

"Don't even begin to imagine that you'll work anywhere else in this town," he declared. Alifa spun on her heel in shock.

"What did you say?" she demanded incredulously.

"You heard me," he retorted coldly. "If I lose business because you're not here, then so will everybody else. I know them all, Alifa, and I know things about them all that will convince them to listen to me."

"You can't do this!" she protested angrily. He merely cocked a brow and regarded her coldly.

"Just watch."

Animosity crackled between them for a long moment. Alifa couldn't believe what she had heard, but Hakim's expression left no doubt in her mind.

Finally he lifted a glass to his lips and took a deliberate sip. The interview was over. Her position was lost. There was nothing she could do.

Certain she didn't want to lose her temper here and now, Alifa stormed to the back of the tavern and tore open the glittering curtain. It was outrageous that Hakim would do this to her! Alifa snatched up a trio of veils she had paid for and jammed them into the pockets of her *chalwar*. Not that she needed them for anything now. Unbelievable! She had been cast out into the cold without any means of providing for herself!

Even more outrageous was the fact that there was nothing she could do about it. Not a cursed thing. Alifa tore a sheer pair of embroidered *chalwar* down from a hook on the wall, hating the very sight of them. Where had this dancing gotten her in the end?

Kasilo wouldn't get his spell. That thought dispelled Alifa's fury for a moment and she froze in the middle of the room in shock.

Kasilo. The children needed her and she had failed them. Again. Alifa's gaze fell on a platter of sweets, and the honey they oozed. Frustrated tears gathered as she knelt down and spread out one of the fine silk veils. She folded it into quarters and methodically piled the sweets in the center. At least they would have one last indulgence.

It might well be their last meal, but Alifa wouldn't think about that.

Her hand shook as she knotted the scarf. She couldn't imagine what she would do now. She had failed her siblings and this time it looked as though there would be no recovery.

It was all the fault of Yusuf Khudabanda. The fault for everything that had gone awry could be laid squarely at his door, Alifa concluded angrily and shoved to her feet. At the very least, he was personally responsible for her having missed another night in the tavern, and she was certainly going to see that he paid for that.

A surge of fear shot through Alifa at the possibility of seeing him again, before she forced herself to sneer with her usual cynical air.

Yusuf was just a man, no more or less a beast than the rest of them. Whatever she thought she had seen last night or tonight had been nothing more than the product of imagination. She hadn't had enough sleep lately, had she? Everyone knew that shapeshifters didn't really exist, despite her mother's old stories.

Alifa hadn't actually seen Yusuf shift, had she? No. Granted, there had been a panther inexplicably in his room. She acknowledged a niggling of doubt, but shook her head stubbornly.

He hadn't changed when she angered him in the streets. And at the tannery, who knew? Men could sniff as readily as beasts. She had seen nothing.

More to the point, she had lost her job. Her family's livelihood was at stake, courtesy of Yusuf Khudabanda. Fear or no fear, Alifa knew that she had no choice other than to set him straight. She would take every single dinar he had. Her lips set with mutinous resolve. That was the least of what he owed her.

Unfortunately for Yusuf, Alifa remembered exactly where they had spent their night together.

Yusuf had the distinct sense that he was being watched.

Every fiber of him came awake in an instant and his hunter's instinct rose immediately to the fore. He willed his eyelids to remain closed and refused to change his breathing until the threat was assessed.

Who was in his room? What did they want from him? Despite the quickening of his blood, he remained stubbornly still while he let his senses fill with his surroundings.

It wasn't his landlady—that much Yusuf knew without doubt. She never disturbed his privacy and could never have remained as motionless as this intruder, even if she had.

He waited for a telltale sign. His fingers flexed in the familiar fringe of the threadbare cushions in his rented room. The warmth of the sunlight that shone into the room only in the early morning heated his bare back. He listened, but the room was silent. The street outside was quiet, too, with that early-morning hush typical of residential neighborhoods.

The room was too silent to be empty. Yusuf dared to inhale and his eyes almost flew open despite himself.

Jasmine. The floral scent flooded his lungs and awakened him with a vengeance.

Alifa wore jasmine. Alifa alone of all the women he knew. In fact, some vestige of her scent still clung to the cushions around him. Yusuf inhaled carefully once more, immediately reassured that this waft of scent was fresh and undoubtedly carrying to his nostrils from the intruder.

It seemed he would have the chance to retrieve his dinars sooner than he had expected.

Yusuf did not dare smile. The rush of anticipation that rolled through him caught him by surprise, but he refused to read more into his response than it merited. Certainly he was no more than relieved that this business would soon be behind him.

It was the principle of the matter. Certainly he couldn't be pleased at the prospect of a whore finding her way into his room.

The *muezzin*'s high, nasal cry broke suddenly over the morning air, calling the faithful to prayer. A muted rustle of cloth revealed Alifa's location. Yusuf composed himself, rolled over and looked her directly in the eye.

If Alifa was surprised that he was not only awake but fully cognizant of her presence, she hid it well. She arched one brow high with unruffled ease as their eyes met and Yusuf stifled a twinge of annoyance.

"Good morning," she whispered pertly.

Yusuf scowled and ran one hand through his thick hair in annoyance. He sat up, but refused to immediately cover his nudity, out of some perverse desire to shock her into responding. To his disappointment, Alifa seemed not to notice.

But what should he have expected from a woman who earned her living on her back? He was far from the first man she had seen naked, and probably far from the last to whom she had granted her favors.

Even at her hefty price. That thought rankled.

He ignored her presence while he hauled on his *chalwar* and his loose shirt. Yusuf washed carefully, spread his prayer rug and performed the first prayer ritual of his day. Yusuf was thoroughly aware of Alifa's bemused regard, but he deliberately lingered over the ritual.

When he was done, he stood up carefully, shook out his rug and looked her in the eye as he folded it up.

"What are you doing here?" he demanded impatiently.

Alifa's eyes widened slightly, though the way she glanced quickly to the door and lifted one finger to her lips showed that it was the volume of his voice, not his tone, that had caught her attention. Yusuf permitted himself a measure of disgruntled satisfaction that she at least had not expected to be welcomed with open arms.

Sneaking into his room. Disgusting behavior, and certainly far beneath the standards of any other woman he had known. Yusuf folded his arms across his chest, as if to make his feelings on the matter completely clear.

Alifa remained irritatingly unruffled by his annoyance. She leaned back casually against the wall and folded her arms similarly. A glint in her eye warned Yusuf that whatever battle they fought this day would not be easily won.

"I am simply fetching what is due to me," she clarified in the same lowered but even tone as before.

Yusuf snorted. "All that is due to you is a resounding case of the pox, and you won't fetch that here," he growled.

"Then you had best hope I didn't fetch my due more than two nights ago," Alifa snapped, "or you might find yourself with an unwelcome souvenir." Yusuf glared at her, the idea sending a ripple of panic through him before he recognized her ploy.

"You've used that tale before to no gain," he observed coldly.

Alifa shrugged in easy acknowledgment of the reminder. It had been Yusuf's insistence that she confess to that lie that had forced their paths to first cross all those months ago.

Yet he and Alifa had struck sparks right from the start. He had longed to throttle her that first day for her insolence and that had certainly not changed with time. Yusuf wondered if Alifa recalled that heated exchange. The way her lips thinned made him think that perhaps she did and that pleased him in a most curious way.

"Business has been good since then," Alifa said archly. "And you never know what some traveler might drag home." Her words dismissed any romantic inclinations Yusuf might have had and he forced himself to look at the situation with clear eyes. He had to remember what this woman did for a living.

"You seem quite cavalier about the possibility," Yusuf remarked, secretly amazed that she could be so offhand about such a risk. Alifa held his gaze boldly.

"It comes with the territory," she said harshly. Something in Alifa's expression should have cautioned him that she was about to make an accusation, but for some reason,

Yusuf's usual ability to read people was less reliable with this woman.

"Abuse, however, is something I refuse to tolerate," she continued. Yusuf felt his color rise and his anger quickly followed.

"You haven't even shown me this alleged abuse yet," he charged. Alifa's eyes flashed at the implication that she was telling tales and she shoved away from the wall. She discarded her cloak with a savage gesture that left Yusuf mutely admiring her grace. Alifa turned her back on him before dropping her shirt over her shoulders.

"There's nothing *alleged* about these," she snapped.

Yusuf first noticed the golden indentation of her waist, which he knew was not what he was supposed to be noticing. He awakened with a vengeance at the sight, however, his gaze running greedily over the luscious curve of Alifa's draped buttocks.

Had he truly caressed that temptingly soft flesh and remembered almost nothing of it? Would she stop him if he touched her again? It didn't matter—the temptation was too much for him to easily deny.

Yusuf had raised one hand toward her before he saw the angry red scratches. His hand stopped in midair and wavered slightly when he saw the damage he had unwittingly wrought.

His heart sank at the familiarity of the marks. He had done this and he knew it. Yusuf looked between the marks and his distended fingers, seeing the same span between the fingers that would be between the claws.

Did the scratches hurt? He spared a glance to Alifa, noting how rigidly she held her shoulders and how she kept her chin high. She would never admit it if they did. An unexpected wave of admiration washed over him. Alifa was a fighter in her own right and he had to respect that. If there hadn't been a possibility of recompense, Yusuf was certain she would never even have shown him the marks.

Or anyone else.

His gaze dropped to the red scratches once more. Bile rose within Yusuf as he noted the full extent of the damage, the depth of the wounds, the length they traced from shoulder to buttock. He had done this. And he had no recollection of the event. None whatsoever.

It was happening again. The beast had returned to haunt him. After all these years of running from the truth, all these years of thinking the past behind him, the curse was back. Yusuf inhaled slowly, willing himself to remain composed.

The metamorphosis explained his lack of recollection of their night together. Only too well, Yusuf recalled that his memory of those shifted times was hazy at best. Maybe that was how panthers remembered. Yusuf did not know.

But what was past was past. What mattered now was the woman who stood before him. He had hurt Alifa and somehow he had to make amends. Regardless of the kind of woman she was.

Yusuf felt a twinge of remorse that he had finally sampled a woman, a woman he was honest enough to admit he desired and he recalled nothing of it. He reached out and tentatively touched Alifa's warm flesh beside the rightmost mark. She flinched, then trembled, but did not move away from the weight of his finger.

An unexpected wave of tenderness assaulted Yusuf. He could make this right with more lovemaking. Impulsively he considered the possibility of carrying Alifa back to bed and soothing her hurt. Sunlight flooded the room and the quiet of the morning would be a perfect setting.

Here in the light, he could not shift. He could look into her eyes, committing the moment to memory forever. He could make her forget the harshness of the world she dwelled in, even if only for a little while. Yusuf could readily imagine peeling off Alifa's remaining garments, bathing her wounds and spending the remainder of the day making her forget about them. His body stirred with the promise as he stared at her silky flesh beneath his hand.

The angry scratches were inescapable.

"Does it hurt?" Yusuf asked quietly. Alifa said nothing, but he looked up in time to see that she nodded once.

Guilt suffused him and he looked back to the place where his finger rested. Her skin was so soft that even now it tempted him to touch her more. Yusuf dared to let the others join the first in resting against her warmth before he hesitated uncertainly. Alifa seemed to hold her breath and Yusuf let himself be encouraged.

Slowly, he let the full weight of his hand lie upon her. Still she did not move, and Yusuf's pulse accelerated. He smelled the jasmine she wore, but sought the mysterious, musky undertone that was hers alone. When he caught the scent of her own skin, his arousal redoubled with a speed that astounded him.

He imagined Alifa in his arms with an ease that made him question whether he truly did remember nothing of that night. Yusuf permitted his palm to slide slowly up the gracious curve of her back, following the path of the scratches even as he savored the feel of her beneath his hand.

The sunlight tinted her skin a more golden hue than it was and the hushed silence of the sleeping house filled his ears. Some faint recollection darted elusively within Yusuf's mind before his arousal took the fore. He thought of Alifa beneath him, he thought of his hand on her back like this once before and he could think of nothing but sampling her again.

Again. What if he hurt her again?

Terror that he might repeat his mistake replaced everything else within him in an instant. What if he did more than scratch? Yusuf pulled his hand away and stepped back hastily, putting half the width of the room between them.

As though that alone would diminish her effect on him. He leaned out in pursuit of her scent, but caught himself before he sniffed the air.

Was he becoming the kind of beast his father was? Yusuf's heart chilled at the possibility.

He would not permit this to happen to him.

"I do not remember anything," he said with crisp formality.

Alifa's back sagged briefly with what might have been the realization that he had moved away before she straightened and turned to face him defiantly. Not a hint of any warmth was there lingering in her dark eyes, though Yusuf could have sworn a moment past that she would not have been adverse to another mating.

Despite the scratches on her back.

It was inexplicable for a moment, until the truth hit him. Why he should expect anything different from a whore, he could not imagine. She wanted no more than coin, but Alifa would see no more of his dinars.

Yusuf couldn't afford the risk. It was enough that she affected him.

For whatever reason, Alifa had triggered the reemergence of the old curse. Yusuf was torn between the desire to flee from her effect upon him and an equally strong urge to keep her close, that she might not spread the tale.

He could never risk touching her again.

"It doesn't matter whether you remember or not," she snapped as she viciously hauled her *kurta* over her shoulders. "The damage is done, you're responsible and I want compensation."

The way her lip curled cynically fascinated Yusuf beyond belief. What had made her so bitter? What had she experienced?

Why had she become a whore?

How had he made love to this woman without knowing anything about her? And why hadn't he asked?

Yusuf glanced away. He could not be interested in Alifa. He could not be intrigued by her. The fact that she was forbidden to him was not an adequate reason. Yusuf slanted another glance in Alifa's direction, to find her watching him expectantly. The way her hands were propped on her hips accented her narrow waist, despite the fullness of her garments, and made him aware of the delicacy of her fingers.

He wished with a sudden fierceness that he could remember their mating.

And wished equally as fiercely that Alifa had any other occupation in the world.

Yusuf refused to speculate on why either thought should occur to him. He forced himself to recall her comment and his ire rose more quickly than it might have otherwise.

"Compensation?" he asked with a sneer. "For what?"

"For the fact that I can't work with this disfigurement on my back," Alifa retorted sharply, clearly giving no consideration now to the fact that they might be overheard. Her rising voice was the only outward sign that she was emotionally affected by their argument and Yusuf wondered how much more emotion she was hiding.

Was she still afraid of him? He wasn't sure and he wanted to know that, too.

"Your kind can always work," Yusuf charged disparagingly. There was a reminder that he needed. Alifa was a whore, he told himself savagely. How many had sampled her favors since he had? Yusuf had little doubt that she rose to the occasion every single time with enthusiasm and he loathed himself yet again for partaking of her charms.

Even once, it was inexcusable.

It was even more inexcusable that he wanted to do it again.

"Wrong," Alifa told him. "With this on my back, I haven't got any clients. Without clients, Hakim won't permit me to work in his tavern, and without a patron like Hakim, I have no chance of finding any new clients." Her eyes narrowed as she stared at Yusuf and her voice became bitter. "I've lost my job and my livelihood, thanks to you. You *owe* me."

The charge hit close enough to home to prompt Yusuf's guilt. His answer was harsher than intended, as a result.

"I owe you *nothing*," he maintained flatly. "If you can't spread your legs for a few days, maybe you should take the opportunity to find a decent job."

"A decent job?" Alifa laughed harshly. "You think I do this because I *like* it?" she demanded. "It's the only skill I've got and I have to eat."

Yusuf cast her a disparaging look. "A decent woman would let herself starve first," he informed her self-righteously. For an instant, he thought he saw something remarkably like regret flicker in Alifa's eyes, but the expression was gone so quickly that he wondered whether he had imagined it.

Alifa folded her arms across her chest and regarded him coldly. "Sometimes life doesn't make choices that easy," she snapped. Yusuf frowned uncomprehendingly, but knew she would not explain even if he bothered to ask. Her next words shocked him out of any lingering confusion. "You owe me four more dinars for the week," she charged flatly.

"That's a bargain rate," Yusuf snapped. "The last I heard, it was four for a night."

Alifa's eyes blazed and she held out one palm demandingly. "Four dinars now, please."

Not likely. Yusuf snorted with disgust. "You owe *me* four dinars," he countered hotly.

"For what?" To his pleasure, Alifa was finally surprised.

"For overcharging me," Yusuf insisted. "Four dinars is a shocking sum for one night of anyone's services and it's only your word against mine that you ever delivered. I certainly don't recall anything of note, let alone anything worth four dinars."

Alifa's mouth opened and worked silently for a moment. Yusuf had finally regained his stride. Obviously being awakened unexpectedly had affected his thinking, but fortunately, this callous little discussion had restored his sense. He had been thinking tender thoughts about a whore. Mercifully, she had shown her true colors soon enough that he had been spared the chance of making a tragic mistake.

Yusuf had little opportunity to savor the moment of victory before Alifa recovered herself enough to respond. "You swine!'' she spat furiously. ''How *dare* you imply that I charged you falsely!''

''Prove to me that you delivered,'' Yusuf charged silkily.

''Your landlady saw me leave,'' Alifa retorted, with a defiant tilt to her chin.

''But I'm guessing she doesn't know what happened within this room that night,'' he parried smoothly.

Alifa's eyes flashed and she angrily closed the space between them to shake one finger beneath Yusuf's nose. ''Of all the low and filthy tricks in this world, I thought I had seen each and every one, but this is beyond unethical,'' she informed him coldly. The last word stung, but Yusuf refused to let her see that she had struck a nerve. ''For all the judgments that you are so ready to pronounce on everyone else, it seems that you have a rather inconsistent moral code.'' She spun on her heel and stalked to the door, only to pause for a parting shot.

''I should have known better when I saw you drinking that *eau-de-vie*,'' she said with a sneer. Alifa swiveled to leave, but Yusuf was not yet ready to surrender the fight.

''And a whore like yourself lives blamelessly?'' he demanded. Alifa's eyes narrowed, and the comment she fired over her shoulder might have made a lesser man consider taking back his words. Yusuf held his ground stubbornly.

''If nothing else, I honorably pay what I owe,'' she retorted. That barb hit close to home, but Yusuf held her gaze, surprised to find the task harder than he might have anticipated.

''Then perhaps we should consider the question another way,'' he suggested coolly before he felt compelled to glance away. Alifa regarded him warily, but did not abandon the threshold. Yusuf bent and casually retrieved her belt and shoes from his pack.

''I believe these belong to you,'' he said. Her expression revealed that she both recognized the articles and was surprised to find that Yusuf had claimed them. ''Perhaps you would be interested enough in retrieving them to pay a finder's fee to me,'' he offered and shook the belt so that the coins sewn to it jingled merrily. "Shall we say four dinars?" he suggested amiably.

The blithe words hung between them as the atmosphere in the room became decidedly chilly. Alifa straightened slowly, until her bearing was not unlike that of a queen, and her features set coldly. Yusuf found to his dismay that he could not hold her gaze now, and he looked down to find his thumb tracing the curved instep of her slipper of its own accord.

He had no reason to feel guilty for what he had said, he told himself, but the awkward wedge of guilt remained lodged in his chest.

"You are beneath contempt," Alifa said in a voice so low as to be almost inaudible.

Yusuf looked up in surprise, but she was gone, the last sweep of her full skirts disappearing in her wake. He strained his ears and caught the quiet brush of her bare feet on the stairs. The urge to pursue her rose hot within him and Yusuf was astounded to realize that he wanted to apologize.

Apologize?

There was no time to question the impulse, for as soon as Alifa left the rooming house, he would have no way of finding her.

And she was the only one who knew his secret.

She could expose him!

That unexpected reminder alone was adequate reason to pursue her. Yusuf hastily dressed, jammed his feet into his boots, whipped on his turban and tossed his cloak over his shoulders as he almost flew out of the room. At the top of the stairs he cursed in recollection and ducked back into his room to retrieve Alifa's shoes and belt. Yusuf dived down the stairs, relieved to find no one else stirring, and darted out into the winding street lined with whitewashed houses.

Alifa was just turning the corner far to the left. Yusuf considered calling out after her, but then his gaze rose to the walls in this respectable and still-sleeping quarter.

Maybe it would be better to simply follow her. He had no doubt that they would argue again and for some inexplicable reason would rather that it happen in a less public place. He would not question his thoughts any further than that.

His mind made up, Yusuf ducked down the street in pursuit of Alifa, ensuring that he kept an adequate distance and moved silently so that she would not realize he was there.

The man had a nerve, of that there was little doubt. Alifa gritted her teeth and stalked down the cobbled street, winding her way home without thinking.

To suggest that she had not even delivered her services! She growled and turned a corner savagely. She had known he had been drunk, but that accusation was beyond belief. Honestly, there were moments when she could cheerfully wring Yusuf Khudabanda's self-righteous neck.

And to offer to sell her back her shoes and belt! The man was an opportunist beyond compare. Alifa clenched her hands so tightly that her nails dug into her palms, but she was in a sour enough mood to welcome the pain.

How dare he say such things to her! How *dare* he imply that she was dishonorable!

The abrupt realization that she had no hope of getting four more dinars for Kasilo's prayer, either from Yusuf or from anyone else, was a sobering one. What was she going to do? Too late the import of Hakim's decision struck her and she felt the full futility of her position.

They had absolutely no money. She had absolutely no skills other than the dubious one that she could no longer practice. Hakim had vowed to ensure that she would not be able to work anywhere in Ceuta. And they had no money to ease the road if they were to move elsewhere.

And where would they go?

She didn't even have money to buy couscous for a meal today. Alifa fingered the sweets tied in the veil safely stowed in her pocket and winced at the stickiness of the honey. Not only were the sweets all they had to eat and sure to be disgusting after her travels this day, but the honey would have ruined both the veil and her *chalwar*.

Would anything go right this day? Would anything ever go right again? Tears rose unexpectedly to blur Alifa's vision, but she refused to indulge herself and brushed them impatiently away.

She had bigger problems on her hands than tears could solve. Somehow, in some way, she had to find a solution to this dilemma. How could she get four dinars for Kasilo's healing? With quick steps, Alifa passed through the wooden gate that marked the beginning of the poor quarter of town, lost in her own thoughts.

A shout from the square brought her head up with a snap and she noticed suddenly the large crowd gathered for so early in the day. A large man she recognized as the silversmith climbed up on the stone block regularly used by speakers.

Too late she remembered the silver bracelet in her pocket and her vow to talk to the silversmith this morning. She fingered the silver band even as she put two and two together.

It couldn't be!

Chapter Five

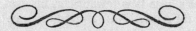

She couldn't be too late! The silversmith dragged a smaller figure behind him, his large hand wrapped around a reluctant wrist. Alifa's eyes widened in horror.

No! Anything but this! Her eyes had to be deceiving her! Alifa ran toward the crowd, her heart in her mouth.

"I have witnesses that this boy stole from my stall!" the silversmith shouted. Angry voices rose in assent. The boy cowered and Alifa could not see his face, despite her frantic efforts.

Was it Jaraw? Or Sinhaj? Or another child she did not know? The crowd shuffled their feet in anticipation and murmured confidentially to each other. Alifa pushed at the relentless row of backs, to no avail. She had to get through the crowd! She had to see!

It couldn't be Jaraw. It just couldn't be him.

Even as the thought echoed in Alifa's mind, she could not stifle the dread that filled her.

"Such behavior cannot be tolerated!" cried someone.

"But he is so young," protested a woman.

"*Especially* in one so young," someone else argued. Alifa flailed at the shoulders of those in front of her, and managed to push closer. Still she could not see the boy and her pulse hammered in her ears at the certainty of who he was.

This could not be happening.

"How will he ever learn?" questioned another dispassionately.

"It is written...." intoned one of the older men. The crowd parted before Alifa just as the boy looked up with terror at his accuser.

"Jaraw!" she cried in dismayed recognition.

Her brother's gaze flew toward her, his eyes wide as he sought her in the crowd. Alifa shoved her way through the remainder of the crowd blocking her path, well aware of the silence that had fallen over the gathering.

The silversmith met her gaze coldly.

"Is this your child?" he demanded. Alifa's heart skipped a beat and she found her usual composure had completely deserted her.

It didn't matter. Nothing mattered except Jaraw's hand.

"My brother," Alifa answered hastily. "He's my brother. Our parents are dead and I have raised him." She was babbling, but she could not stop and she did not care. Alifa reached the edge of the stone and grasped Jaraw's hand, not surprised to find the usually cocksure boy trembling.

She was trembling herself.

"He stole a bracelet from me," the silversmith charged. "And readily confessed to the deed."

"Yes, yes," Alifa agreed quickly. "I found out yesterday and was coming to talk to you about it. Here it is. I wanted to return it and beg your leniency." She rummaged in her skirts and pulled the offending bracelet out of her pocket. Her hands shook as she passed it to the silversmith. He accepted the token, examined it briefly and nodded with satisfaction before pocketing it.

He did not release his grip on Jaraw's wrist.

"You see, it wasn't his fault," Alifa hastened to explain. "I'm sure it was just an error of judgment, a joke among his friends. He's just a boy. I am certain that Jaraw intended to return the bracelet to you...."

"I caught him trying to steal another this morning," the silversmith interjected flatly. His charge effectively halted anything she might have said in her brother's defense and Alifa's gaze fell on Jaraw.

He flushed and looked away. The gesture gave Alifa all the confirmation she needed, and considerably more than she wanted. The crowd murmured disparagingly as Alifa released a shaky breath.

"Did you?" she asked hoarsely, hoping against hope that her brother would deny the charge. Jaraw nodded shame-facedly and disappointment welled up within Alifa. How had she failed him? What had she done wrong? Had she not tried to teach him what was good and right?

"It is the law," the silversmith reminded her. An unexpected gentleness in his voice made Alifa conclude that he had guessed the direction of her thoughts.

It *was* the law and Alifa could make no argument against that. Jaraw had broken the law and he was old enough to no longer be considered a child.

There was nothing she could do. They could not all afford to become outcasts for Jaraw's mistake. She held his hand tightly, forcing herself to think of the others. They needed this home and the security of a stable hearth, regardless of how meager it might be. If she challenged the silversmith's word, if she forced him to release Jaraw unpunished before all these people, they could never remain in Ceuta.

Alifa had no choice.

"Yes," she agreed unsteadily. "Yes, I know." Jaraw raised agonized eyes to hers and Alifa shook her head. How could she make him understand?

"You knew it, too," she whispered. Jaraw's lips thinned and he looked away with an abruptness that wrenched Alifa's heart. Her hand shook as she looked at his hand cradled within it, and she gave his fingers a squeeze.

"I would like to stay with him," she said. The silversmith nodded and unsheathed his knife. Both her words and the older man's gesture seemed to make the situation suddenly comprehensible to Jaraw, for fear finally filled his eyes.

"Alifa!" Jaraw shouted when he saw the blade. "No! You must help me!" Too late it seemed he understood the price he had to pay for his crime. He struggled against the silversmith's grip on his wrist and another man stepped up to aid in restraining him. Jaraw clutched at Alifa with his left hand, his eyes wild.

"Don't let them take my hand! You can't let this happen! I did it for you, after all!" he claimed desperately. The silversmith paused to look at him and then glanced consideringly to Alifa.

"I *never* taught you or asked you to steal," Alifa said crisply, determined to check that thought before it went any further. The silversmith relaxed his stance slightly when Jaraw shook his head determinedly. The boy stilled and the man aiding the silversmith warily relaxed his grip.

"No, no, I wanted to sell the silver," her brother insisted. An unexpected calm settled over Jaraw as he frowned, carefully choosing the words he would use, and Alifa caught a glimpse of the man he would yet become.

Jaraw looked his sister hard in the eye, a determination in his expression that seemed different, for all its familiarity. Alifa was suddenly certain he would say something she wouldn't welcome hearing. Jaraw dropped his voice confidentially and even her expectation did not prepare her for his words.

"I wanted you to be able to *stop*," he confided, putting particular emphasis on the last word.

Alifa refused to believe that he might mean what she immediately assumed he meant. Her brothers and sister knew nothing of what she did and where she went. Alifa had ensured that they knew nothing of her occupation.

"I *know* what you do," Jaraw insisted and his very seriousness convinced Alifa as nothing else could have. "I went to the Jewish quarter," he added ominously.

Alifa's heart skipped a beat. How long had he known? Did the others know? Did they hate her for it?

"And I know that you don't want to do it." Jaraw's lips pressed together in a tight line. He glanced away for a long moment, the gesture making him look much older than his years.

When had he grown up?

"I wanted to give you a choice," he asserted flatly. He looked pointedly at his hand and back to her, his meaning clear.

Jaraw expected her to intervene. Alifa was stunned by the realization that her secret had not really been a secret, and by his expectation that she would flout the law for his benefit. She didn't know what to say. She stared back at him mutely and shook her head.

"It was wrong, Jaraw," she said quietly. Jaraw's eyes narrowed and he turned away, his response making it more than clear that her answer was not the one he had anticipated.

"And what you do?" he demanded archly. Alifa swallowed, well aware of their watchful audience.

"I didn't have a choice," she whispered. Jaraw looked into her eyes for a long moment, then shook his head.

"How do you know that I do?" he charged.

"Stealing is wrong," Alifa said softly, her voice hardening when her brother looked unconvinced. "And you know it." He flicked her a cold look, then granted the silversmith a very adult nod.

"I'm ready," he said calmly and lifted his chin high. "Now that I know where I stand."

Alifa cringed inwardly at the bitterness in his tone, but knew she could do no differently. She could not jeopardize Tabeta and Kasilo—all of them, really. The silversmith nodded and raised his knife. Alifa gripped Jaraw's other hand tightly, despite his effort to pull away. She averted her face, hating her own weakness in being unable to watch.

"I ask you to reconsider," a familiar voice interjected calmly.

All heads turned as one, Alifa probably the least surprised to find a well-dressed Yusuf standing slightly apart from the crowd.

What was *he* doing here? Had he followed her? Yusuf arched a brow coolly to her and Alifa's heart took an unwelcome lurch. She inhaled sharply, unable to fathom why he would interfere, let alone why he was here. Even worse, how much had he overheard?

Yusuf strode to her side with measured steps, the crowd parting before him as though it were the most natural thing in the world. He had presence, that Alifa had to grant him. Her mother would have said he had *baraka,* the aura of kings.

The ancient ones, the shapeshifter magicians, had *baraka.* The thought came unbidden and Alifa forced herself to ignore it.

The entire assembly waited silently to hear what Yusuf would say, despite the fact that he was a complete stranger in this quarter. When he paused beside her, Alifa slanted a sideways glance to his impeccable attire, a new increment of awe in her assessment of him.

Was he what she feared he was? It was unbelievable, but then she noted the similarity between his eyes and those of the panther and wasn't as sure as she might have liked to be.

But regardless of her suspicions, and despite whatever Alifa might tell herself, her first impulse was to be relieved to see Yusuf. It was ridiculous and Alifa knew it, but she could not help but expect that Yusuf, with his air of easy command, would be able to do something for Jaraw.

Something that she had been unable to do herself.

She swallowed a very feminine thrill of pride that Yusuf was standing beside her and taking up her cause before she summarily dismissed the inappropriate impulse. What was she thinking? Alifa slanted a glance to Yusuf and liked his authoritative attitude. She ought to simply be grateful for his interference. Especially if he could aid Jaraw.

Yes, her feelings were no more than that. Gratitude and relief. Perfectly reasonable, under the circumstances.

"Who are you?" the silversmith asked, his tone remarkably less haughty than it had been when Alifa first interrupted him.

A small smile played briefly over Yusuf's lips before he responded. "Call me an interested party," he said smoothly. Alifa marveled that he could be so composed in such a situation. He gestured toward Jaraw eloquently. "You claim this boy has stolen from you?"

"Twice. He was caught in the act the second time," the silversmith reiterated flatly. "I have two witnesses and he readily confesses his guilt." Yusuf looked inquiringly to Jaraw, who nodded once in acknowledgment.

"Have the goods been reclaimed?" Yusuf asked mildly. The silversmith nodded.

"Yes."

"How old are you, boy?" Yusuf asked.

"Thirteen," Jaraw responded with all his usual arrogance. Alifa longed to slap him for not showing better manners to someone who might aid him.

"Old enough to know what he's doing," the silversmith said tightly, clearly seeing where this argument was going.

"And young enough to be impetuous," Yusuf countered evenly. His assessing gaze ran over the boy before lifting to meet Alifa's. To her disgust, she felt herself flush. "Maybe even to make a misguided decision out of loyalty." Alifa's cheeks heated even further, the fact that she was uncertain what exactly Yusuf meant doing little to mitigate her embarrassment.

"Old enough to know better, as I said," the silversmith argued doggedly. "And he came back a second time to repeat the offense."

"It is the law," the other man who had come to aid the silversmith in holding Jaraw said uncompromisingly. Jaraw's gaze rose to Yusuf's and Alifa knew something passed silently between the two of them before the boy looked abruptly away.

"Yes," Yusuf agreed with apparent reluctance. "It is the law." Alifa felt his gaze upon her, but refused to glance up, certain she would find censure in his eyes. "But sometimes the true road is less than clear," he added thoughtfully.

The most self-righteous man she had ever met was conceding that the way could be unclear? Alifa could not believe her ears, but continued to stare stubbornly at the ground. Her feet were bare, reminding her that Yusuf still had her slippers. Such possession felt shockingly intimate to her, here in her own neighborhood, and Alifa felt her color deepen yet again.

"However mistakenly, the boy thought to aid his sister, and that goodwill cannot be discarded," Yusuf concluded.

The silversmith fidgeted. "He stole, for whatever reason, and the price for the crime is his right hand."

"Take only his finger and I will ensure he understands the fullness of his error," Yusuf offered unexpectedly.

Alifa looked to him in shock and Jaraw's head shot up. Alifa was surprised to find Yusuf's gaze on her and a curious heat suffused her at the intensity of his expression. What would prompt him to make such an offer?

And would it be accepted?

If it was, what would Yusuf expect in return? He held her regard unflinchingly and Alifa realized that she did not care. If Yusuf expected her to demonstrate her appreciation for his gesture, the idea was not without appeal. She had rolled onto her back for coin often enough before; surely this was an even better cause.

And a task that held the promise of being a pleasure. It seemed that Alifa could not take a full breath as she stared into Yusuf's compelling gaze. She wondered how much he guessed of her thoughts.

But if Jaraw could lose only a finger for his foolishness and the price was another night with Yusuf, Alifa would pay the price willingly.

"How can you ensure such a thing?" the silversmith demanded.

"The boy will become my ward," Yusuf said flatly. Alifa felt her eyes widen, even as approval for this stranger's words swept over the crowd. Clearly Yusuf was far above Jaraw's and Alifa's station. For him to take Jaraw under his care was no small offer.

The silversmith deliberated for only a moment. "I accept your offer," he said and Alifa wondered if he was relieved.

"I ask only that you sever it cleanly," Yusuf said tightly. Jaraw paled at the import of his words and Alifa could not meet her brother's eyes.

The silversmith nodded and Jaraw's grip on Alifa's hand tightened. Alifa gritted her teeth as the silversmith splayed Jaraw's fingers across the stone. When he lifted the knife, she squeezed her eyes closed and averted her face once more. She jumped when she heard the knife find the block.

Then Jaraw's anguished cry filled her ears.

The boy had fainted.

He slumped bonelessly on the stone, his blood streaming from the place where his index finger had been and forming a puddle around him. Without his cloak of insolence, he was just an average boy, perhaps a little small for his age. The silversmith released his wrist and stepped away, his expression revealing that he would rather be anywhere than here.

Alifa shook like a leaf in the wind, although typically she tried to hide it. Her hair swept over her face, but Yusuf was certain her features would not reflect her usual cool hauteur. Yusuf's gaze fell to the blood once more. He took the boy's scarf and wrapped it around the wound hastily, in an effort to stanch the flow, even as he tried to make sense of his own actions.

What had prompted him to speak for the boy? Yusuf did not even know this child and he certainly didn't care for his attitude—begging Alifa to break the law for him. Yusuf's lips thinned in disapproval. Even now he could not understand his impulse. In fact, the more he thought about the boy's words, the greater Yusuf's certainty that he shouldn't have intervened.

Surely Alifa's distress could not have been enough to compel him to vouch for a brother he hadn't even known she had?

If so, this woman was doing far more to Yusuf than reminding him of what he had been. He scowled, recalling in the nick of time that she was the one who knew his secret. Yusuf felt again that telltale flicker of susceptibility.

Alifa alone could expose him. And to have her decisively in his debt was no small victory.

Yusuf refused to speculate on the fact that he had forgotten that salient point in the heat of the moment. On some level, to put Alifa in his debt had been his plan, he told himself firmly, wiping the image of her distress—and the chord it had struck within him—from his mind.

What was done was done and the reasons were unimportant now. He had vowed to teach the boy and teach him he would. The Imazighen keep their word, he reminded himself proudly. And unless he missed his guess, this one was going to need a good bit of teaching. Yusuf had his work cut out for him here, but he would easily maintain the upper hand over this confident young boy.

That the boy was Alifa's brother was incidental, of course. As was the obvious conclusion that Yusuf would be required to see more of Alifa in future, in order to keep his word.

But that was irrelevant.

At least Yusuf could tell himself that.

Alifa glanced up and there was uncertainty in her eyes for a moment. She looked young with unshed tears in her eyes, almost vulnerable, but then Yusuf blinked and the impression was gone.

Vulnerability. That was a word he had never associated with Alifa and he felt for the first time that he saw her as she truly was. Alifa's lips had thinned and she had turned to survey her brother with what appeared to be displeasure. Suddenly Yusuf wished he could recall some of the harsh judgments he had pronounced on this woman without knowing the truth of her situation.

Alifa looked very small, even with a vestige of her former manner restored. Her hair had worked its way loose, her cloak was draped over the soft curves he knew he had caressed. Yusuf found himself very aware of her femininity and he was seized by an urge to scoop her up and carry her away.

Home. Somewhere away from here. Somewhere private, where they could explore each other at their leisure. Somewhere he would have the time to coax her to smile.

The thought stunned him with its simple truth. When Alifa smiled, she sparkled with youth and vitality. It was her laugh that had first captured his attention, those long two days past.

He wanted to see her laugh again. It was that simple. Yusuf blinked, but his certainty did not fade.

"I suppose I should take Jaraw home," Alifa said in a low voice as she turned away.

She fully expected him to abandon her here, Yusuf realized with a shock. In the next instant, he guessed that she had known nothing else in her life. She had always been left to fend for herself.

No wonder Alifa took care of Alifa first. And, Yusuf amended with a glance to the fainted boy, Alifa took care of her own.

Like this misguided brother.

The excitement over, the murmuring crowd began to disperse and return to their business, leaving Yusuf and Alifa alone with the boy. The silversmith cleaned and sheathed his knife before he hurried away, presumably intent on returning to his shop. The square was noticeably quiet in the wake of the boy's punishment and Yusuf knew they were being left to their own resources.

As befitted thieves and outcasts. It had been some time since Yusuf had been cast aside and he found himself standing taller in defiance of the feeling.

How long had Alifa been alone? How much had she borne alone? He placed his hand on her shoulder and was surprised that she did not step away. Emboldened by her acquiescence, Yusuf let his thumb trace a circle on Alifa's shoulder and she actually took a step closer to him, as though she might welcome his protection, or at least his support. Yusuf was surprised at how heady a sensation that meager trust gave him.

"I *thought* so," a woman crowed victoriously by his elbow. Her unexpected words startled Yusuf out of his thoughts. He turned to look in surprise, his heart sinking as he recognized the woman who had challenged him on his visit to the fountain. She grinned at him crookedly and shook a finger in his direction. "You're the one who came looking for Alifa the other day."

Yusuf felt Alifa's quick glance, but stubbornly remained impassive.

"Really?" he said mildly, hoping his tone was unencouraging. He had no interest in entertaining this woman's confidences and even less in anything she might have to say. Undeterred, the woman nodded vigorously.

"That you did, dressed just as fancy as today." She reached out to finger Yusuf's cloak, but he indignantly flicked the garment away from her grasp. The last thing he needed was some common pauper handling his clothing. "I wouldn't forget these clothes, that's for certain," she confided, an assessing gleam in her eye.

Yusuf stifled a wave of distaste at the unwelcome thought that the woman would see him in the gutter just so that she might sell his cloak. If he ever had the misfortune to stumble in this quarter, he was quite sure opportunists like this woman would pick him clean before he regained his footing.

"Pardon me, but Jaraw needs tending," Alifa interjected firmly. Glad of the excuse, Yusuf nodded and bent to lift the boy purposefully to his shoulder, not missing the way Alifa's brows rose in surprise. He granted her a slow smile and adjusted the boy's weight on his shoulder.

To his astonishment, Alifa blushed with all the softness of an innocent girl. Yusuf's smile broadened, but he checked the urge to touch her again.

"The wound will need to be cauterized," he told Alifa calmly, disliking the pallor her skin took at the news. A protective urge flooded him at the renewed vision of her distress and Yusuf found himself plunging onward before he thought. "Do you live near here?" he demanded quietly. Alifa's eyes flicked to his before she nodded hastily and Yusuf guessed that she was wondering how much he had overheard.

He had heard it all, but would have to wait until later to make sense of it all. It was still amazing to him that this boy was Alifa's brother. Yusuf had never even considered that she might have a family, and once again felt the fool for his assumptions.

But right now, Alifa's family needed tending.

"Wait a moment," the older woman interrupted. Was she still here? Yusuf stifled a twinge of annoyance and turned to her with exaggerated politeness once again.

"Yes?" he asked in his most chilling tone. The woman was undeterred.

"You were looking for an Alifa," she said, evidently still puzzling this through. She squinted and waggled one finger knowingly at Yusuf. "Yes. Yes, I do remember. The other day, when you came to the fountain, I distinctly recall that you said you were looking for a woman named Alifa."

"Yes," Yusuf agreed impatiently, wishing the woman would get to the point.

"*This* Alifa?" the woman asked skeptically.

"Yes," Yusuf said flatly. He gritted his teeth and turned abruptly away, certain the woman's curiosity was finally satisfied and the matter closed. He and Alifa hadn't taken half a dozen steps before the woman called out after them.

"But the Alifa you sought was a whore."

Yusuf halted. Alifa stiffened. He glanced to her and saw that her lips had thinned dangerously. An ominous quiet settled over the square. Yusuf turned slowly to face his accuser, and saw to his dismay that what remained of the dispersing crowd had halted their departure at this unexpected development. All eyes were on them, but Yusuf lifted his chin proudly.

"If you have an accusation to make, please do so," he invited calmly. "The boy needs tending soon."

The woman licked her lips cautiously. "You said you were looking for a whore who had cheated you," she continued. Alifa inhaled sharply and Yusuf could guess her expression without even looking her way.

"Did I?" he said mildly, determined to reveal no more. The woman's gaze flicked between the two of them before fixing on Alifa.

"Are you a whore?" she demanded bluntly. Alifa stiffened.

"No," she said flatly. Yusuf was stunned by her lie, but did not dare show his response. The boldness of Alifa's tone clearly surprised the older woman, for she frowned and took a cautious step backward.

"But the boy said . . ." she began feebly, but Alifa let her continue no further.

"My brother was mistaken," Alifa interrupted her coldly. "I am no whore."

Yusuf did not dare fidget, though the untruth and the ease with which Alifa stated it made him deeply uncomfortable. The two women stared at each other willfully, until the whispers began to filter through the watching crowd. Alifa's lips tightened and she turned abruptly away as the whispering grew in volume.

"I thought you said that Jaraw needed to be tended quickly," she snapped.

Yusuf spared one last glance to the onlooking crowd and turned to match her steps across the cobblestones. Alifa walked with her chin high and he knew that he would get no answer from her about this anytime soon.

"Thieves and whores!" the woman shouted behind them, her audacity restored by their departure. "We have no need of your kind in this neighborhood! Tell us, Alifa, is the tall one your employer? Is that why he took such an interest in your brother? Was it your labor on your back that paid for his fancy clothes?"

Rage filled Yusuf and he would have turned around to contest the charge if Alifa had not snatched at his sleeve in anticipation of his intent.

"Leave it," she advised tersely. "You cannot win."

"I could defend my honor," Yusuf growled, but Alifa's sidelong glance was skeptical.

"Really?" she asked with apparent disinterest before she shrugged. "To what purpose? It is already time to go."

Yusuf frowned and looked to her uncomprehendingly, but clearly Alifa intended to say no more. She strode briskly beside him, her frosty composure resolutely restored and he wondered what she meant.

Tabeta stood up when Alifa entered the house, her eyes widening in shock when she saw Jaraw hanging limply over Yusuf's shoulder. Her gaze flicked curiously over Yusuf, but Alifa had no patience for introductions. She was already too aware, not only of the man beside her, but also of his avid curiosity.

Alifa was in no mood to indulge him.

Was it not enough that an outsider was going to enter her home? Alifa felt cornered, a private part of her open to Yusuf's view. She could not even look at him, somehow thinking that if she could avoid the sight of him here, she could deny that he had ever come. If she had had her way, she thought savagely, Yusuf would not have followed her into the square.

Although then Jaraw would be missing more than a finger. Alifa bit down on the frustrating jumble her emotions had become and frowned at her sister.

"We'll need water from the well," Alifa informed her crisply. "And is there tinder for a fire?"

"Yes, I laid the hearth already for dinner," Tabeta responded, her tone indicating her confusion. She hesitated and Alifa granted her a telling glance that gained no response.

"Go," Alifa commanded in a tone that brooked no argument. Her sister scurried to pick up the water vessel and Alifa knew the precise instant she saw Jaraw's maimed hand. Tabeta gasped and dropped the pottery vessel with a clatter, her hands rising to her mouth.

"He was caught by the silversmith," Alifa explained dispassionately. Tabeta nodded miserably, swallowed and took a gulping breath.

"I told him not to go," she whispered. A single tear worked its way free of her wide eyes and Alifa could not leave it be.

It was not Tabeta's fault that Jaraw was foolhardy. Alifa reached out and carefully wiped the teardrop away. Tabeta looked up at her with beseeching eyes.

"I couldn't stop them," Alifa said before her sister could ask. She was surprised to find her voice unsteady.

Tabeta nodded and took a deep breath before she stepped closer and impulsively hugged Alifa tightly. Alifa's eyes widened in surprise, though she closed her arms around her sister once she felt her trembling. The display of affection surprised Alifa, no less than her sister's words.

"I knew you would try, but he did break the law," Tabeta murmured. "At least you convinced them to only take his finger."

No, she hadn't even done that. Guilt flooded Alifa and she shook her head.

"No, Tabeta. It was Yusuf who convinced them."

Tabeta turned from Alifa to eye Yusuf, who was still standing silently, Jaraw on his shoulder. Alifa followed her gaze, finding it less jarring than she might have expected to see Yusuf standing on the threshold of her home. Astonishingly enough, there was no censure in his expression.

For once, Yusuf had not judged her. He waited silently, his expression speculative as he looked between the two sisters. Jaraw's blood had dripped on his polished boots, but he seemed not to have noticed. Yusuf returned the younger girl's regard unflinchingly and Alifa fancied that understanding flickered in her sister's dark eyes.

"Fetch the water," she whispered. "Jaraw needs us."

Tabeta stirred and nodded hastily, ducking down to retrieve the vessel and disappearing down the winding street. Alifa indicated that Yusuf should enter, wondering what he would think of her simple dwelling. She was unable or unwilling to even speculate about why he had followed her, let alone why he had interfered. His expression was controlled and she could not begin to guess what he was thinking.

"Here," she said simply.

Yusuf nodded and stepped inside. He stamped his feet on the threshold to remove some of the dust before laying Jaraw carefully beside the hearth. He spotted the flint immediately and stuck a flame, lighting the fire with practical ease.

Alifa hesitated behind him, uncertain how to behave with a man in her home and sanctuary, uncertain what she should do. For the first time, she found herself painfully aware of Kasilo's bright gaze taking everything in. The fire sizzled to life under Yusuf's hand, the orange flames casting a flickering light over the whitewashed walls and illuminating Kasilo's curious face. Remarkably, the young boy held his tongue.

"He needs a blanket," Yusuf said. Alifa scurried to do his bidding. She tucked the blanket over Jaraw, and was surprised when her brother's eyes flew open and he clutched at her hand.

"Alifa—" he gasped as his features contorted. "It hurts so."

Her heart wrenched that he was in such pain and that there was nothing she could do about it. Alifa didn't even know what to say and she silently gripped his good hand.

"And it will hurt more before it is done," Yusuf interjected sternly, drawing the surprised gazes of both brother and sister. He leveled a steady glance at Jaraw. "This must be done to clean the wound," he informed the boy. Jaraw nodded uncomprehendingly. Yusuf gripped Jaraw's wrist and before Alifa could protest, shoved his hand into the leaping flames.

Jaraw screamed and fainted again.

"What are you doing?" Alifa cried and dived protectively over her brother. She grabbed Yusuf's arm desperately, but could not pull Jaraw's hand from the flames.

Yusuf was hurting him! Why had she trusted him? Kasilo gasped and Alifa heard the water vessel being dropped on the threshold.

Despite her efforts, Yusuf seared the wound undeterred, not relinquishing his grip on Jaraw until he deemed the task completed. The smell of burning flesh filled the air. Alifa clutched Jaraw's maimed hand to her chest as soon as it was released, checking immediately what Yusuf had done.

The wound was neatly cauterized. Clearly Yusuf had performed this task before, to have done it so quickly and so well. Alifa felt foolish beyond compare at her emotional response.

"Have you brought the water?" Yusuf asked mildly, casting his words over his shoulder.

Alifa swallowed at the realization that he had heard Tabeta's return, as well. The younger girl hastened to bring him the vessel, her hands shaking as she poured the water into a shallow bowl. Yusuf lifted Jaraw's arm, his gaze meeting Alifa's for a charged moment. He arched a brow and she immediately relinquished her grip on her brother, feeling more flustered than she had in years. Yusuf placed Jaraw's injured hand in the water and methodically rinsed off all the blood, taking a moment to examine his work before he nodded with satisfaction.

Now that she realized what his intention had been, Alifa felt ridiculous for having tried to interfere. The wound was closed now, and less likely to fester. Alifa cursed herself for not thinking so practically. She pretended not to notice that she had been sprawled gracelessly across her brother as she sat up with all the composure she could muster.

Then Alifa made the mistake of glancing to Yusuf. The way his green gaze collided with hers was unnerving, to say the least.

"He'll need a bandage," he said calmly.

There was no doubting that she was no longer in charge in her own household, but Alifa did his bidding without re-

flecting on the matter. It was clearly the shock of everything that had happened today that had her acting so
obediently. Maybe a lack of sleep also contributed to her
unusual compliance. It could be nothing more than that.

If Alifa had spared the time to think about it, she feared,
she might have found it reassuring that she was not battling
the fates single-handed. That would have been unthinkable.

Why had Yusuf followed her here, anyway? Surely as
soon as he had what he wanted he would be gone.

He probably only wanted those four dinars. Alifa's lips set
in a grim line. And helping Jaraw was an inconvenience to
be tolerated before he retrieved the coins.

How she wished she had those cursed dinars so that she
could send Yusuf on his way.

And then they could be on their way. Remaining in Ceuta
was out of the question, especially since that last revelation
in the square.

There was something else she could thank Yusuf Khudabanda for. Alifa slanted him a hostile glance, but he was
bandaging Jaraw's hand with more care than she might have
expected. She stopped in midthought to watch his long fingers wrap the cloth and check that it wasn't too tight.

There was that tenderness again. His gentleness with
Jaraw temporarily undermined Alifa's resolve to despise this
man who had destroyed the carefully constructed life she
had built here.

She might have thought she would get used to feeling so
confused around this man. It seemed that she could not
think straight in his presence. The best thing for Alifa's
peace of mind would be to see this man gone from her home
as soon as possible.

His concern was all a facade, she told herself forcefully.
There was no tenderness in Yusuf. What was she thinking?
Alifa would do well to remember the scars on her back and
remember precisely the kind of man she was dealing with.

Whether he was a shapeshifter or not, he had still abused her.

And he had loved her as she had never been loved in her life. Alifa clenched her hands into fists and told herself to forget that part. She had not permitted herself to recall that sense of repleteness she had had; she had not allowed her memory to indulge in recollections of how cherished she had felt in Yusuf's bed.

She had not even permitted herself to acknowledge that his lovemaking had been satisfying enough that she considered not charging him.

Until the scratches, of course. Alifa inhaled sharply and forced herself to sit up straighter. She would do herself a service to remember that particular fact, for it was a pertinent one.

"He'll probably sleep for a while," Yusuf said and sat back on his heels.

He glanced around Alifa's home with polite disinterest, his gesture making her painfully aware of the humble state of her home. Alifa saw Kasilo smile cheerfully and knew Yusuf's gaze had landed on the youngest boy. He said nothing, though, and his gaze swiveled back to meet hers.

"We should talk" was all he said, the way one brow arched high more than eloquent. Yusuf disapproved, that much was clear, although Alifa could not begin to guess what in particular bothered him this time.

And she didn't care. The man had pronounced enough judgments on her to last her the rest of her days.

"Of course," she agreed, as calmly as she could. She lifted one hand and gestured toward the door. "Shall we?"

Yusuf frowned. "Surely the children could leave us?" he suggested coldly. Alifa stood up before he did, her fleeting height advantage bolstering her determination. She was embarrassed to have to explain Kasilo's health in front of the boy, but there was nothing for it. At least she could give

Yusuf a frosty stare for putting her in this position and she did so with relish.

He remained blissfully unaffected by her disapproval.

"Kasilo is ill," Alifa supplied tightly and turned to leave. She felt Yusuf glance to the boy in question, relief surging through her when she heard his steps behind her.

The sunlight was already fading as Alifa left the house, the shadows falling longer in the twisting little street as the sun fell below the city walls. She turned and walked to the end of the street, where a modicum of privacy could be had, folded her arms across her chest and turned to face Yusuf.

Nothing could have prepared her for his accusation.

picked up a lamp, but none of us believed. Who did she think she'd fool?

When she thought of her father, Alifa's throat tightened. He was gone.

"My parents died two years ago," she admitted tightly as she turned the...

Chapter Six

"How many of them are really yours?" Yusuf demanded coldly.

"What?" Alifa's voice was choked with outrage, but his expression did not change.

"It is common, I believe, for women of your profession to insist that their offspring are actually their brethren," he informed her stonily. Alifa could not believe the man's audacity and she fumed. Yusuf mused, apparently oblivious of her simmering anger. "Because of his age, the eldest might truly be your brother, but what about the others?"

Alifa slapped his face as hard as she could. Yusuf averted his face for a moment, licked his lips carefully, as though composing himself, then turned back to face her. His features were impassive, but Alifa did not miss the impatient flicker in his eyes. The imprint of her hand flamed on his cheek, but there was no change in his manner.

"I asked you a question," he said silkily.

"And you have your answer," Alifa spat.

Imagine! Insinuating that she had borne children out of wedlock and was presenting them as her siblings. He was lucky she hadn't given him more of an answer than that! Alifa made to brush past Yusuf and return home, but he grabbed her arm and pulled her to an abrupt halt. Alifa glared up at him, too angry to be surprised when his expression softened.

"Even the youngest?" he asked. Alifa closed her eyes and turned her face away.

"My parents died five years ago," she admitted tightly, well aware of the warm press of masculine fingers gripping her upper arm. Something that she definitely didn't want to feel awakened within her at Yusuf's proximity. "Kasilo is six," she added tonelessly, when Yusuf seemed to be waiting.

Curse the man.

"What's wrong with him?" he asked without even a thread of criticism in his tone.

"I don't know," Alifa confessed heavily before she questioned her impulse to confide in him. She frowned before she continued. "He's wasting away, he coughs throughout the night. Sometimes he can't keep food down."

"And he doesn't walk?" Yusuf asked. His voice was soothing, in an odd way, and Alifa almost believed that he was truly interested in her response.

"Not in the past two months. Before that, he could sometimes."

"Has he seen the shaman?"

Alifa's lips tightened with displeasure at the recollection, but she responded anyway. "He needs more coin than I have to treat Kasilo," she stated proudly. Yusuf's grip loosened slightly on her arm.

"In the mountains, a shaman treats the ill whether they are rich or poor," he commented dryly. If Alifa hadn't known better, she might have thought that Yusuf disapproved of the local shaman. She certainly could not argue with that conclusion. Alifa's lips twisted cynically.

"We're not in the mountains," she said, uncaring that bitterness filled her voice.

"How much does he want?"

"Eight dinars," Alifa said with annoyance at being reminded of the sum. Her anger loosened her tongue and she continued in frustration before she thought. "I thought that he could start when I paid him four dinars, but he wouldn't, even though he kept the coin, the miserable thief."

Too late, Alifa realized that she had revealed too much and checked her unruly tongue. She dared to flick a glance up to Yusuf to find him looking thoughtful.

The sight did not reassure Alifa in the least and her nervous desire to change the direction of his thoughts made her bold.

"Why did you speak for Jaraw?" she demanded abruptly. Yusuf started, then looked down into her eyes. His thumb slid across her arm in an unconscious caress and he shook his head, almost bemusedly.

"I don't know," he admitted and then unexpectedly grinned. He shook his head as though he were as surprised by the revelation as Alifa.

"I don't even know," he repeated thoughtfully.

He glanced down at Alifa, the way his smile broadened making her less steady on her feet than she might have liked. The expression made him look much younger than usual and set a fan of little crinkles around his eyes in motion.

The very thought that Yusuf might have responded impulsively made Alifa feel suddenly much closer to him. She stared up at him mutely and wondered what might have happened if they had met in another time and place.

They stood silently and regarded each other for what must have been a long time.

The wind rising from the sea wound around them, carrying the tang of salt to tease their nostrils. The leaves of the vine climbing the white wall that barricaded the end of the street waved slowly in the breeze, the evening shadows already capturing the lower leaves. It was quiet here and the way Yusuf's smile softened as he regarded her made Alifa suddenly feel that they were alone in the world. His grip tightened slightly on her arm and he leaned closer, prompting her heart to increase its pace.

Was he going to kiss her? Her fervent hope that he would stunned her with its intensity. Alifa shivered and stifled a smile of her own, though Yusuf's next words wiped it away effectively.

"What did you mean when you said it was time to go?" he asked quietly. Alifa could not hold his gaze, but she shrugged as she stared blindly down the familiar street.

They were not in another time or place. Disappointment welled up inside her at the reminder, however unwitting it might have been. They were here in Ceuta. She had nowhere to work, even as the whore and dancer she had become.

Alifa had nothing to offer to a man like Yusuf. He was an educated man—a scholar and a teacher, as likely as not. Such a man did not spend time willingly with a whore.

At least not for long.

The conclusion was more disappointing than Alifa thought it should be. Hadn't she already decided that the man was a savage? Hadn't she resolved that he owed her for the scratches on her back? But somehow, in the face of everything that had happened, Alifa could not summon her anger again.

"We simply have to leave," she said numbly.

"What about the tavern?"

"It seems that my services are no longer welcome there," Alifa said. She realized for the first time what a relief that was, but stubbornly did not look up, for fear Yusuf would guess her thoughts. She was done with whoring. Alifa hoped desperately that she could avoid returning to the trade, wherever they settled.

That was a foolish expectation and she knew it before the thought completely formed. Bitterness filled Alifa and her annoyance with Yusuf began to return.

It was *his* fault that they had to leave. Because of him, she had lost her job. Because of him, the people in the neighborhood knew her profession. They would probably come tonight with stones to finish the accusations that Tudda had begun. She had to get the children to safety.

How Alifa wished Yusuf hadn't come looking for her the other day. Curse Tudda and her good memory, anyway! It was Yusuf's fault, Alifa reminded herself forcefully and mustered as much righteous indignation as she could.

"After all, we can't stay here now," she said acidly. Her voice carried little of its usual edge, but to her surprise, Yusuf fidgeted nonetheless.

"I didn't mean to affect your status," he said. Alifa found her awareness of his scent rising in the shadows and she felt the heat of his skin, so close to hers. Only too easily could she recall the satisfaction she had felt in his arms, but she bit down on that errant whisper of desire.

Another time, another place. How tempting that whimsical thought was.

"It doesn't matter what you meant to do, it's done now." She bit out the words savagely.

"I had no idea your neighbors wouldn't know," Yusuf said quietly. Alifa shrugged, desperately trying to summon her familiar crusty nonchalance.

"Even whores have to live somewhere," she retorted. Alifa glanced up to find a frown puckering his brow.

"Where will you go?" he asked as though he were truly interested.

He could not be. Alifa knew better and refused to be tempted by the thought.

"I don't know," she said defensively. "What does it matter?" Yusuf was undeterred by her manner, much to her surprise. Alifa twisted her arm, but he did not relinquish his grip. His expression had turned thoughtful again and she did not trust the direction his thoughts might be taking.

"Were those the dinars you got from me that you gave to the shaman?" he asked quietly.

Curse him for figuring it out! Alifa swallowed carefully and nodded. So, he knew the truth. What difference would it make?

"Do you have any other coin?" he continued purposefully. Alifa wondered if she had imagined the undercurrent of concern in his tone. She could not even imagine how different her life might have been if there had been another to share the burden, another who was concerned for her troubles.

It had been that way for a long while. She had had love and concern with her parents, but since their demise, even her siblings' presence had not been able to fill the gap.

And she had let them down. That inescapable sense of failure washed over her again. Jaraw had lost a finger. Kasilo was sick. Tabeta was wise in the wickedness of the world far beyond her years. They were being forced to move after all this time and who knew what would befall them on the road?

She had failed her parents. Tears welled up in Alifa's eyes and she stepped away. Yusuf let her go, the warmth of his fingertips lingering on her arm.

"No," she said and shook her head despairingly at the sight of her own bare feet. They were not very well prepared to travel, let alone to begin a new life elsewhere. Alifa said a silent prayer that her parents would forgive her. "No, I have none," she confirmed harshly.

And none of this was Yusuf's concern. She was alone and shouldering the burden herself once again. It would be better if they left this very night.

Alifa walked stiffly away.

"My father is a shaman," Yusuf said when she had taken a dozen steps. Alifa halted, but did not turn, uncertain what he meant. Was he offering her something? She could not be sure. "And you seem to be forgetting that I vowed to teach Jaraw."

Alifa spun on her heel, tentative hope lifting her heart. Yusuf stood as still as a statue behind her, his hands shoved in his pockets, the hem of his cape lifting slightly in the evening breeze. His face was cast in shadow, but she could see his eyes glittering and knew he was watching her carefully.

"What are you saying?" she asked stonily, determined not to let her hopes get ahead of reality. She would know exactly what Yusuf was offering first.

"I have to go home to my father," Yusuf said slowly. "I'm suggesting that you come with me."

Was this pity? Alifa's chin jabbed into the air. She needed no charity from the likes of him. "Why?" she demanded coldly.

"Maybe he can help Kasilo. Maybe Jaraw's hand will need more tending." Yusuf's voice dropped and he took a step toward Alifa, then paused, as though uncertain of her response. Not that Alifa could imagine Yusuf being uncertain of much of anything. "Maybe it would be better for all of you to leave the city and try life in the mountains," he suggested gently.

"We *came* from the mountains," Alifa asserted proudly. Yusuf lifted one brow questioningly and she savored the minute sign of his surprise.

"I assumed you were Arabic," he said carefully. Alifa spat on the ground, eloquently expressing her feelings, and tossed her loose hair over her shoulder.

"Hakim is Arabic. I am Imazighen," she informed Yusuf frostily. "And you would do well not to forget it."

Something that might have been astonishment crossed Yusuf's features before his eyes narrowed and he regarded her shrewdly. "Berber women are not whores," he charged in a low tone. He folded his arms across his chest skeptically and for a moment Alifa did not know what to say.

How could she have been so foolish as to reveal more of herself to him?

"Berber women do what is necessary to survive," she asserted haughtily. She held his gaze for a long moment, then spun on her heel. "We are leaving tonight." Alifa tossed the words over her shoulder, changing the subject so that she wouldn't have to reveal more than she already had. "If you really think that your father can help Kasilo, you may accompany us."

Alifa stalked back to the house without checking to see whether Yusuf followed. Let him come with them or not, she thought with gritted teeth. It was time to leave, either way.

Yusuf watched Alifa retreat in amazement.

She was Imazighen?

As astounding as it was, the assertion explained a lot that puzzled him about this woman. Her strength, for example, her harsh manner, her defensiveness about her younger siblings. Berber women were known for their fortitude and single-mindedness. Yusuf could readily align those traits with what he had seen of Alifa.

Yusuf wondered if the fact that she was Imazighen lay at the root of her obvious displeasure that he had changed his name.

Not that it mattered what she thought of him or his name. Yusuf had no interest in women generally, and certainly not in this one specifically. Even if the half memory of being with her tantalized him almost constantly.

Yusuf had no need of women. Period.

He glanced down the street again, but Alifa had already disappeared into the house. Should they travel together? He was going home to deliver a message to his father. Yusuf tapped his finger on his elbow for no more than a moment as he considered his options, then nodded decisively.

His father could help the boy. Alifa had told her neighbor that she was no whore and it seemed she genuinely wanted to leave that life behind her. Alifa had no place of employment, although if Yusuf left her in the city, she might be forced to begin that work again to feed her siblings.

The thought troubled him deeply.

Of course, that was only rational. Had he not played a hand in the loss of her employment? It was perfectly reasonable that he should feel a twinge of responsibility. For pulling the rug out from beneath Alifa's life, Yusuf owed her the opportunity to make a choice, at least. And there was no shame in traveling with her, now that she had abandoned her profession.

He would take her home to the mountains. That was, after all, the decent thing to do. And he was going there already. Despite his rationalization, the thought prompted more of an emotional response than Yusuf was certain it merited.

Certainly he couldn't be proud to be traveling with a whore? He felt nothing but disgust for their kind. Certainly he couldn't feel any responsibility toward this family? Families were burdens for which Yusuf had absolutely no use. Certainly there was nothing of merit in spending more time in this particular woman's company? Hadn't she already shown herself to be sharp-tongued and difficult? Yusuf scowled at the cobblestones, dissatisfied with his own explanations, until inspiration dawned.

Of course, in the mountains it would matter less if Alifa told anyone what she had seen. There. A simple matter of personal safety. He breathed a sigh of relief.

Yusuf's secret would not be scandalous in the mountains. His father was there, and others like him, and there had been still more back over the years since time began. Surely it was only natural to feel relieved that a threat to his respectable scholarly life was being removed.

And, of course, he would not be staying in the mountains. If Alifa chose to stay, that was her decision, but Yusuf quite definitely would return to town. He had a future here, as a respectable scholar. Such futures needed to be cultivated and tended.

In fact, even lately he had heard that there would be an invasion of Andalusia in retaliation for the loss of Toledo to the Christians. Should Toledo be reclaimed, or even stability established in the south of Andalusia again, opportunities for an educated man like himself would abound.

Certainly Yusuf had little time to waste. The sooner he reached the village where he had been born and returned to Ceuta, the better. And this time, he would shake the dust of that backward little village from his feet for good. Matters would be closed between himself and his father. There would no longer be any reason to go back.

Of course, he would have to admit himself a failure first. Yusuf frowned for an instant, before he realized that he would be a failure in his father's terms only. Yes. And what did it matter if he was less than an acceptable shaman's son? Such things were behind him now. He wrote and spoke five languages. He was an urban man. Yusuf nodded to himself with satisfaction.

Unaccountably he recalled the luscious golden sweep of Alifa's back bared before him this very day. The resultant prickling in his palms made him grit his teeth in denial. An impish voice in his mind wondered whether Alifa would have *urges* after abandoning her profession. The prickling intensified unbearably.

No! Returning to the mountains meant nothing to him, Yusuf reminded himself savagely. Nothing! He had no interest in reasserting his Berber traditions. None whatsoever. And the prospect of seeing his father after fourteen years prompted no emotional response within him at all. None. This was simply a question of duty.

Somehow Yusuf imagined his father would come to quite a different conclusion. He cursed silently, fancying that he could hear the old man's cackle echoing in his ears. Yusuf shoved his hands into his pockets and stalked back to Alifa's house, determined not to give his imagination too much credence.

The laughter had been a trick of the wind, no more than that.

Alifa turned to find Yusuf framed in the doorway of the house, his features hidden in the shadows. She wasn't sure whether to be relieved or disappointed that he had followed her and she cursed the jumble that her emotions had become. Hadn't she always been the clear-thinking one? Since Yusuf had reappeared, it seemed that she could not string two thoughts together to save her life.

Alifa licked her lips and considered the unconscious phrasing of her last thought. Would she need anything to save her life if she went into the mountains with Yusuf? He stood silently on the threshold, his expression unreadable. Alifa suppressed a shiver as the silence stretched between them, fully aware that he was watching her, even though she couldn't discern his eyes.

What had possessed her to accept his offer? She would be taking her siblings into the mountains with a virtual stranger.

She had no choice, Alifa reminded herself savagely. And she would do her best to ensure that Yusuf didn't change his mind, either.

"Changing your mind?" she demanded archly, hoping her harsh tone would hide her growing trepidation.

Yusuf snorted and stepped into the house. "I shouldn't have to tell you that the Imazighen keep their word," he said. For all the smoothness of his voice, his words stung.

"I know," Alifa snapped. "But I wasn't certain whether you had forgotten that along with your father's name."

The words had the effect she intended, for Yusuf's lips thinned to a grim line and he shot her a hostile glance. Surprisingly, watching her barb hit home was less of a victory than Alifa had expected. She shrugged off the unwelcome sense of guilt. She was just overtired. And they had miles to go tonight before she would have a chance to sleep.

Alifa was well aware that Yusuf was watching her gather kitchen implements, his arms folded across his chest, his feet braced wide against her floor. She sorted the necessities and began jamming the crockery into a bag. Alifa knew that she was doing a more clumsy job of packing than she might have under other circumstances and prayed that Yusuf did not attribute her haste to his presence.

She had known that he would not let the comment pass, so when he finally spoke, it was almost a relief.

"An interesting comment from an Imazighen woman who rents out her services," Yusuf murmured. Tabeta gasped and Alifa could cheerfully have wrung Yusuf's neck.

"My former occupation is none of your concern," Alifa countered blithely. "And I certainly am in no need of your judgment." She began to fold a blanket, frowning at the other blankets as though her entire mind were absorbed with the task of counting them.

"But you would judge me?" Yusuf demanded skeptically.

"I only commented that you had changed your name."

"As you changed your ethics." Yusuf's voice dropped to a silky purr. "Yet my change seems to be particularly loathsome in your eyes. Perhaps you would be so kind as to explain your contempt."

"There is nothing further to discuss," Alifa retorted stonily. She was only too aware that they had an audience, despite Yusuf's evident disregard of that fact.

"Ah, but I think there is," Yusuf responded mildly. Alifa knew well enough to dread his next words and she darted a surreptitious glance in his direction. "It seems we have both made changes to our lives, yet you seem to find my choice particularly contemptible.''

"As you clearly find mine," Alifa snapped. Yusuf arched a brow.

"For obvious reasons, I would think," he asserted so coolly that Alifa longed to slap him. Instead, she glared at him.

"Your denial is far greater than mine," she declared. Yusuf folded his arms across his chest and his eyes narrowed. Alifa could no longer hold his gaze. She began folding blankets to cover her discomfort.

"Perhaps you could explain the difference to me," Yusuf suggested smoothly.

The difference?

Alifa spun to face him, the condemnation in his expression sending her temper soaring again. The children's presence was forgotten. "The difference?" she demanded coldly. "You want to know the *difference?*" Alifa heard her voice rising and decided that she didn't care.

"The difference," she informed Yusuf coldly, "is that I made a sacrifice when I had no other options to ensure that my siblings were fed. You, on the other hand, changed your entire life for no good reason at all."

There was a charged silence in the single-roomed house, but Alifa turned deliberately away from Yusuf. She continued folding blankets with a vengeance, ignoring the annoying tears that blurred her vision.

"What *precisely* do you mean?" Yusuf finally inquired. His voice sounded dangerously even, as though he were keeping control of his temper only with the greatest effort. Alifa was angry enough that she refused to be daunted. She cast the blanket aside, stalked across the room until they stood toe-to-toe, then tipped up her chin and stared him in the eye.

"Your face may say Imazighen," she confided, "but the resemblance stops there. You are no more Berber than my old employer, Hakim.'' The accusation was delivered with a sneer that did not go unnoticed. "Being Imazighen should mean something to you—it is not something to be casually tossed aside.''

"I have not tossed anything casually aside,'' Yusuf gritted out.

Alifa's chin snapped up at the assertion and she boldly held his gaze. "Are you *ashamed* to be Imazighen, Yusuf Khudabanda?'' she hissed.

Yusuf's eyes flashed, and before Alifa could step away, his hands locked around her upper arms. He lifted her to her toes and glared at her angrily. His hands were shaking with repressed anger and Alifa was suddenly aware of how much larger he was than she.

Fear flashed through her as she remembered her suspicions of Yusuf's shapeshifting. Would he change here and now? Would he devour her and the children? Why had she ever allowed him into her home?

Nonsense. There was nothing special about Yusuf Khudabanda and Alifa knew it. What she thought she had seen the other night had been just a dream. Maybe a nightmare. He was not going to change shape and attack her before the children, whatever her imagination maintained. He couldn't change. He was just a man, no more, no less, and she had known plenty of men.

The fact that he was a man who denied his roots only earned him her scorn. He was *less* than a man for that.

"Look at what I am and then at what you are,'' Yusuf finally growled. He arched his brows as he held Alifa's gaze and she knew what he was going to say. "Who should be ashamed?'' he asked in an undertone.

Too incensed by his words, Alifa took refuge in action. She spat. Yusuf's lip curled in disgust, and he gave her a shake before tossing her aside.

"I should leave you here to your whoring," he growled with narrowed eyes. Unaccountably relieved to be free of his touch, Alifa arched a brow with her usual air.

"Yes," she agreed mildly. "It would be typical of a man not truly Imazighen to break his word." Yusuf's nostrils flared and he strode to the doorway, pausing on the threshold to look back at her. Alifa could feel the anger emanating from him.

"I *will* leave you if you are not ready when I return," he snapped.

"And I will leave alone if you don't return by sunset," she retorted acidly. Yusuf made some sound of frustration under his breath, and then, with a swirl of red, he was gone.

And good riddance. Alifa exhaled shakily before she guiltily met the wide eyes of Tabeta and Kasilo. She had half a mind to *not* be ready, just to show Yusuf, but there was no doubt that he would do as he threatened.

And Alifa desperately wanted to get out of town. Like it or not, she would be ready and they would leave with this annoying man.

In fact, she hoped he did return by sunset. If he didn't, Alifa was honest enough to admit that she would be disappointed—although only because then she would have to risk the road alone.

Her hope certainly had nothing to do with the prospect of traveling with Yusuf himself. Nothing at all. The man was unbearably pompous.

By the time Yusuf had packed his belongings and purchased a donkey in the *souk,* his temper was returning to normal. Though he knew that one more accusation from Alifa would set him simmering again.

What was it about this woman that so annoyed him? If she had been as callous as she pretended to be, it would have been easy to dismiss both her and her charges against him. Her accusations hit too close to home for comfort.

But there was more than that to Alifa. He had glimpsed vulnerability in her eyes more than once, and maybe even a shimmer of tears. The way she had endeavored to protect her family from the truth of what she did to earn their keep spoke of a different kind of woman from that she would have him believe she was.

Their home was clean and well tended, for all its simplicity, something about it powerfully evocative of the homes he had known in the hills. That alone made Yusuf fidget. If he could have ignored the sounds of the town outside, he might well have thought they were back up in the mountains. Alifa's home was no tent, to be sure, but still there lingered a reminder of that way of life in the arrangement of the belongings there. The house was a home and exuded a kind of dignity that Yusuf had not expected.

Surely that was not the way most whores lived.

The house troubled him. He had felt immediately comfortable there, despite their quarrel, and that troubled Yusuf even more. If she hadn't been so determined to have an argument, he might have taken off his boots without thinking and settled before the hearth.

He refused to speculate further on the matter.

Yusuf could still see Alifa pleading for Jaraw's hand and the image twisted his gut once more. No, there was more to Alifa than met the eye. And Yusuf was more curious about uncovering her secrets than he might have liked to admit.

Yusuf set his lips determinedly as he turned down the alley that led to the house, bracing himself unconsciously for another battle as his mind filled with doubts. What would he do if she wasn't ready? Was he really prepared to abandon her here in Ceuta? Who knew what her self-righteous neighbors might do in the middle of the night? Or where Alifa would end up if she took to the road alone?

But Yusuf had vowed to leave her if she wasn't packed.

What if she left without him? He spared a glance to the setting sun, relaxing slightly when he saw that he still had time.

Unless she had changed her mind, as women were wont to do.

Despite himself, Yusuf's pace increased. He licked his lips carefully as the house came into view. The doorway of the house was dark and quiet. No packs waited outside and Yusuf knew a moment of trepidation.

Was she gone?

Naturally, his sole interest was in having company on the road. It really didn't matter at all to him whether Alifa had changed her mind, much less whether he was forced to leave her behind. Something twisted within Yusuf at that thought and he straightened. He acknowledged that it might disturb him somewhat to break his vow to the boy.

A matter of principle. Men of his quality did not break their word. Men of any kind. The principle itself had nothing to do with being Imazighen. Nothing at all.

Chapter Seven

Never would Yusuf have expected the scene that greeted his eyes. Tabeta beckoned him inside with a shy smile, and he immediately noted the pile of packs assembled beside the door and breathed a small sigh of relief. That was not what caught his attention, however.

It was Alifa, bending to lift Kasilo into a length of cloth knotted and slung over her shoulder. Not only was the sling of a traditional sort used by Berber women—though it usually bore an infant, rather than a small child—but Alifa had changed her clothes. Her garb was more modest, less colorful and fuller cut, in the way of the mountain women.

Alifa *was* Imazighen. There could no longer be any doubt in Yusuf's mind. The clothing suited her and she wore it with an easy familiarity that was more eloquent than her simple assertion had been. She wore a red-and-white-striped skirt and a shawl of similar wool over her full white shirt. A single silver necklace was draped around her neck. A trio of heavy amber beads were strung on the necklace and heavy silver earrings hung from her earlobes.

That Alifa had such a small collection of jewelry was eloquent in itself. She must have sold all of the rest, for both she and her mother, and perhaps Tabeta, would have had much more when they originally arrived here. It was the way. Alifa's hair was covered and when she glanced up, Yusuf saw that she had veiled the lower part of her face with traditional red.

Only her eyes and hands remained uncovered. He imagined that the expression in those beautiful dark eyes changed when she noticed his surprise.

And Yusuf *was* surprised. Alifa looked perfectly and utterly Imazighen. Her appearance struck a chord within Yusuf that stunned him with its intensity.

She looked like a woman a man might take to wife. The transition confused him, more than anything else, and momentarily he didn't know what to do or how to act or what to say. Yusuf could not reconcile the cocky whore he had known with this demure mountain woman. Her clothing recalled the old ways to him and instinctively, after that first glance, he could not even bring himself to meet her eyes. It was improper. It was wrong.

This was the Alifa who had writhed beneath him.

With its increasingly characteristic tendency toward troublemaking, his imagination summoned up another of those fleeting memories of the night he and Alifa had spent together. This time he caught a glimpse of her lying beneath him, her hair cast beneath her in a glorious tangle, her eyes closed as she let loose a low sound of pleasure.

Yusuf blinked, but the demure Berber woman still stood before him, those same mysterious dark eyes watching him curiously. His mind fought the truth. Yusuf simply could not reconcile the two images.

"We are taking only this," Tabeta informed him solemnly. Yusuf gave his head a shake and nodded hastily.

"I bought a donkey," he said, hearing his uncertainty echo in his voice and hating the sound. Curse Alifa, he sounded like a boy again. With a mere change of garments, she had stolen decades away from him. Yusuf flicked a tentative glance to Alifa. "It seemed best for Jaraw and when he recovers, Kasilo can ride. And the beast will serve me well on my return journey."

"I can carry Kasilo," Alifa interjected calmly. There was even a softness to her voice that undermined any possibility of Yusuf speaking directly to her. He felt inexplicably warm inside, uncertain of himself in a completely unfamiliar or half-forgotten way, and didn't know quite what to do about it. Yusuf dared to glance to Alifa again, only to find those fathomless eyes fixed upon him still.

He fidgeted, his gaze casting about the house for somewhere safe to look.

Instead, he noticed her bare feet.

Desire ripped through him, almost setting him off balance with its unanticipated intensity. He had the heady sense of having seen something forbidden and his world spun. Alifa's feet? Surely she had bared more to him before. Just this morning, he had seen her back exposed.... Yusuf reached out and gripped the solidity of the wall in what he hoped was a casual gesture.

It seemed suddenly that this journey would be overly long and difficult.

"You have no shoes," he commented in a tone that he hoped sounded offhand. Alifa shook her head and he could tell by the way her eyes changed that she had smiled behind her veil. Curse her.

"It doesn't matter," she said mildly.

"Of course it does," he countered irritably, hating the sense that her smile had broadened. "I have your slippers here in my pack." Yusuf turned away, grateful for the distraction as he rummaged in his goods.

"I have no coin to pay for them," Alifa said hastily. Yusuf froze for a moment before he hastily continued. Her words recalled his impetuous demand all too readily and suddenly Yusuf felt that he had treated this woman unfairly. His ears burned and he could not look at her.

"It doesn't matter," Yusuf muttered. He produced the shoes and turned around hastily to face her. "Here, take them," he said when she didn't move. When Alifa still didn't step forward, Yusuf dared to look at her. She shrugged as she met his gaze and pointedly juggled the weight of Kasilo.

"I won't be able to put them on," she said apologetically. Yusuf licked his lips and looked from the shoes to her half-hidden feet several times to summon his resolve.

"Of course," he said with what he hoped was some of his usual composure. He knelt in front of her, hoping she couldn't even begin to guess how his heart was hammering. Alifa lifted one foot.

It was as graceful a foot as Yusuf had ever seen and every bit as delicate as he recalled. He remembered vaguely the softness of her skin and was tempted for a moment before he recalled the presence of the children. Yusuf swallowed and stretched out to slide the leather shoe over Alifa's foot. She wiggled her toes in a most distracting way to adjust the fit and Yusuf could not tear his gaze away.

Alifa shifted her weight and lifted the other foot expectantly. This time, when Yusuf slipped on the shoe, he dared to let his hand linger. The temptation to touch her was simply too strong. The heady scent of jasmine wound its way into his nostrils.

Feeling incredibly bold, Yusuf let his thumb slide over her instep. Alifa shivered and pulled her foot away, but not before Yusuf had confirmed that her skin was as soft as he remembered.

"We should leave before it gets dark," she said hastily. Yusuf glanced up, wondering if she was more affected by his touch than she wanted him to believe. The expression in her eyes was unreadable, but still he took some measure of encouragement from her words.

Maybe there was more softness to Alifa than even he had anticipated.

"Certainly," Yusuf agreed as he straightened and forcibly collected his thoughts. "Did you bring all your salt?"

Alifa nodded hastily, her gaze flicking to him. "Of course," she said, but her voice still lacked its previous sting. Instinctively he knew that she understood why he had asked and felt a wave of appreciation for her practicality.

Alifa thought like a good Berber wife.

Yusuf blinked at the unexpectedness of that thought and resolutely turned to the array of packs. It was the second time since he had returned to the house that *Alifa* and *wife* had appeared together in his mind.

Her change of clothes had addled his thoughts more than was certainly reasonable.

"We didn't have much, but it's packed," Alifa added.

"Good. We can sell it in the south if we need to," Yusuf agreed with a brusqueness he was far from feeling.

In fact, he felt a little out of breath, although there was absolutely no good reason for it. He must just be anxious to get out of town.

So that he could get back quickly, of course. He was certain there must be translations awaiting his attention even now, maybe even a student anxious to learn Hebrew or Latin. Truly, time was of the essence.

Kasilo coughed as if to reinforce the point. He seemed unable to stop, but Alifa did not appear surprised, even though concern immediately lit her features. The boy was more ill than Yusuf had thought and needed a blessing soon, if it was to be effective. When Kasilo stopped coughing, he looked to Yusuf with tear-filled eyes.

Yusuf could not deny the boy an encouraging smile.

"My father will have exactly what you need," he assured him. Kasilo smiled tentatively and locked his hands around Alifa's neck with an affection that wrenched Yusuf's heart.

"Will I be able to run and play again?" he asked wistfully. Yusuf stood and ruffled the boy's hair.

"I certainly hope so. My father is a very powerful shaman. If anybody can help you, it will be him."

Kasilo grinned. "Then let's go!" he crowed. Alifa smiled, but Yusuf could not meet her eyes. He spun away from her and stepped back out into the street to take a gulp of fresh air.

If he wasn't careful, Alifa and her family would wind their way into his heart. And that would never do.

With Tabeta's help, Yusuf quickly loaded the donkey, grateful for the distraction of mundane tasks. Jaraw moaned when Yusuf lifted him, but did not awaken. Well aware of Alifa's watchful eyes, he tried to make the unconscious boy comfortable in the saddle. Yusuf checked the bandage, but the bleeding had stopped, at least for now. He could only hope the wound would heal quickly, despite the fact that they would be traveling.

"*Yallah! Zid!*" Yusuf encouraged the donkey in Berber, without ever intending to do so.

How long since words of that cursed tongue had left his lips? He scowled and slanted a glance to Alifa, blaming her completely for reminding him of his past.

The past he had deliberately left behind.

Just as she was leaving Ceuta behind now.

They left in a small, silent procession, Yusuf leading the donkey and the others following behind. Neither Alifa nor her siblings looked back on the house as they turned the first crook in the alley. That alone Yusuf thought indicative of their life here. There were people lingering in the *souk* when they passed through the quiet market, the shadows falling long across the cobblestones.

No one spoke to Alifa and Yusuf could feel their condemnation like a dark wave that washed over them. Seemingly unaware of their censure, Alifa held her head high as she crossed the square, glancing neither to the left nor to the right, not changing her pace one bit as she left the quarter. She walked like a queen. Admiration rose within Yusuf at Alifa's fierce pride and he was suddenly glad that he had been able to offer an option to her and her siblings.

Hopefully his father could help Kasilo. But even if the old man couldn't effect a cure, Yusuf knew, Alifa would find a way to stay in the hills. She might marry a decent Berber man and settle down.

The idea nearly wrenched Yusuf in half. He cleared his throat and frowned at the road, telling himself that he was only concerned that she might deceive the man about her past.

That would be unethical. Certainly that was why the thought troubled him. Yusuf had never had any tolerance for people with loose ethics.

He would have to ensure that he kept a close eye on Alifa. For the protection of the other men in the mountains, if nothing else.

A wheezing laugh rang in Yusuf's ears with a clarity that could not be denied. He gritted his teeth and struggled to ignore the annoying sound, knowing all the while that the effort was a futile one.

Alifa could not sleep.

Of course, she was camped in the hills high above the sleeping town of Ceuta, with a man she was fairly certain couldn't have done what she thought he had done that first night. It simply made no sense.

Shapeshifters held court in old fireside stories, not in real life.

At least that was what she had told herself in town. Up here, outside the city walls, the old tales suddenly seemed completely plausible. The wind whipped around them and the Mediterranean glittered darkly far below. It was easy to believe such tales out amid the rocks and stunted junipers. Alifa frowned to herself in the darkness as she recalled that she had no other explanation for the scratches on her back.

She licked her lips carefully and refused to indulge her imagination. Yusuf was just a man. An annoying, handsome and arrogant man, but a man nonetheless. Alifa repeated the refrain twice, fully aware that her imagination was not convinced.

She rolled onto her back and folded her hands behind her head as she stared blindly up at the stars. The crisp scent of the junipers filled her senses and invigorated her in a way she had almost forgotten all these years in town.

They had stopped when the darkness had completely fallen and Tabeta could walk no more. The donkey Yusuf had brought had been relieved of its burden and staked to graze a short distance away. Jaraw had slumbered the entire way. He stirred now in his sleep and mumbled, but did not awaken.

Kasilo had fallen asleep on Alifa's shoulder as they walked out of town. There had been those who came to watch her departure, as she had expected, but she had ignored them all. No doubt they only wanted to see what belongings she had chosen to leave behind so that they could squabble over the leavings in advance.

Alifa did not care.

Yusuf had said little more to her. They were going to his father and Alifa did not know where that was.

She found she didn't care about that, either. Yusuf's father was a shaman who might be able to help Kasilo. Surely nothing else was relevant.

Certainly not the twinge she felt every time Yusuf made it clear that he would be returning to Ceuta as soon as possible. Alifa understood clearly that this trip was an inconvenience for him. She supposed it was merely feminine pride that pricked at the reminder that she was part of that inconvenience.

Clearly, he might have traveled more quickly alone.

But his presence helped her and she would not complain. Alifa had felt younger as they passed beneath the long shadow of the city walls and she had immediately lifted her face to scan the distant peaks of the mountains. Far, far to the south, in the dying sunlight, she had been able to detect the faint blue smudge of the mountains she had known as a girl and had known a thrill of anticipation.

They were doing what she should have done years ago.

They were going home.

They had not gotten far before Tabeta tired, but Yusuf had made camp without complaint. Alifa had eyed him warily, certain he would have something judgmental to say about the traveling speed of women and children, but surprisingly he had held his tongue.

Then he had walked away. Without an explanation of any kind.

He had yet to come back. It had been so long that Alifa could not keep her mind from forming the inevitable question. Did he intend to abandon them here? Had he continued south without them?

Had this been his way of supplying her with a donkey without argument? Though why Yusuf would consider it his responsibility to supply a beast that she desperately needed to move Jaraw but could not afford, Alifa could not even guess.

She stared at the winking stars overhead and chewed her bottom lip thoughtfully. What if Yusuf didn't come back? Could she make her way into the mountains alone? Alifa took an inventory in her mind. She had mint tea and sugar and the salt and what was left of their bread. She remembered how to make a fire out here and thought she could recall how to make the flat bread that baked so well outside. Surely they could find water on the way, at least while they were still so far north.

Unfortunately, Jaraw was the best shot of the four of them, so they might not have meat for a while. Alifa couldn't accurately pitch a stone for any cause, but Jaraw had a knack for it. Until his hand healed, however, they would get by. They would have to.

The first and most difficult step had already been taken. Surely the best option was to continue now and face their destiny here. Sooner or later, they would find a village that would take them in.

Alifa closed her eyes against the starlight and prayed that it would be so easy.

Jaraw cried out suddenly and thrashed in his sleep. Alifa rolled over immediately, fully intending to tend him—until she met the bright green gaze of a black panther.

She froze. She would have recognized the beast anywhere, although her mind fought against the inevitable conclusion.

It could be another panther, Alifa told herself wildly, even as she stared into the creature's knowing eyes. It blinked slowly, no wildness in those eyes, and she imagined it might slowly smile in a very familiar expression.

Alifa's heart began to gallop and she could not move. It was *not* just any cat. The way its heavy tail lashed slowly at the night air was vaguely reminiscent of the hem of a red cloak fluttering in the breeze. Its eyes widened knowingly before its ears flattened against its sleek black head. It snarled as it crouched lower, its gaze unwavering from hers.

Alifa swallowed carefully. What did it want from her? This was the same cat that had scratched her back. She was certain of it, as illogical as that idea seemed.

But how could this be? Surely she had imagined that encounter? Surely Yusuf could not...did not... But the panther was here and Yusuf wasn't. Just as it had been before. Something about those wary and watchful green eyes told Alifa that she had not guessed wrong.

This was Yusuf. He *was* one of the ancient ones. Hadn't he said that his father was a shaman? Hadn't she thought he had *baraka?* The pieces dropped into place and it all made horrific sense.

She had coupled with a shapeshifter. She had been witness to his ability.

Suddenly Alifa was flooded with fear as to Yusuf's intentions. What would he do? Would he finish what he had begun with her back? Had he brought them into the hills so that none would hear their cries as they were devoured?

The panther moved.

Alifa gasped, but found herself paralyzed with fear. It seemed all the will had left her body and she could not move. Stealthily the beast approached Jaraw, all the while sending cautious glances Alifa's way, as though he did not know what to expect from her. She hardly knew what to expect from herself and she trembled powerlessly.

To her astonishment, the panther crouched beside the sleeping boy, his dark coat blending with the shadows so completely that she had difficulty distinguishing where the cat ended and the night began. Her heart skipped a beat.

Not Jaraw. Please, she begged the panther silently. Please don't hurt Jaraw.

The great cat hunched lower, spared her a telling glance that she might have thought was intended to be reassuring. That made no sense, she thought with annoyance, as the beast bent leisurely and licked Jaraw's hand.

Alifa's eyes widened. Jaraw stirred, but did not move away. The panther settled onto his haunches with a grace vaguely reminiscent of another she knew and methodically began to lick the boy's wound.

The bandage Yusuf had fashioned was gone and Alifa wondered when it had been removed. Had Yusuf planned this? But to what purpose? Jaraw rolled to his back and left his hand sprawled out before the creature, apparently soothed by the rhythmic motion of the panther's tongue.

The ancient ones had the gift of healing. She abruptly recalled part of her mother's tales and sagged with relief. Astonished, Alifa released the breath she hadn't known she was holding.

It seemed he had no intention of hurting the boy. If anything, the cat's manner seemed protective. Alifa dared to relax as she watched the beast's leisurely movements.

To her surprise, the rhythmic licking soothed her nerves, as well. Alifa found her eyes drooping closed as the moon rode higher in the sky. She shook herself awake repeatedly, only to find the cat still crouched beside her brother. That tongue continued in his relentless labors, the angular head tilted first one way and then the other.

Finally Alifa fought her exhaustion no more.

When she awoke, the sun was already edging over the mountains, though the children slept on.

The panther was gone. Though that did not surprise her, her other discovery of the morning was an unexpected one.

There were two freshly killed partridges left beside her belongings. Alifa had seen enough of the world to know a gift when she stumbled upon it. By the time Yusuf strolled whistling into their makeshift camp, the children were up and the meat was roasted.

Alifa did not have the nerve to ask him where he had been all night and Yusuf volunteered nothing. It should have been enough for her that Jaraw's pain was greatly diminished and his hand already showed remarkable signs of healing.

And she was not certain she was ready to have Yusuf confirm what she already knew was the truth.

She knew.

The awareness of that pricked at Yusuf like a sharp sliver. Alifa knew. There had been no shock or disbelief in her eyes the night before. A moment of surprise, perhaps a flicker of fear, but no more than that.

Alifa had seen him on that first night. It was true. He struggled to focus on the meat she had prepared as the children awakened, unable to stifle a sense that he stood unnaturally revealed.

He had been right, though the confirmation did not reassure him at all.

Yusuf had suspected as much. Certainly, the reason he had shifted the night before had been to test his theory, but to have confirmation of his worst fear affected him far more than he had expected. Maybe he had hoped that he had been wrong.

But that didn't matter now. Alifa knew. He could not come to terms with the realization.

Yusuf felt naked. He felt vulnerable. He liked neither feeling.

No one had known his secret since he had left the mountains far south of here fourteen years past. Even then, there had been few who knew the truth, even in his father's village. Now he was traveling with a woman who not only suspected the truth, but had seen him shift. Yusuf slanted a glance in Alifa's direction and could discern no outward sign of her thoughts.

That did little to reassure him. Though, truly, she seemed much more mysterious to him since she had changed her garb, for all the sense that made.

He was lucky he had seen the benefit of removing her from town. Yusuf could only imagine the damage such a rumor would have wreaked upon his reputation. He permitted himself a self-congratulatory moment. If this had not exactly been his plan, it might as well have been, considering how smoothly it had been executed.

Although his plan to get home and back as soon as possible showed markedly lower signs of success. Yusuf chafed to leave, but unfortunately, he had four others to wait for this morning.

So, despite his impatience, Yusuf sat, politely eating roasted meat that he did not want as he tried to divine the direction of a woman's thoughts. Yusuf scowled in Alifa's direction, hating that he could not discern her thoughts. From her manner, one might have imagined that nothing was amiss.

Maybe she wanted him to believe that she had not guessed the truth. Yusuf snorted under his breath at the thought. He knew better. He had seen understanding and fear in her eyes the night before, and he knew what it meant.

To his annoyance, the fear bothered him.

Jaraw rolled out from under his blanket and stretched leisurely. He should have been up already, helping Alifa, to Yusuf's mind. He gave the boy the benefit of the doubt, hoping that Alifa was being indulgent of his injury.

Yusuf's hope was quickly dismissed. Without a glance elsewhere, Jaraw spotted the meat. Yusuf stifled a wave of irritation when the boy dropped down and devoured half of one of the birds without a second thought.

An Imazighen man did not act so thoughtlessly. They were all dependent on one another, and the men, in particular, should see that the others had their due. It was the way.

"No one else has eaten yet," Yusuf advised him. The boy glanced up and his eyes narrowed as he met Yusuf's regard.

"I'm growing," he maintained boldly. He held Yusuf's gaze and defiantly bit into the second leg. Anger flashed hot within Yusuf at Jaraw's insolence, but he schooled his features carefully and reminded himself to bide his time. Tabeta joined them, her pretty young face fresh and clean. Alifa carried Kasilo back from the stream and Yusuf strode to take the boy from her.

"He's too heavy for you," he said chidingly. Alifa smiled and becoming color stained her cheeks.

"You haven't eaten," she said, rebuking him mildly. Yusuf was suddenly aware of how like a small family they must appear.

"I'm hungry," Kasilo confided with a ready grin. Yusuf welcomed the distraction of the boy's sunny disposition and scooped him up high.

"Then you shall have to eat some of your sister's fine cooking," he said as he sat down and placed the boy on his knee. Yusuf granted portions of the other partridge to the two younger children, fully aware of Alifa's presence behind him. She bent to hand chunks of bread to the children and he caught a tempting whiff of her sleepy scent.

Yusuf blinked and swallowed carefully, unable to dismiss an errant image of Alifa's hand trailing boldly up his thigh. Then it was gone, leaving him with an aching hollowness.

Jaraw continued to eat the other bird, his expression no less than mutinous. Yusuf glanced to Alifa, but she was blissfully unaware of his perusal.

The woman would drive him mad with desire.

He scowled, and his gaze landed on Jaraw again. Yusuf realized abruptly how much the boy was eating, without regard for anyone else, and his annoyance found a ready outlet. Had the boy no manners at all? His manner was disrespectful to Alifa and to Yusuf himself. It was unacceptable behavior.

His father would have had words with Yusuf if he ever dared to act in such a manner.

Yusuf tried to school his rising annoyance with Jaraw. Two birds should have been plenty, but he had not counted on the boy making a glutton of himself. He hoped that Alifa did not deem him responsible for the shortage of meat.

"Come and eat, Alifa," Yusuf invited. She hesitated only an instant before she sat beside him, her brows pulling together in puzzlement as he handed her the remainder of the meat.

"But you need to eat, as well," she protested. Yusuf shook his head and held her gaze stubbornly.

"I've already eaten," he murmured in a voice low enough that she alone would catch the words. Alifa's eyes widened slightly as she understood his meaning and then her gaze dropped to the roasted meat.

"I see," she said weakly and Yusuf knew that she did. She was not surprised. There was his answer. Yusuf flicked a telling glance to the young man sitting opposite him.

"And it seems that some of us are quite hungry this morning," he added acidly. Jaraw's mouth opened and closed again, as though he would argue the point but thought better of it. Yusuf coolly held his regard, feeling Alifa glance questioningly between the two of them.

"It has been some time since we have had partridge," she commented hastily. Yusuf's lips thinned when Jaraw did not even look up. That was no excuse for his boorish behavior.

The meal was completed in awkward silence.

It was time Jaraw began his lessons, Yusuf concluded sourly. He was going to live with the Imazighen and the greatest service Yusuf could do the boy was to teach him the rules of community life. Even if Jaraw didn't want to learn. That had been Yusuf's promise, after all. He would be doing no more than fulfilling his debt.

Still, he hesitated to interfere.

Yusuf observed the boy's manner carefully and resolved to wait for his moment. Alifa was certain to be overly protective of Jaraw—in fact, that was undoubtedly part of the boy's problem.

When the children were finished, Yusuf rose and kicked the coals from the fire to scatter them in the dust. He watched from the corner of his eye as Jaraw rose and spared not a hand to the packing. The boy brushed off his *chalwar*, then sauntered over to the donkey to heft himself onto its back. Jaraw sat there like an impatient monarch, waiting for his dutiful but slightly inept courtiers to see to his goods.

That was enough.

Yusuf turned to address the boy, summoning an expression of apparent surprise at finding him already astride the donkey.

"The donkey is for Kasilo," Yusuf said as though the matter were beyond question. Jaraw folded his arms across his chest, making the awkwardness of his right hand deliberately obvious in the movement.

"I'm riding," he said insolently.

"You're walking," Yusuf corrected flatly.

"I rode yesterday."

"And now that you're fully rested, there's no reason you can't walk today." Yusuf fixed the boy with a hard glance. "Kasilo cannot walk," he reminded him forcefully.

"Alifa can carry him," Jaraw retorted. Yusuf shook his head.

"He's too heavy for Alifa."

Jaraw's chin shot up. "Then *you* can carry him," he argued insolently. Yusuf strode to the donkey's side and grasped Jaraw by the ear, lifting him slightly from the donkey's back. The boy's eyes widened for an instant before he reassumed his usual confident expression.

"No," Yusuf said mildly. "You can walk. As I already told you."

Jaraw sneered up at Yusuf. "You can't tell me what to do," he snarled and brandished his bandaged hand. "After all, I'm wounded."

"Wounded as a result of your own foolishness," Yusuf snapped impatiently. "Saved from losing your entire hand by *my* willingness to speak for you and brought this far on *my* donkey's back." Yusuf fixed Jaraw with a steady eye. "I think you should dismount," he suggested in a dangerously low tone. The boy's chin shot up in proud defiance.

"No," Jaraw said stubbornly.

Evidently the boy was simple. And Yusuf had never taken well to defiance. He jerked the boy's ear so hard that Jaraw lost his balance and slipped from the donkey's back. Jaraw stumbled to regain his footing when Yusuf abruptly released him and shoved him aside. Yusuf nodded with polite formality, as though Jaraw had dismounted by choice.

"Thank you for your graciousness in seeing matters my way," he said. He turned to face the others, but not before he glimpsed the open hostility in the boy's eyes.

Yusuf met the uncertainty in Alifa's eyes and his determination faltered slightly. She and the other children stood silently regarding the pair of them and he fancied that her demeanor was judgmental. Had he interfered where she thought he had no right?

But Yusuf had vowed to teach the boy and he had no intention of putting his promise aside. Jaraw's insolence was intolerable. Yusuf would teach Jaraw, with or without Alifa's blessing. And the boy would learn the Imazighen way, whether he wanted to or not. Jaraw's behavior did not befit any father's memory.

"Alifa," Jaraw whined in a tone that belied his age and made Yusuf cringe inwardly. "Don't you think I should ride?"

Yusuf watched Alifa's eyes flick to her brother and back to him. He could not read her expression and was suddenly afraid that she would not agree with him. She straightened in a way that encouraged him, for he recognized the stance as the one she took when she was about to make a pronouncement that might be unpopular.

Unpopular with him or with Jaraw? The question undermined Yusuf's relief.

"You have the better part of your hand because Yusuf vowed to teach you," Alifa said quietly. "Perhaps you had better attend his lessons." Relief surged through Yusuf, but the way that Alifa turned away to scoop up Kasilo left him uncertain of his victory.

"Does this mean that I get to ride the donkey?" Kasilo demanded as he clasped his hands affectionately around Alifa's neck. The little boy's enthusiasm effectively dispersed the tension among them and Yusuf found himself smiling with the others.

"Yes," Alifa said simply.

Jaraw's expression was sullen and Yusuf knew this battle was far from over. He glanced to Alifa and breathed a silent sigh of relief at finding her lips firmly clamped together.

For once, she appeared to have nothing further to say. Yusuf felt a little surge of pleasure that they were of one accord on this subject, at least.

Finally, *something* was going according to plan.

He watched her settle Kasilo and tuck blankets around the protesting boy with care, her concern for the child's welfare revealing to Yusuf that intriguing softer side of her personality once more. Maybe she would let down her guard more often. Maybe she would come to trust him by the time they reached his home.

No, not his home, Yusuf reminded himself irritably. His *father's* home. Yusuf's home was in Ceuta and that was where he would return, soon enough.

It was high time they got on the road and put this journey behind them.

Chapter Eight

By some miraculous stroke of fate, Alifa managed to hold her tongue until the children were asleep that night.

Of course, there had been precious little chance to take Yusuf to task throughout the day. They had come far to the south on the old road, despite the temptation of golden beaches down the steep cliffs to their left. In the heat of midday, the sparkling azure water far below had almost been too much for Alifa and she knew the children had glanced down longingly more than once.

How dare Yusuf speak to Jaraw that way! If nothing else, Alifa's annoyance had kept her putting one foot in front of the other throughout the long day. Each step brought her closer to the moment she could speak her mind.

The air was cooler now that the sun had dropped lower. The sky was turning indigo as Alifa squatted beside a quick stream to rinse the kettle and wash out the crockery and utensils from dinner. Despite her exhaustion and the ache in her back, her anger remained undiminished. Mercifully, as soon as they made camp, she had been free to discard her veil and hood. The wind from the sea tousled her hair over her shoulders and Alifa welcomed its cool touch.

Her temper, though, was far from cool. All day long her ire had been building and now that they had finally stopped, it was simmering steadily. She dumped the dishes into the water and savored their noisy splash.

Yusuf had gone too far this time! Had he no compassion in his soul? Jaraw was wounded. He had been hungry—surely there was no harm in that. Jaraw was a growing boy. The rest of them could accommodate his needs easily, for they had been doing so for years.

Yusuf had overstepped his mark by far.

"Dinner was good," the man in question said unexpectedly from behind her.

Startled by his presence, Alifa jumped and dropped a knife in the river. The water rushed over it as it sank to the pebbled bottom and she cursed her own skittishness.

Yusuf, however, appeared to take her slip in stride. He squatted down beside her and plucked the knife from the water with consummate ease. When he presented the knife to her with a flourish, Alifa was immediately suspicious. What did he want from her? She slanted a glance in his direction to find that slow and confident smile creeping over his features.

Her heart lurched and she snatched the knife from him, even as her distrust of him redoubled. Wasn't she angry with him? One charming smile wasn't going to change that. And Alifa had seen him smile so seldom that she knew the gesture heralded something she would not like.

Yusuf wanted a favor. Alifa's eyes narrowed as she concluded precisely what kind of favor he wanted from her.

After all, there weren't many other whores plying their trade up here. Alifa set her lips tightly, willing herself to wait. Let him ask. If Yusuf dared to do so, he would get a response he was far from expecting.

If only the idea could have been completely without appeal, it might have been easier to ignore him. The kettle seemed to take on a life of its own, the battered old lid fighting Alifa as she struggled to wash it nonchalantly.

"Thank you," she said tightly. Yusuf's brows rose and he settled back on his haunches. Alifa was painfully aware of both his perusal and her own clumsiness as she continued to wash the dishes.

"I didn't think couscous could taste so good," he mused.

His casual reference to the traditional steamed semolina she had prepared and served mixed with the few wild vegetables they had found en route did little to soothe Alifa's nerves. The lid from the kettle clattered uncooperatively. Alifa jammed it back on the pot and stifled a curse.

She hated Yusuf for being so relaxed in her presence. His manner was in marked contrast to her own agitation, even though his compliment on her cooking had launched a warm glow inside her.

Mind your step, she warned herself. He's just smoothing the way with sweet words before he makes his request. There was no need to fall readily into his trap, if at all. And furthermore, Alifa knew that she was no more than an adequate cook, never having had the time or the interest to learn more than the most rudimentary culinary skills.

It had been a plain meal, well suited to people who were famished. Under any other circumstances, it would have been left untouched. Alifa had no illusions about her own limitations.

After all, if she had been able to cook, she would have gone into domestic service of a more honorable persuasion.

"You were probably just hungry," she countered dismissively, certain that was the case. Alifa felt her color rise when Yusuf's speculative gaze landed on her once more. She could see the toes of his boots in her peripheral vision and scolded herself not to be distracted. A crockery bowl leapt into the stream and Alifa cursed roundly.

Yusuf chuckled, the vile man.

"You seem to be a little out of sorts tonight," he commented easily as he retrieved the bowl, as well. He handed it to her and Alifa was certain it was no accident that their fingers brushed in the transaction. She refused to meet his eyes. She snatched the bowl and clamped her lips together, determined not to give him any indication of the tingle that tripped along her skin at his most casual touch. Yusuf frowned.

"Are you tired?" he asked with what appeared to be genuine concern.

Ha! Alifa knew exactly the source of his concern and it had more to do with his pleasure than with her comfort!

"Did we walk too far today?"

"Jaraw certainly did." Alifa bit out the words, glad to have them out in the open. Yusuf said nothing for a moment and she glanced at him warily. He looked surprised, but she declined to let her resolve weaken. "There was absolutely no reason why he couldn't have ridden today," she added churlishly.

There was another moment of silence, although this time it was markedly less amiable. Alifa determinedly chased the last vestige of pale yellow couscous around the cooking pot.

"He couldn't ride today because I said he couldn't," Yusuf finally responded silkily.

Because he said so! Now there was a reason she could respect! Who did this man think he was? For someone who was destined to be a part of their lives for a very short time, Yusuf seemed determined to make the most mess of every moment.

"Oh!" Alifa exclaimed. "So, now you are in charge of our lives! Shall we bow and scrape at your every word and whim?"

She glared at Yusuf and watched his lips tighten. He inhaled and made a sound under his breath that might have been a growl of frustration before his eyes narrowed.

"No," Yusuf said with carefully controlled calm. "It was only right that Jaraw should walk today." He paused and held her gaze for a long moment. "I had thought that we agreed on this matter this morning."

This was her reward for refusing to argue in front of the children. Alifa slammed the last clean utensil onto the pile and shoved to her feet.

"Well, you thought wrong!" she snapped.

She would have swept the dishes up and stomped back to the camp, but Yusuf snatched at her wrist and drew her to a halt. Alifa set her lips mutinously and would not meet his eyes. She tapped her toe impatiently, certain the gesture would annoy him further, and savoring the welcome possibility.

"You could not have carried Kasilo all day," Yusuf insisted. Alifa tossed her hair and tugged at his grip on her wrist, knowing all the while that he would not release her until he was ready to do so.

"I could have and I would have," she asserted determinedly.

"And hurt yourself in the process," Yusuf retorted. "He's too heavy for you to carry and you know it."

"I would have—" Something clicked in Alifa's mind and she froze in shock. Kasilo was ill. Yusuf was a shapeshifter, which meant he was one of the ancient healers. Her mouth dropped open and she pivoted to face him. Yusuf watched her warily, evidently unaware of the thoughts that had filled her mind.

Yusuf could have helped Kasilo himself! Rage rolled through her that he had decided not to intervene.

The man's audacity was unbelievable! She propped her hands on her hips. "At least I would do *something* to help him!" Alifa snapped. "If you had deigned to help him, no one would have had to carry him!"

Yusuf stared at her for a long moment, although she was certain he had immediately understood. "What do you mean?" His tone was low and considering, and Alifa knew he was weighing the risk of what she knew.

Well, she knew it all! And Yusuf had better be prepared to defend himself! There was no excuse for leaving Kasilo to suffer. Alifa's heart pounded and she lifted her chin to hold his gaze in challenge.

"I know what you are," she said, carefully enunciating each word, despite the anger rolling through her. She did not miss the flare in Yusuf's eyes, even though he recovered quickly. "You could help Kasilo!" she accused and her voice rose slightly. "You could heal him! You could do it here, instead of our traveling all the way to your father."

"I don't know what you mean," he asserted with false bravado. Alifa shook her head slowly.

"You know *exactly* what I mean. You're one of the ancient ones, just like your father." She licked her lips, shocked by her own audacity, but she could not stop now. She leaned deliberately closer and Yusuf's regard flickered from hers once again. "You shift," she whispered.

Yusuf relinquished his grip on her arm with a haste that might have been born of aversion. He stepped away and ran one hand hastily over his brow.

"You don't know what you're talking about," he told her hastily.

"Well, I know exactly what I'm talking about. Your father is a shaman and so are you," Alifa said flatly. She heard the accusation in her own tone and knew Yusuf would guess the reason for it. He stiffened, but did not turn. "How dare you force Kasilo to take such a long trip, a trip that might be too much for him?" she demanded. "How dare you not use your power to help him?"

"I have no power."

"What?"

Yusuf glanced over his shoulder and his eyes narrowed. "I am not a shaman," he said carefully.

The simple words took Alifa so by surprise that her anger abandoned her in an instant.

Then she realized that he only lied to her so that he would not be obligated to help her brother. It was a despicable move. Alifa's lip curled with disgust.

"What do you mean?" she cried when she had recovered her indignation. "How can you deny this? Only the ancient ones who can shift have the power to heal. You're a healer and a shaman, Yusuf. *I know you can change shape!* How can you deny this gift?"

Yusuf turned slowly and granted her a tolerant look. "I refuse this gift," he said calmly.

Alifa was incredulous. Refuse it? How could he deny being what he was?

Was she mistaken? It wasn't possible. She had seen him in panther form. There was no other explanation. And the eyes that panther had... Surely there could be no doubt!

No. Clearly Yusuf was playing games. For whatever reason, he simply didn't want to help Kasilo. Alifa had no intention of letting the matter pass without a fight.

"But you can't just ignore your gift," she protested. "It's part of what you are and a blessing to all of us. You are Imazighen. You know that it is your responsibility to share your gift. You *know* that is the way."

"I've told you the answer is no."

Alifa folded her arms across her chest. "Is this because I have no coin?" she asked with open hostility. "Do you have the same requirements as the shaman in Ceuta, who would do nothing without his eight dinars?"

"This has nothing to do with coin and you know it," Yusuf snapped. He pointed back to the distant town emphatically. "I told you there that a decent shaman would treat someone regardless of whether they had coin and that's the truth."

"Then why won't you help him?"

Yusuf glared at her for a moment before he averted his face with a jerk. "It's not my place."

"It is precisely your place!" Alifa cried in frustration. Honestly, the man would drive her mad with his pointless equivocating! "You are a shaman. Kasilo is sick. It is your responsibility to tend him. *It is the way and you know that!*"

Yusuf spun on his heel with an abruptness that took Alifa's breath away. His eyes flashed dangerously but she did not dare step away. "It is *not* my way! It may be the way of those backward people in the hills, but I am not one of them!"

"Well, of course you are," Alifa retorted crossly. As excuses went, that one was pretty poor.

"Of course I am *not!*" Yusuf shouted. She watched him with growing alarm as he flung his arms wide. "I am not a shaman! I will not accept this so-called gift! It is a curse that I have left behind." He stepped close to Alifa and jabbed his finger into his own chest. "I am a Muslim and a scholar, a civilized man who considers logical matters of import," he asserted through gritted teeth. "Not some backward tribesman from the hills with his head crammed full of petty superstitions."

Alifa looked down at the ground. She had never seen Yusuf so agitated and she didn't know quite how to proceed. Clearly, he felt strongly about the matter, but so did she. She set her lips and looked him in the eye once more. "I didn't see a superstition the other night," she ventured to comment. Yusuf growled in annoyance and stalked away.

"You saw what you wanted to see," he asserted.

Alifa snorted. "I don't think so."

Yusuf slanted a glance in her direction. "It doesn't matter. Whatever you saw, you won't see it again," he said firmly.

Alifa's heart sank. There was her answer. A shaman had to shift to work his magic. Only in his alternate form could he reach the spirits who could intervene in this world and effect a healing.

Yusuf would not help Kasilo. She blinked back her tears, unwilling to let the matter go easily. She had to at least ask.

"Then you will not help Kasilo?"

Yusuf shook his head decisively and folded his arms across his chest. "I cannot."

He could not! That claim pushed Alifa's tolerance too far. Kasilo was only a child in need of help. That Yusuf would refuse to heal him was selfish beyond compare, regardless of whatever difficulties he might have with the burden of his gift. He could certainly agonize over that *after* Kasilo had been healed, to her mind!

"No," Alifa muttered, her voice low with anger, "you *will* not."

Yusuf's head snapped around so that his gaze locked with hers. "What does that mean?" he demanded. Alifa jabbed her chin into the air.

"It means that you are the most selfish and lowest individual I have ever had the misfortune to meet," she said deliberately, glancing over him with disgust. "And trust me, I've met more than my share of gutter slime."

With that, Alifa turned to pluck the dishes from the ground and stalk self-righteously away. The man was not worth their trouble. Anyone who would not help a child in need was someone Alifa did not care to know. If Yusuf chose to abandon them here tonight because of her disgust, so be it. They would be better off without his kind.

"You know nothing about it," Yusuf snarled. Alifa ignored him and continued walking. A civilized man? He was a snake. She heard his footsteps trail quickly after her, but stubbornly did not change her pace.

When he snatched her elbow and spun her around, Alifa was not surprised. Her expression remained impassive, even when two of the bowls danced from her grip at her abrupt spin and rolled across the ground.

"You have no idea what this is like," Yusuf asserted hotly, his eyes blazing into hers.

"And I don't care." Alifa shrugged. "It has nothing to do with me," she said with feigned disinterest. Yusuf's grip tightened on her elbow and he gave her a little shake.

"It has *everything* to do with you," he claimed inexplicably. "*Everything*. That is the problem." Alifa frowned in confusion, but he evidently had no intention of explaining. His gaze danced over her features, the very intensity of his expression warming Alifa inside.

What did he mean? What could his power have to do with her? Alifa made the mistake of scanning his face in an attempt to find an answer. She could not step away once she dared to meet his eyes and was snared by that emerald regard.

Instead of the answer she sought, what she found was her own body responding to Yusuf's proximity. Her heart swelled at the determination in the set of his handsome features and something melted within her as the scent of him flooded her nostrils. His grip tightened on her elbow and Alifa suddenly wanted to feel his hands work their magic upon her.

Right here and now.

She wanted Yusuf again. The conclusion was stunningly unexpected, for all its validity, and shockingly inappropriate.

Hadn't he just shown her that he thought of nothing other than himself?

Yusuf leaned closer and Alifa hoped against hope that he would kiss her. He hesitated, his lips a finger's breadth from hers and it was all Alifa could do not to close her eyes and melt against him.

He was so close that she could virtually taste him.

"Do you want me to teach Jaraw?" Yusuf whispered. His breath on her cheek was so distracting that it took Alifa a moment to comprehend his words.

She swallowed, desperately trying to recall her frustration with him. Wasn't she angry with Yusuf for refusing to help Kasilo? Why was she thinking about him kissing her? Was she losing her mind? Never had she let a man affect her like this. Why did it have to be this particularly exasperating one who prompted her deepest desires?

The idea of coupling with Yusuf again was foolish, to say the least. The realization that she didn't want to merely provide a service to Yusuf made it even more so.

Yusuf was a respectable scholar, Alifa reminded herself. Such men did not associate with whores, at least not for long. And Yusuf knew beyond a doubt what Alifa had done for a living. There was no place in his life for a woman like her.

And there was no place in Alifa's life for a man who would deny a child something that could be so easily granted. Clearly, there was no future in her inappropriate desires.

Better that they continue to argue. She took a deep breath and plunged on before she could change her mind.

"You took that vow upon yourself," Alifa retorted as sharply as she could manage. Something flickered through Yusuf's eyes at her harsh tone, but Alifa refused to be swayed from her path. She stepped away for the sake of her own sanity and propped one hand cockily on her hip. "Since you had no interest in my approval then, why do you want it now?" she sneered.

Yusuf did not move. "I will leave him be, if that is what you want," he said quietly.

What? That took the wind out of her sails. Alifa raised her eyes dubiously to meet Yusuf's intense gaze. "But you gave your word," she protested in surprise. Yusuf cocked one dark brow and his eyes seemed to darken with some unspoken intensity.

"And I will break it, if that is what you want," he murmured, his deep voice barely audible over the sparkling gurgle of the stream.

Alifa was stunned by his assertion. For a Berber to break his word simply because she wanted it so was a greater gift than she had ever been granted. She was so amazed that she forgot her intention to begin an argument with him.

Alifa stared up at Yusuf for a long moment as she tried to fathom what would prompt him to make such an offer. Of course, there was little to be read in his expression.

But he could not be doing it to gain favor with her. Why would he bother?

Maybe he was trying to tell her something. Maybe she was wrong about Jaraw. Alifa frowned slightly, uncertain what to think.

Could she be wrong about Jaraw? There seemed to be no other possible explanation for Yusuf's unexpected offer.

"You think he needs to learn?" she asked doubtfully. If Yusuf was surprised by her change of manner, he gave no sign of it.

"I think he takes advantage of you," Yusuf replied with an immediacy that told Alifa he said what he believed.

Was it true? Did Jaraw take advantage? Alifa nibbled at her lip and tried to consider the facts dispassionately. It was certainly true that Jaraw did only what he desired to do and no more. It was also true that even she had noticed a growing tendency for Jaraw to see to his own needs at the expense of all others.

Was it possible that he needed a stricter hand than hers? Could Yusuf be right?

Alifa looked to Yusuf once more, not surprised to find his expression determined. She nibbled her bottom lip as she thought furiously, and finally acknowledged that it made too much sense. As much as she hated to concede the point, Yusuf might be right on this matter.

And if anyone could show Jaraw a strong hand, it was this man, she concluded easily. Alifa smiled at the simple ring of truth in that statement as Yusuf blinked. She had no business making him revoke his vow. In fact, it would likely be best for all if she granted Yusuf a free hand with Jaraw.

For now.

"You may be right," she admitted. Yusuf's brows rose, but he said nothing. Alifa cleared the unexpected thickness in her throat at the recollection of the generosity of his offer. He might deny his heritage, but keeping his word was important to him nonetheless. And Alifa would not cavalierly discard his suggestion, for she guessed what it had cost him. "I would never ask anyone to break their word," she said carefully, "but thank you for offering."

Yusuf nodded once in acknowledgment, though he said nothing. They stared into each other's eyes for a long moment and Alifa again had that curious sense that time had stopped just for them.

Night was falling, and the mountainside was hushed in anticipation. Alifa's desire returned unexpectedly to torment her. A smudge of orange outlined the crest of the Rif mountains to the west. The little stream chortled merrily to itself beside them, the donkey tugged determinedly at the sturdy grasses, its tail sweeping continuously. The wind from the sea caressed the coast and carried a hint of Yusuf's scent to Alifa's nostrils, fueling that dangerous tingling within her.

Why had he offered to break his word for her? Was this as close to an apology as she would get for his refusal to help Kasilo?

Was it possible that he truly couldn't help her youngest brother?

Alifa didn't know. In fact, she wasn't aware of much of anything except the bright gleam of Yusuf's eyes. He had offered to break his word. That was no small thing among their kind.

Without questioning her impulse, Alifa stretched to her toes and pressed a chaste kiss to Yusuf's tanned cheek. His skin was warm, his scent reminding her of greater pleasures, but Alifa was not immune to the effect of her changed clothes, either. Her role was no longer that of the seductress.

Alifa would have pulled away if Yusuf had not caught at her hand. She glanced down at her trapped fingers and watched the lean strength of his outline each finger in succession. His tan was darker than hers and the difference was discernible even in the shadows. His touch was firm but gentle, recalling only too well the weight of his caress on her skin.

Alifa dared to meet Yusuf's eyes and was stunned by the passion blazing there. His hand cupped protectively around hers and he leaned closer, his obvious intent making her heart beat a staccato.

"Alifa," he whispered and his breath fanned across her lips.

Alifa could not deny him. Everything within her surged in anticipation of his kiss. Just one taste, she told herself as her eyes fluttered closed.

Just one, for what might have been in another time and place.

Alifa slipped one hand around the nape of Yusuf's neck to pull him closer and let her head drop back as his lips closed over hers. He was warm, his lips demanding yet requesting her permission with gentle persuasiveness. Alifa opened her mouth and her hand slipped to cup the side of his face.

Yusuf's arms closed possessively around her at her sub-mission. His kiss was dark and sultry, like the night claiming the mountains around them. He tasted of forbidden spices, of hidden secrets, of nameless treasures to be found buried in the dark.

It was too easy to lean against him, too easy to surrender to the surety of his touch. Alifa felt her meager resistance dissolving, just as she knew she could not have turned away from Yusuf to save her life. He tore his lips from hers and she whimpered unwillingly, wanting no more than that he should continue.

"Alifa, I want you," Yusuf whispered, his voice hoarse against her cheek.

His words recalled Alifa to her senses. She remembered suddenly her earlier certainty about his intentions and her cheeks burned with shame.

Fool! She had almost been deceived! He only wanted to use her, as he had before. How could she have been so na-ive? Alifa planted her hands against Yusuf's chest and pushed hard. She felt his surprise even as he stepped back and was well aware of the weight of his questioning gaze upon her.

Alifa could not have looked up for any price. Her voice, when she spoke, vibrated with suppressed anger. "I am not a whore anymore," she whispered unsteadily.

Yusuf said nothing.

Had she hoped for some reassurance? Fool! Alifa had been right in anticipating the direction of his thoughts. She was convenient, no more than that. Tears blurred her vision as she spun away and she fumbled with the dishes as she hastily picked them up. Gathering her skirts, Alifa stormed back to their little camp, unable to look back to the man who stood silently behind her.

Yusuf did not return to the camp that night.

His palms prickled after Alifa's kiss with a vengeance he

flatly refused to acknowledge. He never lost his temper, yet that was another accomplishment he could chalk up to Alifa's charms. The old barbarian had broken through his consistently perfect control, leaving Yusuf disoriented and uncertain of precisely who he was.

And it was all Alifa's fault. He gritted his teeth as she walked away, the swing of her hips doing little to ease his temper. Seductress.

Knowing he could not possibly sleep in her vicinity, Yusuf turned in the opposite direction and strode off into the night. Hours passed and still, tirelessly, he walked.

In fact, he paced and prowled as better befitted his other form, though he did not shift on this night. When the first tinge of the new day stained the horizon, Yusuf found himself on a rocky crag far above the camp. He sat restlessly and turned a disinterested eye on the rising sun.

What had possessed him to kiss Alifa?

The move had been poorly conceived, to say the least. It had been illogical. It had been the complete antithesis of his plan. The woman had him turned inside out and uncertain of what he should do. There was, however, absolutely no reason to pursue intimacy with her at all. In a month or so, he would leave Alifa to return to Ceuta and would probably never lay eyes on her again.

The thought did not provide the reassurance that Yusuf expected. She was a whore, he reminded himself vehemently, but Alifa's angry denial followed quickly on the heels of that thought.

She was right, he conceded reluctantly. That life was behind her, but the knowledge of it should have been enough to keep Yusuf's base desires in check. He stared at his boot unhappily.

At the time, kissing Alifa had seemed the most natural thing to do. Beyond natural, it had been inescapable. And more enjoyable than Yusuf would like to admit.

Yusuf recalled his own whispered confession and squirmed. Even worse, he knew the murmured words had been true. He *had* wanted her. A whore. Surely that was not the sort of urge an ethical, respectable man should have. And even if he should have a base desire of that kind, surely it would not be prompted by either a whore or the rural Berber woman Alifa now appeared to be?

It was inappropriate.

Of course, it had happened before.

Yusuf inhaled sharply and stared at his itching palms. Was it possible that the beast within him was gaining the upper hand? Was it possible that he was fighting a losing battle in his determination to become a respected man of letters?

After fourteen years, he had thought he might have accomplished that very objective. Meeting Alifa had proved him wrong.

Was going home, however briefly, a mistake of the worst kind?

Yusuf frowned and glanced downward, only to find himself just above the camp. He squinted and readily discerned the four sleeping figures around the extinguished fire. Yusuf picked out the largest of the four quickly and his gaze clung to Alifa's sleeping figure.

Was she truly asleep? How could she sleep after that kiss? Yusuf drummed his fingers on his knee and felt his lips thin. He resolutely looked back to the rosy dawn.

The problem wasn't so much that he had kissed Alifa. The problem was that the sweet temptation of the kiss had left him longing for more.

It made no sense. And definitely had nothing to do with his plan. He was supposed to be accompanying this ragged little family to his father's village, and incidentally trying to teach Jaraw some decent behavior, by virtue of his own inexplicable offer to do so. Certainly his plan had nothing to do with kissing Alifa or talking to Alifa or wondering what

Alifa was thinking or recalling sudden images of their night of lovemaking. Certainly not.

Certainly he had had no business confiding in her that the shifting had everything to do with her presence. That wasn't even true, or at least it hadn't been absolutely proved to be true. Such an assertion could only give her ideas about her role in his life.

It was a good thing he had declined her request to help Kasilo. That would have left Alifa believing that she could control him. Yusuf's gaze was dragged unwillingly to the sleeping figure of the young boy, and he gritted his teeth against the wave of guilt that assailed him.

He *couldn't* help Kasilo. He simply couldn't. To do so would require him to embrace the bane of his legacy. He couldn't do that for any objective, however worthy it might be.

Alifa clearly didn't know the sacrifice that had to be made to invoke the shaman's "gift." He had never healed. He had never shifted on purpose. He had never requested anything of the spirits who whispered in his ears when he was in his other form.

He couldn't. Yusuf knew what they would want in return for their favors. It was barbaric and he refused to participate.

Yusuf shoved impatiently to his feet. If he was going to get back to Ceuta quickly, it was high time they got on the road this morning. Alifa could sleep once they reached Yusuf's father's village.

After all, there was little else to do there. He snorted and began to climb down to the campsite again.

Yusuf's troublesome imagination summoned an image of Alifa sleeping, her hands curled before her, her expression curiously childlike. He stopped, stunned by the wave of warmth that swept through him. Yusuf allowed his gaze to skitter to the sleeping figures far below once again and he took a deep breath to steady himself.

It might be illogical, but there was something about the woman that intrigued him.

If a night in her arms had invoked the return of his curse, maybe another night could close the circle and return him to the blissfully normal state he had enjoyed these past fourteen years.

Now there was an idea with appeal. Yusuf paused and pursed his lips, desperately trying to slow the unsteady pace of his heart. Could it possibly work? He stared unseeingly over the valley as his mind plunged forward.

It made perfect sense. In fact, it was the most logical thing he had conceived in quite a while.

And it would not be without its advantages. Yusuf whistled as he jumped down to the next rock, letting his optimism grow as he revised his plan.

Chapter Nine

Unfortunately, Yusuf's plan did not proceed quite as well as he might have hoped.

The way had been narrow all morning and they had been forced to continue in single file, which left little opportunity for exchanging confidences of any kind. As the path broadened in the late morning, though, Yusuf found himself trudging alongside Tabeta.

Alifa, he noted, seeing her in his peripheral vision, lingered close to Kasilo's side, while Jaraw led the donkey. The boy was obviously doing so under protest, but Yusuf didn't care. He matched steps with Tabeta and she flung a cautious smile his way.

"This must be quite an adventure for you," he commented idly. Tabeta shrugged, her attention apparently focused on watching her step. "It has been fourteen years since I went to Ceuta," he said. Tabeta glanced up and he was encouraged by her expression to continue. Mercifully, this one didn't seem to share her sister's harsh manner. "But it doesn't seem as though much has changed in these old mountains."

"Did you come this same way?" Tabeta asked.

Yusuf nodded companionably. "But in the other direction," he clarified in an amiable tone. Tabeta giggled.

"I knew that," she scolded laughingly, before she sobered. "Do you remember what it was like where you were born?"

Only too well, Yusuf thought, but he didn't dare voice that thought. His mind filled with the purple circle of snowcapped mountains that had surrounded his childhood on every horizon, as though their village lay at the base of a mountain-rimmed bowl. Yusuf could not recall a moment when he had not longed to see what lay over those distant mountains, once his father had confided to him that they did not mark the edge of the world. He smiled in reminiscence and shook his head.

"Yes, I grew up there, so I remember it well," he contented himself with saying.

Tabeta spared him an assessing glance. "How old were you when you left?"

"Sixteen."

"Oh. You were *old*," Tabeta informed Yusuf. "Even older than Jaraw." He smiled despite himself at her assessment, but she was concentrating on the path again. "I was only two when we went to Ceuta," she confided.

"Oh." Yusuf said, mimicking her tone. "You were *young*." Tabeta laughed and gave him a friendly shove. "Do you remember your village?"

"No." She shook her head and frowned in thought for a moment. "Well, maybe a little. Mostly I remember that Ceuta felt different."

"Different in what way?"

Tabeta's lips thinned. "It wasn't safe there," she said in a low voice.

Yusuf wondered if this had really been her own impression or whether she had picked up the apprehensions her mother must have felt in an unfamiliar setting. Yusuf knew that he had had a hard time adjusting to the noise and bustle of people on every side when he first went to town. It had been shocking to live so close to indifferent strangers, after having spent his entire life with the same dozen families.

And men did not work at home in town. If their father had gone to work all day, his absence would only have fed their mother's feelings of vulnerability in an unfamiliar place.

"I don't think it's less safe," Yusuf said practically. "I think it's just different."

Tabeta's eyes brightened in curiosity. "What do you mean?"

"Well, in the mountains, you can always be attacked by animals or not catch enough to eat and find yourself starving. In town, there are no wild animals and you can always go to the *souk* to buy a morsel for dinner."

"If you have any silver," Tabeta corrected self-righteously.

"Of course," Yusuf agreed, uncertain whether she was referring to their poverty or Jaraw's recent experience. He glanced back to the trio with the donkey and decided to take a chance on asking. "Alifa always had silver for food, didn't she?"

Tabeta shrugged. "Sometimes more, sometimes less." She flicked Yusuf a glance that was stern beyond her years. "She worked very hard in Ceuta, you know," she informed him with some of her sister's fierce pride.

"Oh?" Yusuf asked, uncertain how to proceed. Tabeta shot him a glance of disdain that did not prepare him for the unexpectedness of her claim.

"Of course she did. She worked for a cloth merchant in the Jewish quarter."

Yusuf's mouth worked for a moment, without his articulating any sound. What tale was this? Tabeta watched him, evidently waiting for some response and he struggled for a reasonable question.

"Doing what?" he inquired weakly.

"Selling cloth." Tabeta scoffed at Yusuf's apparent lack of worldliness. "She had to roll it and measure it and help the customers choose which color they liked best." Tabeta darted a glance over her shoulder to her sister, then leaned closer to an astonished Yusuf. He bent lower to catch her words, wondering what she intended to confide next.

"Sometimes," Tabeta whispered, "she even worked all night."

"No?" Yusuf demanded with mock skepticism. Tabeta nodded.

"Yes. And sometimes they just worked so late that Alifa stayed to sleep there." Tabeta pursed her lips disapprovingly as she turned forward again. "You know, it isn't safe for a woman to be out in streets alone after dark."

"I had heard that," Yusuf agreed sagely.

He didn't know what to make of the story Alifa had told her siblings, though he could readily understand her reasons for doing so. Did they all believe it? It seemed to him that Jaraw had known something else in the square, but Yusuf couldn't be certain.

"You know, she never liked working there," Tabeta continued in the same confidential tone. Yusuf's head shot up.

"She didn't?" he asked as innocently as he could.

"No, but my mother made her promise," the little girl confided, then abruptly stopped talking. Yusuf looked down to find Tabeta's eyes glazed with tears. She looked deliberately away from him, scuffing her toes as she walked.

"Made her promise what?" Yusuf prompted gently. Tabeta shot him a glance that was all too reminiscent of her sister for his comfort.

"To take care of us. It's the way, you know."

Yusuf did know, though the reminder did his refusal to indulge in Berber whimsy no favors. Had he had so many reminders of tradition in the past fourteen years as he had had in these past few days with Alifa?

It occurred to him suddenly that Alifa and his father might see eye to eye on many matters. That was not a comforting thought.

"When your mother died, you mean," Yusuf prompted, as much to evade his own thoughts as to continue the conversation. Tabeta nodded vigorously and he saw a trio of tears catch the sunlight as they fell. She sighed and sniffled once, then impaled Yusuf with a forlorn glance.

"I don't remember that very well," she confessed. "I do remember that it took Alifa a long time to find some work. She was very sad about it, even when she was hired by the cloth merchant." Tabeta's lips thinned and she frowned thoughtfully. "I think she had hoped for something better."

"I can imagine," Yusuf muttered sardonically. He flicked a glance over his shoulder to find Alifa's brows drawn together in concern and her gaze fixed on them.

Evidently she had overheard something. Yusuf's heart sank of its own accord and he dreaded whatever she might say.

"Tabeta?" Alifa asked sharply. "Are you crying?" Tabeta glanced back, her eyes still brimming with unshed tears.

"No..." she said in a wavering voice.

He would never get out of this alive.

Yusuf heard Alifa catch up with them in a purposeful bustle. He glanced toward her, not in the least reassured by the fact that she was demurely veiled and hooded again. Dread welled up within him at yet another reminder of the traditional.

How could he defend himself, let alone argue with her, when she was dressed so modestly? Yusuf could see only her eyes, which made him uncomfortable enough, especially when they glittered in anticipation of a fight, as they did now.

"What have you been saying to make her cry?" she immediately demanded. It was not reassuring that she instantly assumed Yusuf to be responsible.

"Nothing," Yusuf protested, feeling his ears heat. "We were just talking."

"Talking would not make the child cry," Alifa snapped. She stepped between the pair of them and gathered Tabeta protectively against her side.

"He was asking about Mother and Father," Tabeta said quietly. Alifa shot Yusuf a glance that could have turned him to stone and he braced himself for her attack.

"What earthly reason would you have for upsetting Tabeta?" she asked hotly, before understanding dawned in her eyes and stilled her tongue. Her voice dropped to an indignant whisper. "You were prying!" she accused.

"I was not," Yusuf retorted indignantly.

"What, then?" Alifa demanded.

Yusuf waved one hand vaguely. "Just curious."

"Ha!" Alifa jabbed one finger into his shoulder to emphasize her point. "You were prying and there are no two ways about it." Her eyes narrowed dangerously. "I won't have you making Tabeta cry. Anything you want to know about us, you ask me. Understand?"

Yusuf drew himself up taller. "I understand perfectly," he said stiffly. "But I thought you were busy with Kasilo and I did not see the harm."

Alifa arched a skeptical brow. "*I* see the harm and that is enough. My sister is too young for your *friendship,*" she said harshly, putting particular emphasis on the last word. Outrage flooded through Yusuf at her evident meaning and his ears burned.

Mercifully, Tabeta seemed to have no understanding of what her sister meant, for she looked between the two of them with confusion.

"I would never—" Yusuf began to protest in a low voice, but Alifa's cold laugh interrupted him.

"But you have," she taunted. The devil's own twinkle in those dark eyes reminded Yusuf more than adequately not only that he had, but that *they* had. Together. He wondered uneasily if Alifa was laughing at him behind her veil. Alifa leaned closer and Yusuf knew enough to dread her next words. "And, furthermore, I *know* you have."

Yes, he certainly remembered that salient fact. Yusuf stubbornly stared at the path ahead as he walked and refused to acknowledge his imagination's summoning of another vision of a delightfully nude, purring Alifa.

"We were simply talking," he informed her frostily. "It's a shame you can't lift your mind up out of the gutter."

Alifa looked away for a moment, but then her gaze locked with his and her expression was resolute. "What could you possibly have to discuss with my sister?" she demanded coldly.

"We were talking about you," Tabeta interjected. Alifa's eyes blazed for an instant before she softened her expression and turned to her sister. Yusuf cringed inwardly, inexplicably feeling he had been caught at some dastardly deed.

"Talking about me?" Alifa asked sweetly. She brushed a slender finger across the girl's cheek affectionately. "Now why on earth would you two talk about me?"

Tabeta smiled and tucked her hand into her sister's as they walked together. "We were talking about moving to Ceuta. I said you didn't really like going to work for the cloth merchant, but that you had promised Mother you would take care of us." Yusuf didn't need to look up to be aware of the sharp look Alifa fired in his direction.

There was a moment's silence. "I see. And why were you talking about moving to Ceuta?" Alifa inquired mildly.

Tabeta shrugged. "Yusuf was just talking." She paused pointedly and glanced to her sister. Her voice was slightly accusing when she continued. "I thought it was all right to talk to him. He *is* your friend."

Yusuf looked to Alifa in surprise at the unexpected comment. Her wide gaze locked with his and they stared at each other for a timeless moment. *Friend?* Hardly the word Yusuf would have chosen. Acquaintances at best.

Except for the small complication of the intimacy they had shared. Yusuf felt the back of his neck heat, and wrenched his gaze away.

Friend . . . How many friends had he seen writhe beneath him?

"Then why did you cry?" Alifa asked Tabeta gently. Yusuf was only vaguely aware of her words as he fought to regain his control.

"I remembered Mother dying. It wasn't Yusuf's fault." Tabeta sniffed one last time and summoned an almost cheerful smile for her sister. "You aren't mad at him, are you?" Yusuf caught his breath and unabashedly listened for the answer. He felt Alifa's gaze sweep over him and knew in his heart that her expression was not encouraging.

"We'll see," she said enigmatically. "Will you walk with Kasilo for a while? It's dull for him to ride without anyone to talk to."

The little girl agreed amiably and skipped back to her siblings, seemingly reassured, leaving Alifa alone beside Yusuf as he walked. He could not look at her and concentrated on placing one booted foot in front of the other.

He didn't have long to wait for the storm to break.

"If you have anything to ask of me, you ask me directly." Alifa spat out the words as soon as Tabeta was out of earshot.

"We were making conversation," Yusuf protested. A quick glance to his side convinced him that Alifa was having none of that excuse.

It seemed his little plan was doomed to fail if this atmosphere prevailed.

"You were prying," she accused. To his dismay, Yusuf had to look away.

"I was curious," he asserted proudly. Alifa snorted.

"You have no right to be curious," she snapped. That remark defied common sense and Yusuf straightened as his own anger rose to the fore.

"I have every right to be curious about the people I am traveling with," he bit out.

Alifa laughed. "Yes, not knowing about my parents' deaths is a genuine threat to your personal safety," she retorted and continued with a sneer. "The road may be dangerous, Yusuf Khudabanda, but it is not *that* dangerous."

He was certain she had used his name deliberately. Alifa was waving the flag of his second name before Yusuf in a blatant attempt to anger him.

It worked.

"It is perfectly within reason for any traveler to want to know the identities of anyone he would travel with so closely as this," he informed Alifa coldly.

Undeterred by his demeanor, she stared down at him, her eyes glittering. "There are things more dangerous about you than your name," she accused in a low voice. That struck a nerve, just as she must have known it would.

"I don't know what you mean," Yusuf responded curtly.

"Yes, you do," she argued. "Just as you know that this arrangement is more dangerous for me than it is for you."

"You don't know what you're talking about," he said dismissively. Alifa's eyes flashed again.

"No? Fine. Play your games, but we both know what I'm talking about. We could be devoured in our sleep, but what is the threat we pose to you?" Her voice rose slightly, though she did not seem aware of it. "You already know the worst of it. If it's your respectability that you're concerned about, what could be worse than traveling with a whore?"

That she should question the need to maintain a respectable reputation was too much. Yusuf had worked hard for that reputation, not that a woman like Alifa would understand the value of a good reputation. His eyes narrowed and he glared at her as he uttered the first and most hurtful thought that crossed his mind.

"Traveling with a *former* whore, indisputably."

Alifa raised her hand to slap him, but Yusuf was ready. He caught her wrist and let his fingers close tightly around her as he gave her a shake. Alifa unrepentantly jabbed her chin into the air.

"The truth will come out," she said with a curled lip and he was amazed that she never relinquished a fight. "You only agreed to travel with us because you expected consolation on the road."

"Don't fool yourself," Yusuf growled. "A king wouldn't have enough dinars to sleep with you every night."

He didn't see her knee coming until it was too late to move.

"Bastard," she hissed between her teeth, as Yusuf doubled over in pain. Alifa twisted her wrist from his grip and darted out of range.

When he stood up, the others had halted behind them and the four of them were watching him warily. It seemed even that the donkey regarded him with trepidation. Yusuf straightened despite the pain and brushed off his clothes fastidiously.

Clearly, his plan was proceeding perfectly. Yusuf gritted his teeth and allowed himself the luxury of a stream of profanity, at least within his mind, for the mess he had made of things.

He should never have lost his temper. He should never have allowed Alifa to provoke him. Already he felt ashamed of his own behavior, but it was too late.

It seemed he would be doomed to live with the beast that Alifa had awakened. And it was his own fault.

"Perhaps we should stop while the sun is high," he suggested cautiously. They had already stopped, in fact, but there was no reason not to take a break.

"Perhaps not," Alifa snapped. "The less we rest, the sooner we'll be free of each other."

There was that. At this point, Yusuf would cheerfully have rid himself of all four of them. But he had made a promise to take them to his father and he would see the matter through to its conclusion, regardless of the price.

"Fine," he said tonelessly. "We will continue."

Yusuf turned back to the path and set a quicker pace than they had taken so far. To his mingled disappointment and satisfaction, Alifa and her siblings matched his pace without complaint.

They hadn't gone far before Yusuf was surprised to find someone directly behind him. He swiveled to find a determined-looking Jaraw glaring at his back. Yusuf arched a brow and the boy waved his bandaged hand in Yusuf's direction.

"You touch my sister again, or make either of my sisters cry, and I'll kill you," he threatened in a low growl.

"I haven't touched your sister," Yusuf maintained coldly. The boy's eyes flashed.

"Liar!" he charged wildly, then shot a quick glance over his shoulder. Yusuf followed his gaze guiltily and hated himself for breathing a silent sigh of relief when he saw Alifa concentrating on something Kasilo was telling her. Mercifully, she did not seem to have noticed this exchange. Jaraw lunged closer and the hostility in his eyes astonished Yusuf.

"I *saw* you touch her last night!" he declared.

"You had no right to watch," Yusuf growled.

"I have every right to protect my sisters," Jaraw retorted. "Especially from people like you."

"Obviously you've been doing such an excellent job of taking care of them so far," Yusuf challenged smoothly. The boy's eyes narrowed. "Was that part of your plan in getting caught stealing the silver?"

"I'll kill you, I swear it," Jaraw reiterated.

The two glared at each other until Yusuf permitted himself a calculating smile. "You wouldn't know how," he charged softly.

The boy's lips twisted angrily. "I'll learn," he vowed with a solemnity that sent chills through Yusuf. "I'll learn and I'll hunt you down, Yusuf Khudabanda. Don't touch her again."

Fourteen long days and nights later, they arrived in Fez, locked in the same incompatible silence that had joined ranks with them that afternoon.

Alifa had never been so exhausted in her life. The children could not have been any less tired, but none of them were willing to interrupt the terse silence, even to complain. And Kasilo was coughing more. Clearly, his illness was progressing. At first, Alifa had been infuriated with Yusuf for his failure to help the boy, but increasingly she was too tired to care.

She prayed Kasilo would not die before they even reached Yusuf's father, but each day she felt those prayers were more and more futile.

As their ragged little group entered the fortress of Fez, she glanced back and noted how haggard Tabeta looked. Alifa waited until Tabeta was alongside and slipped her arm about her sister's shoulders in silent support. Hopefully they would rest soon, but Alifa would not make promises she could not be certain to keep. She continued doggedly onward, taking the time to shoot a hostile glance in Yusuf's direction.

The man, typically, remained blissfully ignorant of her displeasure. He might as well be made of stone.

In fact, he had ignored everything about her for the past two weeks, Alifa thought with growing annoyance. He might have been traveling alone, for all the notice he took of the four of them. He had them up before dawn every day, walking all day, despite the heat and the steep incline of the path, and not stopping until darkness fell. Half of the time she would finish preparing a meal in the evening only to find the three young ones asleep where they sat.

Yusuf had disappeared every night, which Alifa supposed she should have expected. The night after their argument, she had feared he had abandoned them. Oddly, the sound of a great cat yowling close by had reassured her that night, even as it made her flesh creep. The morning offering of fresh meat clearly showed his intentions and once Alifa knew she could rely upon him, she had worried less.

However unconventional he might be, it seemed that Yusuf had taken responsibility for them.

What Alifa had worried about the rest of the way south was the troubling fact that this apparent claim of responsibility reassured her. How could she be relieved to be under the care of a man who was not always a man and who in his other form was fully capable of killing them all? Even when he was a man, Yusuf had to be the most exasperating man she had ever met.

Alifa could not help but feel that relying on him was a dangerous proposition indeed. Completely at odds with that conclusion was the way her memories of their night together had begun to haunt her with new vigor. Had she really experienced that sense of tender completion with this same man? Alifa was sorely tempted to repeat the event, just to lay all doubt to rest.

And what did he mean when he said that she had "everything" to do with his changing? It made no sense.

That Yusuf was thoroughly disinterested in her when her thoughts were so preoccupied with him did no favors for her pride.

But now they were in Fez. Never had Alifa dreamed they would come this far. Her family had only come from the Rif, closer to the coast—three or four days of solid walking to Ceuta, at most. But they had come all the way to the reputed marvels of the city of Fez.

And who knew how much farther they had to go from here?

Finding herself in the great city she had heard so much about made Alifa suddenly feel rather provincial. Her eyes widened at the bustle of activity that swallowed them as soon as they entered the city's sheltered streets. The chatter of voices was disorienting after so long in the silence of the hills. The mingled smells of cooking, perfume, perspiration and refuse was almost enough to turn Alifa's empty stomach.

Yusuf, however, did not hesitate. And if he could stride nonchalantly, then so could she. Alifa would not give him the satisfaction of losing them in these twisted streets. Her lips thinned and she gripped the donkey's reins more resolutely. She picked up her pace before the sweeping red of Yusuf's cloak could completely disappear in the throngs of people.

Curse him for not even glancing back to check that they were there.

Alifa stumbled on something spilled on the cobblestones, but did not bother to identify it. Surely she was better not knowing. They turned down another twisted street and the light changed abruptly to a softly filtered and shadowed coolness.

Loosely looped skeins of wool hung from lines strung across the width of the alley, obscuring the late-afternoon sun. Each line was hung with wool of a different color. Indigo, saffron, carmine, loden and brown wool waved slightly, just above their heads. Men shouted into the crowd, hawking their wares, while others haggled over prices, their voices rising and falling in the din.

Alifa felt suddenly confined. It seemed the city's embrace had tightened and threatened to suffocate her. The walls on either side of the street felt oppressively close. The wool dangled too low. The sounds were overly loud, the air was too warm and stale. People nudged her on every side and she had the urge to bolt back out the city gates.

"I will take the donkey from here," Yusuf said from an unexpected proximity, his low voice interrupting her thoughts. Alifa glanced up in alarm and found something remarkably like understanding in his eyes. The press of the crowd nudged them closer and she could smell the mingling of dust and Yusuf's skin. Alifa's pulse skittered and she looked abruptly away, even though she knew that it was only her fears that fueled its pace.

She felt Yusuf's gaze slide away and peeked up to find his brow furrowed in a frown. "We'll try to stay at a caravan-serai just ahead," he informed her.

"A what?" Alifa knew her ignorance was showing, but she was too tired to pretend she knew what he meant. Yusuf almost smiled.

"A caravanserai is an inn specifically for the caravan drivers," he told her quietly. "There are stables for their beasts and storehouses for their goods, clean rooms and simple food." Alifa exhaled shakily, feeling her nervousness unaccountably dispel as he talked.

"So, we're a caravan?" she teased with a tired smile.

Yusuf chuckled as he passed a glance over their group. "Not quite," he conceded. When his eyes met hers again, Alifa was astounded by the warm humor lingering there. His gaze danced over her veil, as though he could truly see her features, despite the obstacle. The intensity of his expression made Alifa's mouth go dry and she dropped her gaze nervously.

Yusuf cleared his throat. "We will be able to find transportation more easily there," he explained. Alifa was so surprised that she glanced up into the cool green of his eyes before she could catch herself.

"Transportation?"

Yusuf nodded. "It's too far for the young ones," he mused. Alifa felt her eyes widen in surprise. He *had* noticed their tiredness after all. The realization made her think better of Yusuf than she had in quite a while.

"If it can be managed, I would like to join a caravan for the next part of the trip," he continued. "We'll still have to walk the last few days, but I think it will be worth the price." He paused, and Alifa felt him glance expectantly down at her again.

We must look like a couple, she thought suddenly. The way they were standing close together and quietly discussing their plans might lead an observer to that conclusion. Alifa didn't look up, but her cheeks heated. She was painfully aware that Yusuf said nothing else and desperately sought some reason for his silence.

Was he waiting for her to offer to pay their share? Alifa stiffened at the possibility.

"I have no coin," she reminded him awkwardly.

"I know," Yusuf said, his manner characteristically unruffled.

The silence stretched between them again. What was he waiting for? Alifa shuffled her feet in agitation, only too aware of the weight of Yusuf's gaze upon her. He couldn't expect— Surely she had made it clear that she had abandoned her profession?

Only his continued silence goaded her into asking.

"You're not asking me to work here to earn the money, are you?" Alifa demanded in breathless shock.

Yusuf looked no less surprised by her thought than she had been. He frowned and took a hasty step backward.

"No! Of course not!"

"Then what are you waiting for me to say?" Alifa demanded frostily.

Yusuf shook his head despairingly before he met her accusing gaze and he almost smiled. "That the caravanserai is a reasonable idea," he said unexpectedly.

He was asking her *opinion?* Alifa ran one hand over her brow in frustration. Since when had that been important?

Honestly, the man changed direction more times than the wind in a summer storm. Would she ever be able to guess his thoughts?

Not that it mattered. Yusuf would be leaving them shortly and Alifa would never see him again.

"I hardly think my opinion is relevant," she snapped, taking refuge in anger once again. "You will do what you want, whether I agree or not."

Yusuf's lips tightened. "I think it *is* relevant or I wouldn't have asked."

"How could it be?" Alifa demanded, flinging out her hands in annoyance. Several passersby spared her surprised glances. She jammed her hands into her pockets in embarrassment and dropped her voice to a hiss as she leaned toward Yusuf. "It's your money, after all," she reminded him. His expression remained impassive.

"You don't think I should ask you?" he asked quietly.

Alifa shook her head hastily. "It's bad enough to rely on someone's charity without being consistently reminded of it," she gritted out. "You haven't asked before, so why start asking now?"

Her churlishness seemed out of proportion, even to her, particularly when Yusuf remained so calm, but Alifa could not check her unruly tongue. Why was she behaving this way? She kept her face averted so that Yusuf couldn't guess what she was still uncertain of, but still she knew the instant that he stepped away.

"Fine," he said tightly. His fingers brushed against hers as he relieved her of the donkey's reins and Alifa savored the brief contact.

She had missed talking to him.

The thought was stunning, all the more so because it was unassailably true. She didn't want to argue with him. She wanted to talk to him. The man had asked her opinion, opening a perfectly reasonable topic of discussion and she had snapped at him. Alifa watched Yusuf lead the donkey down the street, both astonished at her revelation and disgusted with her response.

Unless she missed her guess, it would be a long time before Yusuf began a conversation with her again.

And it was her own fault.

"Where are we going?" Tabeta asked as she slipped her hand into Alifa's. Alifa shook her head and glanced down to her sister, not surprised to find Jaraw close behind.

"A kind of an inn," she said.

Tabeta nodded, but Jaraw scowled. "A caravanserai isn't an inn," he scoffed with all the unassailable certainty of a thirteen-year-old. Alifa looked to him in confusion, not at all liking the way his sneer transformed his handsome features. "It's an inn where whores work," he snarled before his gaze lifted knowingly to meet Alifa's.

She looked abruptly away, easily following the path her brother's thoughts had followed. Was this Yusuf's way of telling her how he expected her to pay their share? He clearly didn't expect her to take clients, but did he expect her to welcome him between her thighs again?

Was that why he had suddenly tried to talk to her again? Was Yusuf as methodical and self-motivated as Alifa had suspected he was?

An aching longing to experience his tenderness again flooded through Alifa and left her rooted to the spot in surprise. He was dangerous, she reminded herself forcefully, but to no avail.

She wanted him. And he had already said that he wanted her. Would she be able to turn him away if he approached her?

"Jaraw, don't be silly." Tabeta gave her brother a playful swat. "Yusuf wouldn't take us anywhere like that."

Jaraw looked unconvinced and Alifa could readily understand his suspicions. She heartily wished in that moment that she was half as certain of Yusuf's motives as her trusting sister.

* * *

Yusuf would have dearly loved to wring the woman's neck.

Had he ever met anyone so stubborn in his life? Or a woman more determined to remind him of something he would prefer to forget?

Yusuf *knew* that Alifa had been a whore. Clearly. She had taken four of his dinars for her favors, so he was unlikely to forget why. In fact, remembering why was tormenting him.

Not to mention trying to remember the event itself.

He wanted her. He wanted her more than he had ever wanted anyone before. Yet she persisted in exasperating him beyond human endurance. Why did she have to argue every little matter? Why did she have to take every opportunity to remind him of her former occupation?

By the heavens above, Yusuf remembered that well enough.

And if Alifa's torment wasn't enough, his dark side was getting stronger. Yusuf fought its rise, but recognized a losing battle when engaged in one. He could not trust himself to remain in the camp with them at night. He had shifted twice more, completely unwillingly, and was not amused by this development.

It was Alifa who did this to him. Or, more specifically, it was wanting Alifa that did this to him.

Yusuf could not fathom why. Alifa was the antithesis of what he wanted and needed in a woman. If he had stayed behind in his father's village, if he had chosen the traditional way of his forebears, then maybe she would have had appeal. But his future lay elsewhere and his ambitions demanded that he find a suitable, urban wife. The daughter of a powerful imam or a scholar or a trusted confidant in a sultan's court. Marriage for Yusuf would be about social connections, not about slaking his desire for a Berber whore.

But, unfortunately for his peace of mind, that desire showed no signs of abating. Yusuf's palms itched with a vengeance as he tied the donkey impatiently in the caravan-serai's courtyard. Was his father's influence reaching him already? Was the old man tormenting him? Yusuf knew that the beast had grown in power as he drew closer to home and could easily lay the blame at his father's door.

The only question remaining was what he would do about it.

Or how much choice he would have in the matter. The unwilling shifts troubled him deeply. Yusuf glanced back to Alifa and her siblings and his heart clenched.

He had never shifted involuntarily before he had slept with her.

Was it possible that Alifa had cast a spell of her own? Was there any possibility that coupling with Alifa again would reverse the spell?

The possibility was tempting, if decidedly unlikely. How on earth would he present the idea to her? And would he survive her response? Yusuf suspected not. If nothing else, Alifa had a gift for making her thoughts most clear.

That, at least, he could count on in this world. Affection flooded through him and Yusuf chuckled under his breath before he realized what he was about.

Affection? Regarding Alifa? Surely he was in dire need of some food and sleep. He knotted the reins hastily and stepped quickly into the inn to make arrangements.

Affection. Yusuf snorted in the cool shadows. Just two weeks out of the city and already his wits were addled.

Chapter Ten

The common room at the caravanserai was crowded that evening. The babble of different tongues wound into Alifa's ears, even as the acrid smoke rising from the narghiles stung her eyes. Oil lanterns flickered, the shadows they cast shrouding countless merchants and their lackeys as they ate, smoked and told tales.

It reminded her a little too vividly of the life she had left.

Alifa was only too aware of the speculative gazes that raked over their little group. She stiffened, but kept her eyes downcast, certain that more than one eye lingered on her. Despite the fullness of the clothes she wore, Alifa felt more naked in this company than she had when she danced.

It seemed that everyone must know what she had done in Ceuta to earn her keep. Alifa panicked at the thought that someone here might recognize her, as irrational as that was.

What had happened to the bravado that had sustained her all these years? A simple change of clothing had completely stolen it away.

"I cannot eat here," she whispered tersely to Yusuf. He turned and Kasilo's questioning gaze met hers from his position on Yusuf's hip. Alifa swallowed carefully, uncertain how clear she wanted to be about her objections before this young audience. Tabeta grasped her hand, but Jaraw swaggered behind them at enough of a distance to leave it unclear whether he was with them or not.

"Why?" he asked, though Alifa guessed he knew the reason. She cursed him silently for demanding an explanation before the children. He would never have considered eating in mixed company if she hadn't just abandoned the profession that she had. Decent women ate in private.

The realization that Yusuf didn't think of her as a decent woman rankled and Alifa's chin shot up proudly.

"It would be unseemly," she said acidly.

"Surely it wouldn't be the first time?" he asked mildly. Alifa bit down on her frustration with an effort.

"Maybe not, but there will be no next time," she asserted in a tone that brooked no argument. Yusuf's gaze lingered on her for a moment, as if he were surprised by her attitude. He glanced to Tabeta, then nodded once and turned away.

"They will have a private room," he assured her. Alifa sagged with relief that something had been resolved without a battle between them.

That was a refreshing change.

Even if Yusuf apparently had made the choice for Tabeta's benefit. Alifa gritted her teeth as Yusuf snapped his fingers.

"Newly arrived, are you sir?" The keeper of the caravanserai bustled up at the summons and cast a professional eye over the group of them. "I trust your beasts were stabled in the courtyard? Looking for lodgings? Dinner? A lovely little family, sir, if I do say so myself. I am certain we can make you comfortable tonight." He pressed his fleshy palms together and smiled with practiced ease as he awaited a response.

"Dinner," Yusuf said flatly. "And lodgings for the night."

"Yes, I see. I do have one large room available tonight. More than adequate space for a family of such size as yours, sir, and far enough from the common room that the little ones will have no trouble sleeping.''

''And dinner can be served there?''

The keeper looked shocked before he shook his head. ''No, no, no, sir. That may be the way of your kind, but we cannot permit food upstairs, sir. No, no, completely impossible. The common room is for eating.'' Alifa's ire rose at the man's reference to the obvious fact that they were Berber. She thought something flickered across Yusuf's features at the comment, but he did not deign to respond. Certainly, though, she detected a cooling in his manner toward the plump proprietor.

''I would prefer, for the sake of the women, that we eat in private,'' Yusuf said. The keeper's gaze swept instantly to Alifa and Tabeta and his eyes widened slightly.

''The women. Yes, well, yes, of course.'' He cleared his throat and Alifa distinctly disliked the way his gaze clung to her. ''Certainly we have a room in the back where your family can be served in private.''

''That will be fine.'' Alifa wondered if she imagined the thread of displeasure in Yusuf's tone. But then the men negotiated the price and all was business again.

Alifa could not help but hear the sum of silver agreed upon, and her color rose as she wondered how Yusuf would expect to be repaid.

It seemed that the keeper's gaze lingered on Alifa before he turned to bustle away, though she wondered if her imagination was overwrought. Surely she saw desire where there was none. Surely she was simply too nervous in this setting.

Surely she was just worried about the silver.

Yet Yusuf bristled before the man left them. That alone made Alifa certain her original conclusions were correct and she felt a tingle of pride that he had seen fit to be affronted on her behalf.

Maybe his judgment of her wasn't quite as harsh as he would have liked her to believe. For some inexplicable reason, the idea pleased Alifa, though she knew that Yusuf's approval of her was of no relevance whatsoever.

"Oh, dear lady, you are as lovely as a flower," the proprietor gushed when Alifa shed her veil in the private room. She threw him a glance of such hostility that Yusuf restrained his impulse to intervene.

Alifa would surely cut the man to ribbons for his inappropriate flattery.

"Thank you," she said tiredly.

Yusuf frowned at the uncharacteristically pallid response and glanced at her. Alifa sank onto a cushion beside the low table in the center of the room, looking as though she were too exhausted to be bothered to argue with the man.

Impossible. Alifa always had enough fire for a fight.

Except tonight. Did she truly not mind that the man was behaving inappropriately? Yusuf had deliberately restrained himself from correcting the keeper's persistent use of the word *family* in reference to this little troop, but now Alifa would allow the man's insult to pass without comment. It was all the encouragement he needed and considerably more than Yusuf thought appropriate under the circumstances.

Well. What had he expected? Yusuf had thought Alifa had abandoned her old ways. That had clearly been an assumption. It would certainly appear that he had been mistaken. He put down Kasilo and discarded his cloak with a frown, feeling more disgruntled than the situation certainly merited.

"And you are so young!" the proprietor exclaimed. Yusuf rolled his eyes, then guiltily glanced to the children in the hope that they hadn't noticed his gesture. "Surely these cannot be your own children?"

Alifa slanted the keeper a wry glance, then looked to Yusuf. She arched one brow in an eloquent expression of disbelief, but he refused to be relieved that their assessments of the effusive keeper were as one.

It was of no importance whatsoever.

Even if the weight of Alifa's regard upon him made the room suddenly warmer. Yusuf stubbornly maintained an impassive expression, knowing all the while that she was expecting him to respond. A frown finally puckered her brow and she glanced back to the proprietor, her lips thinning.

If Yusuf hadn't wanted to encourage her, then why did her displeasure make him cringe inwardly? He met the hostility in Jaraw's attentive gaze and straightened.

The sooner he was rid of them all, the better. Then he could be back on his way to Ceuta and never lay eyes on this little family again. Yusuf decided to seek out a caravan before he retired this very night.

"They are my siblings," Alifa responded with terse precision. There was no missing the gleam that lit the proprietor's eye at that revelation. Yusuf stifled an inappropriate urge to set the man straight.

"And the children are very tired and hungry," he interjected before he could stop himself. The proprietor jumped at the reminder and clapped his hands to summon the servants. Alifa smiled at Yusuf and his heart took a funny little leap.

"I do apologize," the other man gushed to Alifa. As she turned toward him, her smile faded in a manner that pleased Yusuf greatly.

"If we could eat shortly..." she began pointedly and the man scurried off.

The private room filled with an awkward silence in the keeper's wake. Everyone avoided each other's eyes. Yusuf wondered if he was the only one to notice that the silence that had hung between them on the road seemed even more pronounced in the cozy confines of this room.

He knew that he could not be the only one relieved when servants appeared to set the table for the meal. Steaming bowls of water with wedges of fresh lemon floating in them were brought, along with luxuriantly thick cloths so that they could wipe the mire of the road from their skin before the meal. The citrus scent filled the room and Yusuf felt invigorated, despite his exhaustion.

Kasilo splashed in the water with more vigor than the others. Yusuf spared the boy a glance, only to choke back a laugh. Kasilo had bitten into one of the lemon wedges and the yellow flesh hid his teeth from view. He grinned with pride when he met Yusuf's eyes, the span of yellow so unexpectedly displayed instead of his teeth that Yusuf struggled not to laugh.

"Kasilo!" Tabeta giggled outright when she spotted his trick. "Let me try!"

"No! It's mine!" Kasilo bit harder into the fruit as his sister reached for it and squinted in surprise as he evidently received a mouthful of lemon juice for his trouble. At that, Yusuf could no longer restrain his chuckle. Alifa spun to find the source of amusement and he could not help but watch her reaction.

She laughed outright and his heart clenched.

"Kasilo, you clown! You don't even like lemons!" she charged. Her eyes danced, and Yusuf caught his breath at the unexpected glimpse of the young, carefree woman who so captivated him.

"I forgot how sour they are," Kasilo complained behind the wedge of fruit. Tabeta scooped another lemon out of the bowl victoriously and mimicked her brother. She grimaced at the tartness of the fruit, then grinned proudly.

"You try," she prompted Yusuf and offered him a wedge. Yusuf shook his head, but before he could respond, Alifa interrupted.

"Dignified scholars don't play with lemons," she informed her sister stiffly. Was it Yusuf's imagination that she took an affected tone? Was Alifa mocking him? Tabeta's smile faded and Yusuf felt churlish for declining to play their games.

"Of course we do," he retorted. He plucked the wedge from Tabeta's hand and popped it into his mouth before his dignity could demand that he change his mind. Alifa regarded him in shock and he grinned widely to display the piece of fruit, then wiggled his eyebrows.

Her lips twisted, as though she were reluctant to laugh at the spectacle he had made of himself, but she lost the battle in short order. When Alifa's laughter pealed forth, Tabeta and Kasilo immediately joined in.

"Your turn!" Yusuf scooped another wedge from the bowl and offered it to Alifa.

"I won't!" she declared, that mischievous glint in her eye taunting Yusuf to change her mind.

He squeezed the lemon so that the juice squirted at her. Alifa squealed when it struck her cheek. Kasilo hooted. Tabeta gasped in surprise. Then they all laughed together.

"You beast!" Alifa laughed and swatted Yusuf across the shoulder.

"We'll make you do it!" Kasilo cried. Tabeta grabbed Alifa's hand playfully and Yusuf snatched at her other one without thinking. Alifa laughed as she tried to twist away and her hood fell back from her hair.

Suddenly she seemed to realize how close she stood beside him and her gaze darted uncertainly to his. Yusuf was abruptly aware of the delicacy of the wrist within his grip and that desire rose hot within him again.

He winked at her before he could stop himself.

Alifa seemed to stop breathing and her eyes widened. What had he been thinking? Alifa flushed scarlet and suddenly turned away.

"I think that's enough for now," she said quietly.

Yusuf was shocked by his own actions. He had been cavorting like a fool! He noted Kasilo's and Tabeta's disappointment that the game was ended so soon and looked up in time to see Jaraw scowling from the far side of the room.

Yusuf plucked the wedge of lemon from his mouth with what he hoped was a measure of his usual dignity and laid it aside. He flicked a glance to the demure woman who had once again shattered his facade, apparently without even trying to do so.

He had better find a southward passage for them tonight.

The smell of roasted lamb was a welcome distraction.

Yusuf, however, might have been more relieved if the arrival of the meat hadn't been accompanied by the return of the effusive keeper.

"Dear lady, I hope our humble fare is adequate to please," the proprietor enthused. "We are quite unused to having such lovely guests."

Alifa summoned a thin smile in response that was lackluster enough to please Yusuf.

Although, if she had refrained from smiling at all, that might have been preferable.

"I'm sure the meal will be lovely," she said politely.

The proprietor bobbed a bow. "But I would like to personally ensure your pleasure."

Alifa blinked. Yusuf stiffened at the inappropriateness of the comment and the keeper hastily recovered himself.

"With the meal, of course," he added in a breathless rush of words.

"Of course," Alifa said firmly. The keeper's color rose.

"Yes. Well. I am quite proud of our fare here. You see, we use only the finest ingredients...." The proprietor hovered by Alifa's side, pointing out each vegetable, and presumably every herb, in the stew. He fidgeted, shifting his weight from one foot to the other, until Alifa frowned.

"Perhaps you would care to join us?" she asked politely. Yusuf's head shot up in outrage that she would welcome such a creature to share a meal. Alifa's expression was coolly aloof, which relieved him slightly, but the proprietor was oblivious of any nuances.

Any other fool would have understood that the woman was simply being polite.

The proprietor, however, accepted her invitation with delight and settled himself directly at Alifa's side.

Yusuf muttered something uncomplimentary under his breath. He dropped down to sit beside Kasilo, who granted him a sunny smile. Tabeta plunked down on his other side and tore the bread for everyone with maternal ease. Jaraw sullenly condescended to join them and for once Yusuf thought he and the boy had something in common, if only this sour mood.

"*Bismallah,*" Yusuf said tightly. Tabeta flushed at the reminder that she had forgotten to wait for grace before starting. The keeper shot him a glance that he made sure to meet. Yusuf held the man's gaze for a long moment, willing him to understand that Alifa was not his to charm.

The keeper tilted his chin and broke Yusuf's regard with a resolute blink. He turned back to Alifa.

"Here is a lovely tender piece of meat. You must try this," he urged, offering Alifa a morsel on his fingertips.

Alifa, curse her, took the meat.

By the time the couscous came, Yusuf was ready to throttle the proprietor. If he had flattered Alifa once, he had done so a hundred times. To her credit, Alifa looked too tired to care what anyone thought, but Yusuf was insulted by his presumptuousness.

How dare the man regard a decent woman this way? The proprietor had no way of knowing Alifa's status. To assume that she was eligible was wrong, to say the least.

And it helped little that Yusuf was fully aware that Alifa was eligible. She was free to agree to any of the proprietor's advances. Yusuf was certain that she wouldn't, but when the man continued and she took less trouble to deter him, he was no longer as sure of that. The possibility rankled and the prickling of his palms made it difficult to concentrate on consuming his meal. By the time the sweets were placed on the table, Yusuf was bristling.

"Perhaps the lady would like to see our gardens before retiring?" the proprietor invited, his eyes gleaming with what could only be lust.

Yusuf straightened, certain he needed no imagination to guess what would transpire in those gardens.

"We are all quite tired," he said, deliberately misunderstanding the invitation as including all of them. The other man smiled and Yusuf did not like his expression at all.

"I had assumed that you would join the men for a smoke and that naturally the children are ready to retire." His voice hardened slightly as he made his point. "My invitation was for the lady, as I said."

Yusuf met Alifa's eyes across the table for a long moment, but he could not decipher her expression. Then she turned to the proprietor with a polite smile.

"I am quite tired," she murmured. The man leaned closer and Yusuf's ire rose.

"The blooms are quite lovely this time of year," he said in a wheedling tone and donned what must have been his most fetching smile.

That was enough.

"My wife has already declined your offer," Yusuf said coldly. All eyes swiveled to him, but he stubbornly stared back at the proprietor.

"Your wife?"

"You heard me," Yusuf said silkily.

"Your wife? I had no idea." The keeper flushed and stammered his apologies as he shoved to his feet and backed to the door. "I—I am sorry. I had absolutely—absolutely no idea. I never would have dreamed of giving affront...."

When he ducked out the door, the room was enveloped by another awkward silence.

His *wife?*

Where had that assertion come from? Why had he said such a thing? What had he done? Yusuf could not even begin to understand what had prompted his impulsive words. He swallowed carefully and stood before he risked a glance at Alifa.

She seemed to have been waiting only for that.

"What on earth do you think you are doing? If you think that I will stand by and—" she began, her voice low and angry. Yusuf held up one hand for silence and flicked a telling glance to the curtain that separated their room from the common room.

"We will talk later," he said tightly and bent down to retrieve his cloak.

"We certainly will," Alifa growled, leaving no doubt in Yusuf's mind as to her opinion.

As for himself, he needed the next few minutes to assemble his jumbled thoughts. What had he been thinking?

And why was he consistently making impulsive offers in this woman's presence?

"I don't know who you think you are, but this time you have crossed the line," Alifa spat as soon as the door to their room had closed behind them. Truly, her anger could not be contained any longer. Alifa was fuming. The man was unbelievable! How dare Yusuf make such an assertion without her consent!

To her increased annoyance, Yusuf just flicked her a disinterested glance.

"Keep your voice down," he advised.

That was enough to send her temper soaring. She was not some poorly behaved child acting out of turn!

"Keep my voice down?" Alifa repeated angrily. "You expect me to be *meek* when you blatantly disregard my opinion?"

Yusuf removed his cloak and granted her an indulgent glance. Alifa's chin rose. His manner was that of someone dealing with a difficult youngster. "As I recall," he said smoothly, "you requested that I do precisely that."

It didn't help that he was right.

"You knew what I meant in the street," Alifa accused angrily, hearing her voice rise higher. "Don't play games with me! *That* was a lot different from deciding where to stay at night!"

Yusuf looked pointedly to the door and braced his hands on his hips. "I asked you to keep your voice down," he repeated calmly.

Curse him for being so composed! Just once she would like to see Yusuf flustered.

"I will *not* keep my voice down!" Alifa shouted. "I will *not* be manipulated like this! I don't care if the whole world hears that I'm not your—"

She got no further before Yusuf's hand clamped uncompromisingly over her mouth. His eyes glittered like broken glass as he lifted her to her toes and gave her a little warning shake.

"I do care." He gritted out the words deliberately. Alifa's eyes widened. There was no doubt in her mind that he was serious. Too late, she feared that she had pushed him too far. What would he do? Her heart began to pound. She did not even dare to imagine.

"And if you had a bit of sense, you would care, as well." That was all he said, the words delivered in a smooth monotone that made her despise his control all the more.

How she hated that she had absolutely no effect on this man!

"And if *you* had a bit of sense, you would not be touching my sister," Jaraw interjected hotly, close by Alifa's side. "I warned you already not to touch her!" Both Alifa and Yusuf's heads jerked up in surprise. Before she could stop him, Jaraw had planted his fist in Yusuf's belly.

"Jaraw!" Alifa cried in astonishment. Yusuf's eyes widened with mingled shock and pain.

"Brat!" he muttered. Yusuf released Alifa abruptly and spun around. Another of Jaraw's misdirected punches found its mark, though the impact just made the older man growl in frustration. There was a brief tussle before Yusuf managed to pin the boy's arms to his sides from behind. Jaraw twisted violently and Yusuf's lips thinned. Alifa saw his grip tighten around the writhing boy and was suddenly afraid.

Yusuf was too much bigger than Jaraw! He would hurt the boy before he knew what he was doing!

"Don't you dare hurt him!" Alifa warned hotly.

"I am not hurting him," Yusuf snapped impatiently. Jaraw writhed and half twisted out of Yusuf's grip. Yusuf swore and grasped the nape of the boy's neck.

Jaraw cried out when his hair was pulled and all of Alifa's protective instincts rose to the fore. She launched herself at Yusuf and beat at his hands. Jaraw struggled and the pair twisted out of her way, leaving her pounding on Yusuf's broad shoulders with all her might.

"You let him go! He's hurt!"

"He's not hurt if he can throw a punch that hard," Yusuf retorted irritably. Jaraw almost worked his way free and Yusuf cursed as his turban was dislodged. Alifa clutched at Yusuf's neck in a futile attempt to restrain him and when he bent over Jaraw, her feet lifted off the floor. Alifa locked her arm around his neck and held on as she pummeled him.

How dare he raise a hand against her brother!

"You bastard!" Jaraw snarled. "I told you to keep your filthy hands off my sister!"

"No! You'll hurt Yusuf!" Tabeta screeched unexpectedly and launched herself into the fray. She flailed at her brother with her tiny fists. Yusuf swore. Alifa grabbed a fistful of his luxuriantly wavy hair and tugged hard.

"You are a cursed lot," Yusuf growled. He tossed a be-leaguered glance over his shoulder to Alifa.

Alifa couldn't help it. The sight of Yusuf, out of control, rumpled and uncertain what to do about it, did her in. She chuckled when she caught his eye and dug her knees tighter into his sides.

"Yallah! Zid!" She whispered the encouragement Berbers used for their mules mischievously before she considered the wisdom of the words. A light flashed in Yusuf's eyes and she thought for an instant that he might laugh along with her.

But he was spared the chance.

"Yeow!" he shouted inexplicably instead.

Alifa's eyes widened when she spotted Jaraw's teeth clamped hard on Yusuf's hand. The assaulted man tussled with the determined Jaraw, trying desperately to free his hand. Tabeta was as much a menace to Yusuf as Jaraw, her fists hitting him as often as her brother.

Yusuf gave a roar of frustration and struggled to cast them all off. Alifa's surprise loosened her grip on him and when he moved she was unceremoniously dumped to the floor. All the breath abandoned her lungs when she landed solidly on her rump.

His eyes blazing, Yusuf tossed Jaraw aside with a Herculean effort.

Cease-fire established, Tabeta took a cautious step back. Everyone breathed heavily and eyed each other warily. The clink of the pipes in the common room below and the low rumble of men's conversations rose to their ears. Alifa regarded the rumpled man glaring at all of them and stifled a highly inappropriate urge to chuckle.

"You're all insane," Yusuf finally muttered with evident frustration.

That did it. Alifa tipped back her head and laughed aloud.

"And you were fool enough to marry us," she quipped unrepentantly.

Tabeta's lips twitched and as soon as she met Alifa's eyes, she lost control. She giggled. Kasilo had apparently only been waiting for another to join in, for he laughed immediately after Tabeta.

Jaraw, for his part, glared at Yusuf and stalked to the window. He braced his hands on the sill and stared out into the deep blue of the night. Alifa could not tell whether he was fighting a smile or not.

But evidently her joke was not appreciated by the man in the middle of the room. Yusuf's eyes blazed as he scanned the group of them incredulously. Then he spun on his heel. He snatched up his cloak and stomped out of the room, his footsteps resounding on the wooden stairs that led to the common room.

Even that was not enough to sober the three of them. Every time Alifa's laughter slowed, she recalled Yusuf's outraged expression, his hair standing awry and she laughed with renewed vigor.

"I don't think he'll be back tonight," she mused, when their laughter had finally slowed.

"And a good riddance that is," Jaraw concluded sharply.

Tabeta's dwindling giggles stopped instantly at her brother's declaration and she cast him a mutinous glance. Kasilo fell silent and his eyes grew wide. The children's responses served to dispel the vestiges of Alifa's own humor in record time.

The children should never have witnessed them fighting, she scolded herself. She should have held her tongue until she and Yusuf were alone, but honestly, no one could make her as angry as Yusuf could. That he managed the feat seemingly without even trying to do so was no excuse.

It did her no favors to realize that his impromptu declaration had not been without its appeal.

Why had he said such a thing? And what, if anything, had he meant by it? Suddenly Alifa wished that Yusuf would come back this night, so that she could ask him for the truth.

Not that she expected he would tell her.

In fact, when Alifa finally lay wide-awake and let the children's breathing fill her ears as they slept, she wondered if Yusuf would return at all this time.

Had they frightened the man away for good with their foolishness?

Alifa never would have expected him to join in Kasilo's game and she smiled in the darkness at the incongruous image of Yusuf with a slice of lemon hiding his teeth. Alifa almost giggled. He had been enjoying himself and in that instant, she had almost liked him.

Liked Yusuf?

Alifa frowned. Yes, incredibly enough. Yusuf could be quite engaging when he forgot to be formal and self-righteous, when he neglected to judge her on every little issue. She wondered whether the uptight man she had first met in Ceuta or the playful man who didn't even notice when he lost his turban was the real Yusuf.

Alifa recalled their night together and bit her lip as her cheeks were suffused with color. Certainly he had been playful that night and the memory of it made her tingle from head to toe.

In fact, that man was someone Alifa could easily grow used to being around.

That was a dangerous thought. She had no interest in becoming involved with Yusuf.

Or had she? The idea was not without its advantages. Certainly Alifa was physically attracted to Yusuf, certainly she respected his intellect and enjoyed his company, particularly when he indulged his whimsical side.

The fact remained that she would have to marry some-body in order to stay in the mountains. The Berber way of life required both a man and a woman to maintain a house-hold. Alifa took a deep breath and frowned at the floor.

She could certainly go to the bridal fair in the fall and try to negotiate for a spouse. There would be the complication of her virginity, however. Alifa was certainly no virgin, yet she could not rightfully claim that she was divorced. She pursed her lips and supposed that she could lie, although there was another answer that was much more tempting.

What about marrying Yusuf?

Her heart took an unsteady lurch just from her having voiced the idea in her mind, but Alifa forced herself to think rationally. Yusuf would make a good husband, except for the fact that he seemed determined to return to Ceuta. In Ceuta, he was unavailable to her. A scholar would never take a whore to wife.

But what if she could convince Yusuf to remain in the mountains? Hadn't he increasingly lost his formal manner the farther they were from Ceuta? Maybe the man she had seen today was the real Yusuf.

Of course, it was probably the real Yusuf who had lost his temper with her, but Alifa did not find that troubling. She would rather an issue be out in the open, even in argument, than watch someone brood over it and be helpless to make a change.

He did seem particularly set on returning to Ceuta, though. And Jaraw appeared to have an unexpectedly strong aversion to Yusuf, although Alifa supposed that was a result of Yusuf's challenging the boy's will. They would come to terms, she was sure of it.

Could she and Yusuf come to terms? Alifa rather ex-pected that they could.

Especially if she made a point of ensuring that Yusuf saw the full merit of her charms. Hadn't he claimed her as his "wife" already? Alifa smiled, knowing that she would ensure that he did not regret that impulsive claim.

The common room was not the place where Yusuf wanted to be.

But without knowing the city, he wasn't about to wander the streets alone at night. He took a table disgruntledly and ordered a shot of *eau-de-vie*.

Why not, after all? Yusuf shoved one hand through his hair, realizing belatedly that his turban was gone.

Too bad. He was not going back to get it. And he was going to have a drink.

The liquor burned a path straight to his toes. Yusuf took a deep breath and savored the momentary tingle.

She ripped him in half when she smiled like that.

Desire rose hot within him and Yusuf signaled the proprietor that he would have another shot. Thankfully, the man seemed disposed to keep his distance now.

The last time Alifa teased him, he had been drinking. And he had kissed her. And Yusuf remembered only too well where that had led.

If not specifically what it had been like when he got there.

The recollection made his body respond in a way distinctly inappropriate to such a public place.

He needed to free himself of the spell she had woven around him. He needed to shake off the beast that she had recalled from his past. He needed to lay these old ghosts to rest and return as quickly as possible to his stable life in Ceuta.

He needed to couple with Alifa again.

The very possibility made Yusuf fidget uncomfortably as his body responded with enthusiasm. His next thought was inescapable, for all its predictability.

Alifa was upstairs. In a room he had paid for. With her belly full of a meal he had paid for. Under his protection, as his "wife." Yusuf would be fully within his rights to go up-stairs.

But he wouldn't. She had left that life behind, by her own admission. Yusuf sighed and downed the second shot.

If only she didn't look so young when she smiled. If only her eyes didn't dance so mischievously that he forgot everything else.

Yusuf's palms twitched, and he grimaced.

If only she didn't remind him of everything he had chosen not to be.

He couldn't force her. He couldn't pay her. But maybe he could convince her to come to him of her own accord. Yusuf's heart skipped a beat.

Didn't it seem that sometimes she desired him? Hadn't she desired him that first night? Could he prompt the same response from her again?

He had to try. For the sake of his own sanity.

Yusuf pushed to his feet and forced himself to examine the crowd of assembled men. They needed to join a caravan destined for Sijilmassa. There had to be at least one here tonight, and now was as good a time as any to make an agreement.

The sooner they headed south, the sooner he could return to Ceuta. Yusuf set his lips determinedly as a wave of desire washed over him.

And, of course, the sooner he could sample Alifa's charms again, the sooner he might be free of this curse.

Chapter Eleven

There was no doubt that Yusuf was astounded to find them all dressed when he stepped back into the room the next morning. He smelled of spirits and smoke, but Alifa did not ask any questions.

"Good morning," she greeted him brightly instead.

Last night's decision made her glance over Yusuf with a new eye, greedy as she was for any minute revelation. He looked as though he hadn't slept well, although clearly he had slept in his clothes. Alifa decided to take that as a good sign, although she could only hope for the sake of her plan that he had been troubled about her. His head was bare, his wavy hair so tousled that Alifa longed to run her fingers through its thickness.

In fact, the sight of Yusuf even moderately rumpled was enough to convince Alifa that her plan was the perfect one. Something about him in this less fastidious state stirred her senses in a way that no other man ever had. Granted, a less fastidious Yusuf was still a much more meticulous man than most.

Yusuf's gaze drifted down the row of bright faces as though he could not quite believe what he saw. His surprise was reasonable for the hour was very early. Sunlight had barely tinged the horizon, but Alifa had wanted to be sure they were ready. The children were washed and dressed, the bags repacked, the four of them, including the ever-reluctant Jaraw, waiting patiently like a perfectly dutiful Berber family.

Alifa had to concede that Yusuf recovered well.

"The caravan will leave shortly," he said, his surprise carefully hidden a mere instant after he stepped over the threshold. He bent and hefted Kasilo to one shoulder, who waved a length of cloth before him.

"You forgot your turban," Kasilo reminded him. Yusuf almost smiled.

"I didn't need it," he corrected mildly.

Alifa's eyes widened but she did not deign to comment. A Muslim always needed his turban. She granted Yusuf a considering glance and tried to recall when she had last seen him at his prayers.

The morning before they had left Ceuta.

Not that he couldn't have prayed while he was apart from them, she reminded herself hastily, although still she wondered.

Was it possible that the cloak of conversion was slipping from Yusuf's shoulders?

Alifa certainly wasn't going to be the one to ask.

"We're going on a caravan?" Tabeta asked as she picked up several smaller packs. Yusuf nodded and Alifa noted that all of the children, including Jaraw, were listening avidly.

"Yes, it will be easier to cover the distance quickly if we ride with the merchants."

"Merchants?" Jaraw demanded. "What kind of merchants?"

Yusuf slanted him a cold look that eloquently echoed Alifa's own suspicions of her brother's curiosity. "Merchants whose business has nothing to do with you. Don't even imagine that anyone will intervene on your behalf again."

"I was only asking," Jaraw protested hotly, but Yusuf's expression remained skeptical.

"They carry salt to trade in Sijilmassa," he supplied tightly.

Jaraw grimaced. "Salt?"

"Yes, salt," Yusuf retorted. "It has tremendous value to people who do not live near the sea."

"Salt." Jaraw shook his head uncomprehendingly and made to leave the room. Yusuf frowned and snapped his fingers impatiently. When Jaraw turned, the older man pointed to several of the larger bundles. Alifa held her breath when Jaraw's expression turned mutinous, but whatever his thinking, he silently followed Yusuf's bidding and carried the packs downstairs.

"What do we get to ride?" Tabeta demanded. Yusuf spared Jaraw's retreating figure one last glance before he smiled at the young girl.

"Camels."

"Camels?" Tabeta echoed. "Aren't they awfully big? And how do you ride on the hump?"

"Camels?" Kasilo asked in evident excitement at the same moment. "What about our donkey?"

Yusuf, to his credit, was not disconcerted by their questions. "They make saddles especially for camels, and even through they're big, they're easy to ride. And they move faster through the drier lands to the south. Our donkey will just have to keep up because we'll need him when we leave the caravan. Would you rather ride him?"

"I want to see the camels first," Kasilo said firmly.

"Are they nice camels?" Tabeta asked. Yusuf smothered a smile and shot a glance at Alifa. Their gazes held for a tantalizing moment, the way his firm lips twisted before he looked back to the children telling Alifa to brace herself for his next words.

"Actually, they remind me of your sister," Yusuf said lightly. He picked up the last of the packs and ushered the children out of the room, the quick pace he set making Alifa wonder if he was deliberately leaving distance between them.

"What do you mean?" Tabeta asked.

"Well, they have the most beautiful big dark eyes, with long lashes," Yusuf began, his conversational tone fueling Alifa's suspicions. "And they spit quite viciously if you try to make them do anything other than what they already want to do."

With that, Yusuf darted down the last stairs in evident fear of retaliation. Kasilo whooped and Tabeta laughed. Tabeta ran after Yusuf, leaving Alifa trotting in their wake.

"You!" she shouted in mock outrage, mostly because she was certain it was expected of her. The others laughed as they gained the courtyard and Alifa permitted herself a smile as she fastened her veil.

How could she be affronted when Yusuf had at least implied that she had beautiful eyes? That the man had noticed anything about her worthy of merit could only be a positive sign. Anticipation trickled through Alifa at the hope that her plan would be successful.

Yusuf could not believe his luck when the old caravan driver insisted on lending his tent the very first night on the road.

"Pretty women cannot go neglected," the driver wheezed and winked at Yusuf. "Even with her veil, I can see your wife is one of those pretty Berber treasures that aren't usually allowed out of the hills."

"She is lovely," Yusuf acknowledged, feeling a twinge of guilt at continuing his lie.

But traveling as a family had been the best way of ensuring passage for them all with a minimum of questions. And a minimum of harassment for Alifa. Not to mention that it left distinct possibilities for pursuing his own objectives.

Although Yusuf hadn't expected his tentative plan to bear fruit so quickly.

"Yes, so take the tent tonight."

"I couldn't possibly," Yusuf objected politely, but the driver waved away his concerns.

"It's a beautiful night to sleep under the stars. Tomorrow I may feel otherwise." He grinned. "Take the chance while you can. Leave the children with us. They'll be fine." He elbowed Yusuf and dropped his voice conspiratorially.

"She hasn't looked away from you all day," he confided. Yusuf's ears burned and he just barely kept himself from turning to look at Alifa. "Just between you and me, women are easier to travel with when they don't feel neglected."

At that, Yusuf did look. He had to. Alifa was a good twenty paces away, so he knew she couldn't hear their conversation. She dropped her gaze so quickly that he almost doubted she had been watching.

Was it possible that the driver was right? Was there a chance that she might not only agree to, but welcome, his advance?

If so, he could not afford to let this opportunity slip away. Knowing Alifa, she would change her mind by the next morning, if only to spite him.

This might be his only chance.

"I thank you for your generosity," Yusuf said politely even as his pulse quickened. The little old man beamed and nodded. "I'll just tell Alifa."

"You do that, boy." The driver winked again, his manner making Yusuf a shade uncomfortable. He wasn't entirely sure he wanted everyone to know what he and Alifa did, but he supposed there was no other way.

The conclusion did not stop the back of his neck from heating.

"And have yourself a good night tonight," the old driver advised.

"Yes. Yes, I'm sure we will."

The driver scurried away and Yusuf watched Alifa for a few moments without moving. Could the man have been right about Alifa watching him? She certainly was doing a superb job of ignoring him now. Yusuf's confidence ebbed away as he stood and he shoved his hands into his pockets with a frown.

But why wait? He might as well weather the storm as soon as possible. For there was no doubt that a storm would erupt at his suggestion or that it would be a violent one. Undoubtedly he would be reminded haughtily that Alifa had left *that* life behind her.

But there was nothing for it. He had to at least try to dismiss the curse of the shifting from his life.

And it seemed that Alifa was the only one who could help. Best put the task behind him. Yusuf took a deep breath and strode to her side.

"The driver wants to lend us his tent tonight," he informed Alifa more abruptly than he had intended.

That was it, Yusuf thought, certain she would make him rue his words. Alifa looked up, apparently unsurprised to find him so close. That prompted Yusuf to wonder if she was truly as unaware of him as she appeared, although that intriguing question would have to wait until later.

First things first.

"How nice of him," she said mildly, to Yusuf's astonishment. "Is it really large enough for all of us?"

Ah. She had misunderstood. That explained her uncharacteristic response. Yusuf cleared his throat, certain that the clarification would unleash her anger. Had she not made it patently clear to him that she was not a whore any longer?

"He's lending it to you and me alone," Yusuf said carefully, hoping she would catch his meaning. Alifa glanced up again and held his gaze for a long moment. Yusuf held his breath, but she merely blinked.

"I see," she said with an eerie calm.

Yusuf tried not to fidget. He would almost rather she yelled at him right away than make him wait. This conversation was pure torture.

"And where are the children to sleep?" she inquired.

"Outside." Again, Yusuf braced himself for her strident protest.

None came.

"Do you think it's safe for them?" she asked simply.

"Yes." Yusuf frowned. "These merchants are reputable and we will not be far." He waited, knowing that all possible questions had been answered and there was nothing to stop the storm from breaking.

Instead, Alifa slanted him a glance that he knew was coupled with a mysterious smile, though he could not see the latter because of her veil. Her expression was so seductive that he immediately felt his body clench in response, though he would not have revealed it to her for the world.

"Then I shall meet you there, husband," Alifa murmured with a curious emphasis on the last word.

Yusuf's stomach dropped from surprise. He stared at her until her eyes lit with slow mischief that left no doubt that his intentions had been understood. That Alifa had no protest made everything quicken within him. She agreed. She wanted him. Yusuf caught his breath before he spun on his heel and stalked away, convinced that he could not have stood there a moment longer and not touched her.

It was only when he had put some distance between them that he doubted his conclusion. Would Alifa truly permit him to touch her tonight? Or would she somehow turn the tables on him yet again?

The tent smelled like sun and wind and camels. Alifa lay back within her own blankets and closed her eyes. The tent also muted the sounds of the camp to a distant murmur and allowed her to ignore the camp's proximity. She savored the rough texture of the wool against her bare skin. Her hair was brushed out until it gleamed and spread across the pillows. Her skin was scrubbed clean and she was alone.

Mercifully, the children were already asleep, although Alifa could not imagine that either Tabeta or Kasilo would have any difficulties with her choosing Yusuf. They seemed to have taken to him immediately.

Jaraw was another matter and one best forgotten for the time being.

Only now when she was ready and waiting, did her trepidation return.

Yusuf was a shapeshifter.

Alifa recalled that salient fact too late to change her mind. She thought of the healed scratches on her back and refused to panic. She saw in her mind's eye the panther crouched over Jaraw, its tail lashing against the night and told herself not to be afraid.

In but a moment, she would be alone with Yusuf again. Nude and defenseless.

Alifa swallowed and forced herself to recall the fulfillment she had felt in Yusuf's bed. She had felt clean, chosen for herself alone—not her occupation.

An occupation that was hers no longer. This match Alifa had chosen to make. She had chosen only Yusuf of all the men whose beds she had shared.

She had desired Yusuf alone.

Maybe it was because of his power. Maybe it was in spite of it. Alifa did not care. She wanted him. She respected him. She trusted him.

Had he not seen to her family's needs all these weeks? Had he not done more for them than Alifa could ever have expected? What were a few scratches against that?

Her pulse leapt at the sound of boots approaching on the ground outside. Yusuf called a good-night to the others. Alifa felt her anticipation rise and wriggled her toes against the blanket.

The heavy wool rustled as Yusuf opened the flap and Alifa propped herself up on her elbows. She felt her hair tumble over her shoulders and knew it glistened in the half-light. When the blanket slid down, she did not stop it from baring her breasts. She knew her charms, and was determined to use them all this night to guarantee the outcome she desired.

She would have Yusuf as her man.

For his part, Yusuf simply stared.

The fading light from outside illuminated one side of his face and she could not read his expression. For a moment, Alifa was uncertain what to make of his response. Was he disinterested? Was he changing his mind? Was he remembering her sordid past?

But then Yusuf swallowed and stepped abruptly into the tent. He fastened the opening, then turned to face Alifa, his silhouette a shadow against the shadows. He shed his red cloak, his boots, the turban Kasilo had inexpertly re-wrapped for him this morning. His eyes gleamed and his gaze never wavered from hers as he disposed of his garments with a relentless efficiency.

Alifa found that she could not look away from that mesmerizing emerald regard. Time stopped. The sounds outside the tent faded to nothing and she was aware only of Yusuf. She could smell him. She wanted to kiss every increment of his flesh as it was revealed. She wanted to bite him and touch him and make him shout into the infinite blackness of the night.

Alifa cast the blanket aside when Yusuf was gloriously nude and rose to her knees. They still had not exchanged a word, but none were necessary. Truly, in this silence, a single word would have been too much. They both knew why they were here.

Yusuf crossed the tent and dropped to one knee before her. His gaze danced over her, as if he had never seen her before and was pleasantly surprised by her form. He lifted one hand as though he would caress her breast, then hesitated, his hand wavering uncertainly before her.

Their eyes met again. Alifa smiled slowly at his uncertainty. Could he not see that she wanted this? When Yusuf still did not move, she took that strong yet hesitant hand within hers, leaned forward and planted a gentle kiss in the breadth of his palm.

Yusuf shivered.

Alifa kissed the inside of his wrist. Once she had started to touch him, it seemed that she could not stop. He sighed as she kissed the inside of his forearm. His other hand rose to tangle in the length of her hair and Alifa felt the strength of his fingers cradle the back of her neck. A tremor rolled through her, but she could not tear her lips away from his skin.

Alifa kissed the inside of his elbow. She let her tongue dart out to sample his flesh and closed her eyes against the heady taste of him. She ran her teeth up the length of his arm and savored the taste of salt. Never had she wanted a man the way she wanted Yusuf. Never had she risked losing control with a man the way she had done once already with Yusuf.

And that would be nothing compared to this night. Alifa dared to raise her hand and let it rest against the wiry hair of his chest. Yusuf did not retreat and she let her fingers tangle in the hair until her fingertips touched the smooth heat of his skin.

He was solid. He was reliable. He had taken care of all of them, despite the harsh words between them. Yusuf was precisely the kind of man Alifa knew she needed and wanted.

Yusuf groaned and folded his arms around her with a possessiveness that made Alifa feel cherished beyond her wildest dreams. The evidence of his arousal made her feel both powerful that she could affect him so and humble that such a man felt desire for her. Yusuf's thumb slipped under her chin and his fingers fanned tenderly over her cheek as he tipped her face to his.

He looked into her eyes for a long moment and Alifa caught the gleam of the tenderness she had felt before. There was no censure in Yusuf's gaze, simply admiration and her heart soared. His thumb slid across her lips in a gentle caress that had Alifa leaning unabashedly against him. Her nipples beaded when they encountered the bristle of his chest hair and she arched her back. Yusuf's nostrils flared and his hands dropped to bracket her waist. Alifa let her hands slide over his shoulders and up his neck until his face was framed in her hands.

Yusuf's gaze dropped to her lips and when he met her eyes again, his gaze was smouldering. Alifa felt suddenly that there was not enough air in the tent, but she did not care. She watched Yusuf's mouth as he pulled her closer, knowing that no one had ever captured her interest so completely.

There was nothing but Yusuf in Alifa's world. Her anticipation redoubled when his knee nudged its way between hers and she felt the strength of his thigh against her flesh. This was the man she wanted, for now and forever, without doubt.

When his lips closed over hers, Alifa knew she could deny him nothing.

She strained toward him and Yusuf scooped her up against his chest. His tongue dived between her teeth and Alifa echoed his gesture, wishing she could meld their very flesh together. He tasted as sultry as the darkness. She wanted him. He wanted her. And tonight they would celebrate their desire.

If there was a price to be paid for this loving, in the morning Alifa would willingly pay. But for tonight, there was only the two of them and the enveloping darkness.

* * *

When Yusuf awoke the next morning, the sky had lightened enough that the tent was suffused with that curious brightness that only comes before the sun has cleared the horizon. Alifa had rolled away from him and he admired the luscious curve of her bare rump as she dozed.

He reached for her just as Kasilo's dry cough rent the morning silence.

Alifa rolled over and sat up immediately, her hair spilling over her shoulders in gleaming disarray. She blinked sleepily and shook her head. Yusuf gripped her elbow, half fearing that she would run nude out to attend the boy.

And there was nothing she could do, after all.

"It's all right, Kasilo." Tabeta's crooning voice filtered through the tent. Kasilo's coughing slowed as his younger sister soothed him and Alifa released a shaky breath.

She glanced down at Yusuf's hand on her arm and Yusuf was suddenly very aware of the silky texture of the skin beneath his fingers. Then her gaze flicked to Yusuf's and the hostility in her eyes took him completely by surprise.

"You didn't shift last night," she said flatly. There was no mistaking the accusation in her tone, though Yusuf found it momentarily confusing.

Surely she should be relieved? Surely she should appreciate the effort it had taken him to avoid doing so?

"I refused to shift last night," Yusuf admitted. He would not tell her how hard it had been to maintain some vestige of control in her presence. The woman inflamed him beyond reason. Yusuf released her arm abruptly and sat up himself, painfully conscious of the space left between them after the night they had shared. Alifa tossed him a skeptical glance. "I didn't want to frighten you," he added, though that was not the whole truth.

He hadn't wanted to hurt her. As he had once before.

Alifa rolled her eyes. "That didn't trouble you before."

"No," Yusuf said tightly. He remembered only too well her frightened response to him and resented her ready assumption that he had not worried about her feelings earlier. "No, that's not true. I couldn't help it before."

Alifa's eyes narrowed. "What are you talking about? Don't you always choose to shift?"

"I *never* choose to shift," Yusuf snapped irritably. "I have never shifted voluntarily. Sometimes it just happens, regardless of what I want."

"I thought a shaman had to will himself to shift," she suggested tentatively.

"You thought wrong," Yusuf retorted and heard his own frustration in his tone. "It takes time and practice to hone the skill. Until then, the shifting just happens whenever it chooses."

Alifa fingered the blanket as though uncertain whether she should ask her next question. Regardless of whatever doubts she might have, she did. "What makes it happen?"

Yusuf slanted her a hostile glance. "When I lose control. When I drink. I'm not sure what else." The last was a lie, but he would not tell her what she did to him.

Alifa tilted her head and stared at him quizzically. He was astonished that she was not afraid and because of his mood, her curiosity annoyed him. "Didn't you have a difficult time hiding your abilities in Ceuta?" she asked as if she genuinely wanted to know.

"There was nothing to hide," Yusuf said tersely. "After I left the mountains, it stopped happening."

"But that night—"

"Was the first time in fourteen years," he confessed irritably and immediately wished he hadn't.

They stared wordlessly at each other and when the seductive smile wound its way across Alifa's features, Yusuf knew she had guessed his secret. He cringed inwardly, but refused to look away.

"Maybe something else makes you lose control, as well," she purred and Yusuf's heart skipped a beat.

Her fingers slid lightly up his arm and she leaned closer. Yusuf swallowed and made the mistake of glancing down, only to find the fullness of her breast brushing against his arm. The nipple beaded as he watched, the peak tightening to a dusky point and he did not know how he would keep from touching her.

"No, you're wrong," he said with no trace of his usual composure. Alifa smiled and rose to her knees. Her fingertips grazed a burning path across his shoulders and into his hair. Her breath fanned his cheek as she trailed a line of kisses along his jaw. He felt her breasts sway against him, just before her tongue rolled in his ear.

The beast roared within him, demanding release.

Its appearance so completely shocked Yusuf that he froze. Hadn't the night of loving Alifa dispelled the curse? How could it still haunt him? How could he have been wrong?

"I must have disappointed you last night," Alifa mused when he did not move away. Yusuf's eyes widened and he regretted his inaction for a brief moment before her fingers began to entice him. His tentative grip on the beast slipped another notch and he knew that if she continued, he would not be able to maintain control.

"Alifa, no," he protested, but her toes wriggled against him in a way that made it impossible to remember why he had ever considered objecting.

"Yusuf, yes," she whispered and her eyes twinkled with the awareness of her own power over him. "I want to see you shift."

"No!" Anything but that! Yusuf shoved her away, hating how ragged his breathing was. Alifa regarded him with luminous eyes that wrenched his very soul. "You don't know what you're asking," he protested hastily and shoved one hand through his hair.

"I've almost seen you shift before," she said. She reached out and traced a delightfully distracting pattern on his shoulder. Yusuf shoved to his feet and paced to the other side of the tent, the meager distance doing little to settle his jangled nerves.

"I could hurt you," he informed her tightly. Alifa shook her head with a confidence Yusuf was far from feeling.

"I don't think so."

"You don't know!" Yusuf snapped, disliking her ready confidence that something he so feared could not happen. "You don't have any idea what you're talking about! Didn't your parents tell you the stories about us?" He glared at her and his voice dropped. "Don't you remember what happens when the shaman shifts?"

"I was young when we left the village," Alifa said. She folded her arms across her chest, which only enhanced the appearance of her breasts, and regarded Yusuf skeptically. "Why don't you explain it to me? Why don't you tell me precisely why you won't help Kasilo?"

Kasilo. If only he *could* help the boy. Yusuf had become inordinately fond of the cheerful youngster. If only it could be done without . . . But it couldn't. Yusuf knew better.

"This is no game, Alifa," Yusuf retorted. He paced two steps and back in frustration, more than ready to tell Alifa the fullness of the tale. She wanted an explanation and she would get one. Whether she liked it or not. "Do you think that I can just shift and ask something of the spirits? That they'll grant whatever *I* ask, just because I've troubled myself to do so?"

"I don't know," she confessed with a frown.

"No, you don't, but soon you will." Yusuf squatted down to stare Alifa straight in the eye as his voice lowered. "As in any transaction, a price must be paid to earn their intervention. Their price is high, too high, which is why I've never asked them for anything. My father, however, has no such compunctions."

"What price?"

"Don't you know? Think about it, Alifa. All of the shamans in my family take a panther's form when we shift.

Panthers are hunters of the highest order. It's no coincidence." Yusuf leaned closer to make his point. "Panthers kill," he whispered. "The spirits want blood."

Alifa's eyes widened, but her response was far from the horror Yusuf wanted from her. He wanted her to recoil. He wanted her to run. He wanted her to leave and take this temptation to become his father away from him. Yusuf was losing his grip on the carefully cultivated urban man he had become. Every step into the mountains brought him closer to home. Closer to his roots. Closer to his father and closer to the trait they shared.

He wanted Alifa to bolt in terror and leave him be.

Conversely, he wanted her to stay.

"No," she protested softly.

Yusuf nodded. "Yes," he said, his voice becoming harsher as he strove to frighten her. "A life for a life. It's an old recipe and one that works." He leaned closer and bit out his next words. "Who would you have me hunt to save Kasilo, Alifa? Whose life is worth sacrificing? Would you make me a murderer and a healer both?"

Alifa blinked and glanced away, but her gaze was sharp when she met Yusuf's eyes again. "That's why you left," she accused flatly. "That's why you hid in Ceuta."

"I could not become what my father is."

"That's why you converted and changed your name," she charged breathlessly.

Yusuf could only nod. "It is wrong to kill."

Alifa leaned forward and Yusuf knew suddenly that she was not going to abandon this argument easily. Disappointment and admiration mingled within him, just to further confuse his feelings. "But after all those years, you suddenly began to shift again," she said intently. Had she guessed? Yusuf granted her a wary eye.

"Yes."

"That night we spent together was the first time?"

"Yes."

"But don't you see that it all makes perfect sense?" she demanded with outspread hands. Yusuf's pulse quickened in fear that she had guessed her effect upon him. "The spirits must *want* you to intervene for Kasilo. They must be summoning you. This healing is meant to be."

Relief that she had missed what he feared to have revealed made Yusuf respond more stridently than he might have otherwise.

How could she insist yet again that he help her brother? Hadn't he explained the situation adequately?

"Alifa!" Yusuf roared, flinging his hands skyward. "I told you that *I would not do it!*"

Alifa shoved to her feet, undeterred by his response. "Maybe they're telling you that your father's way isn't the only way. Maybe you can manage it differently, without the sacrifice."

Yusuf folded his arms across his chest and scowled at her. Had he ever met such a cursedly stubborn woman? "A life for a life, Alifa," he maintained tightly. "That's how it works."

"That's how it works for your father. That's how it used to work," she insisted doggedly. "Won't you at least try?" She gripped his arm and Yusuf glanced over her, hating how her appeal tugged at him. Truly it was a mercy that the woman did not know the fullness of her effect upon him.

"I have never shifted voluntarily," Yusuf reiterated in a disgruntled growl. Could the woman not see sense? "And I will not start now. This is not a part of my life."

Alifa's lip curled with disgust. "Don't be ridiculous. It is more than a part of your life—it's who you are. You cannot simply deny who you are."

That was enough. "It is *not* who I am!" Yusuf cried, not caring who heard him. "I am a *scholar*. That is who I am, despite the misfortune of being born in these cursed mountains."

Alifa shook her head. "You cannot run from who you are, Yusuf."

Yusuf gritted his teeth. If the woman irritated him any more, he would wring her pretty neck. "I am not running from who I am," he told her frostily. "I ran from who I wasn't so that I could become who I am. And as soon as possible, I'll return to Ceuta and continue with my life there."

"This is where you belong," Alifa said with a certainty pitched to feed Yusuf's fury.

"You don't know what you're talking about," he charged hotly. Alifa's brows rose, and she smiled a knowing smile that did nothing to reassure him.

"Then why have you forgotten both your turban and your prayers? Surely a man with the faith burning in his veins would not forget, regardless of where he was."

There was no defense. Alifa was right about that and Yusuf loathed her for it. He had completely forgotten the ritual prayers once the wind from the mountains filled his lungs.

And hadn't even noticed until her reminder. The thought was troubling in itself, though the one that followed on its heels was even more so.

Was Alifa right about more than his faith?

She couldn't be. He wouldn't permit it. Yusuf had left all of this behind for a reason. He had never been like his father. He had never fit in. He had never felt at ease here, had he?

Then why did Alifa, the most traditional Berber woman he had met since arriving in Ceuta, stir his senses like no other?

Could he truly be more of his father's son that he would like to believe? The very idea was terrifying.

"You don't know what you're talking about," Yusuf retorted with an assurance he was far from feeling. "We have been traveling and arguing and any reasonable person could be remiss under the circumstances.''

"I don't think so," Alifa said calmly. She cocked her head as she regarded him assessingly. "In fact, I'm not sure that you ever really converted to the faith in your heart. You've shed the faith as readily as you abandoned your treasured books. What could be more perfectly Imazighen?''

"What do you mean?''

"My mother taught me to adapt as much as was necessary to survive. It is the way and has been for centuries. Conquerors come and conquerors go, and when they go the Imazighen shed the veneer of their ways and revert to what we really are. They never change us inside." Alifa's eyes narrowed as her gaze swept over Yusuf. "Maybe you are more Imazighen than you would like to admit," she mused.

"No! You're wrong!" Yusuf hauled on his *chalwar*, knowing he could not remain here any longer and listen to her bewitching lies. "It's you who have twisted everything around. Nothing has changed. I'm a scholar and soon I will be home with my books and my faith and rid of all of you!" With that, Yusuf hauled on his shirt, grabbed his boots and stomped out into the dewy grass of the morning.

It was not reassuring at all to realize that he felt markedly less than his usually composed, respectable, academic self.

Let alone that he could not quell the itching in his palms.

Jaraw watched Yusuf jam on his boots and hatred filled his heart.

Despite Jaraw's warning, the man had touched Alifa again. Alifa had given up whoring, but she was a woman and therefore weak in her resolve.

It was not Alifa's fault that they had mated.

Quite simply, Yusuf had been low enough to take advantage of a woman's frailty. Jaraw didn't know what story he had spun for Alifa and didn't particularly care. Maybe Yusuf had told her that she owed him for paying their passage south. Maybe Yusuf had threatened to abandon them. Jaraw's lips thinned.

The means didn't matter. The end was despicable enough in itself. Yusuf had been warned, yet he had still persisted.

And now Jaraw would ensure that Yusuf could not repeat the offense.

Jaraw flexed his injured hand, still surprised at how readily he was getting used to being without that finger. He would practice throwing his knife even more diligently when he was alone. And he would watch. One day, Yusuf would relax his guard.

And Jaraw would be ready.

Chapter Twelve

They did not share the tent again.

Alifa did not care what Yusuf told the old driver. From that night on, she slept with the children, not so much as speaking to Yusuf.

She did not get much sleep. Kasilo was growing more ill at an alarming rate. He coughed for the better part of the night and could barely catch his breath. He seldom ate and when he did, little of the food stayed down. He was perspiring heavily and Alifa feared he would lose too much water. She forced liquids into him at every opportunity and worried so much that she could not sleep even when Kasilo did.

Her brother was dying. And there was nothing she could do about it. Alifa had never felt so helpless in her life, regardless of the obstacles that had been set before her.

This one she could not surmount alone.

And the only person who could help refused to even try.

But she would not ask Yusuf for his assistance again. The flame of her anger burned brightly, despite the distance she kept from him. Alifa could not understand how anyone with a heart could deny a child, especially a child as cheerful as Kasilo.

Hopefully they would reach Yusuf's father soon enough to make a difference. Hopefully it wouldn't be too late.

Hopefully Yusuf's unwillingness would not condemn Kasilo.

Yusuf's reservations were understandable. It was his refusal even to try that she could not countenance.

Perhaps Alifa had made a drastic mistake in her assessment of the kind of man he was.

Twelve days after his spectacular night and disastrous morning with Alifa, Yusuf waved farewell to the camel caravan as it meandered down the road to the south. The sun was just past its zenith, although they would do well to get far from the main road before evening was upon them. This last leg of the journey would be the most difficult. The way was narrow and less frequently used, the path steeper and there was no prospect of help en route.

Yusuf cleared his throat and turned to face his companions, although he still could not meet Alifa's gaze. He knew what she was thinking. He had seen condemnation in her eyes and knew she thought him heartless beyond compare.

She was wrong.

Just as Yusuf had been wrong about the result of coupling with her again. If anything, that sweetly memorable taste of Alifa's charms had served to torment him more. There was no hope of the raging beast abandoning him soon.

Every twitch of her skirts inflamed him. Every wan smile she spared Kasilo made him long to have her turn such a smile upon him. The way she tended the sick boy prompted imaginings of her with the child Yusuf could plant in her belly.

This time there were no haunting glimpses to torture him. Yusuf had full-fledged memories of their night together. He knew the exact location of all of her moles and precisely how her softness could curve around him and cradle him against her. He knew the taste of her silky hair and the sound of her throaty chuckle when she was tickled.

Perhaps it had been easier when he couldn't remember.

The merest glimpse of her flesh or flash of her eyes or whisper of her scent was enough to set the beast to raging. Yusuf's palms had never itched as they had these past days and it seemed the malady grew worse instead of better as time passed.

He needed to taste her again.

Yusuf could have dismissed that as raw desire if her silence wasn't annoying him the way it was. He wanted to talk to Alifa. He wanted to see her laugh. He wanted to discuss what they should do about Kasilo. He wanted to reassure her and hold her close and make everything right in her world.

But Yusuf couldn't. He would not shift. He refused to shift. It would be futile.

At least Alifa had not asked him to help Kasilo again. He sincerely hoped that she never did. It would be too cruel to have to deny her to her face once again.

It was better to leave the matter alone, even though it sat between them and refused to let them forget its presence.

"This is the road we must follow," Yusuf said simply when they had stood there long enough.

Alifa nodded and hefted a pack as she turned. It stung that she said nothing but Yusuf supposed he should not have expected anything else.

It was easier this way, he reminded himself fiercely, disliking that the assertion did not ring as true as he might have liked. Yusuf tore his mind away from thoughts of Alifa and forced himself to concentrate on their way.

The ambling path broke from the main road and lazily wound a trail up the side of the mountains. It disappeared high overhead, where Yusuf knew it crested the first rise and began the jagged route across the peaks to the sheltered plateau he had known as home.

Home. He could not completely stifle a flicker of anticipation. They were close now. No matter if they had to walk, it was no more than a few days.

Only a few days until he had to look his father in the eye and admit himself to be a failure. Dread replaced the anticipation in an instant.

The old man was going to laugh himself silly.

Yusuf scowled and shouldered a pair of packs. He checked that Kasilo was well seated on the donkey, then led the way resolutely from the road.

Only a few days until he could leave Alifa behind.

That should have been reassuring, but instead the thought stole all the air from his lungs. Yusuf caught his breath and told himself it was the strain of the altitude. Just another sign that it would be better when he could put his past behind himself for good.

Kasilo's relentless coughing brought them to a lurching halt long hours later. The sun lingered on the crest of the distant peaks like an orange ball that refused to drop and a chill had already started to rise from the earth.

Alifa dropped her pack and pounded on the child's back while Yusuf and the others watched helplessly. When Kasilo finally stopped and gulped for air, Alifa gathered him close to wipe the tears of exertion from his cheeks. She flicked a hostile glance at Yusuf.

"He's cold," she said flatly. Yusuf turned away, knowing well enough what she hadn't said.

"I'll make a fire," he said tonelessly, wishing he could do more. But Alifa was wrong about his capabilities. The sacrifice was the charm and Yusuf could not take that step, even for Kasilo.

And he would not tempt them all with the possibility that anything less would suffice. If nothing else, his father had taught him to respect the voices.

Yusuf wished in that moment that he had his father's conscience instead of his own.

Tabeta skipped away to gather tinder without being asked to do so, but Jaraw, typically, did not lift a hand. He dropped his pack and sat heavily on a rock, his brooding glance fixed on Yusuf as the older man cleared a space for the fire. For once, Yusuf didn't have the wherewithal to fight with the boy. Let him be sullen. Let him be whatever he chose to be. The matter was no longer Yusuf's concern,

Soon he would be heading back to Ceuta.

Alone.

To live alone. To translate books alone. To teach dry, irrelevant lessons to bland-faced students without a spark of wit in their souls. Yusuf set his lips and stubbornly scraped the ground clear. He loved that life, he reminded himself forcefully, refusing to admit that his enthusiasm was decidedly flat.

"Here." Tabeta shoved a bundle of dry twigs toward Yusuf, clearly quite proud of her accomplishment. She had really gotten much better at finding tinder.

"You've done well tonight." Yusuf praised her without thinking, her pride making him smile slightly. "Brush is hard to find this time of year."

"I can find some more, if you like. And there's some bigger wood right over there."

"More tinder would be very helpful," Yusuf agreed solemnly. "I'll get the heavy ones."

"All right. They're right over there." Tabeta pointed again and grinned outright when Yusuf nodded. Then she hastily disappeared, obviously intent on her mission.

"I would appreciate it if you didn't make such an effort to endear yourself to her," Alifa said under her breath as she spread a blanket on the ground beside Yusuf. He glanced to her, but she refused to meet his eyes. "It will only make it harder for her when you leave."

"I was not deliberately encouraging her," Yusuf responded tersely.

Alifa's gaze flicked to his and then away, as though she did not believe him. "Just leave her alone."

Yusuf had nothing to say to that and he distinctly disliked that he felt guilty about those few words with Tabeta. Jaraw's sullen glare weighed upon him and did nothing to improve his mood. Neither did the faint waft of Alifa's scent that haunted his nostrils. He struck the flint and kindled the fire in poor temper.

Alifa carried Kasilo to the outspread blanket and placed him before the fitful blaze when Yusuf had coaxed one of the heavier sticks into catching flame. She carefully tucked another blanket around the boy's shoulders in a gesture that Yusuf found troublingly protective.

All of his doubts returned with a vengeance to torment him. Alifa would make a good wife. Alifa was both tender and practical. Alifa could truly be the ridgepole of the family tent, as the old saying went.

And Yusuf had spent two nights in her embrace without making an honest woman of her. The realization made him writhe.

But how could he do anything else? He couldn't marry her and take her back to Ceuta, where everyone knew what she had been. His carefully cultivated reputation would suffer. It wouldn't be proper.

Marrying Alifa in the first place wouldn't be proper, Yusuf reminded himself in annoyance.

And staying here in the mountains was absolutely out of the question.

Of course it was. What would even make him think of that? His life was in town with his books, not here.

"I'm all right," Kasilo protested beside him, but Alifa shook her head.

"You're too cold," she argued and continued to fuss with the blanket.

"But I don't want to be all bundled up like Tudda in the *souk* in the winter," he complained. Yusuf could readily sympathize with the boy, although he dreaded Kasilo's next words when that bright gaze locked on him. "I want to look like a man, like Yusuf. Yusuf wouldn't sit wrapped in a blanket before the fire."

Alifa frowned, and Yusuf assumed that she was tallying another sign of his poor influence. "Yusuf isn't sick."

"Neither am I," Kasilo retorted. "Because Yusuf's father is going to make me better, so being sick now doesn't count. Isn't he going to make me better, Yusuf?"

Yusuf disliked that a ready assurance did not come immediately to his tongue. In all honesty, he had never seen his father heal anyone who was failing as rapidly as had Kasilo these past days.

The boy's spirit was optimistic, though, and Yusuf could not willfully shatter his faith. That might be the difference needed to effect the cure. His father had always said that the mind was the most powerful tonic.

"Of course," he managed to say with a measure of credibility. Alifa's lips thinned in annoyance. Clearly she was thinking that he could tend to Kasilo here and save them all an arduous few days, but Yusuf knew better.

He would not shift.

"See, Alifa? Yusuf knows," Kasilo informed his sister proudly.

She lifted one brow before she spoke. "You're still cold," she insisted.

"But—" Kasilo began, but got no further.

On impulse, Yusuf stood and swept his crimson cloak from his shoulders. "Let's trade," he offered, the light in Kasilo's eyes all the reward he needed.

"Really?" the boy asked in amazement.

"Really." Yusuf's hands brushed inadvertently against Alifa's as he relieved Kasilo of the blanket, but he could not look at her. He wrapped the boy in the red cloak with a flourish, scooping him high in the process to wrap the wool securely around his feet. Kasilo laughed with delight. Yusuf found himself smiling as he placed the boy before the fire again, though one glance at a heartily skeptical Alifa eliminated that smile. She stood with her arms folded across her chest, apparently oblivious of Kasilo's pleasure in the cloak.

"At least you'll do something for him," she murmured in a voice low enough that Kasilo couldn't hear her words.

Yusuf bit back a hostile retort and spun on his heel to keep from speaking harshly in front of the children. Wasn't it enough for Alifa that he saw them all fed and safe each night? Wasn't it enough that he had traveled all this way with them, just so that Kasilo could see his father?

Apparently not.

Of course, it was partly Yusuf's fault that Alifa had had to leave Ceuta. The recollection did not sit easily and Yusuf almost squirmed.

It had only been a matter of time, he told himself and did not believe a word of it.

"Yusuf, here's some more tinder," Tabeta offered breathlessly. Her cheeks were flushed from her rushing and there was a smudge of dirt across her nose that made her even more fetching than usual.

He was going back to Ceuta to be alone. The thought sent a pang through him.

"Yusuf, don't forget to come and sit with your blanket," Kasilo called. "Alifa will get angry if you get cold."

Yusuf swallowed and turned. How would he leave Kasilo and Tabeta behind? How could he bear to not hear their happy chatter or see how they grew up? He forced a smile for both children, despite his feelings.

"Thank you very much for your help," he said to Tabeta. He bent and wiped the smudge from her nose with a gentle fingertip, surprised to find affection flooding through him.

Tabeta smiled and flushed in a way that made him imagine how pretty she would be in a few years. Every eligible man in the mountains would be at her beck and call, and Alifa would have her hands full.

Although none of that was his concern. Yusuf frowned. He would be back in Ceuta. With his books.

Which suddenly didn't sound nearly as fascinating a possibility as he thought it should.

What if Alifa was already pregnant? Yusuf caught his breath at the tempting possibility. What if they had conceived a child together?

What if she bore him a child up here and he never even knew?

Because if Yusuf went back to Ceuta, he would never know. He was certain that Alifa would not chase him down just to share the news. Yusuf looked at her covertly to find that typically stubborn set to her chin. He stifled a smile.

No. Alifa would adapt as much as she had to in order to survive and ensure that the child survived. She would not chase after him to beg for assistance. Alifa took care of her own. Yusuf decided in that moment that he rather liked her determination. It was reassuring to know that she would not crumple in his absence.

Their child might need that.

Yusuf refused to acknowledge a persistent niggling of doubt. He was going back to Ceuta. It was precisely what he wanted to do.

He squatted down beside Kasilo and wrapped the woolen blanket over his own shoulders. Kasilo watched him avidly and Yusuf leaned closer to the boy as he wiggled his eyebrows. Kasilo giggled. "I wouldn't want Alifa to be mad at me," Yusuf whispered. Kasilo covered his mouth as he laughed.

The woman in question snorted softly, the sound of her breath too close for comfort. Every fiber of Yusuf's being leapt to life at the realization of how near she was and he darted a glance over his shoulder. He met Alifa's dark gaze and floundered, finding himself completely unable to look away.

"It's too late for that," she said in a virtual whisper that nevertheless made her feelings perfectly clear. Yusuf's ears burned and he turned hastily back to Kasilo.

"Leave it alone," he muttered irritably.

Alifa sniffed with indignation. "That would seem to be your solution of choice," she retorted quietly.

"Enough!" Yusuf snapped. He rose abruptly to his feet and cast the blanket aside, taking only the time to glare at Alifa before he stalked off.

"Where are you going?" she shouted after him. He refused to admit that the thread of panic in her tone almost made him turn back. Yusuf clenched his fists, but did not stop. Curse her for not even pretending to be surprised or taken aback by his response.

"To fetch wood!" he bellowed over his shoulder and a blissful silence greeted his words.

Yusuf's palms itched uncontrollably and he cursed the beast within him before he roundly cursed Alifa for awakening it yet again. His memory supplied a vision of Alifa arching her back beneath him as she gasped and the beast's demand grew more ferocious. Yusuf felt its power uncoil deep inside him and his skin prickled in the precursor to the change.

And why not? Who would see? Who would know? Yusuf was tired of fighting the demand. Although he had never consciously chosen to shift, tonight he refused to stop the beast's onslaught. There was a difference, Yusuf was certain of it, and he refused to concede that he had taken another step toward his darker side.

Yusuf snorted to himself as he recalled Alifa's comments. Let the change come, he thought with annoyance. The sky was clear and it was a good night for hunting.

Maybe that would release the tension that had been building within him.

Although Yusuf suspected there was only one act with one particularly vexing woman that would do that.

But he had to at least try an alternative.

The scream rent the silence of the night and brought Alifa's head up with a snap.

It was the cry of an animal in pain and close enough to stop Alifa's heart with shock. It could not be. Alifa scanned the camp, knowing full well what she would find. Yusuf was still gone.

But to her surprise, Jaraw had also vanished.

Alifa dropped the kettle and hastily stood. She had a dreadful sense of premonition. Where could Jaraw have gone? And why? She scanned the shadows on either side of the camp, the embers from the fire doing little to aid her. Kasilo and Tabeta huddled fearfully together and watched her.

Another scream came, this one shrill and clearly human. That way.

Alifa muttered a prayer and looked to a wide-eyed Tabeta as she fumbled with her knife. Her sister looked as frightened as she was, although she caught the knife and scabbard when Alifa tossed them to her.

"Watch Kasilo," Alifa commanded tersely. "Be careful." She waited for Tabeta's nod, then darted into the shadows in pursuit of the sound.

She did not have far to go.

Jaraw swore vehemently just ahead of her and something snarled. Alifa's heart sank at the sound. Anything but this! She burst into a small clearing to find Jaraw and the panther circling each other, in confirmation of her worst fears.

It took only an instant to see what had happened.

Blood dripped from a gaping wound on the panther's velvety black hip. An ornate-handled knife that Alifa recognized as Jaraw's was still buried in the gash. Yusuf was hurt! Alifa's hands rose to her mouth, even as her gaze darted to her brother.

Jaraw sported only a bleeding scratch across his cheek. Alifa shakily released the breath she hadn't known she was holding.

The panther prowled, its eyes narrowed and hostile, its tail lashing impatiently. Jaraw kept his distance, his own belligerent gaze fixed on the knife, his hands outspread.

"What—?" Alifa demanded breathlessly. Jaraw flicked a hot glance her way. The beast did not acknowledge her presence, its regard never wavering from the boy. It snarled with a ferocity that did nothing to ease Alifa's fears.

"Don't worry," Jaraw assured her intently. "I'll just get my knife back and finish the job."

"What?" Alifa demanded in shock. He couldn't possibly mean what she thought he did.

"I told him that if he touched you again, I'd kill him," Jaraw muttered. His eyes gleamed as he braced himself for an attack. "But he didn't believe me and now he will pay."

"Jaraw, don't be ridiculous. You cannot kill him."

Her brother slanted Alifa a look that was chilling in its intensity. "Watch me," he told her.

"You will do no such thing!" Alifa spat with all the authority she could muster. She propped her hands on her hips when Jaraw's lips twisted and he turned away.

"You can't stop me!" No sooner had the words fallen from his lips than Jaraw lunged forward with unexpected speed.

The panther hissed as it saw his intent. Alifa gasped when her brother grasped the hilt of his knife. He twisted the blade. The great cat screamed in pain. It twisted with an agility that belied the evident depth of the wound. Its eyes blazed dangerously as it twisted and its paw landed heavily on the back of Jaraw's neck.

Jaraw fell facefirst in the dirt and stilled instantly, although he did not relinquish his grip on the embedded knife. They froze in that pose for a long moment and Alifa did not dare to breath.

Don't kill him, she prayed silently, knowing without even trying that her voice had deserted her.

The panther's claws gleamed against her brother's flesh, but the great cat hesitated. Alifa saw Jaraw's eyes widen before his grip tightened on the hilt of his blade. She wanted to call a warning, but it was too late. Jaraw jerked and abruptly hauled the knife out of the panther's flesh. He struggled to raise it high but the cat anticipated his aim.

The panther dived down on the hand that wielded the knife with an intent that could not be turned aside. Its mouth locked around the wrist and those long teeth were buried in the boy's skin before Alifa could protest. Jaraw cried out and the knife fell from his grip to dance out of range.

Alifa screamed when she saw the tips of the claws disappear into Jaraw's neck.

No! He couldn't do this!

"You said you wouldn't kill!" she shrieked, certain beyond doubt that the panther was Yusuf.

Both Jaraw and the panther froze at her cry.

Slowly the great cat lifted its gaze to meet hers without releasing its grip on Jaraw's wrist. Everything was achingly still in the clearing—even the creatures of the night had fallen silent—and Alifa did not dare to breathe. Finally, she fancied she saw something change in those crystalline green eyes.

Then the panther gave Jaraw's wrist a shake, as if in warning. It loosened its grip and Jaraw's wrist fell limply to the ground. Alifa sagged in relief. Mercifully, Jaraw did not make the mistake of moving. The panther fastidiously stepped off the boy and snarled once before it leapt into the scrub and disappeared.

There remained only a trail of blood to mark its passing.

Alifa exhaled and ran one hand over her brow as a thousand questions flooded into her mind. Where would Yusuf go? How would he tend his own wound? She was uncertain what to do next.

Jaraw first.

Blood trickled from Jaraw's neck, but the boy abruptly sat up and wiped it away insouciantly. Evidently he was unhurt and once she was reassured, the recollection of Yusuf's injury set Alifa's anger simmering. How dare Jaraw interfere in such a manner? Did he not realize what he had done? He flexed his wrist with supreme unconcern, then granted his sister an accusing look.

"You obviously don't understand...." Jaraw began condescendingly, but he got no further before Alifa interrupted him.

"I understand more than you do," she snapped. "Get yourself back to the camp right now. I think you've done enough damage for one night and I still have to find some way to help Yusuf. You had no right to attack him like this."

"You don't know who or what he is," Jaraw protested indignantly, as though he could not believe her assertion. "I saw him *shapeshift*," he informed her belligerently.

"And?" Alifa asked matter-of-factly. Jaraw looked momentarily surprised before he regained his antagonism.

"You know?" he demanded.

"Of course."

"And you still coupled with him?" Her brother was clearly incredulous.

Alifa did not appreciate the intimacy of the question. "That is none of your business," she retorted formally.

Jaraw grimaced. "I had thought it wasn't yours anymore, either," he snapped. Alifa flushed, but she did not back down. Jaraw's impertinence was unacceptable. As much as she hated to admit it, Yusuf had been right about him.

"Clearly, I shouldn't have stopped Yusuf from trying to teach you some manners," Alifa muttered.

"Well, you don't have to worry about him coming back to teach me anything else," Jaraw assured her cockily. Alifa regarded her brother with suspicion.

"What do you mean?"

"He won't be back."

"Of course he'll be back. Yusuf always comes back," Alifa told him crossly, even as doubt filtered into her mind. How bad had the wound been? She really hadn't been able to tell at that distance and she feared anew for Yusuf's safety.

"Not this time," Jaraw insisted with a confidence that did nothing to reassure Alifa. "I made sure of it."

"What do you mean?"

Jaraw grinned. "He has to find his clothes to change back. I remember that from the old stories Mother used to tell us." He leaned forward with malice gleaming in his eyes. "He's caught between that world and this one without his clothes. We'll never see him again."

"Jaraw!" Alifa exclaimed in shock, only now recalling that facet of the tale. Yusuf would never survive in the wild with that gaping wound. There were other animals that would prey upon him! She glared at her brother, his smug expression making it more than clear that that had been his plan. "What have you done with Yusuf's clothes?"

Her brother folded his arms across his chest and held her gaze defiantly. "They're gone for good, sister dear."

"But you can't do this!" Alifa protested. "He's hurt. It's wrong. How will he have the wound tended?"

"He won't," Jaraw said and his chin set stubbornly. "And that's the point."

"Jaraw. He saved your hand," Alifa chided. Her brother's expression did not soften.

"And he stole your dignity," he argued flatly. "He took advantage of you and is only going to hurt you. I cannot permit that to happen."

Rage rippled through Alifa at his audacity. "*You* won't permit it! Who asked for your opinion? I made my own decision and it is not up to you to question it," she informed him tersely.

Jaraw's expression grew mutinous. "I am the man of this family and I will decide what is best for all of us," he declared.

"You will not make my choices," Alifa argued. Jaraw eyed her for a long moment and she knew him well enough to expect a challenge.

"Then choose for yourself, Alifa," he taunted quietly, though his gaze hardened. "Choose between your beast and your blood."

Alifa was horrified by the thought. She could not choose. She would not choose. How could she choose? "Jaraw, don't make me do this," she warned.

"I think you already have," he mused. "Go ahead, Alifa. Tell me what you want." He leaned closer and there was a mean glint in his eyes. "Choose," he insisted.

Choose.

The answer came more easily than Alifa expected it should have.

"I would take Yusuf to husband, if he would have me," she confessed quietly. Rage contorted Jaraw's features and he stepped hastily away.

"Fool!" he charged. "He thinks he's too good for you, but really the opposite is true. He'll never make you happy, Alifa."

"He's the only one I can be happy with," Alifa admitted, hearing the softness in her own voice and marveling at the truth of her words. "I love him, Jaraw, and you cannot change that."

Jaraw flailed his arms wide and his eyes flashed angrily. "But what about me? What about the family? What about blood?"

"What about compassion? You tried to kill him, Jaraw," Alifa said, still unable to completely believe what she had seen. "That was wrong."

"That was for the greater good. He's no good for you, Alifa," Jaraw stated.

"I'll decide that for myself," Alifa retorted.

"So, you've already chosen, then?"

"No. You're the one who is choosing, Jaraw. I would love both of you—one as brother, one as spouse."

"It's one or the other," Jaraw insisted, but Alifa shook her head.

"Not for me," she insisted. They eyed each other for a long moment, each realizing that the other's opinion could not be changed. "Where are his clothes?" Alifa finally demanded softly.

Jaraw's expression became incredulous as he stared at his sister. "I can't believe this. You really mean to help him? Don't you understand what he is?"

"I have no choice," Alifa said quietly. Jaraw shook his head and backed away, his features twisting into a frown.

"You *had* a choice," he insisted harshly. "And now that you've made it, I see where I stand. Goodbye, Alifa." He turned and darted into the night. Alifa gasped as his silhouette was swallowed up by the shadows, so quickly that she could not see where he went.

"Jaraw!" Alifa shouted. "Where are you going? What are you doing?"

"Don't worry!" Jaraw shouted from far away, anger still discernible in his tone. Alifa could not tell precisely what direction his voice came from and she peered wildly into the shadows surrounding the clearing. "I won't be back to interfere, sister dear. You've made your choice and now you can live with it."

He said no more, though Alifa strained her ears. Jaraw was gone. Even the sound of his footfalls was gone, and there was just the wind rustling the needles of the juniper trees.

And the trail of blood. Alifa's gaze dropped to the incriminating red drops and wondered what she had done.

Yusuf heard the footsteps approaching, but could not move, even to save himself.

He had lost too much blood.

His recollection of events was hazy, as it always was in this form, but he knew it was Jaraw who had attacked him.

Just as he knew that Alifa's cry had halted the hunting instinct just in time. He would have to think about that later, when the pain had faded.

If that time ever came.

For now, he was in torment. The wound prompted him to shift immediately, but his clothes were gone from where he had left them. He was caught between one world and the next, caught as surely as a rat in a cage, and the essence of both lives was slowly easing out of his side.

Yusuf was going to die and he knew it. Here in the mountains, away from either place he called home and without anyone at his side. It was only a matter of time.

His instincts had him bedding down in the shadows, choosing a spot that was rock on three sides, that he might have some chance of defending himself against the marauders that would certainly come. The mountains were full of them.

It was only a matter of time before he would not be able to fight them off.

The footsteps rustled again and his ears pricked up. His gaze sharpened and he peered through the trees, heat flooding through him at a woman's distinctive silhouette.

Alifa had followed him.

Excitement flooded through him, a heady mix of anticipation and dread. What if he inadvertently hurt her? Yusuf felt his ears flatten against his head and he crouched lower in the soft bed of discarded needles. She was already afraid and his awareness of that pricked at his conscience. Yusuf could smell her fear and it brought his hunting instinct to the fore.

He could not afford to indulge it.

Alifa hesitated and he watched her crouch to peer into the shadows where he had hidden himself. Yusuf's heart leapt. Evidently she could not detect him. She scanned the ground with a puzzled frown and he realized that she had followed the trail of his blood.

"Yusuf?" she asked tentatively. Her voice quivered in a way he had never heard from her before and Yusuf realized what this bravery must have cost her.

Alifa had pursued him. Alifa was concerned for him.

He could not think any further than that.

She moved slowly, as though fearing to startle something wild. She crouched and placed something on the ground that he immediately identified. Yusuf's pulse quickened.

"I brought your cloak," she said breathlessly. "And the other *chalwar* that were in your pack. Everything else is gone." Alifa's voice broke and the remainder of her words fell in a little rush. "I'm sorry about your boots and your clothes. I'm sorry about Jaraw. I'm sorry we argued." She paused and took a shaky breath. "I hope you come back," she whispered.

Her hand lingered on the pile of clothes, as though she were uncertain to leave them behind. Yusuf could not leave her in such doubt.

He bared his teeth and let loose a low growl.

Alifa jumped in surprise and her hands flew to her chest. Her eyes widened. The scent of her fear redoubled and everything animal within Yusuf longed to pounce. He schooled himself to remain still and willed Alifa to leave.

Finally, just when he thought he could bear it no longer, she spun and ran.

It took everything within him not to give chase.

Chapter Thirteen

Yusuf was limping when he came back to the makeshift camp.

It was dawn and Alifa distrusted her sight when his figure was first etched against the lightening sky. She blinked in disbelief, but Yusuf limped closer and she rose incredulously to her feet.

He was alive! Yusuf glanced up in that moment and their gazes caught. His features were barely discernible in the early light, but even so, Alifa could see that his lips were twisted in a denial of his pain.

She could not keep herself from running to his side in her relief, but once she was there, her nerve abandoned her. Alifa hesitated an arm's length away, uncertain whether Yusuf would appreciate her help.

She realized that he was wearing only the *chalwar* and cloak that she had left in the clearing before the cornered panther. All night long she had fretted about whether she had done the wrong thing. She hadn't even been able to see the panther when she left the garments. Alifa had heard its labored breathing and followed her instincts.

Then spent the night hoping for the best.

But Yusuf's presence proved her intuition right.

How many confirmations did she need? Alifa wondered crossly. No matter how aware she was of his capabilities, it seemed that each proof was a new revelation.

And even now, as she dared to glance to his face, it was almost impossible to believe that what she knew to be true in fact was true. Yusuf slanted her an assessing glance and she knew she could remain silent no longer.

"You look dreadful," Alifa said quietly.

"And feel worse," he conceded tightly.

What should she do? Clearly, he needed assistance, but would he spurn her help? She hesitated for a moment, then slipped her arm around Yusuf to help him closer to the burned-down fire. He impaled Alifa with a glance that spoke volumes and dropped the weight of his arm over her shoulders. His lips thinned as they walked and Alifa feared suddenly for the depth of the gash she had seen the night before.

"Is it clean?" she asked.

Yusuf shook his head. "I don't know. I can't see it." He flicked her another of those enigmatic glances. "Would you look at it?"

Clearly, they weren't going to talk about the night before. Alifa didn't know whether to be disappointed or relieved. She managed somehow to summon a crisp smile.

"Of course," she agreed, unable to imagine what it had cost this proud man to ask for her assistance. "Just lie down here, on your stomach," she directed and was a little surprised when Yusuf immediately did her bidding. He sighed and ran one hand tiredly over his eyes, his brows pulling together in a frown that wrenched Alifa's heart.

The wound must be worse than she had feared. Alifa peeled back Yusuf's *chalwar* and froze in shock at the sight that greeted her.

There was so much blood.

She gritted her teeth and covered the wound again. "We'll need hot water," she explained in as even a tone as she could manage. Yusuf nodded wearily and closed his eyes as he rested his forehead on his folded arms.

He did not open them again while Alifa stoked up the fire. She placed a pot of water on top of the coals and rummaged in her pack. Her cheeks heated as she removed the *djellaba* she had taken from Yusuf on that first night and she clenched it tightly in her fingers for a moment as she watched him.

Yusuf seemed to sense her regard for he opened his eyes with an effort. His lips twisted into a semblance of a smile as he evidently recognized the garment she held.

"You still have it," he mused, his exhaustion evident in his tone. Alifa felt her cheeks grow hot and she found herself looking down at her hands to avoid his perceptive gaze.

"I forgot that I had it last night," she explained in a rush.

Yusuf merely nodded. "I'm glad that you do," he said. "I could use a shirt."

"I was going to tear the bottom off for bandages."

"Fine. It will serve for both." He closed his eyes again and Alifa did not like how weary he looked.

"Have you eaten?" she dared to ask. Yusuf simply shook his head.

Clearly, Alifa had work to do. Fortunately, Kasilo and Tabeta were still sleeping and would likely continue to do so for a while. With any luck, Yusuf would be more himself by the time they began asking questions.

She would not tell him about Jaraw yet, nor about her fears for her audacious brother.

While she waited for the water to boil, Alifa put the remnants of the previous night's vegetable stew on to heat, as well. She spread some flat bread with the last bit of soft cheese. By the time the food was ready, though, Yusuf looked to be asleep. Alifa watched the rhythm of his breathing and could not bring herself to wake him.

The food would wait. She pulled his cloak over his shoulders and left him to doze.

Once the water was heated, Alifa knelt beside Yusuf. This would awaken him, but there was nothing for it. The cut had to be cleaned. She uncovered the wound again and began to bathe it.

The gash was deep and Alifa winced sympathetically as her ministrations removed the early scabbing. Yusuf's muscles flexed, but he did not move away. The rate of his breathing changed and she knew that he was awake.

"It looks clean," she ventured to comment. He nodded once without opening his eyes.

"Where is he?" Yusuf asked and Alifa knew immediately who he meant. Her lips thinned and she frowned at the almost completely cleaned cut.

"Jaraw?" she asked. She was stalling for time and suspected Yusuf knew as much. He grimaced and nodded, even his silence seeming expectant. Alifa licked her lips, wondering how best to tell him.

Did Yusuf plan to retaliate? What would he do to Jaraw?

And why did she find her heart championing Yusuf's cause over her brother's? To her mind, Yusuf had every right to seek retribution. What Jaraw had done was wrong.

That traitorous feeling did not sit well and Alifa fidgeted.

"He left," she blurted out.

Yusuf propped himself up on one elbow and met her eyes in shock. "He what?"

"He left," Alifa repeated. And she had not pursued him immediately, when there was at least a chance of finding him. Alifa felt that she had failed her parents again. Yusuf scowled at the ground. She felt her tears gather, but would not let them fall.

"Why?" he demanded roughly.

Alifa shrugged helplessly. "We argued and he left."

Yusuf exhaled in evident displeasure and dropped onto his stomach again. "He'll be back when he's hungry," he said dismissively. Alifa shook her head, though she knew that he could not see the gesture.

"He said he wouldn't be," she insisted. Yusuf turned to regard her skeptically again, his expression slowly changing as he saw her conviction.

"What did you argue about?" he asked quietly. Alifa caught her breath and looked into the distance. She felt one heavy tear fall, but ignored it.

"I told him that what he had done was wrong," she whispered. "He disagreed."

A silence followed Alifa's words that she found painfully awkward. She stared down at her hands, well aware of the weight of Yusuf's regard upon her. She could not guess his response to her confession and the uncertainty troubled her.

A bird called in the distance and Alifa realized that the sky had lightened to a rosy blush. The light dew that had fallen during the night glistened on the leaves of the few surrounding trees in the early light.

"You were right," Yusuf told her finally and there was a warmth in his tone that she hadn't known to expect. Alifa smiled sadly and nodded.

"So were you," she admitted softly. She dared to raise her gaze to meet his, surprised to find compassion in those green eyes. "Thank you for trying to teach him."

"You're welcome. I only wish I had met you all soon enough to make more of a difference." Another place, another time. Alifa knew Yusuf meant more than Jaraw's departure by his comment and she wished her heart didn't agree so fervently with him.

Was what she hoped for truly so out of reach? Was it really impossible that they could make their way together from here and now? Yusuf held her gaze for a long moment and Alifa wondered if their thoughts were as one. She barely dared to hope so before Yusuf cleared his throat and turned away again.

"Where did he go?" he asked crisply and the moment was gone.

Alifa sighed in frustration and frowned. "I don't know. I couldn't even tell what direction he went in."

Yusuf pursed his lips thoughtfully and darted a sharp glance in her direction. "Yet you didn't try to find him," he observed.

"No. No, I couldn't," Alifa answered immediately. "It was out of the question. You were hurt and Kasilo is sick and Tabeta needs me." There had been no shirking her responsibilities, but although Alifa believed she had made the only possible choice, not pursuing Jaraw still troubled her deeply. She took a deep breath to steady herself as she voiced the thought that had plagued her all night.

"Jaraw will have to fend for himself, I suppose," she admitted quietly. Failure washed over Alifa and she was certain her parents could never have expected her to make such a mess of the trust they had granted her.

"That might be exactly what he needs," Yusuf said thoughtfully.

Alifa regarded him in astonishment. Yusuf's expression was harsh and his lips were set in a grim line that adequately conveyed his opinion. How could he possibly be so cold? Jaraw was alone! He could be lost or hurt or worse!

She might never see him again. Irrational anger flooded through her at his unexpected response and suddenly it was easy to blame Yusuf for all her ills.

Indisputably, it was all Yusuf's fault. Hadn't he taken a dislike to her brother right from the outset? Hadn't he fairly driven Jaraw away?

"What do you know of what he needs?" Alifa snapped. She pushed to her feet and propped her hands on her hips, ignoring Yusuf's surprised glance. "But then, how could I forget?" she added sarcastically. "You know what is best for all of us. In fact, you probably knew what was best for us before you even met us!"

"Keep your voice down," Yusuf warned quietly. Although his voice was low, his expression made it clear that his temper was wearing thin. Alifa blithely ignored both warnings. "You'll wake the children," he admonished, but she tossed her hair defiantly.

"And that would not be for the best, would it?" Alifa cried. "Imagine how they would feel if they awoke to find out that you had virtually forced their brother to run away!"

She leaned closer to him, overlooking the dangerous glint in Yusuf's eye as she lowered her voice to a taunt. Alifa was pushing him and she knew it, but she didn't care.

Yusuf deserved no less.

And maybe it was easier to fight with him. That way he would never suspect the inappropriate feelings that she harbored in her heart.

"But what are you going to tell them when they do wake up?" she whispered. "They'll probably notice that Jaraw is gone, you know. They may be young, but they aren't fools. And since you're the one with all the answers, it would only be fair for you to conjure up this one."

"I did not drive Jaraw away," Yusuf muttered through gritted teeth. A ruddy tinge began to spread up his neck beneath his tan.

Alifa flicked her chin away. "You most certainly did. From the very beginning, you took an irrational dislike to the boy and did everything you could—"

She got no further before Yusuf interrupted.

"Irrational?" he bellowed, and shoved himself to his feet. Astonishingly, the children did not stir. Yusuf grimaced from pain, but did not falter as he advanced on Alifa. "Irrational? What is *irrational* is the way you persist in protecting that opportunist from the consequences of his actions!"

She had *never* been irrational. Alifa knew that for a fact. She folded her arms across her chest and glared at Yusuf skeptically. "An interesting charge from the one who saved his hand," she observed acidly. Yusuf winced.

"There's something that I've been regretting ever since it was done," he growled.

"Well, you have no one to thank but yourself," Alifa retorted. Yusuf's eyes glinted and he quickly stepped forward to grasp her arm. He lifted Alifa to her toes, but she refused to back down. The strong grip of his fingers launched a tingle over her skin, but she would never have granted him any evidence of her response.

Alifa frostily held Yusuf's regard and tried not to stare at his lips. "You took that burden on yourself," she reminded him haughtily.

"I did that because you wanted me to and you know it," Yusuf charged unexpectedly. Alifa had known no such thing and could not completely hide her surprise.

"Please," she said scornfully when she recovered. "You've never done *anything* because I wanted you to! You do nothing other than what you want to do and don't spare a thought on anybody else."

"Is that so?" Yusuf demanded. He gave her a little shake, but Alifa merely smiled cockily. How she loved it when his eyes snapped! His bare chest was temptingly close, but Alifa did not dare touch him, lest he guess how much their arguing aroused her.

It was exhilarating to know that she could say anything to him and he would rise to the challenge. Never had Alifa had the opportunity, before Yusuf, to spar with a partner who was at least as strong as she.

She realized with astonishment that that was the foundation of her respect for Yusuf.

"Of course it's so," she snapped before he could fathom the direction of her thoughts. "And you know it."

"Fool!" Yusuf hauled her closer and locked his other hand around her free arm. Alifa's pulse took off at a gallop and something warm unfolded leisurely deep within her. She thought of their last night together, the luxury of his caresses and the thoroughness of his loving, and could not look away from his mesmerizing regard.

"Then what am I doing in the mountains with two small children and a completely impossible woman?" Yusuf demanded impatiently. "What possible reason did I have for intervening to save Jaraw's hand? And why would I pledge to teach him anything?" Yusuf's growl dropped even deeper and his frustration was evident as his hands shook in his bid for control.

Alifa's senses were flooded with him and she could barely follow the thread of the argument. The smell of his scent at such proximity was overwhelming, the focus of his attention upon her making her long to throw her arms around his neck and kiss him until he begged for mercy. She managed somehow to shake her head beneath the intensity of his onslaught.

"I don't know," she admitted. Neither did she care at this point.

"You don't know," Yusuf repeated in evident annoyance. It seemed that Alifa's arousal was not mutual. "Do you think I wanted to do any of those things? Do you think I wanted to take twice as long to put this business with my father behind me?" His eyes blazed as he bent over her. "Do you imagine that it didn't take everything within me to *not* rip out Jaraw's throat last night?"

Last night. He had almost killed Jaraw last night.

The reminder brought Alifa abruptly back to reality, but she could not summon an answer. The very idea was stunning. Of course, Jaraw had tried to kill Yusuf first.

The scene deluged her mind's eye and Alifa knew she had not misinterpreted what she had seen.

Yusuf had almost killed her brother. Yusuf was an animal when he shifted. Yusuf was both more than human and less.

The dreadful thing was that the realization did not dampen her ardor one whit.

Yusuf visibly gritted his teeth. *"Do you?"* he demanded when she did not respond.

Alifa shook her head mutely, her gesture more one of futility than of denial. Yusuf leaned closer and she could feel the fan of his breath on her cheek when he spoke. It sent a dangerous tingle over her skin. Alifa did not dare flinch, nor did she indulge her desire to lean closer and run her tongue across his lips.

"I could taste his blood last night, Alifa, and I wanted more of it," he whispered. Alifa's eyes widened and her blood ran cold as she stared up at him. He *was* an animal. Surely it couldn't be so.

"He wounded me. Deliberately," Yusuf continued. "And he would have killed me if he had had the chance. The rage I felt was animal, it was red and blinding. I could think of nothing else but vengeance."

Alifa licked her lips carefully as she fought to come to terms with the revelation. Could Yusuf truly have so little control over himself in his other form? Had she been in more danger with him than she had thought these past weeks? It seemed incredible.

"Why didn't you kill him?" she asked in a voice too small to be her own.

Yusuf's gaze bored relentlessly into hers. "You asked me not to," he said heavily.

For her? Had he really done all these things for her? Alifa could barely believe it, especially when she tried to fathom why.

Surely Yusuf couldn't have feelings for her? Everything quickened within her at the promise of that and to her amazement, her passion rose to the fore once again. Had anyone ever made such a sweet confession? Had anyone ever made a choice purely to please her?

Relief flooded through Alifa and she dared to believe in that instant that Yusuf truly might become her man alone. She let her hands drift up to his shoulders and leaned forward, lifting her lips to his. Yusuf stiffened, but she nibbled at his mouth undeterred, letting the scent of him fill her with contentment.

He had done it for her. He would be hers. She would finally have a man, and one more than worthy of her respect. Alifa framed Yusuf's strong jaw in her hands and kissed him square on the mouth. Yusuf groaned and pulled her closer. He opened his mouth and bent his head, his grip tightening on her arms.

Alifa nearly swooned. It was a taste of heaven. Or perhaps something a little darker, but everything she wanted all the same. This was what she had missed these last weeks. This was the reassurance she had needed since that scene the previous night. Alifa sighed and let her breasts rest against the strength of Yusuf's bare chest.

To her horrified amazement, she became gradually aware of some change in Yusuf.

The texture of his palms on her upper arms changed subtly until their surface was rougher. Alifa tore her lips from his and frowned, not in the least reassured when his expression turned knowing. She held his gaze and her heart began to pound in her ears.

Alifa took a deep breath and glanced down.

Yusuf's palms were black. Though his hands were still recognizably human, his nails had lengthened and there was a dusting of silky black hair on the back of his hands.

He was shifting! Right in her arms! Alifa looked back to his eyes in panic. Yusuf smiled slowly and it seemed to her that his canine teeth were slightly longer than usual.

"See what you do to me," Yusuf whispered confidentially.

"No!"

Alifa shook off Yusuf's grip desperately. She hastily backed away, almost tripping over her own feet in her rush to put distance between them. She eyed him warily, but Yusuf did not pursue her.

It could not be possible! *She* could not be the one who made him become a monster. She had thought shifting to be a gift, a power to be used for good, but Yusuf was showing her a dark side of his ability that horrified her. And *she* provoked this change. Alifa's ardor was dealt a telling blow and it dissipated instantly. She could not be responsible for this!

But as soon as there was space between them, even Alifa could see the change. The black faded from Yusuf's palms and his hands slowly changed back to those with which she was familiar.

Those that had stroked her skin on more than one occasion.

Alifa raised disbelieving eyes to meet Yusuf's regard. He cocked one brow in a very human gesture.

"It's because of you," he said softly. Alifa swallowed, still struggling to absorb the truth. She could not even fathom the reason behind it and she ran one hand over her eyes in a desperate attempt to think clearly.

"We'll leave," she suggested wildly. "We'll continue on by ourselves."

Yusuf's features hardened. "I said I would take you to my father," he insisted. "And the Imazighen keep their word."

Alifa watched him, not at all certain what to make of his confession and less certain that she wanted to travel with him anymore. Yusuf shook his head slowly, as though he could read her very thoughts.

"Don't even think about running away," he murmured. He raised his head and took a deliberate sniff of the air, his manner reminding her of an animal tracking another in a way that she was sure was not coincidental. "I would find you," he said with finality.

The certainty in his words sent a chill down Alifa's spine and she took a hesitant step backward. "And once we get there?" she demanded breathlessly.

Yusuf folded his arms across his bare chest. "Then my word will be fulfilled and we may both continue on our own way."

Alifa breathed a ragged sigh of relief. A few more days, no more than that.

She could do it. Her gaze slipped to Kasilo's sleeping form and her resolve grew. She had to do it. If Yusuf was willing to endure the company of a woman who forced such a change upon him, surely she could tolerate his presence for the sake of the greater good.

She would have to do it.

Just as Jaraw would have to find his way alone. Alifa gestured toward the pot of stew, resolutely ignoring the unexpected blur of tears in her eyes.

"Are you hungry? There is stew left from last night and some bread." Alifa turned away from Yusuf, taking refuge in the mundane so that she would not have to acknowledge the disappointment welling up within her.

Trust her to fall in love with a man who was destroyed by her very presence. It was so typical of Alifa's luck that she should not have been surprised.

Let alone be on the verge of tears.

Three days later, the path began to look achingly familiar to Yusuf. It seemed that even the passage of years could not erase his boyhood familiarity with these hills. He knew that stone and this twist in the path as well as the lines in his own hands. He marveled at how the crooked tree at the crest had grown, taking the moment to brace himself before he turned. Yusuf stilled the donkey with one hand and caught his breath in anticipation before he looked down into the valley.

He could have left yesterday for all the change there had been.

The square buildings were still as red as the hills surrounding them, though both had turned purplish in the dusky light of the sinking sun. More than the buildings' color echoed their surroundings, the jagged ornamentation around their flat roofs making them seem to blend right into the mountainside. Yusuf remembered fearing as a child that the town would melt into the mountains if he dared to look away for too long and he would never find his way home.

But he had. Even after all this time.

A curious sense of satisfaction flooded through him, a satisfaction that he had never expected to feel. His gaze drank in the familiar sight of the women herding a few goats back down from the hills for the night. The majority of the livestock would be out to pasture with the men this late in the season, he recalled. The shadows fell long over the courtyards, the leaves of the peach trees rustled in the evening breeze. Yusuf imagined he could see the green fruit, even from this distance, and expertly assessed the size of the crop.

It had been a good year.

Children cried out to each other and laughed at their games; a woman shouted to summon her brood to their meal. Yusuf felt a slow smile slide over his features as he gazed affectionately down at the valley where he had spent his childhood. Life had been good here. Simple and hard certainly, but filled with good memories.

It had been a good place to grow up. And it was home as nowhere else could ever be.

"Is this where we're going?" Kasilo demanded from in front of him. Yusuf ruffled the boy's hair.

"This is it," he confirmed. Yusuf risked a glance to Alifa to find her expression unreadable. Their eyes met for a moment and then she abruptly looked away.

"It looks lovely," she said simply and Yusuf cringed inwardly.

He had wanted to frighten her and had done so deliberately. So why did it trouble him that his strategy had worked? It had been so easy to let his control slip a little and grant the beast the upper hand for an instant. He had told himself that it would be for the greater good.

Alifa and he had no future together. He could not wish this curse upon anyone and he could not take her back to Ceuta as his wife. Not to mention the fact that Yusuf was not entirely certain that she would go, even if he dared to ask.

And he would not stay here. He belonged in town. Yusuf acknowledged his unexpected serenity at confronting this scene again and struggled to dismiss a dawning certainty that this was precisely where he belonged.

And there was absolutely no question that he could not risk endangering Alifa. His control over the beast was tenuous at best in her presence. So far, he had not hurt her, but he could not be certain that he would be so lucky in the future.

No. He had no future with Alifa. Yusuf told himself that it was only natural to be disappointed. She was a beautiful woman and she reached inside him as no other ever had.

Or probably ever would.

Before his thoughts could meander any further, Yusuf dismounted. He gritted his teeth at the stiffness in his sore hip, but refused to indulge it.

"Surely you're not going to walk?" Alifa demanded. The thread of concern in her tone warmed Yusuf's heart as nothing else could have in that moment. He smiled at her before he could stop himself.

"I'm not going to ride home like a child," Yusuf retorted good-naturedly. Thankfully, he had caught himself before he said "invalid" in Kasilo's presence. The boy was ill enough without having his feelings trampled. Suddenly Yusuf knew instinctively how to ensure that he was not offended.

"Or a woman," he added impulsively. Yusuf stepped forward and grasped Alifa around the waist. It did nothing for his resolve to forget her to realize how neatly his hands fit around her or how readily he could lift her.

"Yusuf! No!" Alifa laughed in that achingly attractive way as Yusuf scooped her high, but he forced himself to place her in the saddle behind Kasilo and release his grip. The children giggled and Yusuf offered his hand to Tabeta. The little girl trustingly slipped her hand into his and he took the donkey's reins, feeling as nervous as if he were bringing his own little family home.

Typically, it was Sarat who spotted them first.

"Yusuf! Yusuf, you're home!" she shouted from her window, which by no coincidence afforded an excellent view of the main approach to the town. Her delighted tone was quickly replaced by one of mock indignation that was welcomingly familiar.

"What has taken you so long, boy?" she demanded. Yusuf looked up and grinned, wondering how she had recognized him so quickly. Surely her eyes had failed even further over this time. Surely she could not have expected him to return here?

"Sarat! Have you no work to keep yourself busy?" Yusuf called, echoing the old joke they had shared. "Don't tell me you're idling away the time with daydreams again?"

Sarat laughed and waved wildly, her smile as infectious as ever. Yusuf returned the gesture, chuckling to himself when Sarat ducked out of sight and he heard her voice rise in a summons.

Soon, more than twenty women had spilled enthusiastically out of the red buildings and rushed to meet Yusuf's little group. Goats and children trailed behind curiously, the goats chewing complacently, the children's eyes wide and their knees dirty. Cheeks were kissed and fingers clasped, tears wiped from lined cheeks with tanned hands. Yusuf was hugged by more than one matron who had spared him a swat as a child and he was introduced to a bevy of new wives who had joined the tribe.

There was a pregnant pause once he had greeted everyone and Yusuf did not need to look to guess the reason. Dark eyes twinkled when they flicked to Alifa and soon a titter of speculation had enveloped the welcoming group.

"And who is this, Yusuf?" Sarat demanded mischievously. "Do you have an introduction to make?" she asked pointedly, her expression coy.

Yusuf felt his color rise as he turned and Alifa, curse the woman, blushed like a young bride. His body immediately responded and he gritted his teeth, wishing Alifa would cease to surprise him with characteristics that made him forget her original profession.

"This is Alifa, her brother Kasilo and sister Tabeta," he explained formally, though his tone was gruff. "They were orphaned in Ceuta and wished to return home to the mountains."

"Yusuf very kindly offered to accompany us," Alifa contributed with a sweetness well outside her usual exchanges with Yusuf. Yusuf granted her a wary glance, but she merely smiled sunnily in his direction. His ears heated and he turned abruptly away.

Sarat's face fell before she managed to smile again. The older woman reached over and patted Alifa's hand maternally. "It is wise of you to come home and find a good man in the mountains," she told Alifa solemnly.

Alifa smiled demurely and Yusuf could not have missed the impact of the look that Sarat fired in his direction. He resolutely ignored both women and lifted Kasilo purposefully from the saddle.

"Kasilo has need of my father's assistance," he said as he balanced the boy on his hip. Kasilo coughed once, but granted the women his most engaging smile. They clucked and assured each other that he was an adorable boy. Sarat pinched Kasilo's cheek and winked at him.

"Kasilo has need of some mountain air and country cooking," she said with assurance.

"Alifa is a good cook," Kasilo asserted proudly. The women melted at his loyalty and exchanged soft smiles.

"Of course she is, love," Sarat assured him. "But you simply cannot get fresh goods in town. Nothing tastes as good as when it is freshly plucked from the vine."

"That is certainly true," Alifa agreed easily. Sarat sent Yusuf another demanding glance and he knew he would hear more about his failure to snap up such an obviously suitable wife when Sarat found a private moment with him.

Little did she know how suitable Alifa really was. Yusuf sobered even as he felt Alifa and her siblings being accepted by the tribe, determined to set matters straight in one regard, at least.

"He needs more than that, Sarat," he said sternly. "Kasilo needs a healing. Is my father out to pasture with the men?"

A ripple rolled over the little group and it seemed to Yusuf that suddenly no one would meet his eyes. He frowned and looked to Sarat, but she was examining her toes with great interest. His gaze flicked to Alifa, not in the least reassured that she looked similarly confused.

Their hesitancy made no sense. Why wouldn't they tell him where the old man was? Surely nothing he did could be that secret—even if the old man had thought it secret, Sarat would have no trouble gossiping. And the woman always knew everyone's business. Yusuf watched the little group in confusion for a speechless moment. There was no reasonable explanation for their attitude.

Unless something had happened to his father.

Yusuf's gut went cold. Such a thought had never occurred to him. The old man had never even been ill.

"Sarat? What is wrong?" he demanded, stubbornly quelling his fear. His father had gone to another village to help and no one knew when he would return. That was all. There was nothing to fear. "Where is my father? Is he not here?"

"No," Sarat said simply.

"Is my father ill?" Yusuf asked hastily.

"No," Sarat admitted with a shake of her head. Yusuf heard her take a deep breath and then she glanced up with an abruptness that caught him off guard.

"I'm sorry, Yusuf. He's dead."

Chapter Fourteen

"Isn't that why you came home?"

The older woman leaned forward in concern, her brow puckered in a puzzled frown. Yusuf was clearly still reeling from the revelation that he evidently had not expected and did not answer the woman.

Alifa was reeling herself. Yusuf's father was dead?

"Yusuf, I am sorry. I was certain that you knew," Sarat said quickly and Alifa glanced up at her agitation. "Your father knew everything that happened to those around him, even when they were far away, and I just assumed..." Her voice faltered as Yusuf fired a quelling look in her direction.

"I am not my father," he whispered tersely.

"Of course not," Sarat said. "But it has always been clear that you have his gifts. Why else would you come back here, if not to replace him?"

Yusuf glanced up with a start, those last words evidently stirring him out of his thoughts. "What?" he demanded.

Sarat shook her head indulgently. "Come along, Yusuf. There's no need to be coy. Naturally you came home to be our shaman. We all know that and welcome you back. You knew we would. We haven't had a shaman since your father died last spring and everyone knows that the task passes next to you. It is the way. It has always been the way."

"No!" Yusuf said forcibly. He glared at Sarat and spoke slowly, as though to make his feelings totally clear. "I did not come here to become shaman."

Alifa saw Sarat's surprise reflected in every gaze.

"But—" the older woman protested.

Yusuf shoved to his feet and frowned angrily. "But *nothing*. I only came home to bring Alifa and to talk to my father," Yusuf informed the astonished group with a firmness that brooked no argument. "I am going back to Ceuta as soon as possible."

Sarat frowned in turn. "No decent shaman practices in town," she scoffed. "What will you do there?" Yusuf shot a venomous glance in her direction.

"I am a scholar, not a shaman," he asserted proudly. This claim was not greeted with approval by his kinsfolk and they murmured discontentedly to each other.

"Why would you do such a thing?" Sarat was clearly confused. "You have a rare gift. Why would you turn away from it to do anything else?"

"I have a rare gift for scholarship and nothing else," Yusuf insisted. Sarat looked unconvinced, as did most of her neighbors.

The words sent a pang through Alifa's heart, as well. What about Kasilo? How would he be healed? Now they were days away from any other assistance and her brother's condition had progressively worsened.

Surely Yusuf would at least have to try to heal Kasilo now, regardless of his reservations. Alifa actually managed to hold that thought for a heady instant before reality checked her enthusiasm.

Hadn't he already declined that path?

"I thought your father was going to help me," Kasilo said in a small voice that did not echo with his usual optimism. He looked to Yusuf questioningly and Alifa was certain she did not imagine the slight tremble in the boy's lip.

Alifa caught her breath, hoping that Kasilo's evident dismay might work some magic, but Yusuf's expression closed.

He averted his face slightly from the child, as though he could not look him in the eye while he spoke.

"He can't help you now," Yusuf conceded tightly. Tears shimmered in Kasilo's wide eyes and he turned to seek out Alifa.

She could not refuse his imploring gaze and she quickly plucked him out of Yusuf's arms. Kasilo locked his arms around her neck and Alifa felt him quiver. For the first time, Kasilo was uncertain of his future and she had nothing to say in reassurance. Alifa could not bear to meet Yusuf's gaze, even when they stood so close, burying her nose immediately in the boy's neck as she hugged him tightly.

She would not ask for Yusuf's assistance again. Somehow they would find a way.

Undaunted by Yusuf's manner, Sarat planted a blunt fingertip in the middle of his chest. "This is wrong, Yusuf. How can you not help the boy? Your father said on his deathbed that you would be back and that you would continue on in his stead."

Yusuf's lips tightened.

"My father was wrong," he said flatly. Alifa knew his denial was meant for her. Her gut clenched that he should feel so little for them after all this time, but she knew there was nothing she could do to change his mind.

Yusuf was denying his roots again and Alifa could no longer bear to watch. She turned wordlessly away, knowing it would be a long time before she was able to banish the ache from her heart.

It seemed that she had made another poor decision for her siblings in returning to the mountains. Jaraw was lost. Kasilo would die. It was a heavy price to pay. This trip south had brought nothing but heartache to her little family. And she could not in honesty blame anyone but herself.

They should have left Ceuta years ago. She should never have taken work in a tavern. She should not have been afraid to face the road alone.

But then, she might never have met Yusuf. The concession was a bittersweet one and Alifa's certainty floundered. Even knowing that there was no future for them, she would not have traded her time with Yusuf for the world.

Alifa felt a tug on her skirts and glanced down to meet Tabeta's questioning gaze.

"Alifa," her sister whispered, though the awkward silence was so complete that her voice carried further than she intended. "I need to go."

The women chuckled sympathetically and Tabeta flushed with the realization that she had been overheard. The tension of the moment eased magically around them and Alifa laid one hand on her sister's shoulder.

"I'm certain we can find somewhere," Alifa assured her quietly. She brushed one fingertip affectionately across her sister's cheek, hoping that nothing would happen to her next. Alifa knew she could not withstand another stroke of bad luck. One of the other women bustled forward purposefully and drew Alifa's attention back to the present.

"Come along and stay with me, won't you?" the woman invited with a friendly smile.

"We couldn't impose," Alifa demurred but the woman laughed.

"Never fear—I'll put you to work," she jested and all the women chuckled together. The woman grew more serious as she touched Alifa's arm in reassurance. "Truthfully, my daughter left recently to be married and I find the house terribly quiet these days. Some children would be welcome and I would greatly appreciate your company."

Her invitation was couched in a manner so reminiscent of their mother that Alifa had to blink back an unexpected tear. Only a mountain hostess could make her guests feel as though they were the ones granting the favor.

The manners were so achingly familiar, and so alien to those of Ceuta, that Alifa felt quite unexpectedly that she had finally come home.

"We would be honored," Alifa accepted.

"My name is Marizu," the woman confided. She tucked Tabeta under one arm companionably and pinched the girl's cheek. "And my home is very, very close," she teased. Tabeta giggled self-consciously. Alifa hesitated as she glanced back to Yusuf. He was still frowning.

"He will stay with Sarat, no doubt," Marizu whispered in her ear. "They will have a lot to talk about."

That was an understatement. One glance to Sarat readily revealed that the older woman was not finished arguing this matter with Yusuf.

Though Alifa did not expect her to make any progress now that Yusuf had clearly made up his mind.

"Of course," Alifa agreed and shifted her weight from one foot to the other.

She lingered in spite of herself. It was time to follow Marizu, but Alifa felt she should say something to Yusuf. But what? She could not ask Yusuf about Kasilo and she didn't know what else to say to him. To thank him for his aid in reaching the town, when it had clearly been a futile errand, seemed ridiculous.

"We will be at Marizu's home," was all she said. To her disappointment, Yusuf did not even look up. He nodded numbly, his disinterest in her departure sending a pang through Alifa's heart.

She had been right in the first place and mistaken to fool herself that there was any possibility with Yusuf. There was no space in Yusuf's life for a woman like Alifa, even if she had left her sordid life behind. He was going back to Ceuta alone. She had known that all along, just as she had known that he cared nothing for her or her siblings. They were an obligation, no more or less.

His lack of response still stung.

Alifa reminded herself that she had known all of that from the very first. Why then did Yusuf's disregard make her ache so inside? The women gathered around him as she watched dumbly, waiting for a sign that never came.

Not even a farewell. Alifa could not believe that Yusuf, the same man who had made her feel so treasured on two separate nights, could now be so indifferent to her. But he was. The evidence was before her very eyes.

Marizu touched Alifa's elbow in a silent summons. Alifa jumped and smiled apologetically and the two women stepped away. It was time Alifa put the past behind her and began building a new life for herself.

Somehow the promise of that did not fill her with optimism as it might have once.

"I'm expecting you'll have your eye out for a nice young man if you are planning to stay," Marizu said merrily as they walked. "Of course, I had wondered about you and Yusuf when you first arrived—probably everyone did, my dear, and it's only natural, after all—but now that I understand your situation, I shall have to think of all the eligible men I know. There are a few who are quite capable herdsmen in the neighboring tribe, although actually there's absolutely no reason why you couldn't make a match with one here, since you aren't blood." Marizu mused for a moment, her index finger tapping lightly against her chin.

Alifa was more than content to let the woman ramble and plan, her own feelings so desolate that she could barely think straight. They had come all this way for nothing. Kasilo was more ill and yet Yusuf would not use his abilities to help him.

She felt betrayed. Life stretched before her as a flat and expressionless wasteland.

"Are you divorced, dear, or have you not been married before? It will be a factor in the negotiations, as you undoubtedly know." Marizu paused, but Alifa was not really attending her words. How could she even consider finding another man after Yusuf? Was she doomed to spend the rest of her days making meaningless comparisons?

"Dear? Have you been married?" the older woman repeated. When Alifa did not immediately respond, Tabeta unexpected chimed in.

"Alifa hasn't been married," she informed Marizu. "Although I wish she would, because it would be fun to have babies to take care of." The woman smiled, the affectionate pat she landed on Alifa's cheek summoning the younger woman back to the moment.

Babies? Alifa blinked and tried to fathom the reason for Marizu's broad grin.

Although she hadn't long to wonder.

"Such a lovely woman and a virgin, too," Marizu declared happily. "You'll have the pick of the lot, my dear."

Virgin? Alifa's eyes widened but she knew she could not deny the other woman's conclusion. Not in front of Kasilo and Tabeta. Nor even in their absence.

How could she tell Marizu the truth? Her life in Ceuta seemed like a distant dream and Alifa knew she would never be able to make these women understand the choice she had made. It was unthinkable that she should even try.

Alifa's heart chilled as she considered the alternative. How would she explain the obvious absence of her maidenhead to a new groom who had paid well for a virgin bride? Was it better to face the consequences of what she had done earlier or later?

Alifa could not say. She hoped for a moment that she might find a man who cared little for such technicalities, but knew the chances of that were slim before the thought had even completely formed.

She would not look back to Yusuf, so concerned with his return to his impeccable scholarly life. He alone of all these people knew her secret. He alone could betray her. She would not awaken him to that salient fact.

In a few days, Yusuf would be gone. Somehow Alifa would concoct a story, though she could not imagine what it might be, a story that would allow her to wed honorably. She needed a spouse to survive here in the mountains. It was ironic in a way that what she had done to survive in town might jeopardize her ability to survive here.

It was the first time since she had left Ceuta that Alifa felt soiled and the feeling was not a welcome one, for all its familiarity.

Yusuf climbed away from the red brick walls of the town, disregarding both the fading light and the height. Sarat was not going to let the matter be and he refused to argue with her any longer.

The woman simply could not see sense.

Her insistence that he had *baraka,* the presence of shamans that his father had possessed, was disconcerting to say the least. Never mind her conviction that the entire tribe was in consensus on his ability to fulfill the task.

An ability that Yusuf was far from convinced he possessed. And even if he did, he was by no means certain that he wanted to use it.

He forced himself to recall his books as he climbed and compiled a mental inventory of their titles.

How dare his father pledge him to this task in his absence! Yusuf let loose what was in his opinion a very reasonable surge of anger. He had chosen not to be a shaman and his father had known it. That was why he had left. In fact, Yusuf was certain his father had understood, for he had not made any plea upon Yusuf's departure, all those years ago.

Now it seemed that the old man had just been granting him enough rope to hang himself.

Yusuf gained a crest that had long been familiar and gazed down at the town, where walls were falling into evening shadows. The wave of remorse that swept over him stunned him with its intensity.

His father was dead. The idea was almost impossible to comprehend.

It was even harder to understand the hollowness that knowledge left within Yusuf. He realized only now how much strength he had drawn from the certainty that his father was here. All these years, that certainty had provided a keystone in some corner of his mind.

But the old man was really gone. Despite any belief his son might have had that he was virtually immortal. Certainly Yusuf had held his enigmatic father in esteem worthy of a minor deity. He had been powerful. He had had *baraka*.

And he had made magic under the moon.

Yusuf could not completely come to terms with his feelings. He had admired his father; he had been in awe of him; he had never imagined that he cared for him. But this unexpected disappointment that the news had unleashed in him could be a sign of nothing else.

Yusuf had been looking forward to talking to the old man. That was astonishing in itself.

Not that he would have learned anything. His questions would have been answered with other questions, and riddles designed to leave him frustrated. His father tormented him and tempted him with possibilities, annoyed him and irritated him so that he lost his composure. But it had been undeniably interesting to match wits with him. Yusuf's father had always been the only one who could keep him on his mental toes.

Until Alifa. The woman could infuriate him even more quickly than his father had, but he shoved the awareness that their paths were parting right out of his mind. Yusuf ran one hand through his hair, liking the cool bite of the wind in his shirt. He shook his head.

He could not think about Alifa yet.

He was not certain he would ever be able to think calmly about Alifa.

Yusuf squinted at the horizon and forced himself to recall his father's wizened features. He saw the tanned and wrinkled visage, the disconcertingly smooth bald pate and those green eyes, so unnaturally bright, and knew a vestige of relief.

Yusuf had never had to admit his failure to the old man's face. There was that small blessing in all of this.

He had not retrieved the book. Too late, Yusuf wondered what his father had wanted with the old alchemical text he had asked his son to find when Yusuf had insisted on leaving. Had that been just an excuse to force him to return one day? Or had his father dabbled in alchemy? Yusuf shook his head slowly. There was so much about his father that he hadn't known.

So much he hadn't wanted to know.

And now he never would.

Yusuf turned his back on the town and crested the rise. He shoved the thought of Kasilo out of his mind, desperately trying to blot out the image of Alifa's shock.

She was hurt, and Yusuf knew it, just as he knew that her hurt was fair under the circumstances. He ached with the awareness that she hoped he would render everything right. But he couldn't. A man had to stick by his values.

Yusuf could not kill, even to save Kasilo. Even to salvage Alifa's opinion of him. He simply couldn't do it.

His lips thinned as he climbed higher. He had been surprised that Alifa held her tongue, but he knew her better than to expect that she would have nothing to say to him if she should find the opportunity to speak. The woman knew her own mind, that was for certain. Yusuf smiled to himself at the thought. Undoubtedly she was just waiting for a more private moment to make her argument.

She never relinquished a fight easily. Yusuf's smile broadened as he hauled himself up to the next crest. He had never liked people who could not stand steadfast in a dispute. Alifa was a remarkable woman.

A wife is the ridgepole of the tent.

The old Berber saying filtered into Yusuf's mind and he smiled. Alifa would certainly hold some man's life together, probably with one hand tied behind her back. She would make somebody an excellent wife.

Why not him?

The treacherous thought halted Yusuf's steps and he glanced back down to the valley before he could stop himself. His blood quickened at the very thought of having Alifa as his partner and he could not honestly deny the idea's appeal.

Could this be love?

Yusuf recalled suddenly what he had felt for another woman and how he had thought that to be love. So long ago and far away. It seemed incredible in retrospect that he had wanted to marry Rebecca, that he would have given anything to wed her.

Had that been just a year ago?

Yusuf frowned and shoved his hands in his pockets as he surveyed the marching line of the mountains. They faded into a purple haze in the distance and the last rays of the sun burnished their peaks gold.

What a travesty that match would have been. Yusuf's feelings for Rebecca were nothing compared to this passion that Alifa ignited within him. Rebecca had never stirred the beast from its slumber. Rebecca had never made him furiously angry. Rebecca had never made him forget himself or lose his composure.

Rebecca had never made him laugh.

He could not have pursued the path of his thoughts further if he had been anywhere else in the world. This peak was where Yusuf had come as a boy to be alone. Here he had childishly thought himself to be at the top of the world and to have all its grandeur within view.

Fez was not even within sight. Yusuf smiled. The world had evidently been much smaller when he was a boy. It didn't matter that his childhood convictions had been untrue; the place still held an awesome power for him.

And offered a privacy he had sorely missed since his departure.

In the solitude of his old haunt, Yusuf dared to peek into the hidden corners of his heart. He knew he should not have been surprised by what he found, but the vigor of the emotion that poured forth at the opportunity astounded him.

Yusuf loved Alifa. With all his heart and soul.

He could not imagine Marizu wedding Alifa to another man, could not imagine her bearing another man's child, could not picture her laughing and flushing beneath another man's indulgent eye.

Yusuf could not conceive of himself being without her.

Did he really care about his reputation in Ceuta enough to deny himself the company of the one woman he wanted to have by his side? Yusuf was surprised to realize that he did not. Let them say what they would. If his peers' opinion of him could be so readily swayed to the negative, they were not people with whom Yusuf wished to associate.

And should any of them make the mistake of saying a word against his wife to his face, Yusuf would ensure that they regretted it.

Yes. He and Alifa would wed. It was blissfully simple. They would make sweet love for nights on end. The promise of it all was intoxicating and he took a deep breath of mountain air before he smiled. Yusuf knew he would be happy and, in this moment, was convinced that he could make Alifa happy. Life would be perfect. He would continue with his studies in Ceuta and she would bear babies with sunny little smiles.

Sunny little smiles like Kasilo's.

His euphoric bubble burst instantly.

If Yusuf could not bring himself to help Kasilo, he suspected he would be without Alifa. Not to assist the boy would be unforgivable in her eyes, he was certain.

But should he sacrifice another, Yusuf knew he would not be able to live with himself.

His stomach churned with indecision. There was no surmounting this obstacle, that he could see. And it stood squarely in the path between him and the goal he sought.

Yusuf turned away from the view with a sigh of frustration and faced the mountain again. He would climb, as he always had when he was troubled. Just a little higher was a spot that had been special to his father. Yusuf knew it well and suddenly it seemed imperative that he pay the old man his final respects there.

Anything rather than return to the village below.

Yusuf had not expected the dreaming.

It had to be a dream. After all, there was no other explanation for the disturbingly familiar silhouette of his father sitting opposite Yusuf in the night. The old man tapped his toe impatiently and Yusuf knew his awakening had been undetected.

Then that disconcerting jewel-green gaze swiveled suddenly to latch on Yusuf. His heart nearly stopped at their impact and the realization that he had misjudged the old man.

Again.

The two adversaries regarded each other silently as the night breathed around them.

Yusuf had reached his father's aerie after dark and had decided to sleep here. Now the moon was high and his father was inexplicably sitting before him.

The man was dead. This had to be a dream.

"Father?" Yusuf asked uncertainly. The familiar snort of derision was all the confirmation Yusuf needed.

It *was* his father. No doubt about it.

But how could this be?

"How typical of you to not believe what is right before your eyes," the old man remarked sarcastically. Yusuf refused to squirm beneath the knowledge that his father had read his thoughts. The old surge of annoyance rippled through Yusuf and he imagined that his father's lips twisted in a wry smile.

"Surely you remember my telling you about the dreaming time?" he demanded. He shoved back the hood of his *djellaba* and flicked his son a deprecating glance. Yusuf's lips thinned.

"Only shamans dream," he said flatly.

"I see." His father nodded skeptically. "You still don't believe that you're a shaman, then?"

"Of course not. I am a scholar," Yusuf commented crossly. "Surely we have had this argument enough times before."

"Ah. Surely." The old man stared at his feet for a moment, but Yusuf was not fooled. When he fired a lethal glance at his son, Yusuf had braced himself for it. "So, precisely why are you here? Surely there are no students or books in my humble clearing?"

Even though the question might have been easily anticipated, Yusuf found his words stumbling from his lips.

"I, uh, I wanted to say my farewells." Yusuf hated that his voice faltered and he saw by the gleam in the old man's eye that his uncertainty had not been missed.

"Ah. A noble gesture," his father allowed before his tone turned waspish. "What took you so long to get here?"

"What do you mean?" Yusuf sat up and ran one hand through his hair, refusing to give any sign of his agitation.

"It's been six moons since I summoned you," his father informed him frostily. "Unless Ceuta is much farther away than I recall, you should have been able to get here in one."

Yusuf shrugged. "I didn't know."

"Ha! Did you not?" his father scoffed before he leaned forward to peer at Yusuf intently. "What then made you decide to come home after all this time?"

"It was the book...."

"It was *not* the book," his father interjected dismissively. "You can tell yourself anything you want, but deep in your heart, you *know* why you came."

He paused for effect, with an ease born of practice, and Yusuf hated him for it.

"It was time," he finally intoned. Yusuf shrugged again, deliberately giving no sign of the shiver that had tripped down his spine.

"I don't understand. Time for what?"

"Of course you understand," his father said with a new edge of irritation in his tone. "You have always understood. You simply refuse to listen to your own knowledge." He shook his head and muttered to himself. "Always too stubborn for your own good. Just like your mother."

"I really don't know what you're talking about," Yusuf maintained tightly. The old man granted him a wary eye.

"Still going to pretend that you're a scholar?" he demanded archly. Yusuf straightened proudly.

"There is no pretending about it."

"Isn't there? When, then, are you going to stop pretending that you aren't what we both know you are? You have a legacy here, one that is yours for the taking, and one that you could fulfill honorably. Would you cast aside everything I have worked for?"

"I am *not* a shaman." Yusuf bit out the words, well familiar with this old argument. His father raised his brows high.

"No? Then what am I doing here?" he asked challengingly.

"This is a dream, no more than that."

The old man spat and shoved to his feet to pace, periodically jabbing his finger through the air at Yusuf to emphasize his points. "This is a *vision,* boy, and you had best learn to tell the difference. Maybe you're right, and you aren't much of a shaman after all. Don't give me that look. *You* summoned *me* here. How many times did I tell you that the dead can be summoned by the living who have the old gifts? How many times?"

"I don't have the old gifts," Yusuf insisted, even though he felt his resolve faltering.

"No?" his father demanded impatiently, and propped his hands on his hips. "Then how do you explain it, Yusuf? Tell me— I'd love to know."

As Yusuf watched, his father began to shift to his panther form. That he should do so deliberately was shocking, to say the least, but Yusuf could not look away. "I suppose everyone in Ceuta can do this," the old man whispered when his teeth were long. His eyes flashed, and the metamorphosis was complete.

A black panther paced back and forth before Yusuf, its very manner making him distrust its intent. It was unsettling, to say the least, that his father had deliberately chosen to shift. Yusuf could not imagine making such a choice, never mind having honed his control over the transition so perfectly.

He could not help but admire the feat in some secret part of his mind.

The creature bared his teeth in what seemed to Yusuf to be a mocking gesture. His eyes glinted knowingly, in a way that left no doubt as to his human identity. Then the great cat sat gracefully back on its haunches before languidly becoming his father again, the expression in those green eyes unchanged.

If Yusuf hadn't known better, he might have thought his father had deliberately prolonged the transition.

The entire event made him deeply uneasy.

"Last I heard, that wasn't a common ability," his father snapped. "Come along, Yusuf, let's have your explanation. What do you tell the women in town when you shift at that private moment? That all men are animals? Are they fool enough to believe you in Ceuta?"

Yusuf swallowed carefully, the telltale pricking in his palms telling him that the beast had been awakened by the presence of one of its own kind. He could smell more in the wind now than he had just moments past and his awareness of the town sleeping below was redoubled. He could almost taste the dual promise and threat of humans in close proximity. His blood quickened as he smelled a sheep wandering away from a shepherd far above them, the predator within more than ready to attack.

But this was not part of Yusuf's world. He would not permit the beast to change his life.

His father's eyes narrowed in an assessing way and he stepped purposefully toward Yusuf.

"You cannot deny what you are, Yusuf," he whispered ominously. "You are one of the ancient ones. The truth runs in your veins and the lineage is melded in your very flesh. You cannot purge it, no matter how hard you try."

"I will not grant the beast control of my life," Yusuf declared through gritted teeth. The old man's brows rose in surprise.

"The beast? What is this you say? Surely you don't think that this ability is a separate creature from you?"

"It is *not* a part of me," Yusuf retorted, not in the least reassured by his father's quick frown.

"But of course it is," he maintained calmly, his antagonism evaporating at his son's evident failure to understand something he found obvious. He hunkered down and frowned thoughtfully as he sought the words to explain. "The beast is your shadow, Yusuf. And if you do not look into your shadow, if you cannot embrace what you find in the dark corners within yourself and turn its power to your purpose, you can never achieve all of which you are capable."

The words made little sense—which was typical of his father's responses. All the same, they sent a chill through Yusuf that could not be easily dispelled.

Yusuf shivered and turned away. "I cannot embrace this," he said tightly. "To kill even in sacrifice is evil."

A silence followed his words and Yusuf feared for an instant that his judgment had driven his father away. He glanced up tentatively, relief rippling through him at the discovery that he was not alone. His father tilted his head and regarded him, a sardonic smile playing over his lips.

"Do you, or did you ever, think that I was evil?"

Yusuf half thought the old man wanted him to say yes.

The question hung for a long moment between them. Then Yusuf licked his lips carefully, knowing that he could not lie. He could not summon the words, though, even to voice the truth. He could only nod. His father's smile widened knowingly and he shook his head.

"You are wrong," he said dismissively and paced the width of the clearing again. "I merely embraced my shadow."

"What you did was wrong," Yusuf insisted.

"How many did you see me heal?" his father demanded. He spun to confront his son and flung his hands out wide. "How many families reunited? How many matches blessed? How many battles won or averted? Was *everything* wrong?"

He paused expectantly, but Yusuf said nothing and the old man made a sound of frustration under his breath. "There are no easy choices in this life, Yusuf, and a leader must always weigh the gain against the loss. And we all make mistakes. Are you telling me that I led our people poorly? Are you telling me that they are not better off than they were before my time? Are you telling me that *you* might have done better?"

"I do not want the task if it requires killing."

"Killing." The old man snorted and spat on the ground. "What is death, after all? As a scholar, you can probably tell me everything you read in some dusty tome."

His father leaned forward and snapped his fingers under Yusuf's nose. "Open your eyes, boy, and *look* for once in your life. Am I not here before you? How final do you think this business truly is?"

He glared at Yusuf, then cleared his throat and began to speak in a more moderate tone. "Life does not disappear, Yusuf—it ebbs and flows, waxes and wanes. Nor is there more of it to mine or fish or retrieve in some other way. There is only so much of the essence of life to be spread between all of us. What goes to one must come from another. If one's need is to be fulfilled, then another must give. There is no other way." He stepped closer and glowered at his son, who was struggling with his enigmatic statements.

"I made my choice," he asserted boldly. "I looked my shadow in the eye and saw that its power could be used for good. I wielded that power as best I was able, and you have no place judging my decision."

"But I have the right to not follow suit," Yusuf maintained stiffly. His father's eyes widened in feigned surprise.

"Who asked you to follow suit?" he asked silkily. "I only expected you to embrace the fullness of what you are. I would expect that of any child, not just my own." He tilted his head again and folded his arms across his chest. "But then, maybe you've become more of a coward than I remember."

That his father should insult him after such a lecture was beyond acceptable.

"I am not a coward!" Yusuf snapped. His father smirked and Yusuf hurled himself in the old man's direction in frustration. He aimed to snatch the old man's *djellaba* and give him a shake, but his hands closed on nothing but dirt and stones.

His father was gone!

Yusuf panicked. There was so much that he still didn't understand. He wasn't ready to be left alone.

"Father!" Yusuf shouted in frustration, not caring that the sound bounced back from the face of the mountain. He stood up and peered into the darkness pressing in on every side, but to no avail.

"Father!"

There was no response. He was gone. Yusuf suddenly felt alone and confused, uncertain what to make of his father's words and convinced that only the old man could make his way clear.

"I summoned you before and I will summon you again!" Yusuf declared with false bravado.

But how could he repeat the feat without knowing how it had been done?

Evidently his father came to much the same conclusion, for the cackle of the old man's laughter carried eerily to Yusuf's ears.

Chapter Fifteen

"Is Yusuf here?"

Marizu glanced up in surprise at Sarat's question and turned to Alifa in confusion. "I don't believe so," she said. Alifa shook her head and they both looked back to the concerned woman on the threshold. Sarat frowned.

"Well, isn't that strange..." she mused.

Yusuf was missing?

"When did you see him last?" Alifa risked the question, hoping no one would suspect her of undue interest.

Sarat shrugged. "He left after dinner last night." She squinted at the morning sun and chewed her lip. "I hope nothing has happened to him," she mused worriedly.

"Do you know where he went?" Marizu asked practically. Sarat shook her head, but Marizu simply smiled. "Well then, there is nothing that can be done. Don't worry, Sarat. Yusuf is man enough to look after himself."

She bent over her sewing again with a confidence Alifa was far from feeling. Sarat summoned a smile and bustled away, leaving Alifa to scan the mountains framed by the doorway in concern.

Alifa had known he would leave and had not really expected an emotional leave-taking. She had thought that Yusuf would at least say farewell, though, and the realization that he cared so little did nothing to improve her spirits.

He was gone. She was alone. And Marizu was making a list from which Alifa would be compelled to choose a mate.

It seemed that her life would go on, without Yusuf.

On the night that the full moon rose, Yusuf summoned the nerve to face his task.

He wasn't certain how many days he had spent prowling around his father's retreat. His belly had been empty long enough that he had grown accustomed to the hollow sensation and he had lost track of how many times he had fetched water from the quick, leaping stream.

His father hadn't returned, although Yusuf thought he had tried every possible way of summoning him.

Every way except shapeshifting.

It was becoming clear to him that that might be the only alternative his father would acknowledge. Curse the old man for his perceptiveness.

Yusuf found himself watching the yellow orb of the moon launch itself from the horizon. The prickling began in his palms and Yusuf instinctively bit down on the urge.

He could not do this thing. Not even for Kasilo.

Not even for Alifa.

He could not willingly surrender to the beast. His father's words reverberated in his mind, though some of his assertions made no more sense than they had before. How could he become a shaman without necessarily following his father's way?

Yusuf acknowledged the changing in his palms with a frisson of dread. He fought against the shift, knowing that he would lose this battle in the end. He was not strong enough, after these days in the sun and wind, to stave off the attack.

The beast was coming. Whether Yusuf was ready or not.

But what about the other? Was it possible that there was more than one way to be a shaman? Had his father's way come out of his own personality?

Had it come from the old man's shadow?

Yusuf could not imagine, but then, nothing else made any more sense. What had his father meant about life passing from one to another?

Did it necessarily have to pass by sacrifice?

An unexpected thought filled Yusuf's mind with an abruptness that took his breath away. His father had mentioned giving and receiving. Was it possible that he could use some of his own strength to restore a balance?

Yusuf straightened in his excitement. Could he give enough of himself, enough of the share of life that coursed within him, to heal Kasilo?

He didn't know. Yusuf wondered what the consequences would be and didn't know that, either.

Surprisingly, he did not care. The solution felt right to him. It was an option that came from within him, not from anyone else, and he instinctively trusted his own inner voice.

This Yusuf could do. In this way, he could help Kasilo. In this way, he could earn Alifa's respect. In this way, he could taste the fullness of the legacy his father had granted him.

This was the only way that he could break the stalemate in his life. If the price was high, so be it. He had to make some choice and move forward. He could not continue to live the way he was now, constantly fearing the outbursts of the beast. Nor could he embrace the traditions of his father. Yusuf was beginning to suspect that he would not be able to live peacefully in Ceuta again, now that the beast within him was awakened. Nor could he stay here without taking up his legacy.

This might offer a uniquely personal alternative.

Yusuf took a deep breath as the moon broke free of the horizon and began to sail into the indigo sky. He could try to heal Kasilo and he fully intended to do so, but there was something he needed to do first. Yusuf suspected he would need all of his strength to succeed at this task and there was only one way to harness it all. His father had given him the necessary clue.

Yusuf had to peer into the dark corners of his soul and acquaint himself with his shadow, as terrifying as the very idea might be.

He stared into the moon for a long moment, then deliberately unclenched his hands.

It was time.

Yusuf took a breath, closed his eyes, and willfully shapeshifted for the first time in his life.

The men returned three days after Alifa's arrival in the village. They came down out of the mountains at dusk in the midst of hundreds of well-fed goats. The goats' bleating filled the evening stillness and was the first indication of their arrival. Women dropped their needlework and laid aside their kitchen tasks to run out into the fading light.

Alifa followed suit, dreading her first glimpse of the men, yet a little curious about the men who matched the names on Marizu's list. The men were almost interchangeable in this light, their skin was tanned almost black, their smiles were dazzlingly white in contrast as they greeted and were greeted by their families. Alifa felt very much outside the celebration, though she willingly lent a hand to the preparations.

There was laughter and food and stories to tell. Fires were kindled, jokes were shared, the height of growing children was acknowledged and admired. Alifa hung on the periphery with Tabeta, both sisters flushing when they were introduced and dozens of curious newcomers glanced them over.

It was easy to forget the legacy of her past in this friendly setting, but Alifa did not dare let herself do so. She avoided the gazes of the few men who tried to catch her eye, knowing without doubt that they must be single. Alifa had no doubt that her past, and the damning clue that would reveal it, would earn retribution from the most tolerant of men.

She was not ready to hasten toward that fate. Let them think her shy.

Mercifully, the welcome did not endure long into the night. It was time for the harvest, after all. The wheat was ripe and that was why the men had come home.

To avoid the heat of late summer, the entire village set to work as soon as it was light. The men wielded the scythes, the women gathered the sheaves, the children and the elderly picked the gleanings. It was an all-consuming and a backbreaking task, but one that would ensure the survival of them all through the cold winter ahead.

The rhythm of the work came back to Alifa with surprising speed. She had been deemed old enough to sheave for two summers before her parents moved to Ceuta, so the task was familiar, if half forgotten. Her shoulders ached by the end of the first day, but she forced herself to continue.

It was by her labor alone that she earned the right to stay in Marizu's home, let alone within the village. If Alifa was useful, she would not be cast out, even if she did not wed quickly. And this was clean work, a task that filled her with a rare pride of accomplishment when they stacked the sheaves in the village at the end of the day.

It had, after all, been a long time since she had been proud of what she had wrought.

"Water?" A masculine voice close by her side made Alifa jump. Her gaze darted to the man's friendly face and he smiled engagingly.

He was the one who had been watching her the previous night. Alifa thought his name was Misra, but could not be sure.

"Thank you." She accepted the tin dipper of water, not making an issue of the way he ensured their fingers brushed, and sipped its coolness gratefully.

Alifa eyed him through her lashes and tried to consider his assets, knowing Marizu would chide her if she did not. He was young enough and tall enough and apparently well mannered enough, but there was something lacking.

He was not Yusuf. And he never would be.

Quite simply, Alifa could not even imagine being with anyone other than Yusuf. She supposed she should put the past where it belonged, but she could not summon the will to do so.

He winked when she handed him back the dipper and Alifa dropped her gaze demurely.

"Would you—" he began, but Alifa hurriedly interrupted him. She could not bear to hear what he might say. Alifa couldn't afford to decline if he made an invitation, but she knew she wouldn't be able to bring herself to accept any invitation with her heart and mind so filled with Yusuf.

"Excuse me, but my brother needs me," she said all in a rush. Fearing he would say something else, she thanked him politely again and stepped hastily away.

It was foolish to be so nervous, but Alifa was not ready by any means to play this courting game. She pretended that she didn't know Misra was watching after her as she hurried away. Prompted by some nameless impulse, Alifa glanced up just before she stepped into the house and her footsteps faltered.

The sight of Yusuf striding into the village did nothing to reassure her about her resolve to forget him.

Alifa stopped, certain she was imagining things. But no, it was Yusuf, more gaunt but definitely as determined as ever. Her pulse began to pound in her ears and it seemed he must have heard the sound. His gaze flicked to hers and she felt suddenly alive beneath his regard. Her heart rolled over lazily as he perused her, and Alifa could not keep herself from smiling like an idiot.

Yusuf was back. He had not simply left her, after all.

It was ridiculous to be so pleased, but she could not check her response. The man cared nothing for her, after all. He might only have returned to say his farewells.

But he had come back. And she at least had this bittersweet and unexpected opportunity to see him again. She gazed back at him, lost in another of those endless moments that seemed to haunt her when Yusuf was in her presence.

Never could she have imagined she might be so relieved to see another. Maybe there was some way to convince him that they might make a future together. Maybe it would not be so bad to go back to Ceuta....

But no. Alifa chastised herself silently. Yusuf would laugh if he ever guessed the foolish direction of her thoughts.

"Yusuf!" cried Sarat from another doorway. He looked away and Alifa felt suddenly bereft.

"I need all your help," Yusuf declared, and he glanced over the slowly assembling tribe.

He stood tall, fairly exuding that mysterious presence that Alifa's mother had called *baraka,* and everyone halted what they were doing to listen to his words.

Baraka could not be earned or bought, Alifa's mother had said, but commanded the attention of all. Alifa watched as everyone waited silently for Yusuf's next words and knew exactly what her mother had meant.

"I need your help," Yusuf said once more. "Tonight, under the moon, in the old ritual spot."

"But it is the harvest," Sarat protested. "We need our sleep."

"No," Yusuf said slowly. He turned to face Alifa again and her mouth went dry when the corner of his mouth tipped in a wry smile. "Kasilo needs us more," he said.

Alifa gasped and her hands flew to her mouth.

No. It couldn't be true. She stared incredulously at Yusuf, but when he made a slight nod of reassurance, she could not restrain herself any longer. It was true! Alifa ran across the space and threw her arms enthusiastically around Yusuf's neck.

"You're going to do it!" she whispered in delight. He caught her around the waist with one strong arm and Alifa was suddenly aware of the intimacy of their embrace.

As well as the interested scrutiny of the entire town. She tried to pull back, but Yusuf was not about to release her.

If anything, his grip tightened around her and Alifa felt herself flush scarlet.

Yusuf sobered as he looked down at her and he brushed the hair back from her cheek, ignoring their audience. "You were right," he said with a quietude that made her heart skip. "I have to at least try."

The moon was hidden behind a smooth blanket of clouds that had been turned an even pearly gray by its light. All of the village assembled silently in the old clearing outside the stretch of the village's shadows as Yusuf paced and collected his thoughts.

He felt vivaciously alive as he never had before. His senses were honed to a fever pitch, his sense of smell particularly heightened. This was not the least of the changes since he had acknowledged the beast as a part of himself. Yusuf knew things with uncanny certainty that he had no business knowing and though he could not discern the source of the information, it did not strike him as alien. It simply was part of him.

His father had been right. Acknowledging his shadow had shown him the fullness of what he could be.

Yusuf was not destined to be a scholar in Ceuta and he knew that now. This was his fate, this was his place.

But first, he had to prove that he deserved his father's legacy.

He heard them all arriving and listened to their footsteps, waiting for the sound of the one he knew well. The sound of Alifa's tread brought a smile to his lips. Yusuf knew she carried Kasilo and that Tabeta trailed by her side before he even turned around. He could see her in his mind's eye, modestly veiled and barefoot in the manner that so fired his blood.

He had been wrong to condemn her when they first met. With a perceptiveness born of his newly accepted abilities, Yusuf saw that Alifa's harsh manner was purely defensive. She had been tested more times than was reasonable and though she had faced each challenge undaunted, the price to the world had been the fortification of her own defenses.

The soft yet steadfast woman he had glimpsed so many times, the woman who enchanted him with her laughter, was the real Alifa. This was the woman he would take to his side. This was the woman who would stand strong beside him, ready to face any challenge that crossed their path.

For Yusuf had no doubt that there would be challenges. His gifts would take their own toll and there would always be those who did not understand. He knew now, with the clarity of hindsight, that it had been fear of losing precisely the kind of woman he had sought that prompted those first scratches on her back. They had been unintentional, all the same.

Once he was assured that she would not run, there would be no chance of that happening again. In fact, he doubted he even needed that much. Had he not immediately heeded her appeal to spare Jaraw?

It was reassuring to know that such a clear-thinking woman had captured his heart and held him in thrall.

He observed that time without him had given her the chance to become nervous. Yusuf met Alifa's gaze as she cautiously closed the distance between them. Even the rustling of the others ceased as they watched, but Yusuf had eyes for no one else.

Yusuf could not manage any sweet confession yet, not until he had succeeded at this task, but he hoped she could guess his thoughts.

"I'll take him," he offered, hearing the surety in his own voice and hoping it would reassure her. Alifa glanced away, then back to him, her trepidation a tangible force.

"What will happen?" she asked urgently, her fathomless eyes readily communicating all her fears.

"I don't know," Yusuf confessed mildly. It didn't matter. They had to try. He spared a smile for the boy now on his hip, but Kasilo remained uncharacteristically silent. "Perhaps we should find out," Yusuf suggested. Alifa looked as though she might protest that, but Yusuf did not give her the chance.

He raised his voice in the ancient cry that was branded into the very fiber of his being. He felt Kasilo's pulse jump and spared the boy an encouraging smile. Kasilo smiled back and slipped his hands trustingly around Yusuf's neck.

Alifa hesitated for a long moment. The men from the tribe quickly stepped into a circle and she stepped away to find her place. The men's hands joined and they began to dance. Yusuf gave Kasilo a tight hug before placing the boy beside the huge pile of gathered brush and finding his own place within the circle.

The rhythm of the dance rolled through Yusuf and he closed his eyes as he let it possess him. His pulse matched the beat and he set the pace. The men's footsteps twined, their feet pounded, the pace of the dance built at Yusuf's behest. He felt the sweat bead on the back of his neck and on his brow, the late-summer heat still clinging to the night air.

His conviction of the rightness of this path increased with every step.

The path of dancers wound a sinuous circle around the brush and the boy. When the moment was precisely right, Yusuf began to sing the old hymn. Kasilo watched the proceedings, wide-eyed, and Yusuf could taste Alifa's trepidation. He resolutely ignored both and focused on the task before him. This would take all that he had and possibly more.

He refused to question whether he could give enough to make a difference.

The ground vibrated, the men's voices rose high. Yusuf's pulse accelerated. He felt the tingle launch over his skin, felt that part of his shadow awaken from its slumber in the depths and take notice of the proceedings. He was dimly aware of the women falling into place behind the men, the swirl of their colored skirts staining his peripheral vision as they joined the dance.

The villagers' cry became louder, echoing in the mountains. The ground pulsed. Yusuf felt the shift begin. He broke from the circle, dancing the intricate steps and singing all the way back to the center. He struck a flint with ceremonial flair, well aware that every eye was fixed upon him. He shouted in the old tongue and his cry was echoed by all as he cast the flame into the tinder.

The dry brush ignited and the blaze flared skyward with satisfying drama. Kasilo gasped and Yusuf spun, savoring the swing of his red cloak as it swirled out behind him. His palms prickled, his flesh tingled, and he welcomed the change. Yusuf embraced the power flowing through him with delight.

He stepped back into the circle and grasped the right hand of the man beside him with his own left hand. The man's pulse leapt to match Yusuf's and Yusuf stared at their entwined hands with amazement. A power rolled through him that was not his alone and his gaze rose to meet that of his neighbor in astonishment. The man stared back at Yusuf and Yusuf knew he did not imagine that their powers were pulsing together.

Maybe he did not have to give to Kasilo alone. On impulse, Yusuf interlaced his neighbor's fingers with his own so that their palms were fixed flat together. He called to the life within that man and felt it flow obediently into him at the summons.

The strength he had for Kasilo had just been doubled. It was intoxicating and Yusuf swayed momentarily on his feet. The man beside him gasped aloud before he hastily grasped the hand of his neighbor in the same manner.

Yusuf smiled broadly at the resultant surge and struggled not to swoon.

He felt taller, stronger, bolder. He felt that his skin would burst with his strength. He felt radiant, as he never had before.

And it was all for Kasilo.

Hands were clasped without breaking the pace of the dance. Yusuf drew from the strength of all, calling to the force until he was certain the air would crackle around him. He felt the surprise of each in turn as they joined their hands, but they did not pull away. Yusuf sensed the women following suit in a circle behind.

Yusuf needed their strength, too, he realized in an instant. The men's circle was rapidly closing and the man on Yusuf's right turned and offered his left hand to Yusuf.

Yusuf shook his head.

The women danced in the opposite direction, all but their eyes and feet covered from view. The women were indistinguishable from each other behind their veils of red, but Yusuf did not need to see to find what, or who, he sought. Yusuf knew suddenly that Alifa was approaching, realizing in the same moment precisely what he needed.

It was right.

He spun on his heel and snatched at Alifa's wrist as she passed behind him. She gasped but Yusuf pulled her close. He tore his left hand from the grip of the man next to him and enfolded Alifa's palm in his own instead. The heat that kindled between their hands clearly startled her and he smiled reassuringly at her.

The pieces had fallen into place. Yusuf had a strong sense that he would be successful this night.

But the chain was broken. He needed the assistance of all. He indicated to Alifa that she should keep her grip on the woman beside her. With his free hand, Yusuf clasped together the hands of the man who had been to his left and the woman who had been to Alifa's right. Their hands were held high over Alifa's head and Yusuf closed his eyes at the power flowing through him. It was enough to make him dizzy.

As the villagers were linked in one large chain, the resultant surge made Yusuf inhale sharply. He tugged Alifa's hand as he began to dance and the line of women passed under the arms of the man and woman whose grip was newly linked.

The rhythm of the dance was quickly asserted again. The circle redefined itself, the line of women slipping inside the circle of men like a contortionist snake, the last woman spinning on her heel to complete the twist. They composed a winding, fluid spiral, with Yusuf at the head, Kasilo and the flame at the center. Yusuf danced, Alifa's hand trapped within his. He traced a path, winding the dancers closer and closer to the flame. He urged their passion to a fever pitch.

Their strength rolled through him, fueling the prickling and the tingling. His very skin vibrated as it never had before. Yusuf fixed his gaze on Kasilo and began to chant a blessing that he composed on the spot.

It felt right. It was right.

It was time.

He reached down and grasped Kasilo's left hand with his right. Yusuf forced their palms flat together and the dancers stamped their feet into the ground as they stood in place and repeated his chant. The words rocked them all, like a call to war, and the smell of perspiration was thick in the night air.

The chant became an incantation that swirled around them, surrounded them, protected them and entreated the powers that be to intervene. The people demanded in one overwhelming but mute voice that Kasilo be healed. The people gave of themselves to see the deed accomplished. The flames from the bonfire leapt high as their entreaty intensified and blazed a path to the very stars.

Yusuf drew himself up taller beneath the mighty pulse of their collective strength, and summoned the change. He called to it, he commanded it, he instructed it, as he never had before. It slipped over him, folding him within its dark embrace, and Yusuf laughed aloud.

He felt himself shimmer on the threshold between forms, but he was not afraid. He looked at Kasilo. The boy was surrounded by an unearthly golden glow that Yusuf knew they had drawn together and he tasted success.

Could anyone else see the halo of light? It didn't matter. Yusuf knew. He prayed for the boy's healing, he recited his blessing over and over again. The life of all of them flexed its strength within him, it roared and grew to flood him so that he was almost overwhelmed. It waxed higher than Yusuf could ever have hoped, and then abruptly waned. Kasilo gasped. The villagers sighed and several moaned.

And Yusuf felt Alifa's fingers quiver within his grip before he was aware of nothing at all.

Alifa was not the first to awaken, nor was she the last.

The fire had burned down to embers and there was a thickness in her mouth that could not be readily identified. She was tired beyond belief and had to struggle to prop herself up on her elbows.

As far as she could see, the huddled shapes of sleeping villagers filled her vision. They were dark shadows against the darker shadows of the night and they all dozed as peacefully as children under the cloudy night sky.

What had happened? Alifa scanned the sleeping forms of her neighbors in amazement. They were scattered in roughly the same circle formation in which they had danced. Some rubbed their eyes as she did, others snored contentedly in the silence of the night. She could remember little after Yusuf had taken her hand, the dancing and the pounding merging together into one event. She could remember the euphoria and the gleam of Yusuf's eyes better than the chronology of what had occurred.

Yusuf. Alifa looked beside her and her heart drooped with disappointment.

Yusuf was gone.

She swallowed and looked beyond the vacancy to Kasilo. No more did he dance on his toes and Alifa wondered if she had imagined that sight.

But he appeared to be fine. He slept as peacefully as an angel, his cheek cradled in his hand. Alifa shoved to her feet and picked up her brother. As she gathered him close in her relief, the sound of his breathing surprised her. She pulled back to look at him, then listened again.

It was clearer than it had been in months. There was no telltale echo of the phlegm that had plagued him lately. Alifa caught her own breath as she dared to wonder—could Yusuf truly have healed him?

But what had happened to Yusuf?

She knew she had been able to feel his hand right to the end, but she had not been able to see him at all. Just an otherworldly shimmer had replaced him by her side. Alifa's heart skipped a beat at the inevitable thought.

Had he made the sacrifice for Kasilo himself? Was that why he had refused to tell her what would happen? Had Yusuf planned this?

Alifa scanned the purple mountains surrounding the little plateau where the village rested, but if they knew the answer, they had no intention of sharing it with her. Stony facades greeted her on every side.

Would she ever know the truth? Or was Yusuf simply gone forever?

Alifa frowned and roused Tabeta, ushering her sleepy sister back to Marizu's home. Both children needed their sleep, as did Alifa, for tomorrow was destined to be another busy day. She had best think about those things she could understand.

Yusuf was gone. Maybe for good this time.

Maybe it was better this way, Alifa told herself as she lay in her own bed sometime later and stared at the ceiling with dry eyes. She would not cry. Maybe it was better to be left wondering than to know for certain that Yusuf had abandoned her. Maybe it was better not to know his fate than to know that he had chosen Ceuta and respectability over whatever she could offer him.

Maybe that had been Yusuf's plan.

Maybe in time she would come to believe that he was right. Alifa clenched her fists and bit her lip, heavy tears squeezing from her eyes as she closed her eyes tightly against the glimmer of the dawn.

She would not cry. She had been alone before.

The snow was creeping down the sides of the mountains by the time Yusuf found what he sought.

He had needed time to think and he had had plenty of it these past few months of tracking and making whispered inquiries. Yusuf didn't like what he heard, but still he followed the trail, determined to lay one more ghost to rest before returning to Alifa.

Alifa. The woman haunted Yusuf day and night, but she could not be his yet. He could not ask her to share his fate until he knew whether he was a success. He could not claim to be a shaman until he knew that his solution had worked.

Otherwise he had no place in the hills. And the hills were where Alifa wanted to be.

The hills were where they both wanted to be. But if Yusuf could not hold up his head and follow his legacy with dignity, then he would return to Ceuta alone.

There were days when he found it amusing that he had once thought returning home to be an admission of failure, when in fact living as a scholar in Ceuta would be the failure of his life. There were other days when nothing about the situation was amusing in the least.

Kasilo's recovery held the key. And no matter what magic Yusuf had wrought, a healing took time. Time that he was reluctant to grant, but he had no choice.

In the moment of the healing, Yusuf had been certain that they could all give a little and heal the boy, rather than one unfortunate giving all. His solution was different from his father's, but on that fateful night, Yusuf had been convinced that it was just as viable.

But as the winter wind forced its icy fingers down his neck and the snow crept into his boots, Yusuf was not as sure as he would have liked to be.

Only time would tell.

There was business to be settled, at any rate. Tales he had heard of bandits on the road to Sijilmassa and Yusuf's conclusion was not imaginative in the least. The one he sought could certainly have learned that the salt from the north on the caravan they had seen was traded for gold in the south. The great "silent trade" was no secret in these parts, where the wind rose with sand in its teeth.

When Yusuf drew farther south and heard about the nine-fingered bandit, he knew he was coming close to what he sought. That this bandit had a reputation for viciousness came as no surprise.

Yusuf crouched in the shadows of the rocks and watched a caravan settle in for the night beside the road below. Yusuf had heard rumors and he waited, more than half suspecting what he would see.

He was not disappointed.

Shadows parted from the hills when the last lamp was extinguished and the camp below had clearly settled to sleep. They moved noiselessly toward their unsuspecting victims, but Yusuf could readily see them. His eyes narrowed, he scanned each figure in turn until he identified the one he sought.

There.

If nothing else, the boy was eating well enough. Alifa would be pleased to hear that much of her brother's fate. The rest of the tale was another matter, though. Outrage flooded through Yusuf as he recognized a much-abused pair of green leather boots.

Thief! Any inclination Yusuf might have had to see the boy healthy and leave unnoticed died in that moment.

He stalked his prey on silent feet, almost smiling in anticipation of the surprise he would spring. Cursed brat. Trust him to have fallen in with this disreputable lot. He deserved the shock of his young life. Oblivious of Yusuf's presence, Jaraw crouched low behind a rock and assessed the distance to the camp. The bandits waited for their leader's signal to attack and there was a moment of breathless anticipation.

It was simply too perfect.

Cape flaring out behind him, Yusuf pounced.

One of the other thieves turned in that moment. He made a strangled cry as he pointed at Yusuf. Jaraw spun and his eyes widened with horror before recognition flooded their dark depths.

"You!" he shouted. Someone tripped over a pot in the camp below and there was an outcry of voices. Jaraw hauled a dagger from his belt with lightning speed, but he wasn't quick enough.

Yusuf was already on top of him. They rolled down the side of the hill, battling over the blade, until Yusuf braced his leg against the rocks and brought them to an ungraceful halt. The bandit leader swore vehemently as the men camped below bellowed to each other and unsheathed their blades. Vaguely Yusuf was aware that the attack on the camp had been foiled and he savored the knowledge that he had contributed to the interruption.

Camels groaned and Jaraw's dagger flashed golden in the moonlight. Yusuf snatched at the boy's wrists and pinned them both to the ground. He leaned on the right wrist hard and Jaraw muttered an expletive as he unwillingly released his grip on the hilt.

The dagger rolled out of reach and glinted innocently. The two of them stared at it for a long moment before their eyes met.

Suddenly Jaraw bared his teeth and Yusuf immediately saw the path of his thoughts.

"Don't even think it," he growled. Jaraw hesitated and met his attacker's gaze suspiciously. He appeared to reconsider his intention, even as he eyed the blade wistfully.

"What do you want?" he demanded with no small measure of hostility. He wriggled his wrists, but Yusuf granted him no respite.

"My boots," he asserted.

Jaraw lifted his chin proudly. "They're my boots now," he said archly. Yusuf let the fullness of his power filter into his eyes as he smiled a dangerous smile.

"Maybe we should finish our earlier business," he suggested silkily.

Jaraw's eyes widened slightly and his voice wavered slightly, despite his bold words. "What do you want from me?" he demanded.

"We need to talk," Yusuf said calmly. Jaraw nodded, more hastily than he probably would have liked to.

"You can have the boots back."

"I know," Yusuf agreed easily. "And I'll have something else from you, as well." He savored the flash of fear in the boy's eyes. Jaraw deserved no less for worrying Alifa so, though Yusuf suspected he would be surprised to learn what Yusuf wanted of him.

Chapter Sixteen

Alifa was sowing wheat when Kasilo ran to tell her that she had a visitor.

She sighed and thanked her brother as she stretched her back. He darted away to play with his friends and Alifa could not help but smile.

He was a different boy this spring. No, she corrected herself silently. He was the playful and busy boy he had been once before.

She wished for the hundredth time that Yusuf could see what he had wrought.

Of course, thinking of Yusuf only reminded Alifa of the almost certain identity of her visitor. Another man come courting, no doubt. And she was running out of excuses.

Alifa supposed she had been fortunate in avoiding marriage thus far. Having arrived so late in the season, she had found it easy to defer suitors before the onset of the cold in September, for Berbers preferred to wed in the fall. That way, the new couple had the winter to grow acquainted with each other before the man went out to pasture in the spring.

But now spring had come again and Alifa knew she would not escape so easily this year. Marizu had already made more than one comment.

She supposed a break from the sowing would be welcome, at least.

* * *

The man awaiting her wore a sweeping red cloak that made Alifa catch her breath. Of course, it could not be. She was seeing similarities where there were none. Her mind was playing tricks on her.

His back was turned to her as he chatted with Marizu and she could not hear his voice. The sight of his tall leather boots, so like the ones Yusuf had worn, immediately shattered any foolish illusions.

Jaraw had destroyed those boots. They were gone. And this man's head was bare. Yusuf always wore his turban. This man's dark hair was ruffled by the gentle spring wind, but Alifa refused to let herself see any further likeness.

She had to put the past behind her.

After all, all Berber men had dark hair. All Berber men were tall and straight. All Berber men were broad of shoulder and lean of hip.

He turned and Alifa's heart stopped.

Not all Berber men had eyes of arresting green.

Alifa had no idea what to say. Shock stole the words from her mouth and left her gaping like an idiot. She simply stood and stared. Yusuf—curse him for his composure—smiled. Marizu disappeared into the house.

"Hello, Alifa," Yusuf said finally. He shoved his hands into his pockets and something about the way he did so made Alifa wonder if he was truly as sure of himself as he appeared.

The thought gave her confidence and unhinged her tongue.

"I thought you were gone," she accused airily. Yusuf cocked a brow at her tone.

"Just for a while," he said silkily. "I had something to do."

Alifa propped her hands on her hips and wished she hadn't come straight from the fields. It would have helped her confidence to be cool and collected, not dirty, with a fine patina of perspiration over her skin. She glared at Yusuf as though that fact were exclusively his fault.

"And now you're back," she snapped. "Forget something?"

Yusuf smiled. "As a matter of fact, I did."

"What?" Alifa demanded, knowing she should let the matter be, but unable to do so.

"Actually," Yusuf mused thoughtfully, "it's more a case of something I couldn't forget."

Alifa sighed with exasperation and shoved her hair back from her damp brow. "Did you really come here to play word games?"

"No," he said crisply, but Alifa knew better than to trust that knowing gleam in his eye.

"Did you come to see Kasilo?" she challenged.

"Not specifically," Yusuf admitted. "But he looks well."

"He's much better, thanks to you," Alifa admitted grudgingly. How did this man manage to confuse her emotions so? Yusuf folded his arms across his chest and watched her carefully.

"Good," he said and they eyed each other for what felt like an eternity. "Aren't you going to ask me what, or who, I couldn't forget?" he finally prompted in a low voice that fed her suspicions. There was something about Yusuf's manner that made Alifa think he was playing a trick on her and she was in no mood for such jests.

"All right," she agreed impatiently. "What did you forget?"

"Who," Yusuf corrected. He waited for Alifa to make the connection and her heart skipped a beat. She stared at him, but refused to jump to conclusions.

"Aren't you going to tell me?" she demanded.

"Don't you know?" Yusuf asked smoothly.

Curse the man! "Contrary to whatever you may believe, I don't have time for these childish games," she snapped and spun on her heel to leave.

Alifa should have known she wouldn't get far. She heard Yusuf's firm tread just an instant before he swept her off her feet. She struggled against the arm locked around her waist, but he held her tightly against him. His breath when he spoke feathered across her ear and made her shiver.

"I came back for you and you know it," he whispered. Alifa spared him a venomous glance.

"No whores wherever you were?" she snapped. Yusuf set her on her feet and turned her resolutely to face him, his hands locking around her waist so that she could not escape. Alifa set her lips stubbornly and refused to look up.

"I'm not looking for a whore," Yusuf insisted quietly. "I'm looking for a wife."

Alifa caught her breath and hoped he hadn't heard the telltale sound. Didn't he know he was dangling the promise of everything she wanted before her? She would not grasp at it just to watch him snatch it away. The temptation of his words hung before Alifa, but she refused to reach for the promise.

Hadn't Yusuf made his feelings about her choice more than clear in the past?

Was he going to make her watch him take another to wife? How would she bear it?

"Then you're in the wrong place," she retorted breathlessly.

Yusuf made a growl of frustration in the back of his throat that was far from the response Alifa had expected. One of his hands slipped to the back of her neck and he tipped her head up determinedly. Before Alifa could protest, his lips had closed over hers with relentless resolve.

Not that she would have protested. Or could have.

Alifa had longed for exactly this for too long. She closed her eyes at the heady taste of Yusuf and sagged against him. The kiss was all the more sweet for Alifa's certainty that she would never experience it again, never mind her fear that this would be the last. He was taking another to his side and this was nothing but a sweet farewell. Alifa was ashamed of herself for being so ready to take Yusuf's leavings, but she strained against him nonetheless.

How could she have forgotten how wonderful his kiss could be? Her memories did not do the taste of him justice. Yusuf lifted his head all too soon and regarded her bemusedly.

"Will you marry me, Alifa?" he whispered. Alifa almost agreed before she caught herself.

Yusuf couldn't mean it. And even if he did, she couldn't just accept. There were so many issues left between them that her choice could not be that easily made. Certainly she could not make such a decision purely on the basis of an intoxicating kiss. She licked her lips and frowned as she struggled to collect her errant thoughts.

This time she would make a good choice.

"I thought you were gone," she murmured.

"I'm sorry," Yusuf said quickly and Alifa dared to raise her gaze to his. His expression was heart-wrenchingly sincere. "I had no idea it would take so long, but he was hard to find."

Alifa's heart skipped a beat at the reference. Surely he didn't mean what she thought he did? "Who?" she managed to ask, although her voice was no more than a croak.

"Jaraw," Yusuf said firmly. He smiled down at her astonishment and traced the line of her chin with one fingertip. "I couldn't let you worry about him," he added in a murmur that could only be affectionate.

Alifa gasped and would have asked about her brother's welfare, but Yusuf planted one thumb across her lips. "He's fine. And after some discussion, he granted me permission to ask for your hand."

"What?" Alifa demanded in outrage. How dare these two scheme over her future behind her back! Yusuf's eyes twinkled at her response.

"I had to ask your family," he explained mildly.

He had asked Jaraw about marrying her before he had asked her? Alifa regarded Yusuf in mingled shock and indignation. "But not me?" she demanded haughtily.

"I did ask you," Yusuf countered reasonably. "But you haven't answered yet."

Alifa was not by any means ready to face that question yet. She deliberately changed the subject, even though she felt the transition was hopelessly clumsy. "Where *is* Jaraw?" she asked, immediately distrusting the way Yusuf's expression changed. "What is he doing? Are you certain he is fine? And when can I see him?"

"I promised him that I wouldn't tell you," Yusuf said carefully.

"You *what?*" Alifa said angrily. "How could you do such a thing? Of course, I want to see him—" That thumb landed on her lips again and Alifa reluctantly met Yusuf's concerned gaze.

"He's fine," he said in a tone that brooked no argument. "Let him go, Alifa. He'll be fine. And when he's ready, he knows where you are."

"Well, that's a feat," she snapped irritably, easily shaking off the weight of his thumb. "I don't even know where I'll be."

"You'll be with me," Yusuf concluded too readily for her taste.

Alifa tossed her hair defiantly. "I don't think Jaraw will go back to Ceuta," she maintained haughtily.

Yusuf shrugged with an indifference that immediately made her suspicious. "I don't know why he would bother." Alifa met Yusuf's gaze, barely daring to believe that he meant to stay here.

The expression in his clear green eyes told her differently and she dared to indulge the tiniest vestige of hope.

"But your books . . ." she protested.

"I'll send for them," Yusuf countered easily. "Not that I imagine I'll have much time. I understand being shaman is quite demanding." He lifted his head and gazed over the village with studied disinterest. A frown puckered his brow. "Then, of course, there is the question of conceiving an heir," he mused. "I'm certain that will take up a good bit of time."

"Assuming you have a wife," Alifa felt obliged to point out. Yusuf smiled down at her, but she saw that his smile did not reach his eyes.

He wasn't entirely certain of her response and that fact alone gave Alifa the confidence she needed to accept.

"Yes, assuming that I have a wife," Yusuf conceded quietly. Their gazes clung for a long moment and he swallowed carefully before he spoke again. "Will I?" he asked with an uncertainty that tore at her heart.

Alifa sighed in a mock concession. "Well, I suppose it's the only chance I'll have of getting those four dinars that you owe me," she said with a sad shake of her head. Yusuf regarded her in disbelief for an instant before he laughed aloud and swung her high in a triumphant arch.

"You're the one who owes me four dinars," he retorted playfully. Alifa laughed in turn as she locked her arms around his neck.

"You'll never get it from me," she whispered mischievously when her feet were on the ground again. Yusuf hauled her close with a purposeful gleam in his eye and her pulse quickened in anticipation.

"I suppose I'll have to marry you, then," he purred. Alifa locked her hands behind his head and pulled him closer for a kiss.

"It's too late to change your mind now," she whispered. Yusuf smiled.

"Good," he murmured. "I have no intention of letting you change yours, either," he added just before his lips closed over hers.

* * * * *

Harlequin® Historical

WOMEN OF THE WEST

Exciting stories of the old West and the women whose dreams
and passions shaped a new land!

Join Harlequin Historicals every month as we bring you
these unforgettable tales.

Don't miss any of our **Women of the West!**

RUGGED. SEXY. HEROIC.

OUTLAWS *and* HEROES

Stony Carlton—A lone wolf determined never to be
tied down.

Gabriel Taylor—Accused and found guilty by
small-town gossip.

Clay Barker—At Revenge Unlimited, he *is* the law.

JOAN JOHNSTON, DALLAS SCHULZE and
MALLORY RUSH, three of romance fiction's
biggest names, have created three unforgettable
men—modern heroes who have the courage to fight
for what is right....

OUTLAWS AND HEROES—available in September
wherever Harlequin books are sold.

HARLEQUIN ®

OUTH

PRIZE SURPRISE SWEEPSTAKES!

This month's prize:

BEAUTIFUL WEDGWOOD CHINA!

This month, as a special surprise, we're giving away a bone china dinner service for eight by Wedgwood**, one of England's most prestigious manufacturers!

Think how beautiful your table will look, set with lovely Wedgwood china in the casual Countryware pattern! Each five-piece place setting includes dinner plate, salad plate, soup bowl and cup and saucer.

The facing page contains two Entry Coupons (as does every book you received this shipment). Complete and return *all* the entry coupons; **the more times you enter, the better your chances of winning!**

Then keep your fingers crossed, because you'll find out by September 15, 1995 if you're the winner!

Remember: The more times you enter, the better your chances of winning!*

PRIZE SURPRISE
SWEEPSTAKES
OFFICIAL ENTRY COUPON

This entry must be received by: AUGUST 30, 1995
This month's winner will be notified by: SEPTEMBER 15, 1995

YES, I want to win the Wedgwood china service for eight! Please enter me in the drawing and let me know if I've won!

Name_____

Address _____Apt. _____

City   State/Prov.   Zip/Postal Code

Account #_____

Return entry with invoice in reply envelope.

© 1995 HARLEQUIN ENTERPRISES LTD.   CWW KAL

PRIZE SURPRISE
SWEEPSTAKES
OFFICIAL ENTRY COUPON

This entry must be received by: AUGUST 30, 1995
This month's winner will be notified by: SEPTEMBER 15, 1995

YES, I want to win the Wedgwood china service for eight! Please enter me in the drawing and let me know if I've won!

Name_____

Address _____Apt. _____

City   State/Prov.   Zip/Postal Code

Account #_____

Return entry with invoice in reply envelope.

© 1995 HARLEQUIN ENTERPRISES LTD.   CWW KAL

OFFICIAL RULES

PRIZE SURPRISE SWEEPSTAKES 3448

NO PURCHASE OR OBLIGATION NECESSARY

Three Harlequin Reader Service 1995 shipments will contain respectively, coupons for entry into three different prize drawings, one for a Panasonic 31" wide-screen TV, another for a 5-piece Wedgwood china service for eight and the third for a Sharp ViewCam camcorder. To enter any drawing using an Entry Coupon, simply complete and mail according to directions.

There is no obligation to continue using the Reader Service to enter and be eligible for any prize drawing. You may also enter any drawing by hand printing the words "Prize Surprise," your name and address on a 3"x5" card and the name of the prize you wish that entry to be considered for (i.e., Panasonic wide-screen TV, Wedgwood china or Sharp ViewCam). Send your 3"x5" entries via first-class mail (limit: one per envelope) to: Prize Surprise Sweepstakes 3448, c/o the prize you wish that entry to be considered for, P.O. Box 1315, Buffalo, NY 14269-1315, USA or P.O. Box 610, Fort Erie, Ontario L2A 5X3, Canada.

To be eligible for the Panasonic wide-screen TV, entries must be received by 6/30/95; for the Wedgwood china, 8/30/95; and for the Sharp ViewCam, 10/30/95.

Winners will be determined in random drawings conducted under the supervision of D.L. Blair, Inc., an independent judging organization whose decisions are final, from among all eligible entries received for that drawing. Approximate prize values are as follows: Panasonic wide-screen TV ($1,800); Wedgwood china ($840) and Sharp ViewCam ($2,000). Sweepstakes open to residents of the U.S. (except Puerto Rico) and Canada, 18 years of age or older. Employees and immediate family members of Harlequin Enterprises, Ltd., D.L. Blair, Inc., their affiliates, subsidiaries and all other agencies, entities and persons connected with the use, marketing or conduct of this sweepstakes are not eligible. Odds of winning a prize are dependent upon the number of eligible entries received for that drawing. Prize drawing and winner notification for each drawing will occur no later than 15 days after deadline for entry eligibility for that drawing. Limit: one prize to an individual, family or organization. All applicable laws and regulations apply. Sweepstakes offer void wherever prohibited by law. Any litigation within the province of Quebec respecting the conduct and awarding of the prizes in this sweepstakes must be submitted to the Regies des loteries et Courses du Quebec. In order to win a prize, residents of Canada will be required to correctly answer a time-limited arithmetical skill-testing question. Value of prizes are in U.S. currency.

Winners will be obligated to sign and return an Affidavit of Eligibility within 30 days of notification. In the event of noncompliance within this time period, prize may not be awarded. If any prize or prize notification is returned as undeliverable, that prize will not be awarded. By acceptance of a prize, winner consents to use of his/her name, photograph or other likeness for purposes of advertising, trade and promotion on behalf of Harlequin Enterprises, Ltd., without further compensation, unless prohibited by law.

For the names of prizewinners (available after 12/31/95), send a self-addressed, stamped envelope to: Prize Surprise Sweepstakes 3448 Winners, P.O. Box 4200, Blair, NE 68009.

RPZ KAL